T0196515

COPPERHEAD WALES

A Novel of New York City during
the American Civil War

C. D. Webb

iUniverse, Inc.
New York   Bloomington

COPPERHEAD WALES
A Novel of New York City during the American Civil War

Copyright © 2010 C. D. Webb

This is a work of fiction. All of the characters, names, incidents, organizations, and dialogue in this novel are either the products of the author's imagination or are used fictitiously.

iUniverse books may be ordered through booksellers or by contacting:

iUniverse
1663 Liberty Drive
Bloomington, IN 47403
www.iuniverse.com
1-800-Authors (1-800-288-4677)

ISBN: 978-1-4502-5215-7 (pbk)
ISBN: 978-1-4502-5218-8 (cloth)
ISBN: 978-1-4502-5216-4 (ebk)

Printed in the United States of America

iUniverse rev. date: 9/12/2010

to Inge Heckel
colleague, mentor, friend

Author's Preface

The fictional plot of this novel, involving eighteen major characters, is a product of the author's imagination and should not be construed to represent actual persons present or past. The story is imagined, however, in the very real context of New York City during the American Civil War. The abundant allusions throughout this novel to historical facts and details are believed by the author to be relevant, accurate and well documented. These references include some of the period's key leaders and personalities, governmental actions and policies, international incidents, battle statistics, ethnic and racial discord, riots, political partisanship, the Copperhead movement, financial and monetary schemes and malfeasance, social manners and customs, sexual attitudes, fashion, cultural attractions, the urban landscape, commerce and trade, and other aspects of life in Manhattan in that most stressful and momentous era.

ONE

Chad read his mother's letter one more time, then hurriedly stuffed it into his valise. When he decided to stay on for a few weeks after graduation to enjoy the privacy of a nearly deserted campus, he anticipated no such complaints from her. He took solitary walks beyond Princeton's leafy quadrangle to the edge of town, where orderly streets gave way to broad fields and distant spires. Once in late July he wandered all the way to the station, strongly tempted to board the next train for New York, burst in on Clarissa's father, and demand the right to marry her at once. As the train chugged closer, he lost his nerve again, shoved his hands deep into his pockets and sullenly returned to his gray stone dormitory.

He wanted Clarissa so much it was hard to concentrate on his Greek and Latin texts. When he translated Ovid, the ancient erotic overtones aroused and distracted him. Yet his post-commencement languor stretched on and on. He justified his absence with brief letters home, citing his determination to improve his German and French and Italian in preparation for a "grand tour" of Europe. Many of his classmates had already embarked, students with whom he felt equal, both socially and economically, at least until he received his mother's unwelcome note:

> *Dear Chad,*
>
> *I've only had three letters from you all summer, and your father hasn't come back from Virginia in over six months. Rumor has it he got into some financial trouble after he lost his old family home. There's talk of war down there and I wouldn't be surprised if he's behind it. I'm sure his affection for me has diminished. To make matters worse, my father came down from Boston last week*

to demonize me again just because I've befriended an abolitionist preacher in Brooklyn who helps me while away my lonely hours by working for a noble cause. Father has frozen our trust funds and cut my income in half. How long do you think a rich beauty like Clarissa will wait? All the young men in town are after her. We should hope for a speedy marriage, otherwise it means an even greater loss for us since she already has an immense fortune in her own name. You spend all your time reading those Greek and Latin books and pay no attention to your Mother's problems. Won't you please come home right away? Otherwise at least be kind enough to telegraph. I really can't wait for a letter.

Your loving Mother

The crowded New York train, engulfed in swirls of white steam and black smoke, sped him northwards through the blur of New Jersey's vegetable gardens and factories. Stalwart teams pulled heavily laden wagons and fancy carriages. Wide marshes under snippets of blue harbored a random heron or crow, their alternating black and white suggesting the paradoxes in his head and in his country. The future was supposed to be an endless parade across the vast continent towards California and the foaming Pacific. Railroads pushed farther into the western lands, barges floated down the Missouri and Mississippi, tall ships with both boiler and sail plied the oceans of the world, flying the proud banner of the United States of America. Europe wanted their raw materials and shipped them elegant goods in return. Hawthorne and Emerson spearheaded a literary maturation to be proud of and people like himself, educated and well connected, boldly pursued the promising dawn of an American Century. But dark clouds gathered on the horizon. Was his dream of America about to turn into a nightmare?

October 1860

Chad looked out the tall window at the yellow and brown leaves on East 10th Street, soaked by a gray morning mist that darkened the drawing room. A carriage rattled by, muted by the rain and the leaves. He could feel his mother's eyes behind him as he spoke.

"If you hadn't sent that letter I'd have stayed on in Princeton a little longer."

"What about Clarissa?"

"She said her father thinks we're too young."

"That's ridiculous. I married your father when I was only 20."

Chad adjusted the gaslights, rubbed his hand across the polished spinet, looked at his mother again, and then sat down abruptly in his favorite old wing chair in front of the fireplace. Perched primly on the settee, her arms folded in her lap, his mother avoided his gaze.

"I overheard you and Grandfather Laymus arguing in this room when I was about eight. I peeked in under the doors to see what was going on. He was very critical. And Aunt Marilyn said I was such a healthy baby to be born seven months after the wedding day. Did you think I'd never find out?"

"You have no right to talk to a woman in that fashion. Especially your mother! Your father and I felt strongly for each other—love changes people's behavior."

"Not mine."

"We shall see." She looked, at last, directly into his eyes. "You never could make up your mind about anything. If you wait too long, she may turn you down. Our situation could worsen and Mr. Renfield may oppose the match. He might think you're after her fortune."

"Was father after yours?"

"You're the product of a loving marriage. Neither one of us knew how it would turn out. And when my family took control of my trust funds, it was a slap in the face, it hurt. And your father felt demeaned by it. I think that's when he started to drift away from me."

"At least your dowry paid for this house." He took a small figurine from the piecrust table beside him, turned it slowly in the flickering yellow light, and set it down again gently. "What are we going to live on?"

"I still have access to my trust funds. The only difference is the principal is frozen and the income has been limited. If I'm careful I can make ends meet."

"What about me?"

"If you behave yourself—and I can't expect you'd do anything else but behave—you'll get it all when I go, and by then the principal should have doubled, and the family will likely remove the restrictions. It's probably already set up that way, with the lawyers."

"The Boston lawyers, though, right?"

"Well, yes, and Clarissa's uncle Randall, you've met him. Father engaged him in part to establish a connection for you, with the Renfields. Clarissa's father has known for a long time what's in those trusts and what will happen when I'm no longer here."

"Mother, I'm 22 and you're barely 43. You're still attractive. If Father's really deserting you, if war comes and we're split up, you could find a way to live happily if you tried. I don't hold anything against you. I just want to know the truth."

"And how you're going to live."

"Yes, and how I'm going to live."

"You have the legacy, it was payable on your twenty-first birthday."

"There's not enough to get married on."

"You should work anyway. What are you going to do with yourself?"

"I always thought you and Father would make up my mind for me."

"You had every opportunity. The best schools, the best college, introductions. Clothes. A generous allowance."

"Grandfather sent checks, but he was angry I didn't go to Harvard like the rest of the Laymus clan."

"You shouldn't call them a clan. They're thoughtful and responsible and hard working. Their treatment of me was a mistake, a misunderstanding. I think they've come around a bit, since I wrote you. It's true I got myself involved with the abolitionists here. But how could they publicly criticize me for that?"

"Do you really think they're comfortable with your trips to Brooklyn, unescorted, crossing on that ferry full of God knows what kind of people just to sit in some radical church and cheer this man on, whatever his name is?"

"His name is Reverend Thaddeus Mullen, and Henry Ward Beecher himself has come to hear him. And they say Mr. Lincoln spoke of him when he was here for the debates, back in April."

"Whoever heard of this Lincoln? And what's he doing here anyway? He's got no experience and no education and he's obviously an opportunist."

"He supports the tariffs. That's important to our family business. And so it's important to you."

"What do I care about tariffs?"

"You'll care about them if the money dries up. What are you going to do with yourself? Do you want to go to law school? Would you like to teach?"

"I want to take a grand tour like other young men of my status."

"That's an odd way of putting it, Chad, really. Status? We're plain New England people who don't flaunt our position."

"And don't spend principal. And don't talk about hurried weddings. And don't want their son to think for himself."

"That's not true. Emerson's family has been friends of our people for generations."

"That's hardly relevant. See how you twist everything around? It's all very neat isn't it? You can go off to Brooklyn to wail about slavery while our family gets richer selling slave cloth for the Negroes in the South. You can rile yourself up over the lower classes while we've got twelve-year old children working in our mills in Lowell and Lawrence and Worcester."

"I don't appreciate that tone of voice. We've always been sensitive to the needs of the less fortunate. We'll phase out the children over time, whenever it becomes possible for their families to support them properly and send them to school."

"Why not let the South phase out slavery, then?" Chad wrinkled his brow, clenched his hands together, stood up quickly and then sat down again. "Don't forget I'm only half Laymus. The other side is Wales. Wales! One of the first families of Virginia. The Wales tribe who once had a great plantation in the Shenandoah, an estate I'll not even get to see, much less live on."

"Your father's family freed all their slaves long before they had financial problems."

"Maybe that's why they had money trouble in the first place."

"It was gambling that brought them down. And this insane crusade of your father's, spending all his time down there, thinking he can get Cedar Crest Hall back. He should have stayed here and worked for my family."

Chad looked up from under his black brows and eyelashes, almost coyly, at his mother. "Maybe instead of a grand tour I should just go down there and join him. In Richmond. And then go on to Charleston and Savannah and New Orleans. Life is pretty fast in New Orleans, I hear."

"And let Clarissa marry somebody else? Her brother's friend from Yale, maybe? Have you met him?"

"Who?"

"Schuyler's classmate from Yale. They just got back from Europe and he's staying on in New York for a while. I think he's actually living at the Renfield mansion. Do you know him?"

"Whom are you talking about?"

"Schuyler's bosom friend, as he calls him. His name is Tifton, the Ohio Tiftons. They've got iron ore and ships on the Great Lakes and they're very big in politics. As big as one can get and still live in Ohio, I suppose."

"I didn't know Schuyler had a bosom friend from Yale, whatever that means. At Princeton, we tended to have a lot of friends and not dote on one."

"You shouldn't insinuate anything if this ever comes up with Clarissa or her father. You're on thin ice now, if you really want to marry her. You ought to get it over with. Once you're married, you'll never have a problem. They say she has forty thousand a year in her own right already. You could teach languages or literature, the things you're fond of and live a quiet and secure life. Raise a big family. They've purchased a yacht, you know."

"A yacht? The Renfields? Whatever for?"

"People are doing extravagant things these days. I think it's all this talk of war on top of everything else. The air isn't clean downtown, the streets are dirty and now this Croton Reservoir problem. They say it's not safe. Most of us who can afford it will still buy our water from a really reliable source, no matter what it costs. You must promise me to be careful, Chadwick, about the water you drink. Don't go into any of those places …" She stopped herself short again, afraid to mention anything unseemly to her son, pretending there was no blemish on her or on her family. "And then all these immigrants. I mean, we were all immigrants of course. The Laymus family, when we came over …" She paused, smoothed the pleats in her textured frock, and went on as Chad knew she would, "when we came over on the Mayflower."

"What's downtown like these days? Somebody told me Five Points is the worst."

"I don't dare to drive through Five Points. When I go to Brooklyn the coachman takes me the long way round, then straight down to the ferry. It's in all the newspapers now, these problems. Seems like there's one more newspaper every day. Some of them don't care what they print. And those Irish politicians have got a grip on things. We're overrun by the Irish, you know. One out of four New Yorkers, can you imagine it? Some of them are very decent people, I should say. The folks across the street have two young Irish girls on staff, clean as a whistle and hard workers, too."

"You can be so charitable, Mother!" Chad was impatient with her duplicity, as he called it once when they had a loud and coarse argument. She could praise and damn in the same sentence.

"If you read anything other than those Greek and Latin books—I don't understand why you like that type of writing anyway. And I'm told some of it is unsavory, to say the least." Harriet thought she'd regained the moral high ground. "And those gangs downtown have brawls all the time, public fist fights! And some of these new speculators on Wall Street, they're people you'd never invite to dinner. And there are places where the men …" Her voice trailed off as she realized she was going too far for a mother and son conversation.

"There are a lot of political clubs down there too. Not like the Federal Club, of course. Do you think I should join one of the better men's clubs? Do you think I could get in?"

"Your father got into the Federal Club, as well as Aunt Marilyn's husband. Or did he? Maybe he chose the one where the members mostly stay in all day playing cards."

"Playing cards and drinking. I don't think he would be welcome at the Federal Club."

"There's been very little drinking in the Laymus family, except for Aunt Marilyn." Harriet looked proud, reassured, and raised her chin up towards the high windows, where a sudden surge of light announced a clearing sky. "You haven't developed any bad habits, have you dear?"

"What if I had? Who would care?"

"The Renfields would care, that's for sure. Just watch yourself. You're young and good looking and ripe for trouble. Just like your father was. Avoid those … destinations … I've heard about, above Canal Street."

"They're called brothels, Mother. There are supposed to be hundreds of them in New York. I've never set foot in one and don't intend to."

"I don't think we should talk about such things, not in this house!" She leapt up from the settee and opened the sliding double doors, to see if there was anyone listening. "The maids are upstairs, the cook's gone to market, but you never know. Watch what you say in front of the servants. They get together. From one family to another, I mean. They have their little social affairs and their churches and things, and they gossip, I know they gossip. And I won't have any more talk about our family's difficulties. Most of all I don't want anything to interfere with you and Clarissa. Tonight will be a good opportunity to impress them. It's the first time in over a year they've invited us both for dinner."

"Then I had best get dressed." Chad kissed his mother on the cheek and slid the doors open, careful to close them afterward, while his mother sat there, head erect, perfectly groomed, eyes downcast, and with a hardened face.

* * *

The Renfield mansion was rectangular, with its narrow side facing Fifth Avenue and the main entrance on West 28th Street. The blocks west of Fifth above 23rd were considered socially preferable. Nonetheless, the neighborhood had begun to change even before the massive chateau-like Renfield house was completed. Traffic on Broadway had grown heavy with cabs and omnibuses and milk and water wagons, but Chad liked to walk from his old family home to see Clarissa, even when he was still a teenager. But tonight, with his mother in tow, they summoned their coachman to drive them.

Chad and his mother arrived promptly, only to find the other guests were already assembled in the parlor for sherry. There were nine of them altogether, and they eyed each other in anticipation of an evening of lively—and timely—conversation.

Phillipse Renfield sat on an Empire sofa beside Clarissa. Since he chose not to remarry after his wife's premature death, he allowed Clarissa to act as hostess. He gloated over his daughter, dressed in a pale blue silken gown with off-the-shoulder straps emphasizing her bosom. With her quick smile and musical laugh, she seemed always at the center of Renfield dinners. She was at ease with her role, exuding familial affection and gracious warmth for her guests. But tonight a more pensive expression could be seen, perhaps a trace of anxiety. Chad hoped her excitation was a result of his presence. They'd not been alone together since he returned from Princeton and tonight he hoped to slip into a corner somewhere and talk frankly about their future.

When he was growing up Chad was told not to engage in political or religious conversation at a social event, but in New York, after the panic of '57, these stringent rules were often abandoned. Politics, real estate, and social unrest were on everybody's mind and so it was inevitable that the subjects would arise. Chad was determined to navigate this treacherous course with dignity and detachment. Phillipse himself made the first sortie, hooking a thumb in his silvery brocade vest, smoothing back his ample and still dark hair, and looking around the room with complete self-satisfaction. Now in his late forties, he was considered to be a banker whose success made him the equal of all.

"The election is less than a month away," he announced. "I suppose you men have made up your minds already."

"Lincoln's the one to beat," Schuyler said, his auburn hair curled over his forehead, his dark brown eyes and a dimpled chin making him look adolescent, although he was a year older than Chad. He was squeezed onto an upholstered bench next to a man of the same age, impeccably dressed, with long blond hair and Wedgwood blue eyes. Schuyler looked directly at the man as he spoke. "I wanted to introduce all of you to my classmate from Yale, Marcus Tifton. He's from Ohio. There's a lot of political maneuvering going on out there."

Mark placed a hand on Schuyler's shoulder and laughed. "In New Haven I learned to keep quiet about Ohio. You Easterners still think we're living on the edge of the wilderness."

"I don't agree with that," a short and stocky man responded quickly, an edge of aggression in his voice. He was standing behind a black-haired woman with dark eyes, seated on a Duncan Phyfe chair, swirls of her expensive dress puffed around her, jeweled ear-rings glittering and her angular face twisted upwards to hear her escort speak. Chad had already met the lawyer Randall Renfield, Clarissa's uncle, but the seated woman, who was apparently with him, was a stranger.

"We've all got our eyes on Ohio," Randall Renfield said. "Those ore boats are part of our future, and now this young John Rockefeller—I think he's only 24—is planning a refinery. And you've got chemicals and iron in Cleveland, rich farmland stretching all the way south to Cincinnati, with a lot of beer barons and pork purveyors squatting on the edge of the river, and from there to the Mississippi and on to New Orleans! Of course, we'll see which way you're leaning politically, but my brother and I—I think I may speak for Phillipse on this issue—would like to keep close ties with Ohio."

Randall looked directly at Mark and then Clarissa when he spoke, making

Chad's spirit sink as he accepted the possibility that Schuyler's "bosom friend" from Yale might actually be a contestant for Clarissa's hand. Would the Renfields prefer to link with the West, but not the South? He presumed that his ties to Virginia were significant to Phillipse, whose desire to avoid civil strife and possible secession was well known.

The guest seated in front of Randall looked up at him again and then spoke in a low but confident voice. "Perhaps you men won't pay much attention to the political opinions of a woman, since you do not allow us to vote. But my father thinks our economic future lies beyond cotton and tobacco. He thinks we'll see heavy industry, iron and oil and chemicals. Railroads crossing to California. Wall Street is looking to the West right now. So it might not be too bad to have a man from Illinois safeguarding our interests." There was an embarrassing hush, but the woman showed no trace of regret about her remarks.

Phillipse quickly responded. "Susan is privy to much information that's valuable to all of us here. It's my privilege to work closely with her father on a number of initiatives. Solomon Steinmann is a legend in our city, and we can all raise a glass to his family before him. It was the House of Steinmann that financed much of our war of independence and all Americans owe you a debt of gratitude."

Glasses were raised, and Schuyler and Marcus shouted in unison "Hear hear!" Harriet remained uncharacteristically quiet.

Phillipse seemed eager to avoid any further awkwardness. "These are complex times and people of our class have a responsibility to foster not only what's right but also what's best. Most of us are uncomfortable with the institution of slavery. Many of us, nevertheless, have no ill will towards the South, with which we have such important economic ties. These rumors of a split in our nation are, I hope, unfounded. This Lincoln, on the other hand, is aware of our position on tariffs. Without tariffs we couldn't compete with these cheap goods being forced on us from abroad. Without tariffs, you ladies would walk into Lord and Taylor's new emporium and find everything in it was made in England or France. Worse still, you'd not be able to look forward, as Miss Steinmann and her family do, to the great industrial growth that lies ahead for our country. This is a time for circumspection and for caution. But right now, I think the time is ripe for dinner. Gentlemen, let's escort our ladies into the dining room. We can talk of pleasanter things."

Phillipse extended his arm to Susan Steinmann. Before Chad could cross the room, Marcus Tifton took Clarissa's elbow and walked towards the door. Randall was beside Harriet, so Chad looked towards the only remaining woman in the room, whom he'd seen at parties, and was about to offer his arm, when Schuyler stepped in front of him and bowed to her. "Miss Van Der

Venner, if you please," he said, somewhat pompously, Chad thought. But he knew who the small, thin, young and doll-like woman was. Her Dutch name proclaimed her position in Old New York society, and though she rarely said a word, people always deferred to her slightest wish.

Chad ushered himself into the large dining room. A massive table, carved in dark wood, was set with silver and porcelain and flowers, the gas fixtures slightly dimmed to allow numerous candles to light their sumptuous dinner with Phillipse Renfield and his flock.

After the men had smoked their cigars and sampled Phillipse's French brandy, they joined the ladies in the drawing room. Clarissa allowed Miss Steinmann to pour tea and coffee and several guests sipped cordials as they talked, the atmosphere more relaxed now after a five-course dinner with three different wines. There was laughter, the voices were louder, the women flushed and animated. Chad glanced at Clarissa, who returned his gaze surreptitiously as she talked with her brother Schuyler and his friend Marcus. Chad nodded towards the double French doors to the garden. It was still early October and the air was warm, slightly humid, and the moonlit sky was striped with gray mist and an occasional star.

Clarissa nodded furtively, and Chad moved towards the open doors. Nobody paid any attention as he slipped out to the terrace, and walked among the shrubs and flower beds, casually arranged around a bronze ornament reminiscent of Diana.

In a minute Clarissa joined him, pulling a thin silk scarf over her bare shoulders and wrapping it above her breasts. Chad took her hand and they stood close together in silence. Chad's heart was beating fast and he felt bolder, inspired by the wines and brandy and his growing anxiety that he might let opportunity pass him by.

"I welcomed your letters from Princeton," Clarissa said, nestling her hand in Chad's warm, gentle grip. "But they were no substitute for seeing you in person. Did you miss me at all?"

"I missed you a lot, Clarissa. My reasons for staying were complicated, some family matters, and as you know I had hoped to tour Europe like Schuyler and Marcus. Some of my friends are over there now. I improved my languages and did a lot of reading."

"What do you want to do with yourself now? Father's been pressing me for an answer. He thinks a young man, even at 22, should have a sense of direction."

"What I want is you, Clarissa. Do you remember when we went riding up Fifth Avenue, when they first started working on the new park? Do you remember what I said? What you said to me?"

"I thought you were very bold that afternoon."

"I apologized."

"And I told you I was glad you were bold. I want you to be bold now." She moved closer, scattering the white gravel under her feet, into the shadows of arborvitae, sheltered from the view of her dinner guests and her family. She still had her hand in his.

"I can be as bold as you want, Clarissa."

"I'm more than fond of you, Chad."

"Would you be willing for me to talk to your father right now?"

"Hush," Clarissa said as she touched her lips to his cheek, and then let him put his arms around her and kiss her. Finally Clarissa pulled herself free.

"We'd better stroll back into the light or Father will send somebody out here to get us." She laughed and twirled around on the gravel, her hands on each end of her scarf, moving it back and forth over her bosom.

"You didn't answer me. Shall I talk to him?"

"Chad, you mustn't think I'd deceive you or put you off. But I know my father. With all this political uncertainty, he's preoccupied. He'll tell you to wait, to become more certain about your future career. He'll want to know where you stand if the worst happens. Everybody knows you're half Southern."

"You're the only thing I'm sure about."

"There's going to be a very active social season this year, despite all the trouble. The first big event is at the Academy of Music. The Prince of Wales is coming and Mr. Belmont is sponsoring a lavish dinner for him. I told Schuyler I'd go with him and Marcus. You can meet me there. We can dance and talk. It will be crowded, so we can have some time to ourselves. Then you may start calling on me regularly, in the afternoons, while Father's at work. And we can go to the opera and to the theater. I think I'd like to attend one of your Aunt Marilyn's evenings, too, to meet all those writers and artists she knows."

"Some people don't approve of my aunt."

"If I go, it will lessen whatever talk there is. We have nothing to hide from each other. I know you'll be torn apart by your mixed parentage if this North and South situation grows worse. But with Father getting used to you, it'll be easier. We could possibly ask him in December and announce it at our big New Year's Eve party. The house will be full of all the right people."

* * *

"Our ties with the British are strong and enduring," Phillipse Renfield said loudly. He raised his glass, "Let us drink to the health of His Royal Highness, the Prince of Wales." Glasses were raised and voices in unison could be heard throughout the Academy of Music: "His Royal Highness, the Prince of Wales," they bleated.

Organized by August Belmont, the wealthy financier whose close ties to the Rothschilds gave him international credibility, the formal dinner for visiting European royalty was the most publicized gathering of the year. But 1860 was to begin a series of many large gatherings, most of them in the public squares and crowded streets of the city, many of them boisterous, some of them violent. Phillipse, who had arrived on East 14th Street in his finest carriage and with his best horses, was not unaware of the hostile demeanor of the crowds who pressed around the Academy to see the rich folks hobnob with a prince. He cradled his arm carefully around Clarissa as they entered, fearful there might be an eruption of some sort, but determined to take part in the celebration, which he viewed as one more link in his economic chain, binding his bank and its industrial and mercantile patrons to the South, to England and France, and to his own westward-thrusting nation. He had made it plain that if war came, he wouldn't want England to side with the Southern renegades, as he was convinced she might well do, both on the basis of the cotton trade and the Southern market for British goods. He also believed the Southern class system, more stringent and visible than that of New England, was also more to the liking of the landed gentry who still exerted powerful influence in the Parliament, despite the rapid expansion of the industrial barons of Manchester and Leeds and Birmingham.

For Clarissa, dressed in the finest new French fashions, with diamonds at her ears, around her wrists, and gleaming from the tiara atop her beautiful head, the festivities had nothing to do with international relations. Chad was there, waiting to fill her dance card, and with such large attendance, they could be lost from view and censure if they bent their heads close together to talk about their future as man and wife.

Schuyler arrived separately from his father, in another family carriage, with his friend Marcus. Harriet Wales had decided not to attend, so Chad considered himself to be part of the Renfield entourage, which also included Randall and Susan Steinmann and Eliza Van Der Venner.

At the punch bowl, Chad vowed to be especially talkative with Schuyler and his friend. While he couldn't quite understand why Marcus had decided to remain in New York, without career and without rooms of his own (there being no question about his welcome in the Renfield mansion), Chad nevertheless wanted to cultivate him. A friend of Schuyler's was, presumably, a friend of the Renfields. Anyone who aspired to become a member of that family should set out, as his mother had instructed him to do, on a campaign of amiability.

"This is the most extravagant party I've seen since I left Paris," Marcus began. "Certainly outdoes anything we poor Ohioans could put together. Of course, when I was in London, I had letters of introduction to some key people in government. I was able to meet many members of the royal family and to dine, once, at a state dinner with Queen Victoria herself." When he finished his declaration, Marcus drained his glass and refilled it while Schuyler gazed at him with admiration and pride.

"That was the only time we weren't together," Schuyler said. "I was mortified to find out there wasn't a chance of even one more guest at that dinner. You see, Chad, we stayed together most of the time, to exchange impressions and guide each other. But I think I liked Paris best, especially the artists we met, and the writers. Mark, remember when we went to Madame de la Tour's salon and met that painter, what was he called, the one who had a studio near the Sorbonne, which he shared with that writer, what's his name, the poet who knew Baudelaire?"

Squeezing Schuyler's shoulder, Marcus looked straight into Chad's eyes, as if he needed some kind of confirmation. "Both of us are artistically inclined, I paint a little bit—believe it or not we've got some good artists in Ohio—and Schuyler, well, I've been encouraging him to write ever since we roomed together at Yale. Not fiction or poetry, that's too rarified, but essays, travel impressions, a gentleman's view of the cultural world. I think we might decide to live in France ourselves, in order to share expenses and help each other along, as we absorb the new cultural developments." He paused, keeping his hand on Schuyler's shoulder, and said, as if in sudden sympathy with all the deprived New Yorkers dancing the night away, "You don't even have an art museum in this town."

"It's a pity, don't you think, Chad, that people of our generation and our class have to go to Europe to be exposed to the fine arts in a meaningful way? That's why I want to continue my education abroad. I'm not ready to marry yet and neither is Marcus, although there are plenty of girls in Ohio and right here in New York who'd like to snare him. Best to wait, I told my father, and try bachelorhood for a while." Schuyler and Marcus were both facing Chad now. Mark had removed his hand from Schuyler's shoulder and now Schuyler pressed his palm to Mark's back. "How about you, Chad? I know you're fond of my sister and she of you. Should I expect to have you as a brother-in-law anytime soon?"

"Of course that's up to your father, and to Clarissa, to decide," Chad said. He spilled some of his drink on the tablecloth and fumbled for a napkin. "I don't deny my strong feelings for her. I respect her and I respect you, so I want to proceed in a way that would be acceptable to your family. And in my case, I have strong interests in literature, too, but I haven't made a career decision yet. I haven't even been to Europe."

"Dear boy, you must go," Marcus and Schuyler said, almost in unison, as Clarissa joined them, flushed and animated.

"What are you gentlemen up to," she asked, nudging Chad's vest with her fan. "Everybody's dancing, the Prince himself. How can you men just stand here drinking when there are so many people to meet! Come away, Chad, right this instant. I want to show you off!"

Chad looked at his two friends with an expression both sheepish and proud as his Clarissa took him by the arm and led him through the bobbing heads and waving arms, towards her father, who was standing next to the Prince of Wales.

"Do you think it means anything to him that my name is Wales," Chad whispered in Clarissa's ear as they headed to the guest of honor. "I don't want to do anything to embarrass you. I love you, Clarissa, I absolutely love you."

* * *

Chad and Clarissa joined Phillipse in the family coach and rode back to the Renfield mansion, where he said goodnight to his beloved in a very proper fashion while her father looked on. They offered to have the coachman drive him home but he demurred, saying he wanted to walk a bit, it was only fifteen blocks or so, he felt safe enough, and he needed the exercise. In truth, he wanted to clear his head. The evening had been a blur of opulence and power and music and wine. He craved solitude and a chance to think, so with his walking stick as a weapon if he needed it, and with his top hat securely on his head, he walked fearlessly off. When he got to 23rd Street, he decided to take Broadway towards Union Square, then on to 10th Street, and his quiet home and his mother, who was likely to be waiting up for him, planning the next step in her siege of the House of Renfield.

Broadway was shadowy and there wasn't much traffic at night. But he could hear loud voices in the distance, blended into an underlying hum, punctuated from time to time with angry shouts. At 19th Street he could see the flames of a hundred torches. Too curious to be fearful, he quickened his pace. At the northern edge of Union Square throngs of people pressed together, holding placards affixed to poles, visible in the light of the torches, their legends scrawled with crude black letters large enough to decipher even at night. Chad waited at the edge of the unruly crowd, which seemed to consist mostly of working class people. Political banners proclaimed the merits of this or that politician. Using speaking tubes, the leaders exhorted the crowds, which grew larger and more animated by the minute.

"Down with Lincoln," they shouted. "Free and sovereign states," they cried. "No war, more jobs!" "Leave the South alone!" One poster was inscribed in Latin, which Chad assumed most of the crowd couldn't translate. It was the motto of his father's home state of Virginia, "*Sic semper tyrannis.*"

November 1860

Marilyn Laymus Blaine's house on East 25th Street was looked upon with suspicion by her neighbors. Since she rarely went out, and even more rarely invited neighbors in, her "evenings at home" were thought to be highly improper, if not sinister. Most people on the block didn't even know what she looked like. But there was a steady stream of visitors knocking at her door, framed by fluted columns surmounted by a broken pediment crown, with a carefully carved pineapple in the middle. Marilyn neither knew nor cared what her neighbors said about her, but she was aware that the maids and cooks and liverymen gossiped. Deep down, she relished the attention.

When she presided over her effulgent group of mostly young acolytes, she did so without bothering to get up from her tufted chaise, angled between a front window in her parlor and a large fireplace. There was hardly any wall space left uncovered, since she was the recipient, week after week, of gifts of oil paintings and watercolors, porcelain and bronzes, and a constant flow of fresh flowers sent in gratitude by the breathless young artists and writers who vied for her invitations. Only an old gilt girandole over the mantel looked backwards to America's past. Marilyn Blaine, it was said, looked only to the future.

But it was also acknowledged that her mornings were spent trying to recover from her evenings. Her diet of pastry and chocolate, washed down by cordials imbibed at intervals all day long, hadn't been kind to her figure, nor her moods. From breakfast to lunch she devoted painful attention to her household affairs and her accounts, instructions to her small domestic staff, a brief report to her from "Cook" about the status of her larder, and a quick perusal of book reviews and exhibition notices and commentary on concerts and the opera, which she'd not attended for several years, mostly because it was entirely too tiring to heave her frame into a balloon of a dress and waddle to her coach for a drive to the Academy of Music. Some of her artist friends described her as "Rubensesque," in a fashion era that preferred, instead, the small waist and the barely hidden bosom.

Her nephew Chad was of course always welcome, with or without a specific invitation. But he'd spent little time with her and her *entourage*, preferring to visit, when he was a boy, with his mother during the day, after his great-aunt had pummeled herself together in the forenoon, and was not yet stretched out on her chaise to "receive" her evening crowd. Chad's mother harbored ambivalent feelings towards the woman and her house, since it was there that she first met Franklin Wales and was swept off her feet, quite literally, and blessed in a short time with progeny.

But Clarissa wanted to go there, so now Chad did too. An invitation was issued, at his request, to Clarissa and her brother, and her brother's bosom friend, for a gathering on November 8, only two days after the national election.

Chad dressed himself a little more fashionably than usual, pursed his lips, tried out a variety of smiles, and even attempted to look worldly and solemn in front of the full-length mirror in his old bedroom on the third floor of their East 10th Street house. He knew he could hold his own if the conversation were substantive. He was more fluent in languages than most of them, after all, and could quote Catullus and Virgil and Parmenides with ease. But he was mostly indifferent to interior decor, cared little about antiques, and confined his discussion of current painting and *belles lettres* to those works that attempted to encapsulate matters formidable and grave. And now, two days after the nationwide vote which some papers termed a carnival, or a lottery at best, any political comments were likely to be serious indeed, since the gangly untutored one-term congressman from Illinois who ran as Honest Abe had actually gained the presidency, with only forty per cent of the national vote, and only a third of New York voters.

But despite his preparations, Chad didn't really know where he stood. Tariffs were important to him, his mother admonished. The South was being lacerated, opined his father in his most recent letter. His lovely Clarissa remained mostly mute, but her father seemed to straddle the fence with the grace and assurance of a circus bareback rider. As he rushed noisily down the stairs and out into the street, bound for an assignation with his beloved (and of course with her brother and her brother's friend as chaperons), he decided it might be best if he just listened.

It was not difficult to keep silent in Aunt Marilyn's parlor, overstuffed with guests who kept their eyes trained on their overstuffed hostess, since the reigning lady of the chaise discouraged any conversation except the one she was currently engaged in. People with differing opinions about Melville or Thoreau or Bierstadt or Cole or North or South had to wait their turn. To allow multiple conversations meant diversion of eyes away from Aunt Marilyn's ample form, and it dawned on her nephew as he stood alone beside a *bureau plat* laden with books and unanswered letters, that this nourishment of words directed to her was in fact the only thing she looked forward to. This assumption filled him, momentarily, with pity for his Great-aunt Marilyn, a depression soon lifted when he heard the maid open the front door to the melodic laughter of Clarissa Renfield.

Chad sneaked out into the hall and took Clarissa's hand after he patted both Marcus and Schuyler on the back with perhaps too much enthusiasm. He led them into the parlor where the buzz of talk abruptly diminished, and found himself the focus of all eyes, since it was to be he who introduced this stunning woman to Aunt Marilyn's edgy coterie. At the same time it seemed to Chad that Schuyler and Marcus were viewed with a familiarity that belied their status as new initiates to the ceremonies of the house on East 25th Street, so much more frequented than any others on the block. Nevertheless, he rapidly made the introductions and the two first-timers blended immediately into the crowd, with ease and grace, while it was left up to him to escort Clarissa to his great-aunt's prone body and pursed lips, so he could present to her the object of his love and the portal to his future.

When the discussions commenced anew, Chad looked more closely at the assembly and discovered he'd failed to recognize, seated in the far corner, both Susan Steinmann and Eliza Van Der Venner, *en tête-à-tête*. Unlike the other ladies, Miss Steinmann wore a long rectangle of a skirt made of tweed, and a form-fitting but decidedly severe jacket of a woolen substance very like the coat worn by Chadwick Wales. At her throat was a black ribbon looped like a necktie, and in it a pin of lustrous cameo, yellowed with age. Miss Van Der Venner, of diminutive stature and inclining head, looked at the floor while Miss Steinmann whispered something in her ear. It was the first time Chad had seen the two women without his soon-to-be uncle-in-law, Randall Renfield, an eligible bachelor who had long escorted the pair to those drawing rooms that welcomed the daughter of one of New York's richest and most respected investment bankers, and a young lady whose old Dutch name was all she needed to flourish in society.

"I'm so glad this election is over with," Aunt Marilyn said. "Now perhaps we can talk about matters of more interest. My nephew Chad has recently returned from Princeton where he distinguished himself, and is now lolling about his New York house trying to plan his future."

"The future and the past are intertwined in Europe," Marcus said. "I suggest he make a grand tour before this talk of war prohibits it."

"An interesting but irrelevant past," Marilyn retorted. "I say the future lies with America and the West. Look at that newest painting there, the small one next to the girandole. It's a little landscape, but an important one. It's the West as seen by one of our most promising painters. And if you pay for admission to that gallery on Fifth Avenue, you can parade up and down in front of another version fifteen feet wide and eight feet high, I'm told."

"I've seen it," Miss Van Der Venner said quietly. "It's a magnificent vision of our destiny."

"We've only just set foot on this continent but the future is ours," Marilyn continued, hardly pausing to allow her petite and small-voiced guest to comment. "Not for the generals and the politicians and the bankers—begging your pardon, Miss Steinmann—no, the future belongs to you artists and writers who will give us structure and form. You'll pave the way to our maturation. You'll discover for us our latent purposes and our ill-formed conscience. *Viva brevis, ars longa*, as my nephew, so proficient in Latin, would say. Isn't that right, Chad?"

"It's actually *vita brevis*," Chad said, feeling ashamed for sounding pompous and eager to correct the impression. "I really don't think I've found my convictions either, any more than the country has. I haven't even been to Europe yet. Clarissa's brother Schuyler and his classmate from Yale have just returned from Italy and France and England. I believe they're more qualified than I am to comment on the future of our cultural landscape."

"You're so attractively modest, Chad," Schuyler said. "But it would be an inadequate judgment of my sister's good sense not to see in you some uncommon strength."

"I cherish her good opinion of me, as I do yours, Schuyler," Chad said, feeling more assertive. "All of you know that my father is a Virginian and my mother from Massachusetts. I'm rather like a no-man's-land where these opposing sides can meet and maybe merge in a productive fashion. I see no harmony in the declarations of a new President who doesn't seem to understand how tariffs oppress the South, nor how many of us here in New York and in New England are at the same time uncomfortable with slavery."

"Well said, dear boy," Marcus Tifton exclaimed. "I'm an Ohioan, closer to the frontier than most of you. And my recent trip abroad has given me another perspective. We're naive as a people and unsophisticated as a culture."

"Surely not," Marilyn said. "We're already experiencing our very own literary and artistic renaissance. Some of these soon-to-be-appreciated artists are right here in this room."

"But we can't be reborn until we've suffered our adolescence," Marcus said. "Despite our Hawthorne and our Emerson, we're too full of untested ideals and too quick to welcome a presumptive savior when political strife appears. Moderation, reflection, patience, and a sense of compromise—that's what's needed for a nation coming of age."

"Your European sojourn should have convinced you of the primacy of the artist." Marilyn didn't reveal a hint of anger on her plump face but her tone was testy.

Marcus showed no awareness of his hostess's impatience. "I agree, Mrs. Blaine, that it's the writer and the artist who will give form to our souls. Schuyler and I, while we've just returned from Paris, are planning to go back soon. I want to try my hand at the easel, perhaps apprentice myself to an up and coming atelier, and Schuyler, I've determined, has always been interested in the written word. He writes, as a matter of fact, quite well. So we think it will be an economical extension of our education if we share a studio and expenses in France and try to get a more tempered view of the destiny of our homeland."

"Perhaps you might allow Mr. Renfield to speak for himself," Aunt Marilyn said, shifting on her chaise and rummaging around in her chocolate box.

"Yes, Schuyler," Clarissa said with an air of confidence and defensiveness combined. "Our father has given us some strong guidance, and has consulted such eminent financiers and statesmen as Solomon Steinmann. Father thinks all philosophical and political discourse eventually boils down to economics. Trade, he says, is always the issue. Did I get it right, Schuyler?"

"I don't always agree with my father. What son does? But I recognize trade to be paramount. I feel I could hold my own in a financial position, but it may be to my advantage, and to my family's as well, if I join Marcus in Europe once again, so we can learn more about older and more powerful nations, and how they integrated their thinkers and artists into the body politic. Especially France. Isn't that true, Marcus."

"Absolutely, dear boy." Marcus put down his glass of sherry, got up from his chair and walked towards the window, where he loomed over little Miss Van Der Venner. "First the Dutch and then the English, and then the advent of a new nation, and then hordes of immigrants, and then the blessings and curse of international trade and disputes and vested interests. These little conflicts are but foamy crests on an ocean swell. It's the artist and the writer who will point us on our way."

"Tell me, Mr. Tifton, do you talk that way when you're back in Ohio?"

"Only when I'm alone with myself, Mrs. Blaine."

Nervous laughter relieved the tension. Maids brought in more sherry and tea and cakes and chocolates and green and red and yellow cordials, and one of the young men slipped away to the spinet and began to play a Beethoven sonata, and everybody in the room, grateful for the right to abandon the repartee, breathed more easily.

Chad leaned against the wall and gazed at Clarissa, certain he'd handled himself well, and more certain than ever that she would be his.

December 1860

"He's coming back." Harriet said. She held the letter in her lap, gazing over Chad's head towards their tall parlor windows facing the street. Large snowflakes drifted gracefully on a windless morning. The pavement was already covered and the steady silent snowfall calmed them, as if in response to the spirit of the December holidays and the growing need, in the Wales household, for some signal of peace.

Chad took the letter from his mother's hand. Harriet looked into the fireplace, eyes fixed on the orange and blue flames. "We ought to buy the tree this week, so we can decorate it before he gets here."

"Do you think he'll stay? This letter's a mystery. No indication why or how long, not even when he'll get here. Is he coming up from Virginia by steamer? Will he take the train? He could at least have told us that. We could send the carriage for him."

"Your father's always been impetuous. A lot like you, Chad. You even look like he did the day I met him at Aunt Marilyn's."

"I thought you said I've got the Laymus eyes."

"That's true dear, green and hard like diamonds. But your beautiful black hair and the way you twist your mouth around when you smile, your restlessness. That's all a gift of your father."

"It would have been thoughtful of him to be more explicit."

"The point is he's coming back. We can talk to him. You need to straighten things out between you."

"With you, Mother. That's more important." He placed his hand gently on her shoulder and gave her back her letter.

"I'm willing to accommodate …" She stopped in mid-sentence, pressing her knotted fist against her brow.

"There's no point in crying, Mother. He may just want to settle his affairs here. You shouldn't get your hopes up too high, it will hurt when he dashes them on the rocks again."

"He's leaving Virginia and coming home for Christmas. We'll have him in the house for the holidays, like we did when you were little. I'll ready his study upstairs. You and I will do the tree together like the old days. Oh, Chad, we have to take this whole thing a little bit at a time. It's just too much if we don't."

"What should I tell Clarissa? You know as well as I that what happens between you two could affect my chances with her. She wants me to spend more time there during the holidays. She thinks I might talk to her father in a few days. If he gives his consent we'll announce our engagement at their party on New Year's Eve. You'll have to be there, Mother. It would look good if Father were there with you."

"I'll try to convince him, even if it's only for appearance. He's so resentful if I try to force him into anything. And how about my feelings? I'm the one he abandoned."

"Last week you said he'd abandoned us both."

"Your future is what matters. You must tell him that, when he's here in this house. Just the two of you. You must tell him of your love for Clarissa and that you have a chance to become part of the Renfield family. Knowing you're secure and happy and that our family is back where it belongs should mean a lot to him. No scandals, no gossip, about …" She broke off again and rose up with jerky movements, pacing around the room. "Chad, you have to have it all out with him first."

"We never talked much."

"He's moody like you. But he's not seen you for over a year. You're so handsome, you're so smart."

"He made me feel as if he didn't approve of me."

"That's just your imagination, you'll see. You've grown up to be a son he can take pride in. And when you marry Clarissa it'll be the talk of all New York!"

"I don't want to be the talk of all New York. I just want to know where I'm going. Mother, you never listen to me when I try to explain this. Neither did he."

"Dear boy, you must stop punishing yourself like that."

"I don't know if I'm Northern or Southern. I don't know if I'm going to be financially secure or not. I don't know if I'm a Republican or a Democrat. Back and forth and up and down, all my life."

"You can't hide out in your books forever."

"How else am I going to put two and two together? There's been tension in this house from the time I crawled up to the sliding doors that day when grandfather Bartleby accosted you and said those cruel things."

"Your grandfather was worried about me, not about you. Our family has a special place in Boston's history. We're looked up to but we're also under attack. First the rum and slave trade allegations, then the privateers in 1812 and then the young workers in our factories. People don't understand. We were part of the times, we did what was necessary and we profited. Bartleby Laymus has given hundreds of thousands to charity. To the church. To Harvard. Help for the poor. Working in our factories put bread on the table for hungry immigrant families. We built New England and New England built the nation. But there are those in Boston who still hold back from us, as if our money isn't as old as theirs, even though most of it came from the same places ours did."

"Calm down, Mother. I don't need a lecture about the economic growth of New England. I'm perfectly aware of how your family developed. No body listens to me. Nobody!"

* * *

"Clarissa's busy upstairs right now, Mr. Wales. She told me to ask you to wait for her in the back parlor. There's a nice fire going and I can make you some tea." The Renfield's housekeeper wore a simple black dress and a white apron, not quite a uniform, but an indication to any chance visitor that she was in command, though not really a Renfield.

"I don't mind waiting." Chad was burdened with brightly wrapped packages that almost obscured his face. He was afraid he'd drop them and crossed the threshold with relief, spilling some of the smaller boxes onto the bench in the front hall. "Could I just put these under the tree?"

"I'm afraid it's not up yet. It's a Renfield tradition to wait until Christmas Eve to do that."

"I'd forgotten. But I want to deliver these packages now. My father's coming back from Virginia and I may be tied up for a couple of days. We have so much to talk about." He gulped down his last few words, thinking it inappropriate for him to become overly familiar.

"I'm sure Miss Clarissa will be pleased and can tell you where to put them. Leave them here for now and let me offer you some tea."

The back parlor of the Renfield mansion was large but informal. Embers glowed bright red in the fireplace and there was a comfortable armchair beside it. He sat down anxiously, not yet accustomed to being alone in the great house, which he assumed would soon be as familiar to him as his own.

The housekeeper brought him a steaming cup. "Most of the maids and the groom and stableboys are away this morning. Miss Clarissa felt they should have a little time of their own to get ready for Christmas. She's so very kind and thoughtful. But of course I expect you know that already, Mr. Wales."

She was being more intimate than she should, he thought. "Thank you for the tea," he said stiffly. The housekeeper sensed his withdrawal and curtsied, turning her back to him and closing the double doors. He sat down and took a sip of tea, so hot it burned his lip. He put the saucer down on a leather-topped table, rattling the porcelain and spilling tea over the side.

A tall-case clock ticked steadily in the corner. Not another sound, except for the sputtering fire. The silence made him uneasy. Why was Clarissa keeping him waiting?

He put his cup down and walked around the room. Large landscape paintings arranged in tiers, flickering gaslights and the warmth and coziness of the room calmed him. He must learn to be relaxed and confident in this house, he told himself. He studied his image in the large gilt mirror by the door, straightened his clothes, practiced a smile. Then he sat down again. The clock seemed to tick louder. The fire was burning down, should he stir it? Should he ring for the housekeeper to do it?

There were newspapers on the sofa table. He glanced through them absent-mindedly. "Tension Mounts in South," one headline proclaimed.

"South Carolina Legislature Debates Secession," another one warned. "Lincoln to Visit New York on Way to Inauguration." Chad wondered if his farther would read such stories in his Virginia papers or on the boat or train bearing him homewards to his family.

Why was she avoiding him in this big house? He opened the sliding doors a crack and peeked out, the edge of his nose sticking through the portal. Not a sound. He stepped out into the hall, dimly lit in the dark December afternoon. He could hear nothing. There was an upstairs sitting room, where he'd joined Clarissa more than once. Schuyler, too. It was their personal parlor, they told him. When they were children they'd dress up and take their tea there with prim little Clarissa, acting her role as hostess for her father in his grand house and with his great guests.

Perhaps he should take the gifts he'd wrapped for Clarissa and Schuyler and deposit them in that intimate and personal sitting room. He picked up a few packages from the bench and ascended the grand stairway to the second floor. The lights were dim here too. Several doors off the upstairs hall were closed. He nervously realized both Clarissa and Schuyler had bedrooms on this floor.

He inched farther down the hall towards a pale light under the door on his left. He carefully tested the doorknob, which opened with such ease and quiet that he'd entered the room before he realized it. There was a sputtering fireplace here, too, and radiant tapers on the bureau and on a pedestal table. The gas was turned low, a faint bluish flicker adding to the haze. When he saw the carved knobs of a large antique four-poster, panic overtook him as he realized he was in somebody's bedroom. He froze in place, afraid to move.

Two forms were intertwined on the bed, and as his eyes adjusted he could see a ruffled head of hair and bare arms. Bare feet and legs extended from under the covers nearest to him. Without thinking he cleared his throat. One of the figures sprang up, completely nude. It was Schuyler.

"Oh, I'm so sorry, Schuyler, please excuse me." He was still standing stone-like in his tracks. Another head, ringed with blond hair, appeared. "Marcus! Forgive me, please!" At last regaining mobility he hurtled out the door, closing it tightly behind him. He raced down the stairs.

"Mr. Wales," the housekeeper said, as she closed the door to the front coatroom. "Is there something the matter?"

"I'm afraid I forgot my appointment today at the Federal Club," Chad explained, almost out of breath. "I thought the packages might best be left in the sitting room upstairs. Please tell Clarissa I dropped off the gifts but I had to get on to my appointment. Thank you for the tea. I've got to go now, Madam."

The housekeeper held his hat and coat out to him, a puzzled look on her face. He slipped one arm into his greatcoat as he closed the door behind him, hat and walking stick in hand, one glove on and one glove off, racing down Fifth Avenue, hoping to find a cab or an omnibus or anything to carry him away from the scene he'd just witnessed, etched forever, he knew, in his already troubled brain.

But no conveyances were in sight. It was late afternoon and the streets were already dim and gray, but he lowered his head against the falling snow and walked, as briskly as he could, down the avenue.

There was commotion in Madison Square, a group of people under flaming torches, chanting slogans and waving the American flag. Throngs of newsboys crossed back and forth, hawking a special edition. "Extra, extra," they cried. But he couldn't bother with whatever news they proclaimed. He'd encountered a situation that he thought existed only in the pages of his Greek and Latin texts, the sections they never discussed in class. Now this strange condition had invaded his life, possibly his future family. He'd heard, over the years, crude jokes and vague allusions to the phenomenon and some of his literary idols had even accused the popular poet Walt Whitman of advocating this practice. Chad's own feelings were vague, almost neutral, so caught up was he in his father's predicament and his mother's anguish and his own prospects as a possible member of the Renfield dynasty.

Walking usually cleared his head but he grew more agitated with the snow and the cold afternoon darkness. He slogged stubbornly towards the familiar stoops and railings of 10th Street.

A carriage waited in front of his doorstep, the driver bundled up in cap and scarves, his breath white in the cold, and the horse, too, breathing fog into the late afternoon air. Squares of brightness fell on the sidewalk from the windows of his parlor, where the upper shutters were still open. As he rushed up the front steps he saw a man standing at the window, looking out at him, and recognized, even in the hurried instant and through steamy glass, the face of his father. Franklin Wales had indeed come home.

He found the door unlocked and pushed into the hallway, throwing his hat and coat and gloves onto a bench. Taking the sliding doors in both hands, he pushed them open and stood in anticipation on a thick patterned rug, dripping moisture and chilled from his frenzied walk. His father stood silently with his back to the room, gazing out into the street. He held a small cigar, not much bigger than a pencil, in his hand. At last he turned and faced his only son with a troubled gaze.

"We didn't think you'd get here until the twenty-third," Chad said. "You could have sent a telegram."

"I've been here for several days," his father said. He puffed his little cigar again and put it down in a crystal ashtray on the sideboard.

"Several days and you didn't even let us know? How could you do that? I haven't seen you for over a year."

"Don't take it too personally, son. I had business to transact. And certain future arrangements to account for."

"Where are you staying? Mother got your old study ready for you. We expected to spend our holidays together."

"Your mother assumed too much. I'm at my club. And there are people there, members of the Federal Club, to see. I've got to negotiate certain arrangements concerning the political dilemma."

"What political dilemma?"

"Your mother told me of your pending engagement. I suspect you're too caught up with the charms of Clarissa Renfield to pay any attention to what's happening to your country. Or perhaps I should say, both your countries."

"But it's already the twenty-first of December! We've put up the tree and there are presents. We hoped to host a small dinner. There's not much time until Christmas Day."

"I'm well aware of that," Franklin Wales said. "Indeed, yesterday was December 20th, 1860. I suggest you note that day in your diary, if you still keep one. It's a day that will live in history."

"Whose history?"

"The papers have published special editions today, although the news came in on the telegraph last night. The legislature in South Carolina has voted to secede from the Union. There will doubtless be similar actions in other Southern states in the next few weeks. I've got to make sure my contacts with certain sources in New York are firm, and then I must get back to Virginia as soon as I can. Tomorrow, if possible."

"Tomorrow? Mother will be devastated."

"I've already told her. She's upstairs in her room. We've said our farewells."

"Farewells?"

"Son, there are things you must accept in this world. Your mother and I were not compatible here. And my heart is in Virginia. In fact, there's a Virginia woman whom I hope to marry. This morning I asked your mother for a divorce."

"There's never been a divorce in our family! You'll ruin her health and her reputation and you'll compromise me, too. Phillipse Renfield won't look kindly on this. He may not permit us to marry. How can you do this?"

"You'll learn that a man must do what he must. In terms of my personal life, I could no longer stay here in the North, looked down upon by her self-righteous family. I couldn't tolerate the hypocrisy of those New England textile kings who spout abolition sermons from their mouth while they take our cotton and slap tariffs on our imports. It was a voluntary union of independent states and South Carolina has taken the only honorable path. Others will follow, no doubt, including my home state of Virginia."

"But what about me? I expected to visit there in the future. With Clarissa's money I thought we might get Cedar Crest Hall back."

"A touching gesture, and I'm moved. I know I've not been the father you deserve. You were an unexpected blessing in my friendship with your mother. That doesn't mean I've not loved you. But I can't give up my heritage, especially now. If war comes and Virginia has joined a new confederacy, I'll be needed. I'll serve. And we shall win!"

"This will kill Mother. Damn you!"

"I'll not chastise you for cursing your father. These issues are bigger than either of us now. No, your mother is strong, her family is resilient, and there's a lot of money that will eventually come to you. They'll grow even richer if there's a war, even when the South defeats them."

"Do you have to leave right now?"

"There's a carriage outside the door. I've waited expressly for a chance to tell you all this in person and to say goodbye, and to tell you that, as painful as it may be for you, it's probably for the best."

"I'll come with you, then. If there's a war I'll fight for the South. The Renfields don't want war. The Laymus family doesn't want war. If I fight alongside you and we win quickly, I can come back a hero and maybe Clarissa will marry me, even if there's a divorce hanging over our family!"

Franklin moved closer to his son, shook his hand, and put an arm around his shoulder. "You're upset and you have the right to be. You're intelligent and well educated and you have the potential for a bright future. An academic, perhaps, or a writer. Perhaps the Church. But not the battlefield. No, my son, you must stay here and comfort your mother. Go ahead with your engagement. Even if your mother agrees to grant me a divorce, it won't be public knowledge for weeks or months. And by then, there may be world-shaking events that will make our little rift seem a trifle, indeed."

"Lie to Clarissa?"

"You wouldn't be lying since there's nothing to report right now except the very personal negotiations between my wife and me. You needn't even admit you know about it. Treacherous times are before us, and there may be bloodshed. The nation will be reshaped. Some people will prosper and others won't. Many may die. I beg you to stay here, look after your mother, and go ahead and get married. You're a good boy and with the right connections you'll survive." Franklin took his gold watch from his vest. "And now I must go." He hurried out of the room, pulled on his cloak and cap, and opened and then solidly shut the front door. Chad watched from the parlor window as his father's carriage drove off down the cold winter street.

* * *

Every window of the Renfield mansion sparkled in the frigid night air, including the circular panes of the huge ballroom on the third floor, usually unlit. Carriage after carriage pulled up before the grand house to discharge its well-dressed passengers. The guests came in twos and threes and fours, the women covered with furs and jewels, the men in their most formal finery. Extra servants had been engaged, every fireplace in the mansion blazed, both parlors and the drawing room and library were thrown open to all, and a small orchestra was tuning up on a stage at the end of the ballroom.

As was customary on New Year's Eve, Phillipse Renfield and his son and daughter stood side by side in the main foyer, greeting their guests. Coats, hats, walking sticks, and gloves were carefully stored. The three-person receiving line did its best to hurry people along with the quickest and warmest of greetings and then up the stairs to the ballroom. There was a bountiful buffet, and an endless supply of punch and champagne.

After a proper wait for last minute guests, Phillipse instructed his senior staff to welcome and direct stragglers, and with Clarissa on one arm and Schuyler on the other, ascended the broad curved stairs to join the crowd. It was said that everybody who was anybody in New York would be there.

Chad stood near the main doorway to the ballroom, with his mother alongside him. She was subdued in demeanor but dazzling in dress, having spent some of her Christmas money on new clothes, in an attempt to keep up, for Chad's sake, an image she now considered to be a hoax. She smiled and talked and tossed her curls in laughter. All of it was not feigned, of course, since she was with her handsome son, the only certainty left to her as 1860 came to a close.

Chad was bursting with both pride and apprehension. He'd followed his father's advice and said nothing about his family's trials. He'd sat with Phillipse in the library and poured out his heart to him. And Phillipse had listened sympathetically, betraying no doubts about his daughter's feelings for this young man. He had other worries now. He'd been in meetings all week with his banking staff, with their major customers, and by telegraph with key centers in the South. A personal visit to Solomon Steinmann was especially fruitful, he said cryptically. Everything had to be done fast, to protect his empire. Chad understood, for he knew that in Boston and Worcester, the Laymus family was retrenching, planning to make the most of the coming rupture in their land.

Schuyler and Marcus stood together near the punch bowl, and greeted him without reservation. Chad was too timid to look either one in the eye. There'd been no occasion to discuss with them the effect or significance of his intrusion, and in fact, Chad wished it had never happened.

Clarissa left her father's side and stood with Chad and his mother. The attractive young couple enjoyed a dance together, conscious that many eyes were on them, for there was a rumor that Phillipse Renfield intended to make an important announcement this New Year's Eve.

As her father prepared to silence the crowd for his little speech, Clarissa took Chad by the arm and marched him over to her father's side. Bells were rung to silence the guests, and the orchestra was instructed to play a fanfare and then stay silent until further advised. Phillipse stood on the small stage and looked out over the crowd.

"Dear friends, honored guests and colleagues. It has been a pleasure for my family to host these New Year's Eve dances for many years. You honor my family and me by coming out in the cold to spend the few remaining minutes of the year with us. Before we begin the countdown to 1861, I have a special announcement I wish to share with you, something personal and public simultaneously, but perhaps an occasion that's in danger of being overshadowed by recent events."

"As you know, one of our sister states has voted to leave the Union. And on the day before Christmas, our Federal government ordered the garrison at Fort Moultrie in South Carolina to be transferred to Fort Sumter, overlooking the Bay of Charleston. I hope this deliberate provocation doesn't signal portent of violence and disruption. I shall do all in my power to maintain our mutually beneficial relationships with all and each of the Southern States. Let us put this anxiety out in the open and perhaps lay it to rest, at least for now."

"I offer you as a token of my optimism some special family news. My daughter, Clarissa, my cherished jewel, is embarking on a great adventure that provides a chance to further strengthen our family line through an alliance with a bright and worthy partner, Chadwick Wales. Chad is the descendent of an honored New England family, and one of the first families of Virginia. It's a hopeful sign, I think, that his blood and my daughter's will be joined in matrimony, for Chadwick has asked for my daughter's hand and I've willingly given it to him. Let's toast the newly engaged couple, and let's remember as we do so that we're all one family, North and South, East and West. Let the years ahead bring us together, not apart, and let my daughter and her husband-to-be prosper and be fruitful, as a symbol of American unity and as a blessing on the House of Renfield."

There was an enormous cheer, glasses were raised, and the orchestra struck up a jaunty tune. Chad and Clarissa stepped out on the floor in a close embrace, dancing their way to the middle of the room. As they dipped and swirled and skipped, Chad felt the knot of apprehension in his stomach once again. Nothing was what it seemed to be, not even his promised marriage. Was he going to be wed to a beautiful woman or to a bank? Was his brother-in-law to be a friend and ally, or a harbinger of shame? Was his father a hero or a traitor? Could his mother muster the strength to endure the multiple attacks on her security and her honor? Would there ever be anybody he could turn to?

TWO

January 1861

There had been rain and then snow and then rain again earlier in the month, and now on January 14, Chad hoped a long walk might clear his head. But his plans changed when an unexpected note arrived at nine in the morning. His eyes lingered on the meticulous penmanship and embossed initials on ivory paper.

His mother watched him, trying to decipher his reaction. Chad slid the heavy folded notepaper back into its envelope, offering the entire package for his mother's inspection. "Did you know Uncle Caleb is in town?" He looked at her as if she were part of a plot.

"He came to see me yesterday evening, while you were out. I'd have told you but you didn't get in until late, so I went to bed. Where were you?"

"I was with Clarissa, of course. We dined together in the upstairs sitting room. It gave us time to be alone and accommodated her father, as well. He had a house full of bankers and merchants and factory owners, Clarissa said. Apparently they were going to discuss the tariff situation, now that Lincoln has been elected."

"Mr. Lincoln is in town too. They say he's going to the opera tonight."

"Then I suppose I'll see him there. Clarissa and I are going, with Schuyler and his friend."

"He's an imposing and thoughtful man. I heard him debate Mr. Douglas at the Cooper Union. There's something secret about him, though."

"I should think so, Mother, he's a politician."

"No, some inner sadness. Even when he was waiting his turn for a rebuttal, he sat there with his long legs crossed and looked out into space like a lost child."

"The man knows exactly what he wants and how to get it."

"You're so quick to judge people, Chad. I hope you'll grow more mellow after you're married."

"You fail to tell me your brother Caleb is down from Boston and now you say he called on you here, and twenty minutes ago I get this hand-delivered message demanding I have lunch with him."

"I should think 'demand' too strong a word."

"Did you know about this, too?"

"I did not."

"Why does he want to see me? And he says Clarissa's uncle will be there."

"It makes sense, doesn't it? Randall Renfield represents clients who do business with our family. And you're about to bridge the divide by joining Laymus and Renfield together. I should think the three of you would have a lot to talk about. Just watch your step. My brother's not a forthcoming man, and Randall's a lawyer, after all. Neither one of them is all that bright, just between you and me. At least Randall has a sense of humor. You should weigh every comment and not commit yourself to any position until we've had a chance to discuss it here."

"You don't think I'm capable of discussing weighty issues? Like money? Or tariffs? Or my place on the bridge between the Laymus textile mills and Phillipse Renfield's bank? I'm not worldly enough because I 'hide out in my books,' as you usually put it. No, Mother, if I go I'll speak for myself." He flashed a defiant smile. "If I go."

"Of course you'll go, after you calm down. You're just as excitable as your father. Besides, I already alerted Higgens that he needs to get the carriage out and deliver a note to Randall Renfield's office in the next hour. You'll want to dress very carefully for lunch with the two of them at the Federal Club. Do you think you're getting too fancy in your dress, Chad? I hope you're not influenced by your future brother-in-law. Schuyler's a year older than you and richer than you, at least for now. But he's a little too fashionable, don't you think?"

"Why should Higgens get the carriage out? He could walk or take an omnibus."

"It would look better if he took the carriage. Perhaps you'd like to go along, wait outside in the carriage while Higgens delivers your response, and then have him drive you to the Federal Club early. Your father's a member. You could sit in the main lounge and read the papers, perhaps say hello to people you've met before. Let them get used to seeing Chadwick Wales in the flesh, the man who's going to marry Clarissa Renfield and join together two of the most powerful families on the Eastern Seaboard." Her voice rose in a pride that verged on hysteria. "What about your clothes?"

"My clothes are really rather conservative. I'm in good shape, everything fits, Mother. And I'm quite able to advance your purposes without further training."

"My purposes?"

"Do you want me to ask the Federal Club if it would be acceptable for a woman to join us in the dining room today, so you can make sure it all goes the way you want it to go?"

"Chad, a sarcastic demeanor is not at all attractive. You've got to watch yourself. You're smart and you're well educated. But most people don't read Greek and Latin and they don't want to sit in their room all day thinking. Decisiveness! That's the quality you want, and now more than ever. Caleb told me last night that he's sure there's going to be trouble. He said there'd be chaos if states continue to secede."

"Mississippi, Florida and Alabama so far this month. Georgia is debating it and so is Louisiana."

"But not Virginia," Harriet sighed. "Your father will be dashing about in Richmond trying to work them up, I'm sure of it. He thinks somehow a war might make it possible to get Cedar Crest Hall back. I told him if there's a war there may no longer be any Cedar Crest Hall."

"Suppose I go along with Higgens while he delivers my acceptance. Have you written it up yet, Mother? You could just say 'My son accepts your invitation to lunch at the Federal Club with you and Randall Renfield and I've instructed him on what to wear, how to behave, and what to say.'"

"I really don't like this trait in you, Chadwick. You and your father …"

"If you don't like my clothes, Mother, perhaps you could have something worked up for me in one of your textile mills. Something fashionable, maybe, but made out of slave cloth."

Harriet clenched her fists and bowed her head. She trembled and sobbed quietly.

"I know it's hard for you, Father not coming back. You have to find other ways to confront your despair. That's what it is, despair. I'm sorry. Please …"

Harriet reached out her hand towards her son who dutifully kissed it. "So you'll go then. To the lunch?"

"Yes, Mother, I'll go."

* * *

The uniformed attendant at the front door looked him over carefully, but Chad had exuded confidence and ease, although he was an hour early for his luncheon. The main lounge of the Federal Club had high ceilings, simple wainscoting painted white, two chandeliers and numerous gaslights. He sat down in a big chair near the window and looked out at the wintry day. There were several other men in the room, reading or dozing off. A clock ticked. The wind rattled a window. From time to time soft vague voices could be heard from the staff.

Chad got up again and walked to the long table spread with *Harper's* and *Leslie's* magazines and a dozen different newspapers, including a few from abroad, more than a month old. He glanced at the headlines in a London publication, which warned of "Disorder Brewing in Former American Colonies". He took a more recent paper in hand, strode back to his chair, and perched on the edge as he read the ominous news. He was, after all, capable of making up his own mind. But he didn't quite realize what it was he had to make up his mind about. After a while he spread the papers on his lap and leaned his head against the padded high back of his chair and closed his eyes. There was too much pressure on him, he concluded. Best to think of other things. So he mentally recited to himself several lines from Lucretius, and one of the more political of the poems of Catullus.

A hand on his shoulder roused him from his reverie. It was Randall Renfield, his dark hair peppered with flecks of gray, his boots polished to a dazzling shine, his silken vest adorned with a gold chain. He was looking at his watch. "I've arrived early, but not early enough to outdistance my future nephew," Randall said.

When Chad rose to his feet he saw his uncle Caleb Laymus standing immediately behind Randall.

"Your mother told me how well you've turned out, Chadwick. We're proud of your achievements at Princeton and even happier to learn of your engagement to Clarissa Renfield."

"Yes," said Randall, "We have many issues to examine with you today, not the least of which is the timing of your wedding and the vocation you hope to take when you've made up your mind about a career."

Each man took one of Chad's arms, guiding him out of the lounge and into the main dining room, where high ceilings looked down upon rows of portraits of past club members who had distinguished themselves in battle or board room or, through wise marriages, in the bedroom.

"Well my boy, what will you eat? I recommend we start with a cup of our excellent *bisque*, and perhaps a small fowl of some sort, and plenty of vegetables. I've learned that you can judge a man's health and his longevity by the amount of vegetables he eats." Randall Renfield folded the menu and handed it to the waiter, who rightfully assumed he'd ordered for all of them.

Another uniformed server hovered nearby with a polished silver tray filled with popovers, and biscuits, and sourdough bread.

"You were reading the papers, my boy." Uncle Caleb said. "Did you find anything of substance therein?"

Put off by his uncle's overly formal language, Chad felt he was about to be assaulted, and answered nervously. "More news about the problems in the South. Most of the other states down there are discussing secession. And of course they feel they've been discriminated against, economically."

"How do you feel about that," Randall Renfield asked. He'd lifted a knife to put butter on his popover, but now suspended it like a weapon, in midair, aimed at Chadwick's heart.

"I don't know how I feel exactly. I am, as you know, half Southern. My father has discussed the situation often with me. He values my opinion, he says. He said because I'd studied the ancient languages so thoroughly, especially Thucydides and Herodotus and of course Pliny and others, he said he thought perhaps I might add a perspective to the political crisis now threatening us."

"And what is that perspective, if I may ask," Randall continued.

"The South has three main exports, cotton, tobacco and rice. It buys everything else from the North or from abroad. High tariffs make it hard for them to compete, much less prosper. So they're against Mr. Lincoln because he has made it clear how he stands regarding tariffs."

"There are two sides to every story," Uncle Caleb said.

"More than two," Randall added.

"Yes, but we need to look at these things from every point of view. Take slavery, for example. It's disgusting and reprehensible and ought to be illegal. Even my father says that—his family freed their slaves decades ago. But we've got other kinds of servitude in the North, from indentured servants to little children working long hours in the mills and factories alike."

"You seem to be taking a strong position on these controversies already, Chad." Uncle Caleb said. "We must be practical and we need to be fair. There may be a place for you in this controversy, especially in light of your coming marriage to Mr. Renfield's niece."

"Let me make it clear for you, Chad." Randall shifted his weight on the upholstered seat of his delicately carved early American chair, and looked directly into Chad's eyes. As he spoke he made flourishes with his butter knife. "The issues are clear. Without tariffs we can't prosper here in New York and New England. If the South secedes we must still collect our customs duties. Most of the Federal budget comes from that source, you know. And the Federal government will require more money in the months and years to come. We need a central bank. There's too much uncertainty in the currency markets. As to slavery, we all agree it's despicable. Abe Lincoln's meeting at this very hour, I might add, with leaders of the Republican Party—that's indeed the real reason for his visit to our city prior to his inauguration." Renfield stopped himself, took a deep breath, put down his butter knife, and took a good long drink of the Federal Club's pure cold crystal-clear water.

"I thought he was meeting with the mayor," Chadwick interjected, taking advantage of the mute Renfield whose throat bulged and whose Adam's apple pulsed as he drank his water down.

"He did," said Caleb. "Fernando Wood is as corrupt a politician as you'll find. He urged your own city council, just recently I believe, to vote to permit New York to secede as a free-trade city. He thinks it would be good for commerce and New England be damned. You've been well educated and you show a marked propensity, your mother told me, for abstract thought. Now put it together in that young head of yours. There are always circumstances that certain factions deem unjust, but these can be worked out over time. Right now we want to preserve our markets, keep tariffs high, allow the South to deal with its own challenges, and maintain our supply of cotton."

"Yes, and tobacco and rice," Renfield added. "And kerosene from Ohio. And this most excellent *bisque*. And these apples from upstate, aren't they fine? We've worked for well over a century to produce this way of life, my boy, and it will be up to your generation to maintain it. Whatever it takes."

"Yes," Caleb said, "Whatever it takes."

"I'm grateful you asked me here and honored you want my opinions," Chad said.

"Let's get to the point. You're about to be married to my niece, daughter of the most powerful banker in New York. At least he thinks he is," Renfield laughed. "We all must be permitted to overvalue ourselves a little. But you see, whatever happens, it will take a more— shall we say 'adventurous'—attitude to reap the biggest rewards. Your Uncle Caleb and I see things in much the same way. No matter what happens there's going to be a big change in this country. Much of the focus will be on the West. But we've got mills all over New England. They must be kept busy. From a humanitarian point of view."

"A humanitarian point of view?" Chad tried to conceal his consternation.

"Yes. We employ people who otherwise couldn't put bread on their tables. And where else could they work and still have relative freedom? If the system is disrupted in the South, these jobs would be the first to go—either the factories close down or the blacks come north to get the jobs. The Irish are afraid of that. That's why they hate Lincoln."

"The Irish hate Lincoln because of the blacks who might take the jobs in New England factories?" Chad's voice trailed off uncertainly.

"Don't strain yourself with the details, my boy, look at the overall picture. That's what you're good at. Let me be explicit," Randall said. His lips were tight, he was staring into Chad's eyes, his fist was again clinched around his butter knife and his face was taut and flushed. "Let me make it simple: one, Northern mills must prosper and endure; two, tariffs make it possible; three, slavery is an abomination but we can deal with it later; four, without a central bank we can't control the currency and if we don't control the currency we can't maintain our ruling position."

Caleb joined in spiritedly. "Yes, and five, there's bound to be conflict and where there's conflict there's opportunity."

Randall relaxed a little. "Yes, and six, that's where you come in."

Both men had the air of trial lawyers who had rested their case but Chad didn't get the point.

"What can I do?"

"Don't worry, my boy, we'll tell you what to do. We're in the process of setting up a number of new corporations. The ink is hardly dry on the charters. They'll be holding companies to allow us to deal in food and clothing for the war effort, should it come. And manufacturing of arms and transportation. And the raising and lending of funds to support a war that might cost a million dollars a day!"

"Think of it!" Caleb said. "A million dollars a day!" He stabbed his quail with his fork and slashed it to pieces with a sharp silver-handled knife. Chad decided to attack his bird too, just to keep them from hectoring him, but when he did so the small fowl slipped off his plate, staining the tablecloth, and propelling a jet of buttery sauce onto Randall Renfield's formerly spotless silk vest.

"I'm so sorry," Chad said, attempting to wipe Renfield's waistcoat with his napkin.

"Never mind," Randall said, impatiently. "You're young and unknown and able to see the big picture. And you're half Southern and half Northern. We'll install you as head of one or more of these new companies we're setting up. All you have to do is go to the office from time to time and attend board meetings. Much of the time you can just stay home and read Greek. Of course, either Caleb or I will chair the boards of these companies. It will earn you the approbation of the financial community and you'll surely please Phillipse. Phillipse has high ideals. Even so, when we more practical men show him what's necessary, he's smart and swift to act."

"Might I add, Randall, that Chad is still young and may not fully appreciate the financial dilemma. Remember that the panic of '57 plunged us into an economic mire. Lost revenues, unemployment, a threat of inflation. Now it's happening again. Already in this new year we're seeing a business downturn. Bankruptcies up. Wages down. We need stimulus. And to do that, we need strong Federal leadership, a central bank, and more tariffs. And a President who knows how to make a really great speech and still act in the way we tell him to."

"What would my title be," Chad said, hoping to cover up his clumsiness.

Randall was too fired up now to worry about the grease on his clothes. "We'll call you President or something like that. Of course, not all the companies will remain in business."

"What's the point of starting them if you already know some of them will fail?"

"There'll be a cheapening of the money market. Money will flow like water in the Croton Reservoir! And much of it will find its way into investments. And what better way to invest than in a promising new company? We'll make a fair profit on the initial stock offering. If the company prospers we'll make even more. If it fails, we'll take our bounty and reinvest it."

"Even if all this is based on a bloody war?"

"We're not politicians. If war comes we'll support it on principle and participate for profit."

"It's the patriotic thing to do, all things considered," Caleb joined in.

"Yes, and there's no nobler mission in man than love for, and sacrifice for, one's country. As you might put it, Chad, *dulce et decorum est pro patria mori.*"

* * *

Chad sat next to his bejeweled Clarissa in her shimmering new dress, purchased specifically for their first night at the opera as an engaged couple. Her shoulders edged out on either side, her slender neck was covered in pearls. Although it was still January she carried an elaborate black fan with ivory insets. He couldn't help feeling a possessive pride as she sat beside him in the Renfield box. He watched as the orchestra seats filled slowly, and blushed with pride when he saw men gazing at his fiancée, then turning to their guests in animated conversation about what they saw: one of the most beautiful, and richest, young women in all New York, leaning her head towards him with a smile. Below the railing, out of sight, he held her hand. His excitement made him warmer, his pride made him bolder, and the afterglow of his lunch at the Federal Club made him more confident than ever.

"What did Uncle Randall have to say," Clarissa asked.

"It wasn't just your uncle, mine too. My Uncle Caleb from Boston. He's important in the family hierarchy, second only to my Grandfather, Bartleby Laymus. You'll meet him, he's promised to come to the wedding."

"But what did they want?" She squeezed his hand in anticipation.

"I guess your uncle and mine are setting up a number of new enterprises. Financial combines, commodities, import-export. I think it would be another stage of the Laymus operation and your father's bank. They said the country is about to change and they want to take advantage of every opportunity."

"There were hints about new developments when Uncle Randall dined with us a few days ago. Are you too modest or are you going to turn out to be secretive? I wouldn't like that, Chad, if you kept things from me."

"The truth is, Clarissa, they'd like me to head up several of these companies. Act as President. They're eager to have my expertise and my connections. They think I could help them with the South if these secessions are permanent, and they believe my mother's family would look favorably on my taking such a position. And your family, too, would benefit, which means you and I would benefit."

"I'm so proud of you, my darling. I told Father you weren't just a bookworm."

"What do you mean by that?"

"Nothing, dear. You know you have a reputation for bookishness. That's all right. This new man from that bank in Hartford, the one whose father sent him off to Germany to be educated, they say he's very well read, speaks several languages, collects art, and is as much at home on the family yacht as on Wall Street."

"Whom are you comparing me with?"

"In my heart no one compares to you. I love it when you touch me." She looked deeply into his eyes, turned her gaze to the audience below, and then spoke again. "J. P. Morgan."

"What?"

"J. Pierpont Morgan, that banker from Hartford. He's just as educated as you and not much older. They say he's made of steel, under his polished veneer. And he doesn't even need an adviser for his art collections. He picks most of it out himself. And he loves books more than anything!" She smoothed her skirt and adjusted her bracelets. "Oh darling, we'll have such a great life. I know they'll settle this tariff controversy soon and the Southern states, how could they prosper without us? You're not the only man here tonight, I'd wager, with complicated parentage."

"What are you implying?" In his mind's eye Chad was eight again, peeking under the parlor doors, seeing only the hem of his mother's dress swinging back and forth as his Grandfather Bartleby raged and scolded.

"Don't be sensitive, Chad. You're half Southern, everybody knows that.

But there are honorable people in the South just as there are in the North. Even in the West—look at Marcus, and he's from Ohio! Now you're almost a symbol of it, the two sides coming together, under the flag of the House of Renfield. We'll have such a great life and we'll be one of the richest young couples in New York, maybe the richest of them all when you get all those trusts."

"How did you know about that?"

"Chad, my family would never permit me to marry without investigating my preferred suitor. You were preferred, so you were investigated. Did you think it would be otherwise? When the Laymus family settles in with mine, the restrictions on your mother's trust funds will be lifted and when you're thirty you'll come into even more than that legacy you're living on now."

"You know more about my affairs than I do."

"Don't be angry, darling. You've snared the best catch in *tout* New York. I love you and respect you and I know we'll be happy. We'll have a lot of children and Father will build us a grand new house up by the new Central Park. The governess can take our children to play there. You can race your trotting horses against my father in the new park." She looked deeply into his eyes, then slightly frowned. "He loves to race but he doesn't like to lose."

"Clarissa, I haven't got any trotting horses."

"You will, my dearest, you will."

The door behind them opened and closed as Schuyler and Marcus took their seats. They were almost identical in dress, and both seemed flushed and excited.

"You'll never guess who we saw in the lobby," Marcus said. "Solomon Steinmann, at the opera! They say he almost never goes out anymore. He's got his daughter Susan with him."

"The way she's dressed I thought at first it was his son," Schuyler said.

"That's very naughty of you, Schuyler," Clarissa said. "She wears tailored clothes, and all those tweeds, to hide her figure. They say she has a very fine figure but her race is more modest than we."

"And Lincoln's here," Marcus went on. "He was downstairs talking with the Republican bigwigs. He ought to be taking his seat any minute now. The curtain should go up soon, it's already late."

Chad had shared with no one the scene he'd discovered in the Renfield Mansion just before Christmas. Neither Marcus nor Schuyler had approached him on the subject, as if by common consent it should be relegated to some prankish childhood memory, and would make no difference whatsoever to the newest member of the Renfield family. He decided to change the subject.

"You saw Lincoln downstairs?"

"Oh yes, he's here to meet with the power brokers, the ones who wanted him nominated in the first place. There!" Marcus rose to his feet. "There he comes!"

As the tall thin man in an ill-fitting frock coat took his seat, there was a murmur and bustle among the crowd. About half of the audience stood until the President-elect was seated. Others continued to look at their programs. Chad borrowed Clarissa's opera glasses. Lincoln's face was inscrutable.

Chad turned his attention back to the program. The evening's offering, translated as "A Masked Ball," was one of the most popular of the Verdi operas to cross the sea. Chad read the summary, confused as to why an Italian composer would set this tale in colonial New England. It involved a political assassination at a costume party. He doubted if the Laymus clan or any other old New England family would permit, much less attend, such an ostentatious event.

"Marcus, do you know why this Verdi fellow would set an opera in New England?"

"Censorship, my boy. The noble houses of Europe, the ones who rule, would never permit a play to be performed, or an opera, in this case, which seems to make it possible for a political leader to be gunned down in the midst of a crowd by upstarts."

"It's not very realistic," Chad said.

"Of course not, dear boy, it's an opera."

April 1861

Chad and Clarissa decided to take tea with his mother. Although he'd grown accustomed to tension and anxiety in his East 10th Street home, it was calm and peaceful compared to the Renfield Mansion. For the first two weeks of the month, Clarissa told him, the house was in a furor night and day. Messengers delivered heavy envelopes full of reports and contracts and news of the foreign exchanges. Merchants and lawyers, shippers and factory owners, bankers and old money dowagers came and went throughout the day, and groups of partners and collaborators and ambitious businessmen eager to participate flocked at night to the home of Phillipse Renfield. For now it was not just gossip. War had come.

Chad welcomed the chance to offer strength and safe harbor to his bride-to-be. His town house was not a mansion, but it was large and respectable and well maintained. They had a library and fine furniture and oil paintings, some of them primitive renderings of his mother's 17th and 18th century ancestors, including Great Grandfather Corbin Chadwick, the fiery Puritan parson-turned-patriot during the War of Independence, a privateer in 1812 who later sat as a judge and then invested in the Laymus mills, forming a liaison that eventually joined his name and theirs in Chadwick Laymus Wales.

"Clarissa, dear, have some tea and try to relax. Your father's not ignoring you, it's this war. Our world is changing so fast we'll find it hard to keep up, and it's in times like these that family is so important. I'm receiving news daily from my relatives in Boston and Worcester. I expect to hear soon from Chad's father. But Virginia seceded yesterday, so even that's uncertain now." Harriet poured tea in Clarissa's cup and handed her a plate of sweets.

"What else could we expect," Chad said. "The minute South Carolina fired on Fort Sumter, Lincoln and his cronies in Washington got the excuse they needed. It was General Beauregard who gave the order to attack. Do you remember him, Mother? He was Commandant at West Point. He visited the Renfields once when we were there. Now they say he's head of the Confederate army."

"Father said the war should be short," Clarissa said, "but he's suggested I leave New York anyway. He thinks rebels may sneak into the harbor and shell the city from the East River. There's panic everywhere downtown. Panic in the streets and panic on the market. Stocks went down yesterday and Father says it will get worse. Bonds too."

"Leave? Clarissa, I want you near. I want to take care of you myself. I couldn't rest easily if you were out of my sight for very long." They were seated side by side on the larger sofa, facing Harriet, who took her usual place on her settee, her full skirt spread like a blanket over the cushions.

"Father thinks I'll be safer at Yellowfields. We've got a large staff. It's close to the river but there's a huge cliff there. Only one way up and it's guarded night and day. There are many prestigious estates nearby. There's a new steamer that makes a round trip in a single day. We've assembled a fine library, there's a garden. It ought to look very colorful and fresh right now, with the forsythia and tulips and dogwood blooming. I don't like what's happening here. I don't like it at all."

Chad took her hand. He'd never seen her so unsure of herself and it brought out his protective instincts. He looked at his mother as he spoke. "Yellowfields is a great estate and the militia of Westchester and adjoining counties keep close watch. But what about renegades? There may be bands of raiders on the loose. I can't permit it, my darling. I simply can't let you out of my sight."

"Chad, you really ought to let Mr. Renfield make these decisions. He must know more than we do what's best."

"Mother, the Seventh Regiment's been called up and they're leaving for Washington tomorrow. The Seventh! People from the best families are in the

Seventh, and now they're leaving for the capital. The Southerners will likely invade Washington first, not New York. They need us. They've got bank accounts here, they need our letters of credit and bills of transport. They can't wait until their cotton gets to England to get paid. The banking houses are critical. Why would they bombard us? At least half of New York is on their side anyway. It's this warmongering Lincoln that's causing the trouble. And it's all about the tariffs. Uncle Caleb and Clarissa's Uncle Randall have filled me in on all this. After all, it's likely that I'll have to accelerate my involvement with their new companies. New York City is the undisputed center of the economy and the economy is what fuels the war."

He stood up, stretched, and positioned himself behind Clarissa, still staring at his mother. "Of course, I may have to go to Richmond, to look after certain negotiations there. We're expecting Southern investors in these new companies I'm in charge of. I'll have to decide when the time is right. Clarissa, if I've got to go to Virginia, maybe it would be best for you to stay at Yellowfields. I'd worry about your safety here in New York if I were out of town."

"Chad, you'd best leave these decisions to Clarissa's family. Actually, it should be Phillipse we listen to. Begging your pardon, Clarissa, Randall's not as knowing as he pretends to be. Neither is my brother Caleb. Both of them live in the shadow of an older and more accomplished person. Son, you're still young and inexperienced in these matters. You have no military training. Older and tougher people may be needed."

"I was highly praised in my boxing class at Princeton, Mother. I was first in fencing. I'm in excellent physical condition, and besides, I've got a reason to be strong." He placed his hand gently on Clarissa's bare collarbone. "Clarissa is my betrothed. It's I who must assure her safety."

"Your grandfather Bartleby played a key role in 1812. He commandeered a privateer and went to Washington after the British burned it. We've heard stories about the Revolution, what can happen to rich young women left at home in a big city where hordes of immigrants and other rowdies are likely to riot. They burn and loot and kill, in a war. I think Clarissa's right. Why don't you just go with her to Yellowfields? It will be so pleasant upriver in springtime. You can plan your wedding. You can study your Latin. You can run your companies from there."

"First of all, Mother, I've got a responsibility to protect you as well as Clarissa. And how do you think I can run all these new companies from a Hudson River estate? There's only the telegraph line and the rebels may cut it. The river boat may be suspended if the Confederate warships break through Fort Clinton and head up the river."

"What a horrid thought," Harriet said. "You have such a colorful way of speaking, Chadwick, that it seems to me you might serve your country better by writing some interpretive essays. Based on your knowledge of history, you might draw significant parallels. We're all split up here. Mr. Lincoln received only a third of our votes, and the street gangs downtown are out in force. Shopkeepers are afraid, there are reports of vandalism, and Negroes are assaulted every day. Some of them are freed blacks with their own little businesses. Somebody threw a brick through the window of a carpentry shop near South Street. Even the fishery workers are divided. What's to become of us?"

"Mrs. Wales, you're welcome at Yellowfields. It might be the best possible thing for you."

"You've already become the daughter I never had. But I must stay here, whatever the cost. If there's real violence, one of my family's agents will take me to a steamer bound for Boston. I'd surely be safe in Boston."

"Mother, the rabble in Baltimore has already attacked the Massachusetts regiment. Before it even got to Washington and Maryland hasn't even seceded. Lincoln can't afford to lose Maryland, it surrounds the capital. The South is fighting for its life. It's united, they think and act as one. The North is divided. There's too much disagreement. Your abolitionist friends are trying to make slavery the issue in this war, or at least they'll try to, if I'm not mistaken. No, I'll stay in New York to tend to my new business affairs. If Clarissa feels better upriver, I'll go there on weekends. You, Mother, had best stay right here. It's I, your son, who'll spirit you off to a Boston-bound steamer, not some clerk in one of your shipping offices."

Chad turned his back on both women and circled the room, hands clasped behind him, looking for all practical purposes to be Phillipse Renfield and Franklin Wales rolled into one.

June 1861

"There you are, Nephew." It seemed that Marilyn Blaine had not moved one inch from her position when Chad last visited, more than six weeks ago. She eyed him across the room. "Did you not bring your fiancée? Aren't you afraid not to have her by your side during these dangerous days? Should I address you too, Schuyler? Where is your lovely sister?"

Before answering his aunt, Chad quickly decided it was his place to speak for Clarissa now. "She's gone upriver to the Renfield estate. She wants some peace and quiet and to enjoy her gardens."

"She's a rare flower herself. I should think you and Schuyler might be concerned. Look at what's going on! Where will it end?" Marilyn fanned herself and reached for a bonbon. "I'm told they recruited a dozen regiments after that rally in Union Square. Can you imagine? They say there were 200,000 people. How could that be? It's only eleven blocks away and I didn't hear a thing. And they've—what's the word—they've 'bivouacked' them at the Battery and in City Hall Park and all over town. It's like we were living through the French Revolution! Aren't you boys worried about a beautiful woman left to her own devices in the warm sunny air of Westchester?"

Schuyler had been engaged in a private conversation with Marcus Tifton, but he turned quickly to defend Chad and himself from this unexpected attack. "I can assure you, Mrs. Blaine, that my sister is safe and sound. The air is clean, the food is fresh. We've acquired an ample staff, and the militia keeps order in the area night and day. There are a number of substantial estates in the region, including the Van Der Venner's old Dutch house." Schuyler looked around the room expecting to see Eliza Van Der Venner in her usual little chair, but spied only the formidable shadow of Susan Steinmann, dark against the bright shutters that filtered the clear June sunshine of another New York afternoon. Despite her anxious tone, the hostess seemed as comfortable as ever, beached on her chaise.

"I see that you've gathered all your regular guests here today. I should have thought that many of your young male protégés might be bivouacked as well, having felt compelled to join the troops." Chad's remark was greeted with silence and he was sure Susan Steinman, a dark silhouette against the window, was glaring at him. But he didn't care. He was, after all, about to become a major force in the economic life of the nation.

"Say what you will, I'm concerned. That's why my *soirées* have become *après-midis*. Did I say that right, Chad?"

Sensing her defensiveness, Chad was determined not to be drawn in. "I suspect your schedule change was needed to facilitate the presence of some of your newfound friends, Aunt Marilyn. I see people here I've not met before." As he spoke, Chad was examining a most unexpected presence in his social world, standing near Susan Steinmann. He was a young priest—Chad assumed he was Catholic, and not Episcopalian as his family and the Renfields were. He wore, in addition to his clerical collar, a gold colored cross.

"Well, dear boy, you must meet Father Fineas Flaherty. Father Flaherty is a Jesuit, and highly educated, so I suspect you and he might have many common subjects to talk about. Father Flaherty's also immersed in life downtown. He can tell us more about the stability of the lower classes than we'll ever read in all these newspapers. They only print what they want to, and only if it supports their views, either radically pro-Lincoln, or obsessed with commerce and trade. Didn't we all agree in this very room that our future belongs to you writers and artists, not to the lords of commerce?"

Father Flaherty seemed embarrassed. "I suspect, Madam, that the future is God's."

"Perhaps so," a deep, unfamiliar voice interjected. "But until we get some direct communication from Him, I think we should all secure our bank accounts, cock our pistols, lock our doors, and then, only then, Father, can we have the peace of mind to pray."

"Chad and Schuyler. And Marcus," Aunt Marilyn said. "Have you met Bynum Bradley-West? He was born in North Carolina but when he escaped from Chapel Hill he decided to live in London for several years. And spent time at Oxford, I believe. Now he's returned home, or at least close to home, and you'll see that he's left his Southern accent in England and brought back a hyphenated name, there being no tariffs on accents or hyphens."

Bynum stood erect before the fireplace, sheltered for the summer by a Hudson River landscape painted on a metal screen. He was in his thirties, Chad guessed, tall, slender, with thick dark hair. He wore finely tailored clothes, probably bought in London. Chad vowed to pay more attention to his own wardrobe now that he might have to journey to the South, or even abroad, in the management of his dozen or so corporations.

"Mrs. Blaine, I'm honored to be here but if my presence offends any of your guests I'd prefer to excuse myself." Father Flaherty's voice was soft but firm. He sounded genuine to Chad, who immediately took pity on him.

"We're all tolerant people here, and our nation was founded by pilgrims seeking religious freedom. Some of them were ancestors of mine. I should think, Father Flaherty, that you might have insights to offer us as a result of your Christian labors downtown." Chad felt more self-confident than ever. "As for the gentleman who has returned from England without his accent, I sympathize. I'm half Southern and was influenced by my father's manner of speech. I recovered from it only after four years at Princeton. In the beginning I even pronounced my Latin with a drawl."

A ripple of laughter spurred him on. Was he becoming, at last, the worldly *raconteur* he had so long hoped to be? "As for this war, well, we're not French and there will be no reign of terror in this country. Peace and freedom are in all our best interests but the rights of states to manage their internal affairs haven't yet been successfully contested, not since the agreements they made in ratifying our Constitution, or the Missouri Compromise or the Kansas-Nebraska Act. Such independence is guaranteed by the very fact, as well as the specific documents, of our Union. Popular sovereignty has been our watchword."

"Your father would be proud of you," Bynum Bradley-West enigmatically said.

Father Flaherty spoke again in his quiet, determined way. "If you want to see patriotism, look at the volunteers camping around Manhattan before we send them off to be gunned down on the battlefield. I was at that rally on Union Square, Mrs. Blaine. Yes, there were huge crowds, and much speechifying and flag waving. But they mustered seventeen regiments, and they came from the Irish and the Hungarians. Italians, Poles, Germans, even the Netherlands. They love America. They feel blessed to be here. And they don't want to see our Union dissolved in a war fomented by the slave states."

"The question of slavery is not the basis of this war, if we're to believe the President of the United States," Bynum said, keeping his voice as well modulated as his opponent. "He's made it plain that he doesn't believe he's got the authority to abolish slavery in individual states. In fact, he proposed at one point that the best plan might be, eventually, to ship these poor creatures to the Caribbean or back to Africa.'

"It was their home, after all," Marcus said.

"Hardly," Bynum said, surveying the room as if anxious to see the effect of his comments. "I've been to Africa, and the conditions are not beneficial. Many slave families have been here for generations. English is their language now. They look to the land for sustenance and to authority for guidance. Indeed, your church, Father, is quite strong in one of the so-called slave states. Georgia, if you're unaware."

"My church is a large one, Sir, and we're known to have different opinions within it."

"Nevertheless," Bynum continued, "this war is about tariffs and economic development, about the dominance of Northern industries and the lack of resources in the South, a three-crop economy with few factories and fewer railways. But they've got spirit and they're determined. In the French Revolution, it was finally the people, I won't say the masses, who translated the Enlightenment into action. And a few years later they welcomed a tyrant to solve their problems. I'd suggest, Father, that you consider your church's historic position on the issue of war."

The normally unflappable Marilyn Blaine was growing uneasy with the rising tempers. "How about their clothes," she said. "All these soldiers, some of them illiterate, I suppose, sign up to lay their lives on the line and the Federal government, who asked for them in the first place, doesn't even have the funds—or the will—to clothe them."

"States have traditionally outfitted their own militia in this Republic, Mrs. Blaine." Bynum was apparently not willing to bow to his hostess on this matter either.

"Yes," Father Flaherty said, "And the state and some private sources have pledged money for that purpose. The problem is who'll be the supplier. Brooks

Brothers got the first contract for uniforms. I suspect most of you young men shop there. But they found they couldn't keep up with the schedule so they delivered inferior goods that fell apart before they were out of the city. Of course, Brooks Brothers is anxious to keep its good name, so it replaced the defective materials. But there are scores of suppliers—not just clothes but food and even weapons—who'll make millions on this war, providing brave men with faulty rifles and rancid food to eat before they fall dead or wounded on the battleground."

Marilyn was eager to stem the flow of controversy. "How about those Zouaves? Their sponsors have clothed them like emirs out of the Arabian Nights. Scarlet and tan, silk sashes, turbans and swords. Is that anyway to go to war? I suspect some of my young friends may decide to enlist after all, if they can dress up like that."

"I'm afraid I can't joke about this," Susan Steinmann said. She emerged from the blurring light of the window and stood closer to Marilyn's chaise. "It's always the same, a mob chanting slogans, bands playing loud march music, flags and uniforms and speeches. But it always ends the same way. No matter who wins, the price is too high to laugh about. My family came here from Portugal before the Revolution and we've supported every war this nation has fought since. But these were wars aimed at establishing our independence and safety. These were wars that sought to guarantee freedom and hope. This war will be different, my father says. This war will tear us to pieces and we'll pay the price for years to come. My father fears we may never be whole again."

Chad had grown to admire Susan but suspected her severe dress and rigid posture indicated a strength and determination that might be considered "unfeminine" by most of his family. He was about to comment when Bynum Bradley-West spoke instead.

"Miss Steinmann is quite right. The price will be heavy. There will be anguish and suffering and death. What is the alternative? Every major war we humans have waged has affected the course of history; but no war has ever changed human nature, not one whit. War, like poverty, will always be with us."

"What a dismal conclusion!" Marilyn almost roused herself out of her supine comfort and then sat back with a sigh. "Progress! Haven't you read these English writers? They've done so much to interpret our history. It's a steady march towards a better world. If there are obstacles along the way, we'll overcome them. Someday, I'm sure, we'll relegate these paltry disputes to the dustbin of history where they belong, and concentrate our efforts on a better life for all. That's what you writers and artists have to do. That isn't just your calling, it's your responsibility!"

Chad didn't want to regress to his former status as a quiet onlooker. "Surely the truth lies somewhere in between," he said. "Challenge, confrontation, resolution, and then another challenge. It's the dialectic of history. You need only read Hegel to understand that."

"Perhaps in the short view," Bynum replied. "Look what happened, all over Europe, in 1848 and afterwards. Blood was shed, treaties were broken, boundaries were disputed, crowds rose up in the streets. But the poor still find their way to the docks of Europe, anxious to board a ship for America. And now, when they get here, they'll find we're as belligerent towards one another as Europe has been for a thousand years."

Marcus Tifton eyed Bynum intently. "Perhaps Mr. Bradley-West doesn't recall a conversation we had in London during my trip with Schuyler. It was at that French embassy party, Madame de la Tour du Pin's niece was there, do you recall, Sir?"

"Indeed I do," Bynum replied. He'd placed his teacup on the mantle, and turned to face Marcus directly. Marilyn shuffled uneasily on her chaise, then soothed her edginess with a cordial. There was a taut silence in the room. Bynum went on. "The discussion had to do with the admission of new states and whether or not they should be allowed to have slavery. I made it clear then, as I do now, that as a Southerner I'm loyal to the right of each state to formulate policy. But I also stated clearly that I'm personally against slavery of any kind, including wage slavery and political slavery, and, please note me on this Miss Steinmann, gender slavery."

"I said to you in London, Sir, that you're before your time. I'll say it again here. But perhaps you'll find a method to reconcile the apparent difference between your emotional loyalty and your rational and democratic convictions."

"When I was ordained and ordered to New York," Father Flaherty said, "I was told politics and religion were not to be discussed socially, even by a priest. I've been here two hours already and all we seem to talk about is politics."

Schuyler seemed taken with the priest and moved across the room and stood beside him, looking at Marcus who was now positioned next to Bynum. "Then let's talk about religion, Father." For the first time Chad detected a gleeful twinkle in his soon-to-be brother-in-law's eyes. "Expiation is one of your tenets, is it not? I understand that these malevolent character traits we humans share, according to Mr. Bradley-West, are easily reconciled by a simple confession. Thereby, as I understand it, the contrite may go forth and do it all over again."

There was a titter of embarrassed laughter. Even Marilyn now seemed bothered and held her cordial glass up to the light, apparently trying to determine what she was drinking. She sat it down and took a chocolate instead. She said nothing and the room grew quiet.

"The troubled spirit's often calmed by a good meal, a few hours of comfort in one's own home, and the unparalleled solace of a loving spouse," Bynum said. "But here in New York, this great city that claims to be in the vanguard of our national progress, there are wretched conditions that would make medieval Europe look like the Promised Land."

"Sir, I must disagree emphatically. Emphatically!" Chad was surprised at his own vehemence since the needs of the working classes occupied his thoughts only when he was disputing with his mother. "We strive to better these conditions. Most of the poor you describe are immigrants, and wouldn't come here if they didn't prefer it to their original homes. America is the beacon, the hope, and the solace for millions, even the ones who haven't got here yet. And as we push on to the West, there will be opportunities never seen in any other country in history."

"Hear hear!" said Marcus. "Indeed!" said Schuyler. "We shall see," said Bynum.

"It won't do to underestimate the despair and privation of the poor in this city," Father Fineas said. "A fourth of them are Irish. Many of them are parishioners of mine. I minister to them daily. I help them bear their burden, or I should say my Church and my faith help them to endure and to find hope. They're crowded into dark tenements, sanitation is wretched, there's not enough to eat and hardly enough clothing to cover their thin bodies. Many of them resort to drink and to violence. Gangs ravage their own communities. But in my Church there's respite, there's asylum. Their spirits are comforted by our sacrament of confession, and their hearts are lifted by the hope of redemption and of a glorious heaven. Would any of you want to take that way from them?"

"Yes!" Chadwick said abruptly. He'd not thought this out but he plunged on. "Does it not say that the truth shall set you free? Truth, that's what I seek. My study of ancient literature and philosophy may seem impractical but it's given me a mission, to continue to think and to reason and to search for whatever it is we can decide is true. And now that I've become responsible for a major section of the Renfield-Laymus endeavors, I believe my practical side has been exposed. So now I must keep alert on two fronts, first against economic chaos, and second, against those who would lure us towards a rosy but false horizon, one that promises much but offers little. The middle path, Mr. Bradley-West. Moderation and skepticism, Father."

"Well, you'll soon have a chance to put your practicality to a test in your financial enterprises. Stocks fall daily with the latest war news. There's an increase in bankruptcies. Thousands have lost their jobs, and those who are working find their wages cut. How long do you think they'll put up with that? And how much of their frustration will they vent on the South and on the Negro, whom they see as competitors for their jobs?" Bynum edged closer to Chad as he spoke. During the ensuing lull in conversation, Marilyn gestured with her fan to a young man perched near her, who seated himself at the piano, where he began to play a melodic but melancholy sonata of Schubert's.

Bynum was now standing next to Chad. He leaned forward and whispered in his ear. "I was with your father in London last month. I've got news of him for you. And some letters from him I think you'll be eager to read. We should meet somewhere, privately. And alone."

THREE

July 1861

Chad fidgeted in the crowded downtown restaurant, although the table Bynum had reserved, conveniently situated in a corner, gave them a soothing privacy. Thick white tablecloths were topped with heavy plates and crisp napkins beside a brimming breadbasket, a small vase with a few fresh flowers, and silver candlesticks glowing in the noonday half-light from the shuttered windows.

"You had no trouble finding this place, did you?" Bynum had arrived early and sat sipping a glass of white wine. Chad hadn't spotted him from the door, but the *maître d'* led him immediately to Bynum's table.

"I received your invitation yesterday morning and planned my day around it. I came down on an omnibus with the crowds. It's changed a lot while I was away." Chad tired quickly of small talk. He knew little about Bynum Bradley-West, whose mysterious comments about Franklin Wales upset him. The whispered invitation worried him even more when Bynum, after delivering his *sotto voce* message, had suddenly grabbed his hat and stick and bid farewell to Aunt Marilyn and her guests, before the thin, young pianist had finished his Schubert. Now he decided to get to the point immediately. "You say you've got news of my father. You must surely realize this causes me considerable frustration. Not knowing you or anything about your news, I couldn't mention it to my mother. She's worried herself into a fretful condition now that the war has come, especially with the news of the latest battle."

"The reaction to Manassas, or Bull Run as some have called it, has been swift and deep. Stocks plunged yesterday and will go down further today. The Southern victory has upset Washington and all the sympathizers with the North. I guess now they realize who they're dealing with."

"Please don't delay, Mr. Bradley-West. What about my father?"

"I'll call you Chad if I may, and you must call me Bynum. Believe me, we're destined to be friends. Your father's well, and you shouldn't worry. The news is complex and I'll explain it as we eat. It's mostly good news so you can remain calm. The waiter will be over in a minute. Let me give you further background. Until the battle at Bull Run, this war consisted of little skirmishes and some coastal confrontations. There were few casualties and no indications about which side was stronger. There were two or three little conflicts in Western Virginia—the sympathies there are mixed and there's already talk of breaking off from Virginia and sticking with the Union. That'll take a long time to happen, if it happens at all." Bynum sipped sparingly from his glass, which reflected both filtered sunlight and flickering candles as he raised it to his lips.

"Let me give you more details because it will affect your reaction to the news I wish to impart. The day before the Manassas battle, the South convened a Provincial Confederate Congress. So there's no turning back. There are many Northern sympathizers with the Cause. And there are those who don't favor the South as much as they fear the erosion of their liberties in the North. I suppose you're aware than Lincoln has suspended the right of *habeas corpus* in what he referred to as "certain circumstances". That means a Federal official could walk into this restaurant, arrest us both as conspirators, and lock us in jail without making any charges, and without bringing us before a judge. The next step, I'm sure, will be to establish military tribunals to try American citizens as combatants for the enemy. All this is in direct violation of the Constitution, regardless of your feelings about secession." Bynum lowered his voice as a waiter approached. "Try the lamb stew. It's a bit heavy for a summer day but tasty. Will you have some cold soup first?"

"Whatever you say," Chad replied. He didn't really enjoy dining out and he was far too preoccupied about this stranger's mixed messages to worry about food. Bynum placed their orders and selected a bottle of red wine.

"In short, the North is scared. Lincoln and his high-tariff Eastern supporters will try to take drastic measures. Congress isn't at all unified on any of these issues. In fact, the day after Bull Run they passed a resolution affirming that the war's being waged to preserve the Union, not to do away with slavery. And the border states are considered to be slave states anyway. It's a very dangerous situation. Kentucky, in particular, will find it hard to remain neutral, especially if Confederate troops invade, which they're sure to do, and fairly soon, I suspect."

"Bynum, please. What of my father?"

"He's a courageous man and you should be proud of him. I know he would have been pleased to hear what you said at Mrs. Blaine's gathering. Yes, it takes courage to do what he's doing." Bynum looked up at the *sommelier* who presented a dusty old bottle, waited while he opened it, savored its bouquet and sipped it delicately, and nodded to the waiter, who poured ruby liquid into both their glasses.

"Your father's a loyal son of the South, and you already know he'd never take any stand against Virginia. He decided he could do his best fighting the blockade. The idea that Lincoln and his cronies would blockade our Southern ports, robbing us of food and staples, depriving us of our export income, reducing us to political impotence, the whole thing is outrageous. Chad, your father has become a blockade-runner. He and his crew will outwit the Northern gunboats and facilitate a lively trade with England. And of course, he'll make substantial but fair profits while doing it."

"A blockade runner? How did you learn about it?"

"My prolonged residence in England was not without purpose. I've acted for several years as an agent for a major Southern bank, and have represented state governments in private negotiations with potential allies in Europe. When the war came, I was asked by a coalition of Southern leaders to work directly for them. I'm being paid, so you can call me a mercenary. The pay is handsome but there are great risks. Of course I'm taking a chance telling you this before I've ascertained your views. But the comments you made during your aunt's party have encouraged me to believe that you'd not betray me, even if you choose not to join me."

"Join you? But I'm already engaged in important work for the Renfield-Laymus interests."

"What are you doing for them?"

"I haven't got an office or anything, or a staff. They're setting up a network of new companies that I'll eventually be president of. We wish to aid those who might protect our interests, people who don't necessarily favor military action, and would probably prefer the Southern states to go their own way. The point is we need each other. My mother's family owns one of the biggest textile combines in the country. My fiancée's family, she's a Renfield, are bankers with deep ties to Richmond, Charleston, Montgomery and New Orleans. We're patriots but we're also practical. We want to preserve order so our economic bounty can trickle down to the people. Is that so bad?"

"Why are you so defensive? Part of my job is to see that the banking and textile interests are served on both sides. As you know there are banks in New York and Philadelphia doing business with the South as we speak. Their cotton is finding its way to your New England mills and your slave cloth is wending its troubled way southward. What I'm going to propose to you won't interfere with your new-found position as head of a lot of hastily incorporated companies with rather ambiguous purposes."

"Sir, we're an honorable family engaged in honorable enterprise."

"Calm down, Chad. I'm your ally. I realized when I heard you speak out at Marilyn Blaine's that you're a thinker. Like many thinkers, your principles are deep. You keep an open mind as long as you can, but when the evidence is in, you're guided by your sense of right and wrong. That's why I think you may want to join me and your father—indirectly of course—in our work, which seeks the same ends that you and your family—and Miss Renfield's family—so desire."

"I've been accused of thinking too much. I admit I may seem to some people to be indecisive. Yes, it's the overall picture I try to examine. But I still don't understand what you're asking."

"I gather information for the Southern leaders, both in commerce and in government. I transmit this information through a network of agents throughout the Eastern States, from Maine to Florida. I arrange for certain transactions to occur. Supplies. Arms. Foodstuffs. I transmit letters of credit for both my English clients and for the South. I work tirelessly for a fair resolution to the conflict, by helping the South to remain strong, so tyranny cannot prevail, and justice can be found despite political in-fighting. This will allow people like you and me, thoughtful principled people, to make rational choices based on tested ideas, instead of falling pray to the rabble, and to the ruthlessness of vested interests who would sacrifice our constitution for a percentage of the profits."

"Are you saying you're a spy?" Chad felt a tremor in his arms and a transient dizziness. He sipped his wine, which proved to be excellent and soothing.

"You're too skilled at languages to pigeonhole yourself—and me—with such nomenclature. You must know better than most that nomenclature is not wisdom. Indeed, words sometimes stand between us and reality. You cited Hegel. Let me cite Kant."

"But isn't it still treason?"

"Treason's a simplistic concept. I seek to help my colleagues in both the North and the South, and to help myself in the process. I believe you'll find, Chad, that you can't always keep yourself on a narrow path that allows no room for moral maneuvering. If we must take a side, let's take it judiciously and secretly, so we may change our opinions if circumstances warrant it down the road. Thoughtful examination of complex issues is not synonymous with treason!"

Bynum sipped his wine with obvious relish and ate quickly from his plate of lamb stew. The lunchtime crowd was animated, probably about the war, and the blend of their voices created a drowsy hum. Chad had ingested more wine than usual. He felt sleepy and confused. He was, on one day set up as a corporate president, and now being asked to serve as a clandestine agent—a spy.

"I just don't know, Bynum. Be assured I'd not betray you. But I must think carefully on your proposition." He'd eaten very little, so he took a few bites. "What about the letters from my father?"

"Ah, here they are, my boy. And here's my card. I've got rooms in Third Avenue at 18th Street." Bynum reached into his vest pocket and pulled out several envelopes tied together with a gray ribbon. There was sealing wax on each envelope and they'd not been opened. "I don't know what he has to say but I suggest you read them and think it over before you share these letters with anyone else, especially your mother. And certainly not Clarissa Renfield."

* * *

His mother's letter had called him home from Princeton less than a year ago, Chad thought, and now he sat in their parlor on East 10th Street once again. This time, it was three letters; they were in his vest pocket; and they were written to him from his father and secretly delivered by a mercenary and spy who, barely three hours ago, had attempted to recruit him as a traitor.

He tried to mask his distress as his mother poured tea. It was an old habit less often observed during this troubled year. But he let her fill his cup, took a finger sandwich from the tray, and eyed the small pastries she'd arranged on a finely detailed silver platter which he recognized as an early 18th century heirloom she proudly displayed in her breakfront, telling all who would listen that it was left her by her maternal grandfather, Corbin Chadwick.

"How did you meet this man," Harriet asked in a low voice. She kept her eyes averted, staring towards the front windows, then glancing down at her teapot. She rearranged some of the pastries. "Where does one meet such a person," she asked again.

"He was one of Aunt Marilyn's guests. I went there to meet Schuyler and his friend. I thought it might give me a chance to cultivate him. As Clarissa's brother, he must wonder about his place in the family business and he may have learned, by now, that I'm to head up these new business operations. That is, if I decide to go on with it. Now I'm not sure."

"Poppycock," his mother exclaimed. "You're to marry one of the richest and most attractive women in New York. They've offered you a rather special position for a man as young as you. What difference does it make what you'll actually do? Even if it's some kind of figurehead, a go-between, whatever, you'll be fixed for life. And you'll have time to do what you like best. You could even have them build you a separate house at Yellowfields. I hear they've got a hundred acres of grounds. An orchard. Their own dairy. Plenty of fresh water. They've even got a maze."

"I may be needed in town. Especially if I have to interrupt my further studies with this proposed position in commerce."

"Eventually there'll be a faster train up there, perhaps along the riverbank, all the way to Yellowfields. Why can't you just let good things happen? If you want to question everything, do it in private. Write something. Emerson writes mostly short essays now. You could replace him, in years to come, as our leading commentator on philosophy and the arts."

"You always make it so simple. You never look at the whole situation. And you blind yourself to anything you perceive as negative."

"Not slavery! I should say, Chad, that I've been repelled by the fact that you're not the least concerned about this great evil. You get excited about these ancient writers—Plato and Aristotle and Hegel—but you don't take a stand on the evil right under your eyes."

"Hegel's not ancient, Mother. And you needn't try to divert me with these lectures about my personal convictions. Bynum Bradley-West came to Aunt Marilyn's expressly to see me. He admitted as much. It was Father who told him to go there."

"Your father? How could your father even know him? I thought you said he's been living in England for ten years, after he left Chapel Hill. That's a state university, isn't it? Do our kind of people go there?"

"See how you categorize everything? Your mind is divided up into little pigeonholes. If it doesn't fit, you throw it out. You worry about issues too large to do anything about while your marriage collapses and your son is left to make up his mind alone about extremely complicated matters."

"With your fine education you've learned to engage in circumlocution far more fanciful and obscure than anything a poor untutored woman like me could achieve. Will you answer my question? What has this man got to do with your father, and why did you allow him to poison your mind with obscene offers and mindless allegations? Tell me, I demand it."

She was verging on hysteria again. Chad reached into his vest pocket and pulled out the three letters, the wax seals now broken but the envelopes still secured with a gray ribbon. "These are letters from Father. Sent from Father to me from London. London! And Bynum was recruited to bring them directly to me."

"Bynum? Are you already on a first name basis with this man?"

"We're a lot alike. I don't have to agree with him to like him. I just like him"

"I assume one of the letters is addressed to me?"

"No, Mother, they're all addressed to me. He does ask in one of them that

I convey to you his continued respect and good wishes, and says that due to the outbreak of the war he'll not pursue the divorce right away."

"He said nothing else?"

"Not about you he didn't. It would seem he's metamorphosed into a loving father if not a loyal spouse."

"You're so cruel, Chad." She pressed her fist against her face. Chad headed her off.

"Mother, that routine isn't going to deter me anymore. I'm sorry for your distress but I had nothing to do with it. Indeed, I've been left to fend for myself emotionally ever since I was eight years old. You changed after Grandfather Bartleby gave you that tirade in the parlor. Shortly thereafter Father started to travel more. It wasn't until I was thirteen or so that he came back long enough for us to get to know each other. He used to ask me to lunch with him when he worked downtown at the branch office of First Shenandoah Trust. His family started that bank!"

His mother removed her hands from her face and fixed him with a cold, direct gaze. "You want me to avoid my own feelings so I can spare yours, is that it? Very well, let me tell you something. I'm stronger than any of you. And I've got connections. And friends. And influence. Although my trusts are frozen, my income is still sufficient to maintain this house and my position. And I've got plenty of secrets myself, some of them could ruin your father, ruin you and Clarissa. My secrets could demolish your chances with the Renfield-Laymus empire. They might even bring down the House of Renfield. Do you think Phillipse consented to your marriage because he was so impressed with you? Do you think he would hand over the richest and most beautiful woman in New York without a second thought because you've so captivated him? That he can't wait to have a Greek and Latin scholar in the family running their new businesses? Do you think for a moment I had nothing to do with it?"

She looked directly at him now. Her lips were pressed in a cold horizontal line. Her hands lay calmly on her lap and her head was held high, as if his news of his father had transformed her into a Medea. If so, was he the child to be sacrificed?

"What do you mean?"

"No, what do you mean," His mother said again. "You may now tell me everything that's in those letters. Otherwise you may leave this house tonight."

Although she seemed to be a new person, Chad didn't take her threat seriously. "Very well then. It really doesn't concern you that much. First, he tells me to trust Bynum, to go to him for advice and for help. Then he says he hopes I'll not fight either for or against Virginia, that I'll stay out of the conflict. He says he hopes my marriage will be successful. But then he makes me a promise. He says he's become a blockade-runner out of patriotism. He says it's dangerous and he may not survive. If so, he tells me that he's also profiting from his new role. And he says that a large percentage of his profits are stowed away in London banks. In my name, Mother. My name! He says that if there's a problem after the war, or even during it, if I need to get away for any reason, if I'm threatened or disinherited or otherwise taken advantage of, I can cross the sea, present one of these letters—actual legal documents, for your information—and I'll have enough money to live on comfortably in London. And if it comes to that, Mother, I'll get free of the lot of you!"

"Free? How do you know the money will be there? How do you know it's sufficient? How do you know your father isn't lying again? He's lied before. To me. To my family. Blockade-runner! A small notch above pirate, that's what he is."

"Pirate? Well, Mother, this new you doesn't seem to remember the old you. How about Corbin Chadwick, the grandfather whose name I bear? Didn't you say he made his money by leaving the Church and becoming a privateer in 1812? Robbing English cargo ships on the high seas. Pirates indeed! And then weaseled his way into the Laymus family just as they were getting out of the slave trade. And helped them build up their textile empire as you call it, selling slave cloth and offering humanitarian employment to twelve-year-old girls."

"You'll lower your voice and you'll apologize if you intend to live in this house. And what do you suppose the Renfields will think if they learn your own mother has driven you away?"

"Mother giveth and mother taketh away, is that it? I'll go to Mr. Renfield tonight and explain your actions to him. I'll tell him that I'm happy to take up my position with the new Renfield-Laymus companies. I'll go upriver, take my Clarissa in my arms, and rush her to the altar. And when that's all done, I'll come back here one more time, pack up my clothes and desert you, just like father did. Now I'm beginning to see why!"

Harriet finally lost her resolve and crumpled on the settee, sobbing violently. She reached her hand out to him without looking up. "Go then, if you want to. Go ahead. There's so much you don't understand."

"I don't enjoy this and neither do you."

"Did you know that I'd stoop to blackmail for your sake? That I'd stand up to all of them, defending your right to be a Laymus, and now to be a Renfield? You say you see the whole thing, why can't you see this?"

She was howling now, and Chad was scared. He moved to the settee and took her in his arms. She leaned her head on his chest, still wailing uncontrollably. "Mother, what is it I don't understand?"

She sobbed more quietly now but said nothing more. He held her silently for several minutes, listening to the wind and rain on the front windows as a mid-summer storm swept across Manhattan from the sea, wind and water bound for the West. His fiery resolve was waning. He was filled with guilt and apprehension again. There was a knock on the parlor doors. The housekeeper entered reluctantly, as if she might have been eavesdropping.

"Master Wales, there's a man here to see you. A stranger. He says he has an urgent message for you."

"Wait a minute, I'll be out. Mother, will you be all right now?"

"I've said too much."

"We can settle this later, when we've both calmed down."

Chad opened the sliding doors and stepped into the reception hall. There was a short man in an ill-fitting raincoat, dripping on their marble floor. He squinted out of one eye, scratching his uneven beard. "Are you Chadwick Wales?"

"Yes, what is it?"

"I've got a message for you from a friend." He handed Chad a crumpled and wet envelope. Chad opened it hurriedly. *"Dear Chad, Marcus and I've been assaulted and robbed near Five Points. We're hurt but not badly. We have no more money with us and we're not in a condition to permit public transport. Can you bring a carriage for us? The messenger has directions. We're in the house and shop of a man named Holder Pratt. He took us in when the mob pursued us down Water Street. Please come as soon as you can. And please do not say anything about this to my family."* It was signed simply *"Schuyler."*

* * *

After giving Higgens directions to Holder Pratt's Water Street address, Chad sat back in silence on the leather seats. It was well past five and the rain had blown out towards the West. In the July heat and glare, Chad absorbed the din and chaos of crowds passing before his eyes like a magic lantern show. He'd spent most of his twenty-two years in this city, had been taken to see his father downtown, had been driven by the family coachman to school and birthday parties and boxing and fencing and piano lessons. There were many evocations of his childhood, and the adolescent years before he left for Princeton. But no matter which way he looked, everything seemed changed now. Faces on the sidewalk reminded him of Renaissance etchings in a big book his mother had given him for Christmas when he was twelve, faces of people long since dead, converted to black lines on white paper, their twisted expressions shielding him from their inner anguish.

The noise and smell of the streets brought him repeatedly back to the present. His life grew more complicated by the day, although he felt a growing self-confidence in himself as a scholar, businessman, potentially a family man, perhaps a clandestine agent, a rescuer of his mother from what she hinted was a dark secret, maybe even a statesman of some sort. An essayist, perhaps, who could see the whole situation and sum it up for both North and South. He could live in a big mansion on upper Fifth, near the new park. People would sue for invitations. There'd be a constant stream of visitors. Foreign bankers would seek his advice because his language skills were so good. Young artists and writers would beg him to comment on their work. The governess would bring, each evening at five, his children for him to speak with before he packed them off separately to their dinners and their beds. Then a few quiet moments with his Clarissa, interludes of passion, and a sound and dreamless sleep.

"Mister Chad? Mister Chad?" Higgens's voice roused him from his reverie. "There it is, the house on the corner. Should I wait for you?"

"Would you please, Higgens," Chad leapt out of the carriage, afraid Higgens would know that "Master Chad is daydreaming again," a comment he'd once made while driving him to school.

The building was at an intersection, framed in wood, with two full floors and another one added on the top, with two small dormers. The door was angled on the corner, and in the windows facing each of the intersecting streets, he saw examples of finely crafted furniture—a ballooning lowboy, a pedimented high chest, card tables and intricately carved chairs. Above each of the two windows was an identical sign, carefully incised, painted green, the letters gilded: *Holder Pratt Fine Furniture and Carpentry.*

The front door was closed but unlocked and a small bell sounded when he entered. The two occupants of the anteroom faced him when he came in, but said nothing. The man was over six feet tall, solidly built, and held what appeared to be scale drawings in his hand, probably the design of a custom item, Chad surmised. The man's face was a deep and gleaming black, outlining his bright eyes and flashing teeth. Beside him was a woman, much shorter, with dark curly hair, a prominent bosom, and a face the color of wet sand.

"I'm searching for Holder Pratt," Chad said, his confidence swiftly ebbing. "I believe there's been trouble of some kind." He searched their faces for a reaction, but neither responded. They were sizing him up, obviously, and Chad tingled with a mixture of adventure and embarrassment.

"I'm Holder Pratt. And you, Sir, what is your name?"

Chad paused, "I'm Mr. Wales. I'm here to help my friends."

"Mary, you'd best go on home now. I'll call on you later tonight." The woman rose on tiptoe and planted a warm kiss on Holder's cheek, smiled conspiratorially, and left by the main door. Holder Pratt eyed Chad again before finally nodding his head. "Follow me, then. They're upstairs."

The ceilings were much lower than the rooms on East 10th Street, the stairs narrow and twisting, and the lighting dim. The late afternoon sun had started to fade. Shadows made the climb more difficult and Chad stumbled when the stairs curved abruptly to the left, before reaching a small landing.

"In here. I'll leave you alone with them."

Holder closed the door behind him. Chad waited for his eyes to adjust to the dim light. A kerosene lamp's flickering flame gilded a bulbous globe. A rumpled form twisted slowly on the bed. In a high-backed chair by the window, another form was crumpled in dejection.

"Schuyler? Marcus?"

"Chad, thank God!" The voice from the window was Schuyler's. He crossed the small room and shook Chad's hand. "We didn't know whom else we could call. It's a nightmare, I'm afraid of what Father and Clarissa may think."

"Are you all right? How is Marcus?" Chad fired the questions quickly, now as curious as he was apprehensive. "What on earth happened to you?"

Marcus untangled himself from the bed and stood up. In the dim light Chad saw bloodstains on his blond hair. His lip was cut.

"Marcus, good God! You should lie down, you look terrible." When Chad turned his gaze back to Schuyler, he could detect several facial bruises and a swelling black eye.

"You've got to help us, Chad. Marcus and I thought it foolish to tour the bad neighborhoods of Europe without knowing what was to be found here at home. We chose our oldest clothes and we tried to blend in. We saw things you wouldn't believe!"

"Who attacked you?"

"It must have been one of those gangs. We stopped in a number of places we'd heard about. There's a cafe a lot of artists and writers go to. I think Walt Whitman is often there. And then we drank too much in one of those taverns. We got rather friendly with the customers. We played darts and a few card games and tried to learn all we could. We went on to another place which I'm at a loss to describe, there were …"

"Schuyler, did you go to a brothel?"

"I suppose you could describe it as that. Chad, we were on a lark, we didn't intend to do anything. And this brothel, well, it was a surprise to us, different from those we saw in London or Paris."

"The truth is, we were followed," Marcus said. "A gang of ruffians chased us down the street and we made the mistake of trying to hide in an alley. They found us there and demanded money. They took our watches and our rings and all of our cash and we thought that would be the end of it. But then they made lewd comments and started to ridicule us. I couldn't permit this, so I took my walking stick and flailed one of them. I suspect I hurt him seriously. Then they all fell upon us and beat us and kicked us and shouted obscenities. We escaped from the alley and found our way to Water Street where we saw this shop."

"I know this shop," Schuyler said. "We bought some furniture for the upstairs sitting room here. You can tell by the window display that it's very finely made. And it's in the great Goddard-Townsend style, the Newport style. Marcus and I both prefer those great classic pieces to this new stuff that's being sold today, with grotesque curves and awkward carvings."

"I agree completely," Marcus said. "Back home in Ohio, we've always preferred the simple styles, certainly nothing more fanciful than Empire. The heavy style you see in these *nouveau riche* drawing rooms is crude, if you ask me."

"I couldn't agree more," Schuyler said.

"Are you here to shop for furniture or do you think you need a doctor? I could drive you to our family physician, Dr. Forrest."

"No," Schuyler said. "He's our doctor too. He's everybody's doctor that we know."

"We can't go home like this," Marcus said, eyes cast to the floor. "Not to the Renfield house."

"And we can't go to your house either," Schuyler added. "Not with your mother there."

"I could take you to Bynum's rooms in Third Avenue. Marcus, you said you had met him."

"Yes, we both met him in London. I think he would be sympathetic to our plight."

"We can all squeeze into the carriage and get there by eight. If Bynum's out we'll just wait for him. Put your coats on and I'll go downstairs to thank Mr. Pratt. Do you think I should offer him money?"

"I don't think so. He does business with most of the families we know. I've heard him discussed several times. He told us his family's been free since before the Revolution. And he reads well. They have their own world, you know, the old freedmen. There are schools and a newspaper and a church. But I think this man, Holder Pratt, mixes with the whites too. He said something about a church in Brooklyn he goes to."

"I'll square it with him. Get yourself together and come on down when you can. I'll wait in the carriage and we'll drive to Bynum's straightaway."

Chad cautiously descended the stairs. Holder was bent over a counter, intent on his drawings. He looked up as Chadwick entered.

"Well, are your friends going to survive?"

"I think they'll be all right. I'm going to drive them home now. We'll have a doctor look them over. I want to thank you, Mr. Pratt, for sheltering my friends after this unfortunate event. I've been told it's dangerous to explore some of the streets down here. I guess we can consider it a youthful prank."

"Perhaps, but they're not so youthful they don't know how to behave. People are attacked in broad daylight in certain sections, but it's not common around here. This is primarily a business address with some people who live above their shops, as I do. We don't often experience this kind of violence, especially not against two grown men who appear to be capable of defending themselves. Do you suppose they may have somehow, inadvertently of course, inflamed one of the gangs in some fashion?"

"What are you implying, Mr. Pratt?"

"I imply nothing, Sir. It's I who took them in. I'm not critical of unfamiliar behavior. It just seems strange."

"I'd like to pay you for your trouble."

"That's surely not necessary. I'm a successful craftsman with an elite clientele. I believe one of the young men has actually been here before with his family, selecting some of our finer pieces."

"Thank you anyway, then, Mr. Pratt. I'll wait in the carriage. They're coming down now."

"Just a minute, did you say your name is Wales?"

"Yes. I'm Chadwick Wales."

"Would you perchance be related to a woman known as Harriet Wales?"

Chad turned from the door where he'd already grabbed the knob, eager to be seated again in his own familiar carriage. He saw no way to avoid further conversation. "Yes, she's in fact my mother. Has she bought from you as well?"

"I know her from a church I attend in Brooklyn. It's Reverend Mullen's church. He's a fervent abolitionist. Although my family has been free for generations, I'm naturally sympathetic to the cause. Your mother often attends Dr. Mullen's sermons."

"I believe she's spoken to me of them."

"She spends considerable time, when she's in Brooklyn, with Reverend Mullen. Some say she's his chief supporter and friend. They're often seen together in discussions and study. And when they hold teas in the parish house, she often acts as hostess. Reverend Mullen isn't married, you see. He's only in his late thirties, I believe. He has a very loyal and devoted following. I'm proud to be a member of his congregation. Please remember me to Mrs. Wales."

"Well, of course. Thanks again, Mr. Pratt. I …" Chad dashed out the door in mid-sentence. He felt his world narrowing about him the way he pictured

Manhattan when he studied maps and pictures as a child. He remembered how the island crunched downward from the north, swelled pregnantly at the middle and then relentlessly narrowed as it pinched itself up at the Battery. He loosened his collar. "Higgens," he said, "I have two friends who'll join us shortly and then you must drive us as fast as you can to Third Avenue and 18th Street. You'd best light the carriage lamps. Darkness is coming on fast."

*   *   *

Chad drank his cognac and slumped in his chair. Bynum, walking quietly so as not to wake Schuyler and Marcus, who were recuperating in the spare bedroom, poured himself another brandy and sat pensively.

"Are they asleep?" Chad's voice had a tremor in it.

"I suspect so. Resting, at least."

"What a day!" Chad felt the need to confide in somebody and wasn't sure if it should be Bynum. "It's too much for me, all at once like this. You take me to lunch and suggest I conspire with you, give me revealing letters from my absent father, after which I have an unsettling dispute with my mother, for whom I have the most tender feelings, deep down, but who drives me mad at the same time. And my fiancée's brother and his friend are assaulted in a manner that arouses grave doubts about their moral character."

"Two things, Chad. First, I wouldn't make moral judgments about Schuyler and Marcus if I were you. You've read the Greek and Latin texts. If your suspicions are accurate, it's nothing new. Best not to think too much about it and let people be human. Second ..."

"Not suspicions, facts." Chad couldn't resist interrupting. "I came upon them upstairs at the Renfield house in a most indelicate situation."

"Are you adult enough to forget that and keep peace in your fiancée's family? It's surely in your best interests to do so."

"What's second, then?"

"Second, your philosophical mind should help you meditate on the nature of time. You may go for days or weeks or months without events that change your life. And then you're given three major issues to deal with in a single day. This war is like that. Little forays and incursions here and there, nothing significant, and then Manassas. Now another lull. But violence, like love and friendship, will flare up when you least expect it."

"You've no qualms at having them as guests?"

"Not at all. I don't share their proclivities but I'm also not unaware of them. I've lived in London and Paris, visited Africa, and I've dealt, in my 'clandestine' work, as you call it, with some of the people downtown who are considered dregs of society. This Holder Pratt, by the way, sounds like a decent man who showed what some would term Christian compassion."

"You say it as if you're not yourself a Christian."

"I pretend to be, to keep up the front. The teachings of Christ are sound and inspiring. But the Church itself is not always possessed of integrity."

"An odd way of putting it. I'd think you either believe it or you don't."

"Come now, you're much too smart and too well educated to pin yourself down like that. A questioning mind, an open mind, and a decisive mind aren't mutually exclusive. If I may be bold enough to offer advice—I'm after all just as educated as you and almost twelve years your senior—I suggest you not make any decision you don't have to make, but be firm in your choices when it's timely and proper."

"Such as?"

"Your opinion of those two boys sleeping in the next room will have very little impact on human history. Your participation, or lack of it, in the current controversies might very well chart the future of a nation. Or two nations."

"I haven't made up my mind yet."

"I'm convinced that the longer you take to decide, the firmer will be your decision. If you do join with us, we wouldn't want ambivalence."

"I was disturbed by what I saw downtown. Violence and hunger, greed and suffering. Prejudice. I feel so much better with my books. I'd rather just stay home and read Plato."

"Yes, but there'd be no place for either you or me in Plato's Republic."

"How can you say that?"

"We're both poets at heart, although I suspect you're a more skillful one than I. We look at the real and turn it into the ideal. But our minds are too stubborn, so we question the ideal and try to turn it into the real. A view of history not unlike Hegel's. But the poet, as you'll surely recall, is expelled from the Republic. Plato, and all those who seek a strong central state, wouldn't permit people like you and me to exist."

"I consider myself a loyal American."

"Your mind is impressively agile, but you're naive about Hegel. His work is cited to justify power, to sanction warfare, and to support authority. You can see that this war is very much about the centralization of power. Do we want a Federal authority reigning over our states? Do we want a central bank controlling our currency? Do we want an attitude of subservience to the usurpation of wartime powers that are plainly unconstitutional? Wait, don't answer yet. Let me guess. You'll probably say no."

"I'm a champion of liberty. When Hegel talks about the state he sees it as the embodiment of liberty. No power is justified without liberty, he says. And he explicitly says war can't be a goal in itself."

"You know as well as I do that Hegel never says anything explicitly. My job, though, is to try to convince you that in the interim, as we work our way along the human road to freedom and fulfillment, we must take certain definite and timely acts, even though we might not commit ourselves to them in the future. Once again, these are essential tenets of your Hegel. Even Hegel tempers his credo with a dollop of democratic optimism. The history of the world, I think he says somewhere, proceeds from an increasing awareness of the possibility of freedom."

"How am I to judge your personal behavior with relation to Schuyler's aberrant inclinations?"

"Be comforted. Although I kept a mistress in London, I find that such considerations are secondary to me right now. Don't forget that I'm a mercenary. But I could just as easily sell my service to the North, which I'll not do because of my principles, which I've just outlined, rather tediously I fear, for your consideration.

"And you're also anti-church?"

"Only because I don't need it. And neither do you. But a church of some sort will always exist."

"Why?"

"Because people are afraid of dying, which makes them afraid of living. They need the hope of another world, another life. But an unsustainable hope produces an enduring despair, so they dare not think too clearly on it. And those who would exploit human weakness for the sake of power will offer them hope, however illusory, in order to restrain them from the despair that produces revolution. Let the Church be, I say, as long as it doesn't intrude upon politics nor dictate to me how I'm to live my very secular life."

"I'm caught in the middle. I love Clarissa, as passionately as ever man loved woman. And I love my country, or thought I did. I'm being forced to make a painful choice. Both sides of my family are after me. One would perhaps lead to riches and comfort and a quiet life of letters and culture. The other challenge is more vague. It's tantalizing. And I'm sure it's dangerous. But I'm accused of being of two minds, and now I must make a choice. Perhaps the benefit of knowing you, Bynum, is that now I can make a choice."

"Your carriage is outside. Take yourself home and sleep soundly. I've dispatched a messenger to the Renfield Mansion telling them that Schuyler and Marcus and I and some cronies are engaged in a night-long card game. They'll chastise him for that, but it's better we give them something to be irate about lest they inquire into the true nature of this unfortunate episode. Goodnight, my boy. Whatever your choice, I'll hold you in esteem."

September 1861

"I can hardly believe September is upon us," Randall Renfield said.

"Nor I," said Chad. "I haven't heard from you in six weeks, except for the check. I've not deposited it. Indeed, I don't know what it's for."

"Consider it a retainer, my boy. It takes time to complete our arrangements but we're almost there. The truth is, I've been away much of the time. Didn't Phillipse or Clarissa tell you I took their yacht away from them for August? I had to stick close to the shore, of course, with gunboats and rebel cutters rumored to be around. It's a sleek vessel indeed, a two-masted schooner with auxiliary steam, marvelously well fitted, teak and brass and mahogany everywhere. Ample quarters for guests and room for the crew as well. I was in Newport much of the time. It's convenient to Providence, where we have both banking and manufacturing interests, and some of our partners-to-be sailed down from Boston to meet me."

They were seated in Randall's office. The chairs were leather, unpleasantly sticky in the humid late summer weather. Randall had opened a window but then closed it because of the noise from the streets. It seemed to be a parade of some sort, a marching band, onlookers shouting patriotic slogans. Chad tugged at his collar and wiped his brow. "I've been engaged in a number of activities. Clarissa is, as you must know, at Yellowfields. I'm planning to take that new riverboat next week and spend time there."

"Be careful with that boat, my boy. They're known to change their itinerary in mid-journey. Once they deposited friends of mine at a dock several miles beyond their destination and then charged them additional fare to drop them off on the way back. Make yourself known to the captain if you can. Tell them you're on your way to the Renfield estate. That ought to do it."

"Mr. Renfield, before I deposit this check I must know more about the arrangements."

"As well you should. It's simple really. We've got three holding companies chartered in Providence, away from prying eyes. One will handle financial issues, one will market goods to the war effort, and the third will engage in certain mercantile and shipping endeavors. You'll be the titular head of all three."

"Titular?"

"We want your abilities as a visionary, a planner. You see things whole. And of course your good name and your mixed parentage will be useful in engaging in certain third-party transactions. We've got a man on Wall Street to help us with that. Name of Grover Appleby."

"I don't wish to seem ungrateful but isn't it possible to give me some inkling of what I'll precisely do? And where I'll work?"

"Your office is being readied right now, just down the hall. You may come and go as you wish, just make sure you're here at least once or twice a week. We'll need your signatures on documents from time to time. And you may have to make calls on the customs people and meet with a banker or two now and then. If it's a complex procedure one of us will accompany you."

"One of us?"

"Your Uncle Caleb or I."

"What kind of documents?"

"They're all vetted by our lawyers here, in this firm, in advance. You really don't even need to read them."

"Why is the name Wales so important to you? Surely you know my father has committed himself to the Southern Cause."

"The names of Renfield and Laymus are well known to both North and South. But the name Wales is not familiar in New England yet. I say yet, because we all have high hopes for you. And Clarissa, of course."

Randall leapt from his chair at the sound of a bell and excused himself. He was gone a full three minutes, time enough for Chad to fidget.

"Sorry to leave you like that. They ring a bell out front when there's something urgent. It's a telegram from the Treasury Secretary. Do you know him, Salmon Portland Chase?"

"I believe I was introduced to him at the Renfield's."

"He's well known around New York. He can't stand Lincoln but he joined the cabinet anyway. Now he's here on government business. Big business, I might add. If we participate it will involve our financial company so you'll have to sign something."

"What does he want from us?"

"What he wants, Chad, is what Lincoln must have. They want fifty million dollars and they're willing to pay 7.37% interest. And the war's costing a million a day. That means they'll be back in a couple of months for more. Guaranteed by bonds, backed by full faith and credit of this Republican government."

"Do we have access to that kind of money?"

"Yes and no. We could pull it together on our own; but why do that? We need a consortium, and some of the participants will be from Boston and Providence and even Philadelphia." Randall noticed Chad's quizzical look at this news. "Philadelphia folk," he explained, "are a little more conservative than the risk-takers here in New York. But they'll join in when they see that interest rate. And we're offering stock in our holding company, the one that deals in equities. Bond trading, too. You'll have a lot of papers to sign when this is up and running. This war goes back and forth every week. It could last for years so they'll need more money, every two months or so. Let's see, every two months is six times a year times four years, let's say, is twenty-four times fifty million, that's one point two billion dollars!" Randall slumped in his chair as if the weight of such figures had drained him of all energy.

Randall sat silently savoring the future and then continued. "Now, government borrowing at that level, along with the increase in demand for goods and services, will force prices up and the dollar will go down. But we've got them there, too. We invest our interest payments in English and French currencies, some bonds here and there, and in certain companies in Manchester and Leeds and Birmingham, who need cotton. So we'll have a return on the interest in a harder currency while offering our Southern partners a continued market for their major crop."

"Whose side are we on," Chad asked incredulously.

"My boy, we're on the Renfield-Laymus side. Blockaded ports are being bridged by maverick merchant vessels. But the goods most in demand now are luxury items, since they're not available in the South. Whisky. Silk. And porcelain, like in the days of the China trade. Your ancestors made a bundle on that, some of your ships out of Essex bringing back all those plates and cups and tureens and useless knick-knacks, made for practically nothing in China and sold at a profit from Maine to Georgia! My God, boy, this is indeed the land of opportunity! Excuse me, I've got to have a drink of water." He walked behind his desk and poured a glass of crystal clear water from a frosty silver pitcher. The drink seemed to calm him down. "Want some?"

"I'm still trying to keep up with you." Chad hoped his face didn't reveal his skepticism, as he remembered his mother's assessment of both Randall and Caleb as lesser men contending with older and smarter relatives.

"Look, Chad, sixty-two percent of our national commerce flows through New York right now. We're bigger than Boston and Philadelphia and Charleston combined. There are new advances everyday. New industries. Advertising, for example. Who would have imagined it? There are over fifteen advertising agencies in New York now. A bunch of creative people like yourself writing and designing advertisements and getting paid for it! Make a note of that, Chad, it might be something we'll want you to look into after the war. We must always think of the future."

"You realize I've had little education in financial matters, although I was tops in my class in mathematics."

"We've got our own man on Wall Street, as I said. You must meet with him soon. Not at the Club, he's not the kind of person you'd want to invite home for dinner. But we need him. You may find him amusing as well as useful, comes from a farm family in the far west of the state. Always says the same thing. 'Hello, I'm Grover Appleby of the apple grove Appleby's.'"

"How will I know how to get in touch with him? Should I meet him in public?"

"Why not? This is a democracy. Try one of the better public restaurants near the Exchange. He'll need you to sign some papers, too. And then you and he'll be going back and forth as we build on our achievements. God, I'm proud to be an American!"

October 1861

She sent him a perfumed note on fine textured paper with cursive initials on the front. But he'd not replied until he got her subsequent telegram. She was less than forty miles away, safe at her Yellowfields perch on the Hudson, with its own landing and a private hillside approach guarded twenty-four hours a day by burly men on the Renfield payroll, armed with pistol and nightstick. They were told to shoot first and ask questions later if they were invaded by outsiders. They feared intruders might emerge either from the rolling fields or stands of virgin trees, or the river itself, as it widened out into a deep, cold fjord along the Renfield shore. Night and day the swift-flowing river was a useful but threatening thoroughfare for anonymous hordes in rafts and small boats and steamers, moving urgently downstream with the current. Others struggled northward towards Albany, where the legislature was in furious debate about the war, the tariffs and the budget, all made more divisive by the rising tide of violence in the state's biggest city, now acknowledged to be America's major metropolis.

She claimed to be morose because he'd not written her. She mentioned the serenity of the estate and the lazy routine of her days. And she ended by saying if he didn't come in early October he might as well not come at all. The leaves had already started to turn red and gold, and soon there'd be frost, cold autumn rains, and then the inevitable snow. Winds could make the Hudson River more perilous, and even the trains were delayed when the nor'easters struck. Why was he not there, she implored?

She was his Clarissa, and he longed for her. He'd now become familiar with neighborhoods where women, at all hours of the day, could be purchased for a coin. He admitted and accepted the reality of his urges. He was not staggered by such needs, but he felt an unquenchable thirst for her. How was he to explain? He'd been persuaded that his actions would broaden his knowledge and increase his appetite for life. Instead he felt he was confined to a muddy field with four neat ninety-degree corners: one for the Renfields, one for his mother and her Laymus breed, the third for Bynum and Franklin

Wales, and the fourth an uncharted space of riots and hunger, war and corruption, treachery among his peers.

What he'd been promised was an orderly nation and a leisurely young manhood. What he received was chaos, made worse, he admitted, by his own indecision. How could anyone decide anything, when there were so many alternatives and so much pressure? If his mother was right, he should have joined Clarissa during the summer, accelerated their wedding plans, and built their own sturdy residence on the eastern edge of Yellowfields, near the old post road, and not far from the new station that would soon be served by several daily trains.

He was determined not to capitulate to opportunism, to short-sightedness, nor to bigotry. If he suffered an inner anguish, it was a luxury compared to the problems of others, including people of a privileged station in life similar to his own. After all, it was he, Chadwick Wales, they turned to, Bynum and Schuyler and Marcus, Caleb and Randall Renfield. He was their fulcrum. His open mind, he decided, was an invitation to assault. His willingness to weigh alternative views was a welcome mat for trespassers who would use him for their own selfish ends.

Alone on the bow of the paddle wheeler, he held onto the iron railings and looked dead ahead. Traffic was steady on a midweek working day, but the decks, vibrating with the churning engines, were mostly deserted. Women with packages and men with portfolios sat primly inside the main cabin. His only companions were children, running back and forth on the deck, pointing to sailboats and rafts, and to the houses atop the riverbanks. He'd intended to stand at the railing all the way up to Yellowfields, but grew too tired, mostly from his thoughts, and went into the main cabin and had a cup of tea and a sandwich. Then he sat down on a hard bench, careful to remove himself from families and groups, and began to quote compulsively in his overactive mind some of his favorite *Georgics* of Virgil, which he deemed suitable for the bucolic vistas sliding past his spray-stained windows.

A crewman aroused him. "Are you the gentlemen what wants off at Renfield landing?"

"I am," Chad muttered, his valise clutched in his hands beside him and topped with his hat and stick.

"Come this way, Sir. We don't often stop at Yellowfields. It's a bit of extra effort for us, if you get my meaning. We can't delay long, you'll have to disembark quickly." He took his hand from his pocket in expectation. Chad pressed a coin into the man's palm and lurched past him. Halfway down to the landing, still swaying on the gangway with the bobbing ship, he saw her, waving to him, a parasol over her wide-brimmed hat, white gloves over her hands and arms, her welcoming smile half-shadowed by a waving arm. All his doubts vanished in an instant.

* * *

The Renfield Maze was the talk of the county. Covering a carefully trimmed acre, its walkways provided both privacy and distraction for those who strolled there. Clarissa held his arm as they paraded down a dead-end alley or turned a corner only to find another unrevealing pathway. The tall hedges were carefully trimmed, and an occasional bench offered rest for those who were tired of wandering, or who gave up, for a moment, their hope of finding a way out.

He kissed her and held her close to him on an old, intricately carved wooden bench. Finally, she spoke.

"What did your mother want with my father?"

"What do you mean?"

"She called on Father back in New York. They were in the library, the doors were closed, but my maid heard them arguing?"

"Clarissa, I know nothing of such a visit."

"My personal chambermaid went down to New York three weeks ago. Annie, you've met her. I wanted her to pack some books and papers for me. She said she saw your mother go into the library with Father and close the door. And then there was a buzz of talk and then shouting. Annie's very candid and I've allowed her to gossip with me about family matters."

"I'm sure Mother would have discussed it with me if it were important."

"Important? We've been engaged for ten months and there's no date set yet. You told me you've been conspiring with my uncle to go into business with him. I don't hear from you for over three weeks. And now your mother makes a mysterious call at my home. Isn't any of this important?"

"I'll certainly ask her, my dear. It's probably something to do with our trust funds. Or maybe she just wanted to help your father plan for the wedding."

"How could they do that without asking me? It's my wedding, after all!"

"I want it to be the happiest day of your life. But our world's changing fast. It's very confusing."

"Are you confused about your feelings for me?"

"Not for a minute!"

"Father doesn't really like Uncle Randall, you know. He thinks he's foolhardy and once he even called him a buffoon. I don't think he even trusts him as a lawyer."

"You knew he and my Uncle Caleb were involved in an enterprise, and that they'd approached me. I discussed it with you before I accepted. You were very enthusiastic."

"I was then. But what is this enterprise and what is your place in it? What is your mother doing calling on my father unbeknownst to either of us?"

"My mother wanted me to spend the summer here with you. She said we might ask your father if we could build our own house on the grounds somewhere, live quietly, safely, here in the country."

"I don't want to live quietly in the country! I want to have our own house in New York. I want to go to dances and give dinner parties and show my friends how happy I am to be the wife of Chadwick Wales."

"With the war and the violence downtown, we may not have such a sheltered life."

"Are you implying that I'm insensitive to the problems in my hometown? Or the poor soldiers being dragged off to war? I'll help make bandages. I'll pack food and clothes for the boys at the front. I'll donate generously from my own funds. I have a considerable amount in my own right already, you know."

"I have a small income already, too. With the new business deals, I'll more than pay my own way."

"I'm not accusing you of that, Chad. I admit I was warned, even before we announced our engagement, that many young men would be after me. Some of them for my money."

"Clarissa, you're the most beautiful woman in New York. I love you and you alone. I can't conceive of my future without you. You know I'll eventually receive some very large trusts. Please let's not argue about it."

"Darling Chad, I always trusted your motives. It's your ..." Clarissa's voice trailed off, as if she were about to say something she feared to disclose.

"Well, say it. Which of my many faults are you concerned about today?"

"I didn't mean to imply ..."

"Yes you did. We both know you've got more money than I do. But I'm independent and I also have considerable prospects. My mother's family is almost as rich as yours."

"It's not about money."

"What's it about then?"

"It's about you. The way you don't make up your mind. The way you isolate yourself. Your books."

"You're objecting to my books?"

"I'm proud that you're smart. And so well educated. You're quite entertaining, sometimes."

"Sometimes?"

"I mean, I wouldn't want to be married to a man who didn't appreciate the finer things. Literature and such. But I'm more inclined to the livelier arts. I want to go to the theater and the opera and I want us to surround ourselves when we're married with the brightest people. We'll be the most envied couple in New York."

"Envy is not a blessing I actively seek."

"So you're accusing me of being small-minded!"

Chad clenched his fists and gritted his teeth. He knew he was going to explode, finally, and say things he didn't really mean.

"Clarissa, you sound like my mother. She baits me until I lose my temper." The thought of his mother's compressed lips and her handkerchief wrapped around her fist distracted him, but he took a deep breath and went on. "Loving you doesn't mean I have no inner life of my own. You've known me since we were children. You used to approve of my interests and my behavior."

"I still do, sweetheart. Try to look at it my way. I want our life to move ahead on schedule. I don't want us to be separated by events, or opinions. We've earned the right to a happy life, haven't we?"

"Your happiness is among my foremost goals."

"Among?"

"What?"

"You said among."

"Clarissa, I'm a man of the world now. I'm well educated. I'm being asked to head up several momentous undertakings with great financial promise. I've been asked to take sides in this conflict. At one point Schuyler's friend said I should enter politics."

"Schuyler's friend? Are you close with Marcus?"

"Close? Of course not. I see him only when he's with Schuyler."

"He's always with Schuyler."

"Maybe he's after Schuyler's money, then."

"That's not funny. Marcus Tifton is as rich as you or I." Clarissa looked across the walkway at a small black and yellow bird, perched on the hedge. "What about Schuyler and Marcus?"

"What do you mean?"

"I sense something at home. The servants. Our head housekeeper."

"Have they said things?"

"They wouldn't dare do that, of course. A laugh, a look. Sometimes when I hear them talking when they don't know I'm around."

"My mother warned me that servants always talk. It's their way of socializing. She says they hold their own little get-togethers, and gossip with the staff of other households."

"Schuyler told me about your mother's visit, too. It wasn't just my maid."

"Schuyler told you what?"

"That your mother had called on Father and that he heard them arguing in the library."

"I thought he and Marcus were here with you."

"Oh they came up two months ago and stayed for two weeks. Then Schuyler came back for a few days and told me about your mother's visit. There's something strange going on, that's for sure. And I got the impression you were involved."

"Involved in what?"

"They came up here because they were afraid of Father. They were both hurt, Chad. Marcus had a cut lip and a bruise on his forehead and Schuyler had a black eye. They said they were roughhousing at their boxing club."

"These things happen."

"Chad, Schuyler's never talked about a boxing club. I don't even know what a boxing club is."

"They're both young men with time on their hands, they're sure to sow wild oats."

"They said you'd done them a favor."

"The truth is, Clarissa, they got into some trouble downtown. They were just out on a lark, and a gang of plug-uglies attacked them. They were robbed, so I went down in my carriage and got them. I took them to Bynum's place and they stayed overnight, to recover. You mustn't tell Schuyler I told you, or he'll cease to trust me. He's on our side, you know. He's happy that I'll be his brother-in-law. He told me so."

"Then maybe we'd be better off living up here after all," Clarissa said, a note of anxiety in her voice.

"Darling, you're just reacting to all the turmoil. Look, there's no reason we can't have our own house in town. You can see your friends. When we're married I'll be with you most of the time, except when I'm attending to my executive duties, of course. I'll want some time alone to pursue my studies. I intend to write, you know. Essays, that sort of thing. Like Emerson. He doesn't work either, I'm told."

"We want to have a family, don't we?"

"Of course we do."

"You think you're one big happy family and then you find out you don't really know each other."

"Now what?"

"Oh not you, darling. It's Schuyler. I'm embarrassed to say it."

"Say what?"

"You don't think there's something unnatural, do you? About his friendship with Marcus."

"I don't know what unnatural is and I don't believe you should allow yourself to think bad things about your brother. He's devoted to you and I'm devoted to you and your father dotes on you."

"Schuyler's more devoted to Marcus than anybody."

"It's good to have a bosom friend. Literature is full of it."

"So you suspect something too!"

"Clarissa you put me on the spot. Schuyler trusts me and I'm his friend. He's our champion in the Renfield home. Let's leave it at that."

"I suppose you look at it from the literary perspective. Family life."

"Well, it's the wellspring of most literary effort. Oedipus. Medea. Lear."

"Happy families all! I don't want to fight with you, Chad."

"I apologize if I've worried you unduly, Clarissa, my love. You and I'll cling to each other no matter what our families do."

"We'll make sure we don't allow anything to disrupt our happiness. Not even our families!" Clarissa looked coyly and with a certain satisfaction at her lover. "Families!"

"Yes, families!"

* * *

"Did you enjoy your trip to Yellowfields, dear?" Chad's mother was in her usual post, on the settee, hands folded in her lap, lips compressed. They'd eaten lunch at home and adjourned to the parlor for a demitasse.

"The boat ride was unpleasant, smoke and fumes and all those people. Noisy children running amok on the foredeck."

"Best get used to it. You'll soon have children of your own, no doubt."

"When I have children I'll always be honest with them."

"Yes," his mother replied. "Honesty is the best policy. But of course policy and practice do not necessarily coincide."

"I always thought you wouldn't mislead me."

"What mother wants to mislead her only son? Mothers are alike on that point, I think. We'll do whatever we must in order to protect our only son."

"You think I need protecting?"

"I think you're given too much to thought. I suspect you're as yet naive in the everyday world."

"You mean to teach me wisdom, then."

"I don't know what wisdom is or how to get it. I deal with things the way they are, one thing at a time. You're still so young, and you've been rather sheltered. You probably don't even realize what I've done for you. Or would do for you."

"Like making a secret visit to my future father-in-law?"

"They told you of that, did they?"

"Not they. Clarissa. She had to learn it from her maid. And from Schuyler. What were you fighting about?"

"Fighting? Nobody has the courage to fight with Phillipse Renfield. Not even me."

"Is it cat and mouse again or are you going to explain yourself?"

"I needn't justify my actions to you but out of concern and affection I'll share my behavior. I simply wanted to talk about the trust fund situation and offer advice about the wedding. I suspect any mother in my position would do the same."

"What is your position?"

"I'm a wronged woman, Chad! I've been subjected to contempt from my father, my husband and my brother. I've been accosted by my son in a most belligerent manner, and I still hold my head high and make the right decisions."

"Why was it necessary to shout at Mr. Renfield?"

"I suspect there was some passing clatter, a carriage or something."

"You can't hear a sound once you're inside the Renfield Mansion. The walls are two feet thick."

"Servants make up tales. Young men like Schuyler make mistakes, too. Or perhaps they want to divert attention from their own misdeeds." She looked at him accusingly.

"What do you know about Schuyler?"

"As much as I need to know and more than I'd like to know." She'd once again assumed her expression of moral superiority.

"Did you learn it from Holder Pratt?" Chad immediately felt ashamed that he'd pierced her armor and was about to apologize, when Harriet turned her face away and sipped from her tiny cup. But Chad could see her hands were shaking, and when she spoke her lips trembled.

"How dare you go prying with those people downtown about my private actions and my political involvements?"

"Those people downtown? I thought Mr. Pratt to be a very decent man."

"He is a decent man, and he's very helpful to Reverend Mullen and me in our work for the abolitionist cause. Can't you accept the fact that your mother has a brain? That she has feelings and beliefs? Principles, even! Though we're not allowed to vote we're the backbone of the nation. Hand that rocks the cradle, as they say."

"I've no objection to your principles, as much as I know of them. Slavery is an abomination; we've been through that before. But you're a married woman, and you're traveling without chaperon or escort to Brooklyn and spending long hours with a younger man, a preacher who, apparently, is appealing to lots of women your age."

"How dare you! Tad is scarcely four years younger than I."

"Tad! I see." Chad felt he'd scored a victory and a loss simultaneously.

"If I wish to devote my energies and my abilities to a noble purpose, and if I have to go to Brooklyn to do it, then that's where I'll go."

"Do you enjoy acting as this preacher's hostess at his little teas?"

"His teas are not little. In fact, they're working sessions of people like me who aren't so caught up with their personal troubles that they forget their duties in the larger world. Their moral obligations. I don't have the desire to lose myself in Greek and Latin histories of wars gone by. We've got a war right here at home. The South ruled over by feudal lords. Worse, really. Even the serfs and vassals had a better time of it. It's a shame and a stain on all our souls. If you want to ignore it, go ahead. But don't you dare to lecture me about righteousness or morality!"

She finished her long speech and arose from the settee, moving towards the door. Chad stood up and blocked her path, his arms spread out on either side of her against the sliding door.

"What's your secret, Mother?"

"Stop behaving like a bad actor in some cheap melodrama and get out of my way!"

"I'll do nothing of the sort. You're in secret talks with my future father-in-law. My father is trying to divorce you. You spend your days alone with an unmarried preacher over in Brooklyn. And you've told me yourself that you've done things, things you didn't specify. You even mentioned you were willing to use blackmail. The evidence is mounting, Mother, and in this melodrama we haven't even finished the first act. Are you going to be honest with me or are you not?"

"I absolutely won't discuss any of this with you while you're acting like a spoiled child. I'll tell you one thing, though. You shouldn't doubt my determination, nor my influence, nor my ability. Unless you step aside and shut your mouth, I'll not bother to speak to you again, about your marriage or your father or your politics or your friends."

Chad wilted in the face of her granite gaze. She no longer sought refuge in tears. She was, to his mind, as furious and as powerful as any of the distraught women in his Greek dramas. And knowing what such desperate women are capable of, he dropped his arms, lowered his eyes, and stepped aside.

* * *

"I think I could learn more from you than all the rest of them put together," Chad said. He picked up a newspaper from the sofa table in Bynum's sitting room and read the headline. "Look, there's further disagreement on the war, right here in New York. Ex-mayor Wood, he's the one who wanted the city to secede, is still agitating people. Members of my own family are selling to the South while waving the Northern flag here at home. My mother has hardened towards me. Clarissa thinks I'm not worldly enough—she more or less said so. And this deal with Randall Renfield and my Uncle Caleb is still unsettled." He folded the paper and put it on top of a thick stack of dailies. "Now the editor of the *Journal of Commerce*—he's anti-war—has been charged with being 'disloyal.' Since when is it a crime to voice your opinion in this country?"

Bynum nodded in agreement. "And that crazy Trent Affair could have cost the North any potential British support. You can't forcibly board a foreign ship on the high seas and remove passengers you claim are under the jurisdiction of Washington, when in fact they're envoys from the Confederate States. The English Parliament is up in arms about it, and the North will have to capitulate. After all, that's one reason we went to war in 1812."

"I wish I was as self-assured as you."

"In truth I'm fickle in action while you're merely fickle in thought. I'm a mercenary, but I try to serve the causes I believe in. But the wind may change, and I can come about because of it. Tacking, if you will, in the stream of current events."

"Don't you believe in anything?"

"I believe in Bynum Bradley-West."

"That's cynical."

"Perhaps. But it's the general position, especially of those who have any self to believe in. It's surely true of those in power, whether their seat of authority be a pulpit or a corporate office or a bench in the legislature. The higher the office, the more they believe in themselves. But they hide it in rhetoric, and then, when rhetoric fails, they take action. But it's action aimed at convincing the people their leaders are right and able and strong. Indicting the editor of the *Journal of Commerce* won't stop the so-called disloyalty. People like me will continue the opposition and people like you, guided by your intellectual turmoil, will continue to seek some form of truth. Since truth is elusive, and ever changing, you're doomed to failure until you decide at some point to put thinking aside and commit yourself to action. Put that in your Hegelian pipe and smoke it."

"Are you turning against me too?"

"To the contrary, I'm on your side. Largely because I think you'll eventually decide to join us. I'm after all a Southerner in the employ of British and Confederate agencies, so I'm more likely to be designated a spy, and if discovered, hanged. Northern sympathizers with the South are everywhere. In Ohio they're especially strong. They say Vallandigham is with us. The scope of the war will surely broaden as impatience grows. Lincoln says he wants to preserve the Union, but in fact they need the tariffs to run the government with. If they decide to allow the South to go its own way, they're put in the odd position of trying to collect customs duties in somebody else's country. Even as skillful a speechmaker as Lincoln can't reconcile that paradox. Not even your Hegel could!"

"Have you had further word of my father?"

"As a matter of fact I have. And I've informed him of your health and happiness. He deems it too dangerous to write you directly now, especially should he be captured at sea by a revenue cutter. Letters addressed to you would bring the authorities to your doorstep in a short time. And even without proof, they could arrest you, now that Lincoln has suspended *habeas corpus*. And they could even put you in a Federal jail, perhaps bring you before a military tribunal, even though you're a citizen of the United States—or what remains of the United States."

"You told me that before and I said it's outrageous."

"People are alarmed. They're angry. They believe in whatever seems to match up with their hearts, not their heads. And the thinking man is virtually defenseless against them."

"I want you to help me, Bynum. I want to learn to put thought aside and commit to action. I can't promise to be an ally in any illegal activities. But I want to learn more. I'd like to meet the people you're working with."

"It would be both foolhardy and perilous to introduce you to the real undercover people. I'd not, of course, betray them. But you should be aware of the hierarchy."

"The hierarchy?"

"In resistance there's organization, just as there is in government. Some people are nameless and say nothing; they move at night, so to speak, and they take actions that would be illegal under any form of government. They set fires and throw bombs and ambush leaders. There are those who carry messages—once they've discovered a message to carry. Spies, if you will, not necessarily the people who'd burn down a building. And then there's the top level, the ones with a public position, who can argue either side without revealing their true partisanship. They're the ones who mostly want to hold on to their current wealth and power and get more while they're doing it. This category would include Randall Renfield and Caleb Laymus. Frankly, neither one of them is as important as Phillipse is. He's playing both sides, I'm sure of it."

"I'm not unaware of the devious schemes of my business mentors. Still, everybody praises me and blames me simultaneously, my own family, the people I love most. All their comments begin 'Yes, but.' I want to be more like you. You're as educated as I. You like abstract thought as much as I, even though you hide it better than I do. Be my tutor, Bynum. Perhaps I'll learn enough of the 'everyday world' as Clarissa calls it to make up my mind. Maybe then I'll join you without reservation."

"Do you know a man named Appleby? 'Grover Appleby of the apple grove Appleby's', he calls himself."

"I believe he's an agent for Randall Renfield."

"Indeed he is. Insofar as he can be an agent for anybody other than Grover Appleby. I know him and work with him. He plays both sides with admirable aplomb. He's nevertheless a dull and crude man, but it would be interesting if you met him. Perhaps we'll go down to Wall Street and lunch with him."

"He'd be sure to tell Randall Renfield or Uncle Caleb, wouldn't he?"

"I don't think so. You see, it would be to his advantage to have a more— shall we call it 'flexible'—relationship with you. He can work with you in a completely straightforward way as it relates to your Uncle and Uncle-in-law's objectives. What they're proposing is obvious to me. Dummy corporations offered to greedy but naive investors. Initial offerings that will prove worthless. Appleby will broker them. He's done it for years. That's why he carries a revolver on his belt and a tiny silver pistol in his vest pocket. One ruined investor already took a shot at him. Fortunately for you and me and our circle, they missed. Sooner or later someone will be more skillful and we'll have to find another agent."

"What more can I learn from him? I'm already involved in the new companies."

"Appleby has helped me with currency transactions and letters of credit. He also acts as a conduit for the funds I receive, for my own accounts here in New York and money to disburse to those in my employ. The real secret agents. We have to support them, you see. Keep up appearances. They're everywhere. One lives permanently at the Fifth Avenue Hotel. Some have rooms in fashionable houses. Others hide in dark and decrepit tenements downtown. Some of them are tied up with the gangs, especially the Irish, who do not want the black man free and do not want a horde of Southern migrants moving north to take their miserable jobs."

"Why do I not know about these things?"

"Because we haven't yet found our own Herodotus to chronicle our history. I suspect we'll never live to see the story told in full. Whichever side wins will influence the historians for generations. Perhaps for centuries. They'll issue information that may not be accurate but will appeal to the existing fears and prejudices of their audiences. People like you may come along from time to time to try to take a balanced view, but one side or the other will label such objective thinkers as traitors or fools or cowards. That's why I've personally abandoned the search for truth. It was a depressing decision and in a way I envy you. Perhaps you can find a way to pursue honesty and practicality at the same time. Nobody else has, though."

"Take me downtown then. Let me meet these people. Let me walk beside you when you enter their neighborhoods. No matter how squalid or cruel or empty or how mean, let me see it all for myself. And when I come out of it I'll either be transformed, or I'll return to my old ways. In either case, nobody, least of all my mother, can imply that I'm not wise to the ways of the world."

Interlude: A Descent

In the turning of a corner and in the wink of an eye, Chad discovered parallel worlds. It was as if a translucent glaze had been lifted and light now penetrated into spaces formerly forbidden to his view. With Bynum at his side he drank beer in crowded bars full of tobacco smoke and stale odors, seated at benches with boisterous men in rags. They walked streets where the pavement soiled their shoes. They saw teenagers with dirty faces running away together to escape a policeman in half-hearted pursuit. Women leaned against doorways, flouncing their skirts and taunting the male passers-by, who often stopped, negotiated and disappeared inside for their trysts.

They looked into the faces of beggars, young women with babes in arms, faces pocked with illness and hunger.

They watched helplessly while a gang of thugs beat an old man until his bloody form was a senseless heap on the cobblestones.

In finer establishments they sat with gaudily dressed businessmen, stuffing themselves with oysters and steaks, gold rings and gold teeth gleaming, money passed under the table, deals made, contracts broken.

They sat in jolting omnibuses with drivers who whipped their overworked teams and drove them at perilous speed across lower Manhattan. On the docks they saw costumes from all over the earth. They heard languages they couldn't even identify, much less understand. They walked the immigrant streets where women washed their clothes in metal tubs on a rickety back porch and spent their allotted time in the common kitchen cooking weak stews for their husbands and sons, who would arrive home after a twelve-hour day hungry or drunk or both.

On every block they were accosted by ragamuffin hordes with hands outstretched for coins. They had their boots shined and their coats dusted and their mouths and stomachs filled in such disparate ways it seemed the entire world had shrunk to a few blocks on the south end of a fifteen-mile island on the North American coast.

Arguments were loud in tavern and alleyway, fights were frequent. They saw a man shot dead on a Five-Points street corner. They watched muscled men roll barrels of beer and crates of whisky into barrooms, and then heard protests from barkeeps about extortionate prices, only to see them silenced with billy club or fist.

They inhaled fumes from distilleries and smoke from tanning factories. They stepped over offal and ordure. They waded through mud.

Once, in a passably clean tearoom, a bright young redheaded girl with moist lips and tempting eyes, placed her hand on Chad's privates and winked, saying, "For you, there will be no charge!"

Chad learned to follow Bynum's lead, to laugh when he laughed, to get out quickly when he did, to steel himself in the face of suffering and to calm himself against violence.

After a few hours he could no longer distinguish barroom from boardroom or friend from foe. Authority and insurrection walked hand in hand. Peace and violence contended on every block. Exhausted and dispirited after a single long day, he gave up. He pleaded with Bynum to show him no more. And he walked all the way home to his stolid street and his haughty house and his cluttered life, convinced that if this be truth, he would have none of it.

FOUR

February 1862

Chad watched absent-mindedly as coils of black and white smoke spewed from a multitude of chimneys. Across the room a round conference table and four Windsor chairs waited, as yet unused. A pen and ink jar rested beside an appointment book. They'd also given him a supply of business cards, with a simple inscription: *Chadwick L. Wales, President, Financial and Industrial Enterprises (FIE)*.

He stored a few books in his desk, including the new edition of Emerson's essays, a collection of Wordsworth, and several Greek and Latin texts. In the chill February weather, he kept the doors closed, but Randall Renfield suggested that as it warmed, he could open the transom to hear the law office bell announce the arrival of important dispatches. Chad's personal signal was three rapid rings and two more after a pause. Once he thought he'd heard this pattern and rushed down the hall, only to discover that the receptionist had actually been calling for the messenger boy.

"You don't need to be here every day," Randall told him. "We need your visionary talents most of all. By the way," he added, "best keep the inner door closed when you're reading those books we found in your desk drawer."

Today he was to host his first conference. He dusted the top of the table and carefully arranged the notepaper and pencils. There would be three participants, including himself. He'd arrived early, and was about to take up his Catullus when the outer door opened and in walked Randall Renfield, red-faced from the bitter cold. With him was a shorter man, balding, his greatcoat trimmed in fur. He removed his kid gloves ceremoniously as he stood by the entry door and spoke before Randall could make the introductions. His voice was loud and raspy, his accent suggesting an untutored origin.

"So you're Chadwick Wales," he said. "I'm Grover Appleby, of the apple grove Appleby's." He stuck out his right hand, raw and ruddy, and adorned by a large gold ring with a jewel reflecting the morning light.

Chad shook his hand and gestured to the conference table, where Appleby settled down with a loud sigh. Randall shuffled several sheets of paper. "What I've got here, Chad, will need your signature. I also hope that the initiatives we've spelled out will inspire your creative mind to come up with other possibilities for expansion. We'll go over them one by one and then Mr. Appleby ..."

"Why not just call me Grover, Randall," Appleby said. "We're all partners here."

Randall made no attempt to conceal his irritation, "Very well. But to the point: our first offering on the Exchange is the Paramount Iron and Forge Company, which will provide weaponry to our boys in the Union army. Once capital is raised we'll start production somewhere in Pennsylvania. Just sign there."

Chad began to read the document, heavy in legal jargon, but Randall interrupted. "As I say, Chad, no need to trouble yourself with the details. Here's the second one, Excelsior Shipping and Transport. Using rail, barge, and a boat or two, Excelsior will be a major conduit for war supplies and as such is likely to grow rapidly. If the war should end quickly, we can convert it to civilian uses in the explosive growth that's sure to follow."

"You think the war will last a long time," Chad asked. "In the paper this morning they say the Union has prevailed in several battles in Tennessee, under General Grant. Ulysses S. Grant." Chad remembered the name because it reminded him of Homer.

"Look at the big picture, Chad. The *official* Confederate Congress convened in January and Jefferson Davis is now the *official* president of the Southern states. It's obvious they're in this for the long haul. Grant's an ambitious man. I met him once. Drinks too much and has a bit of a temper. He'll win a few skirmishes but the South is inflamed with loyalty and confidence. We don't react to the day by day news anyway, except as it may affect our portfolio of stocks in more established companies. Since wars go back and forth, we have to watch for timely opportunities. We've got Appleby here for that."

"Grover Appleby's a name well known on Wall Street, Chad. I'll handle the initial offerings of shares in our new companies. If we have a stockholders' meeting, you may be asked to appear. Your youth, education, and appearance will be a benefit. Youth in management is regarded favorably in these new enterprises. Look at that Rockefeller out in Cleveland. Only 24, a commodities broker but now he's buying up all those refineries. Vision and appearance count."

"And there's more, Chad," Randall said. "The first time we make an offering of stock in one of our new companies, you'll be given a sizable number of shares. So you're not just a front man. Now here's the third, and last one, for today. American National Purveyors and Supply. Foodstuffs and clothes for our soldiers in the field. This one is in New Jersey. Lots of foodstuffs in New Jersey, all those gardens with vegetables and fruit. You can tell a man by his appetite for vegetables, I always say, and after the 1812 war some people claimed that without fruit you might end up with scurvy. We wouldn't want to inflict that on the troops, they've got enough trouble already. I'm hoping to get Mayor Opdyke's family to buy into this one. 'American National' has a patriotic sound, don't you think?"

Chad sat silently while Randall ruffled through the sheaf of papers. Appleby inserted a gold toothpick into his mouth. The room felt hot and stuffy. He remembered passages in both Greek and Latin that dealt with dissembling and fraud. He was convinced these two viewed him as naive and indecisive. He was uneasy with Appleby's brazen manner and the sinister expressions and language Randall employed. Did they think he was a fool?

"I'm not as experienced as you in business affairs, but it seems to me my post here is not integral to the operation of these companies."

"Chad, my boy, we've perhaps been too insensitive in our presentation of these opportunities. The truth is, we need new blood. Of course some of these initiatives are not without risk. And we certainly acknowledge that we're openly seizing opportunities brought on by the war. But be realistic. Wars have always involved new sources of food and clothing, armor in the old days, armaments today. Everybody is out to make a profit, a fair profit of course, on the conflict. But that doesn't mean we're unpatriotic or unlawful. How else can a war be fought? The old idea that an army marches on its stomach probably appears in one of your ancient histories. Idealism is a noble trait, especially in the young. But there are other considerations. You're to be married into our family. You're more or less estranged, for now anyway, from your father. Your Uncle Caleb has confided in me the status of your mother's finances. Indeed, I'm the lawyer who helped negotiate those arrangements. You must trust me. Mr. Appleby here ..."

"Grover."

"Grover and I are sincere in our attempts to involve you and there'll be a definite role for you to play down the road. Don't turn down a chance to make money on your own because you think it might conflict with principles. Accumulate monetary principal first, and you'll be free to practice your other principles for the rest of your life." Randall paused and looked Chad in the eye. "Think of Clarissa. With her money and the money you'll make, you'll be able to live however you please. You'll be indebted to no one. You needn't take orders from me or anybody else. I know that's what Harriet …" Randall stopped himself abruptly. "That's what your mother wants for you, I'm sure of that."

"Have you discussed this with my mother?"

"Your Uncle Caleb's in touch with her on a regular basis." Randall looked down at his papers and seemed distracted. Appleby shuffled in his chair. Chad tugged at his collar in the overheated room. There was a muffled sound of a bell and Randall leapt to his feet. "I must be excused for a minute. The Deputy Secretary of the Treasury is due to visit me today. Another big loan in the making, think of it! The interest rates will be even higher this time, mark my word! Appleby, you can finish up here." Randall closed the door without looking back.

Appleby stared into Chad's eyes with a sardonic smile. He tapped his ringed fingers on the tabletop. "I was hoping we'd have a chance to talk privately. It's my business to know more than other people about any deal that's made downtown. And I wouldn't think of revealing to your future bride's uncle that you're also involved with one Bynum Bradley-West."

"My involvement with Bynum is tentative, at best, at this moment." Chad tried to sound confident and formal but Appleby, sly as he was rumored to be, noticed his awkwardness.

"Bynum is a mercenary who has found a cause that appeals to him. I'm a mercenary, too, in a sense, except I avoid causes like the plague. This business with the Renfields, it may or may not pass muster. Randall and Caleb strike me as simpletons, but they need me because they naively think I'll take the blame if there are any charges made later. Or lawsuits. They want you because you've got a name that's known in the South but not on the Exchange. If the proposed companies work out you'll indeed make some money. At the very least, you'll realize significant amounts on the initial offerings. Be sure you don't sell your shares too quickly. That might attract attention."

"I appreciate your candor, Mr. Appleby."

"Grover. And now, perhaps you and I should go somewhere and have a little lunch. I'm meeting Bynum later today. There are insistent demands here in New York to clamp down on any deals that benefit the rebel states. Of course, every bank, every shipping line, almost every manufacturer and at least half the railroads are reluctant to give up a sizable portion of their business. These new companies may help us if we lose some of our commerce with the South. But you and I and Bynum have another important goal, to provision our former states with both materials and funds. Bynum because he's paid to think that way and you because you're still beholden to your father. And I, Grover Appleby, because I intend to outpace the market and the money brokers, whether it's the House of Renfield or the House of Steinmann.

You don't know yet, Chad, how fortunate you are to have met me. It may be true that you're better educated than me. I spent my boyhood swinging on trees in my family's orchards near the Finger Lakes. But I'm the one who'll teach you how to walk down both sides of Wall Street at the same time."

March 1862

Chad and Bynum decided to skip lunch; the March winds were brutal, and a mixture of snow and ice had made the streets treacherous. Traffic outside Bynum's windows was slight.

"While I lived in England I learned to love cheese," Bynum said. "And on my visits to France I often had a sampling of cheeses and fresh bread for lunch. With a good wine, it's sufficient. The bread's not French, of course, but it's crusty and tastes really good." He sliced off a generous portion of cheddar and cut a thick slab of bread, reaching across the tea table to place it on Chad's plate. Then he uncorked a bottle of red wine and poured it into large stemmed glasses. Chad tasted and chewed and sipped and sat back in his chair. He remained silent until Bynum broke the quiet again, while the rain and sleet dripped down the windowpanes and the wind whistled through the sashes. "So," Bynum said, "You've now made the acquaintance of Grover Appleby."

"He's a loud and insensitive man, Bynum. I felt uncomfortable with him even after Randall Renfield left the room. Can he be trusted?"

"As long as he thinks his best interests are being served. A man like Appleby, you use him only when you need him and you don't include him in anything else. Most importantly, you don't trust him."

"Why are you doing business with him, then?"

"It wouldn't be possible for me to engage the Renfield bank or the House of Steinmann to handle my transactions. And the smaller brokerage houses can sometimes be indiscreet. As long as Appleby has something to gain, he'll serve us well. Later, we'll probably have to get rid of him. He's unpleasant, I agree. Worse, he's dangerous."

"Sometimes I think Randall Renfield is just as bad. Why would he be involved with the Treasury Department in these massive Federal loans? Wouldn't Phillipse handle that himself?"

"I'm sure he does, actually. But remember everybody has an ego. Phillipse Renfield thinks he's the most important banker in New York—a claim that's open to debate—so he needs to delegate some of the preliminary work to somebody else. I'm sure he met with Secretary Chase on his last visit. Actually, he thinks he should deal only with the President."

"The difference between Phillipse and Randall is night and day."

"Well," Bynum said with a laugh, "Randall is after all a lawyer. Remember that he's also the younger brother of a very successful man. He seems quite ordinary—average might be a compliment in his case. I suspect his reach exceeds his grasp."

"They're obviously setting me up to front for them. Insofar as the new companies are legitimate, I suppose that's all right. They already gave me a large check, which I finally deposited in a new account with a different bank. But I know there are questionable practices involved, or they wouldn't need Appleby."

"Some of your Greek historians imply that war brings out the best in men. Others recognize both sides of the coin. War may sometimes be necessary. Sometimes, I suppose, war supports admirable principles. But on the whole it's a paltry and monstrous method to resolve complex conflicts, and as far as I'm concerned it brings out the worst in people. Including me, of course. After all, I'm a mercenary."

"But it's a cause you can support in principle as well as practice."

"You think of yourself as unworldly, but I see in you a different trait. For all your bookishness, and in spite of your keen abstract mind, I see you as a man whose feelings are integrated with his thoughts. It's an attractive condition and should eventually bring you intimacy with wife and family and friends. But it's also rare. Look at Phillipse."

"I look at him all the time and he's still a mystery to me."

"He thinks he's a pillar of society, a financial wizard. He runs the House of Renfield as if he were a Rothschild. These investment bankers think of themselves as royalty. They believe that they, and they alone, are the financial powers behind nations."

"I love Clarissa but I'd be afraid to work for her father."

"Agreed! They pretend to have the highest of gentlemanly standards. A handshake or a word from them is viewed as an unimpeachable trust. 'His word's as good as gold,' they'll say. But what do they do when the chips are down? They resort to whatever methods are needed to protect their position. They close their circle and conspire to preserve not only the fact of their wealth and power, but also the myth of their honor and courage and *savoir faire.*"

"Sometimes I don't know whether to be flattered by your praise or frightened by your view of human nature."

"You see, you're so forthright. Most people don't reveal their true feelings. You'll have to learn to be more guarded. We're about to embark on clandestine activities that put people's lives at risk. People can be hanged or shot for taking the wrong side in a war that grows in bloodiness day by day."

"I read about those two ironclad ships at Hampton Roads. A new form of naval warfare, the papers said. But the Union won. Does that mean the tide is turning?"

"The *Monitor* was built over in Brooklyn, you know. So the North can build more of them, and faster ones too. The *Merrimac* will be hard for the South to replace. I had a letter from your father about it. He was ashore in Norfolk, but managed to get away. He mentions you, in a sort of code, of course, and wishes you well. He repeats his hope that you'll not fight either for or against Virginia. And he indicates those accounts in London, the ones in your name, are growing."

"I think my mother still dreams that one day the war will end and Father will come back to her. I'm convinced that regardless of the war he'll never live with us again."

"When we met in London we spent a long evening in one of those men's clubs—I've got privileges at two of them—and he had more brandy than usual. I gather he's saddened by the rupture in your family but feels he had no choice. Something happened, he said, when you were about eight years old. But even though he'd had a lot to drink, he wouldn't pursue the revelation and I was too much of a Southern gentleman to draw it out of him."

"My mother blurted it out during one of our arguments. She's got a secret, she says. Somehow she thinks she can protect me and make me happy with the power of this secret. All I ever expected from the two of them was affection and honesty. I'm quite capable of looking after myself."

"Of that, dear chap, I'm certain. Otherwise I wouldn't have been so forthcoming with you and surely wouldn't have sought to involve you in our work. If we were in Washington, I'd never have approached you. I respect you too much and would be loathe to place you in harm's way. But here in New York, it's different. Support for this war is weaker here than anywhere else in the Northeast. Even if you should be discovered, it's possible you'd not be prosecuted."

"If that's true why does Lincoln want all these war powers?"

"People seek power for its own sake."

"I've no desire to wield power over other people. I find it repugnant."

"More evidence that you possess a most unusual integrity."

"Bynum, don't flatter me. I'm already committed to helping you. I just can't understand your motives."

"Did you know the Union troops have been victorious in North Carolina? New Bern, that's on the coast, has fallen. New Bern is my hometown. I grew up there, Chad, in an old Georgian house, three stories high, symmetrical architecture, red bricks and white woodwork and lawns and gardens. We had no slaves. They were freed right after the War of 1812. We did have Negroes working on the estate. They were paid. Some of our neighbors who relied on slave labor were suspicious of us, but we were nevertheless part of a special way of life. Gentle, formal, stately. I rode my pony in those gardens. I went to birthday parties in neighboring mansions. I played stickball and rolled my hoop along those dusty lanes in summer, or went to the beach and roughhoused in the surf. I had my first sexual experience in that little town, with a young barmaid, out behind the tavern, in a woodshed." Bynum paused, looked towards the windows awash in rain and poured himself another glass of wine. Then he rose and turned the gaslights up a bit. He sat down again in his upholstered chair and sighed. "You see, I'm as romantic as you. But circumstances have decreed that I shall follow a different path towards preserving my dream. My myth, if you will. The truth is, I think the South will lose this war. I think that their economy will be destroyed, that hundreds of thousands will be killed, and that the very structure of constitutional government—at least with regards to the rights of individual states—will be forever lost. My motives? They don't bear up under rational scrutiny. I know that. But I can't let my dream of a happy childhood and a special place in the history of my home state be destroyed without putting up a fight. And as a practical man, I decided that my fight should also bring me some money."

"Do you really think we'll be in danger?"

"Did you read about that man, Gordon, I think, who was hanged this month? He was the only slave trader ever executed. The only one! Why do you think they hanged one of them at this late date? Let me answer—because war requires examples, sacrifices, warnings. A hanging here, a firing squad there, even the branding of young men with a fiery poker if they show cowardice in the face of battle. They're actually doing that, you know, right now. A far cry from your Spartan heroes."

"Death and torture on an arbitrary basis?"

"War brings everything into the light, the good and the bad. But I'm afraid it's mostly the bad that prevails. Maybe some good can be salvaged. I'd not feel any remorse if slavery were abolished. It's a heinous institution. Even before the war came when I was, like you, a cultivated young man with leisure and happiness before me, my conscience was troubled. No, it won't do to gloss over this evil in the South. There are those who pretend they abhor slavery but support it because it's necessary and in the long run better for the Negro. I know this to be a callous lie."

"One out of four Southerners still has slaves. Why do the other three-fourths not stand up for what is right? Then Washington couldn't really justify this war."

"That issue should have been addressed separately. Lincoln himself said the war is not about slavery and the Congress even passed a resolution saying the sole purpose of the conflict is to preserve the Union. But the question, the fair question, Chad, is a union of what? I think we created this nation out of nothing. *E pluribus unum* is an innocuous slogan. It should read, how would you put it in Latin, "Out of nothing, something."

Chad sat quietly, gazing into his wine glass, soothed by Bynum's sincerity and personal warmth, but chilled by his tone of compromise and accommodation. They sat in pensive silence for a long while, listening to the splash of rain against the glass, the snap and crack of the log fire, and their own occasional deep breaths. After a while, Chad stood up, warmed his hands at the fire, and turned to Bynum, who seemed lost in thought.

"You're only twelve years older than I am but you've become like a father. I know no other person in New York with whom I share so much, in terms of education and literary interests and a certain reverence, call it romantic if you want to, for the things we feel in our heart, things put there by our childhood experiences. I watch you confront the right and the wrong and take a stand, although I can't wholeheartedly agree with everything you say. I guess I seek an ideal that's perhaps unreachable. Like Plato, as you pointed out. People like you and me, people who try to think our way through these so-called practical matters, aren't welcome. But I'll not cease to weigh one fact against another, and as my experience grows, perhaps I'll find an ethical compromise. In the meantime, I'm determined to keep up my charade of a job with Randall Renfield and keep my eyes and ears open. And I'll deal with this Appleby if you want me to. And I'll work with you to see if we can transmit information or advice that might help bring this war to an end, even if it means the South is triumphant. Tell me what you want me to do."

"I've written down a list of tasks, mostly dealing with information, details about financing plans, since the war runs on money. We could exploit any evidence of Northern complicity in the illegal shipment of goods to the South. While such a discovery, if publicized, might cut the Confederate supplies even more drastically, it would undermine the solidarity of the Northern fanatics who prosecuted this war in the first place. What choice did we have but to fire on a strengthened garrison that sought to collect tariffs on our necessary imports? I'd be unfaithful to my friendship with your father if I lured you into hazardous activities. It has to be your decision, based both on your practical concerns and your principles. When you've read the details in this envelope and probed your conscience once again, let's meet and make our final commitments to each other. And now my friend, I must send you out into the cold, for I'm both exhausted and fulfilled by this discussion. We'll meet again soon and at that time, I'll help you decide which assignments you'll accept. Together we may change the course of history and save thousands of lives while we're doing it."

April 1862

Dr. Forrest's face was a familiar sight for Chad's family and friends, either in his consulting room, or around the dinner table. Now in his sixties, distinguished among his medical peers, and revered by many younger doctors whom he'd taught and inspired, he was a tactful habitué of a closely knit "Very Old New York", as Marilyn Blaine called it, not without both envy and scorn.

Although Marilyn was no longer popular among the coterie into which she'd been born, Dr. Forrest remained loyal and nonjudgmental. So when she began to have worrisome symptoms, he went without complaint to her house and examined her there. Whatever he told her was not yet known to the ever-changing participants in her East 25th Street salon. But there was talk, and it was not reassuring.

It was, therefore, both fearful and hopeful that the well-known doctor should appear at one of his patient's gatherings, now held in the afternoons. Chad arrived with Clarissa, Schuyler and Marcus in one of the larger Renfield carriages, with a team of high-stepping white horses, plumes on their heads and opulent livery on their coachman, who waited outside in front of the Blaine townhouse.

Chad was determined to find out more, and since this doctor delivered both him and Schuyler, he felt he had a wedge to help him discover the truth about his colorful aunt's condition. One look at her had alarmed him, for she actually seemed thinner, and he noticed that she hardly touched her cordials and ate far fewer chocolates than usual.

With Schuyler at his side, Chad cornered Dr. Forrest in the foyer, where they spoke in low voices. "The truth is," Dr. Forrest said, "Mrs. Blaine has a serious condition, the nature of which medical protocol forbids me to disclose. I will, out of consideration for you as her nephew and you, Schuyler, as her friend, warn you that the prognosis is not a happy one. My advice is to treat her especially well in the weeks to come and to show her your devotion and respect. I know there are those who consider her behavior to be a little racy, and her marriage to be questionable, but that's none of my business. I hope we can work together to provide a period of happiness, whether or not she pulls through. She's an exceptionally intelligent and cultured woman, which is one reason she's not popular in certain elite circles where women succeed by remaining silent. But she'll not fail to notice unexpected changes in attitudes towards her, so I strongly urge you to keep up the game." With that the tall, gray, slim and regal doctor, professor of medicine, *bon vivant* and *raconteur*, squeezed Chad's shoulder, shook Schuyler's hand, and hurried out the door and down the front stoop to his waiting carriage.

War had brought both evidence and talk of death, even at festive parties and across the dinner table. But Chad's life hadn't yet been touched by the inevitable, so he reacted to the news with his usual combination of deep feelings and long thoughts. While he found it hard to dissemble he would try to keep up a happy front. His past criticisms of this bulbous old dowager now distressed him, but he was smart enough to know that a radical change in his demeanor would simply exacerbate her ordeal. He could now be certain of his ability to play a role, since he was, in his own mind at least, now both business tycoon and spy.

The memory-filled parlor was as crowded as ever. Susan Steinmann and Eliza Van Der Venner sat side by side in front of the fireplace, which remained unlit on a balmy late April day. One of the crowd known as "Marilyn Blaine's boys" sat on the piano stool, facing his hostess. Seated near the famous chaise was Father Fineas Flaherty, whose Roman collar and dangling cross now seemed ominous rather than curious, as if he were prepared to administer final rites to a woman—born and bred in the Episcopal Church—who made known her disdain for religion in general, a declaration that contributed to her precarious position in the society to which she once belonged.

Chad's role playing, as he now thought of it, was made more difficult by the presence of his collaborator, Bynum Bradley-West, richly adorned and carefully coiffed, who stood by the window looking like a carefree man-about-town, the persona he'd told Chad was best for both of them.

Chad took Aunt Marilyn's hand and bent to kiss her cheek. As she looked into his eyes, he suppressed a shudder and convinced himself she surmised little and knew less.

"Did you say hello to Dr. Forrest, Chad," Marilyn said, keeping her penetrating gaze fixed on his green Laymus eyes, which she shared. "He's such an old friend and so well known to most of you that I finally convinced him to attend my salon. Like many cultured medical men he's keenly sensitive to new ideas. I suspect, Chad, that he's as well read in the great classics as you are. But alas, today he had sadder news."

For a moment Chad feared this grandiloquent woman was going to reveal her condition and make it part of their discourse. But that would be out of character, he reassured himself, trying to think of a witty reply when she continued. "Did you know that after the outbreak of typhoid fever last year several doctors died? Did you know that we're now experiencing a shortage of doctors here at home because so many have already left to answer the needs of our armies? Dr. Forrest, as patriotic a man as you'll find, is getting a little old for the battlefield, so he's kindly consented to stay and look after all of us.

I was surprised but delighted that he could spare a little time to join in our discussions today. Doubtless he'll return as this war goes on, for he's keenly sensitive to the daily agony and prospect of bereavement confronting many of our families, including some of the best families in New York."

Her curious combination of reassurance and alarm was a relief to them all, Chad suspected. He decided to support her attempts to keep the focus away from her rumored decline. "I'm not surprised," he said. "The bloodletting that went on at Shiloh for three full days is enough to distress any humanitarian, regardless of political views. That the Union prevailed, some say barely, is small comfort in the face of such unprecedented loss. Casualties for the North were 13,000 and for the South 11,000. Numbers like that were hardly expected by either side and it's changed attitudes everywhere. There are those here in New York who believe that both sides should immediately sue for peace, and gather around a conference table to solve this dilemma before thousands more are killed and wounded."

Susan Steinmann's face hardened at Chad's speech. "Sue for peace? Tell me in what war did opposite sides hurry to the conference table at this stage of hostilities? They both think their cause is just. Both sides think they'll win. Chad, your reputation persuades us that you're amply schooled in classical literature. War is fable, war is myth. The facts escape even the participants. More significantly, few will plead for a peace that threatens their economic benefits. Later on, when both sides have suffered unconscionably, only then will they falter. By that time, reason will have withered up and died. And I dare say both sides will proclaim that God is on their side, even after one of them is defeated."

"We should not deign to place God on either side, or even to say that he's on both sides." Father Flaherty had been leaning forward in his seat but now straightened his back abruptly, appearing tall even when seated. He was a sandy-haired man with pink cheeks and bright, hazel eyes. He had the visage of the Irish, many said, some in approval and some in derogation. "Who among us, regardless of spiritual convictions, would pretend to know the will of God? A mysterious subject, an essence who works through unfathomable means. We can only hope for mercy, and charity, and perhaps a little humility. Most of all, sympathy for the suffering and the bereaved."

"Perhaps, Father, you could find words to justify this carnage when you're pacifying your flock." Bynum smiled graciously but the hostility of his tone didn't go unnoticed.

"The plague of war is a challenge to all of us who wear the cloth. We must disregard the slogans and marches and fluttering flags and devote ourselves to comforting those who suffer. And that's of course our constant role, since war, even a war as brutal as this one, is merely an even more painful metaphor for the human condition. *Bellum omnium contra omnes*, Mr. Wales. I assume you know your Hobbes."

"I both know and disagree with Hobbes," Chad said. "His famous articulation of the war of all against all strikes me as a handy phrase used to excuse each of us, as individuals, from making hard choices. Perhaps we might well think for ourselves, however much we respect, as I'm known to do, the wisdom of the past. Where is it written that we can't change ourselves? Where does it say we can't awaken to a higher mental state, where intelligence and reason are not disdained and where compassion and tolerance are savored? Indeed, who's to say that we couldn't, as individuals, take belligerent actions ourselves, in the early stage of conflict, in order to facilitate a speedier resolution to this woeful antagonism?"

"Well said, Chad." Marcus seemed to address his comments solely to Father Fineas, moving across the room to stand near him and looking directly into his eyes. "Those of us who are Protestants are perhaps less likely to accept ritual, and the behavior which sanctions it, as an excuse to avoid decision making. My home state of Ohio has mustered numerous regiments, while there's simultaneously a backlash against the war. I'm proud of this strong opposition in my home state although I don't personally agree with the pro-Southern sentiment. It's the principles, finally, that matter. Human life is dispensable but principles are with us always. I rejoice that in Ohio, opposing voices are heard. For which of us is to say he knows what's right?"

"There are many Catholics in Ohio, Mr. Tifton, especially among the immigrants. The immigrant hordes, I suppose some of you might say. But these people, many of them forlorn and living from hand to mouth, are hardly what I'd call dispensable. In fact, they're perhaps truer patriots than some of the people in this room."

A general murmur followed an awkward silence, but the clergyman went on with his indictment. "Are you aware that of those volunteer regiments assembled after the big Union Square rally, many were established on immigrant lines? There were Hungarians, and Germans, and Italians joined to advance the war on slavery. And many of them were Irish, as am I."

"It might be expected, then, Father, that our President and his cabinet could speak a little more honestly about the slavery issue, in the border states as well as within the Confederacy. Familiar as I am with the history of your native land, I should think there'd be some sympathy for those who are invaded and suppressed by a more powerful people." A gentle tone cloaked Bynum's irritation, but Father Fineas was not deterred.

"We Irish are also persecuted in this land of the free. They're even more hostile in Boston, the so-called Athens of America. 'No Irish Need Apply' is such a popular sentiment it's printed on handbills and sold to merchants and other businesses in need of employees, to place without shame in their windows. Here in New York, where one in four is Irish, there's a somewhat more promising situation, in that many of my countrymen have advanced in the professions, in business, and especially in politics. Politics being a wordy pursuit, we Irish are especially proficient at it."

It was obvious that Father Flaherty's attempt at humor was meant to soothe ruffled feathers in preparation for even stronger admonitions. "It's true that there's drunkenness and brutality in some of us, but I suspect no more than in other poor wretches who seek a better life in America. Irish blood will flow in this war. And as one of you pointed out to me in a previous gathering here, there are Catholics in the South, especially in New Orleans and in Georgia. And their red blood will be no different from other rebels, whether it's at Bull Run or Shiloh, or whatever more horrific battles await us in this struggle. Does the end justify the means, Mr. Wales? Does your learned background include Machiavelli? Many people, including our president, insist this war is not about slavery, but if it must be fought, and the abolition of slavery is a result, which among you will declare with certainty that it was not God's will?"

Bynum peered out the window and sipped his sherry, then turned to face Father Flaherty. But his gaze swept the room as if he were careful to address his remarks to all of them. "I suspect God has his hands full. We've focused here on our own little universe which is beset with evils, chief among them, I myself believe, is the repulsive tradition of slavery. Abolish it, yes. Perhaps if it could be done no other way, abolish it by war. But I hope you'll keep your facts straight, Father, even though you must by necessity conduct yourself in accordance with a written code that's considered by many to be metaphor at best and myth at worst. I respect the Bible and I know that you can find passages there to justify almost anything. Perhaps I needn't even say 'almost.'"

"I'm not a cleric who'll use obscure passages in our sacred texts to justify war or slavery or murder. But we Catholics are supposed to be ruled more by conscience than doctrine, whether or not, Sir, you accept that fact."

"Your point, as a personal practice, hardly needs debating, Father, but the issue of slavery does. One might look at how the British Empire abolished slavery within its nation and throughout its imperial realm. But we speak here of only the more obvious forms of slavery. Granted, the more apparent evil needs the most immediate attention. But it wouldn't do, Father, to ignore servitude in all its guises, including servitude to a religious tradition that has included, as you must yourself admit, some of the most inhumane actions in history: violence, murder, suppression and repression, and the penalty of death leveled on many whose only sin, or crime, was disagreement."

"Bravo, Bynum. You should move to Ohio!" Marcus looked around the room with a smug expression and sidled closer to Schuyler, in anticipation of his approval.

"I guess I'm more like my future brother-in-law," Schuyler said. "I've reserved judgment and preserved hope for a more peaceful solution. Even if it takes a little longer, it may save us much in the long run. These statistics from Shiloh have put a very different perspective on this war. Are we to expect even greater losses in the future? The thought is staggering and dismal." Schuyler looked at Chad first and Marcus second, started to say something else, then put his glass on the teacart and sat down again.

"We're privileged people in this room, for the most part," Susan Steinmann said. "We women have our own yoke of servitude but at least we're not shot down or hanged arbitrarily. And many of us will retreat from time to time to enjoy what men think are the womanly pursuits, though I favor few of them. I don't sew nor crochet nor embroider and can scarcely boil a pot of tea. I may be a Sunday painter, and I can play the spinet as well as that young man there who has so often delighted us with his talents. You men will have it out, one way or another. You'll eventually talk yourselves onto the battlefield. There's little I can do, except give generously to the Sanitary Commission and to other charities to help the wounded and their families. Other than that, I choose to withdraw. Indeed, my dear friend Eliza has invited me, and I've accepted the invitation, to spend the summer with her at Kuyperkill Farm. It's not far from Yellowfields, Clarissa. Perhaps you'll visit with us."

"I've suggested to my husband-to-be that we spend more time upriver. Indeed, after our marriage we may choose to build our own retreat on the grounds. I'll be happy to visit with you and Eliza, and I hope you'll return the favor by calling on me as well."

"You see," said Chad. "There's room for a variety of opinions concerning our situation. My Clarissa, like Miss Steinmann, works vigorously for war relief and for the poor. Some of us will try to alleviate immediate suffering. Others will join the battle itself. Still others will work in their own private ways to bring this disaster to a conclusion. Don't disparage those who hope to effect reconciliation. For as I recall, Father, it's written in your Bible that 'blessed are the peacemakers.' It doesn't delineate the morality or propriety of the methods used to achieve this end." Chad ended his remarks with a sense of accomplishment, and was chagrined to see Bynum's face, which telegraphed to him and him alone an order to shut up and sit down.

Bynum didn't want the argument to end with Chad's too-obvious proclamation of the right to be subversive. "We've heard a diversity of opinions today. You know that I'm a Southerner and Chad is half one. So what I say may be suspect. But look closer to home. Your own Governor, Horatio

Seymour, has made himself clear and it serves as an effective summary of the paradox. Governor Seymour has proclaimed his support of the Union. But his hostility to Lincoln is well known. He's charged this president with the eager usurpation of unconstitutional war powers. And he's vociferously opposed to conscription. Yes, there are those in the Congress who are discussing a draft law. You might consider that, Father. The volunteer regiments recruited at Union Square were inflamed by rhetoric and charged with emotion. They were made to feel noble and safe at the same time. They didn't expect a war that, in a single three-day battle, would claim 24,000 casualties. But there aren't enough volunteers anymore, certainly not from the upper classes, and not even from your parishioners. The Irish, perhaps more than any of us, know the cost of prolonged violence and oppression, since their country has been occupied, more or less, for centuries. Is it not Shakespeare's Richard II who complains that 'it's these Irish wars' when he tries to find an excuse for misgovernment, and when he's desperate for funds to keep fighting?"

Bynum looked into Chad's eyes as if he expected an answer but didn't pause for one. "In a sense I'm a refugee in a foreign land, and I hope by keeping my mouth shut most of the time, and by behaving myself all the time, you'll honor my life, my freedom and my dignity. But this is still America, or what's left of it. You may want to concern yourselves, on a more immediate and practical level, with the charges that so rile your own elected Governor. Would you sacrifice the Constitution to prosecute a war, not avowedly to free the oppressed, but to maintain the balance of power in Congress and to continue to run the government with money raised almost entirely from tariffs, which have injured and hindered the South for a long, long time?"

Marilyn Blaine lifted her hand and surveyed the room with a weary countenance. "Regardless of the outcome, I shall miss these spirited afternoons. I'm a lonely old woman and my time is not as long as yours. I haven't gone out into society for many a year. I've instead retained my openness to people whose personal habits are maligned but whose artistic talents and intelligent minds have sustained me and will continue to sustain me in the weeks and months to come. Dare I say it? I agree with you all!"

Early May 1862

Clarissa decided to use one of the bigger carriages for their outing in the new Central Park. Most of the trails were open now, and it was already a New York pastime to ride or drive the full length of the Olmsted-Vaux creation, which some critics had termed "a work of art in itself." She told Chad the big carriage would be best because the coachman wouldn't be able to hear them, and the large leather top, folded in back, shielded them from prying eyes from the rear and both sides. "We'll have privacy and it will be so romantic, riding with you in the springtime, in the heart of our hometown!"

Despite the noise of horses' hooves and the rumble of other carriages in front or behind them, Chad still feared their words might be heard, and if so, would soon be shared with the rest of the servants, and then with the servants of other households. So he spoke softly.

"I apologize again for not spending as many hours with you as you'd like. The truth is, my involvement with your Uncle Randall and my Uncle Caleb, in these momentous new business ventures, has monopolized my time."

"Uncle Randall said you don't have to go to your office more than twice a week."

"Of course he might say that, but I take these responsibilities seriously. I don't wish to be an errand boy or a front man. If I'm to serve as head of these companies, I must immerse myself in business affairs. Not only in my office, of course. I spend time downtown, meeting with Wall Street people. And I still have my reading to do. Believe it or not, Clarissa, there's hardly anything in our lives that's not anticipated in literature. Bynum feels my broad background in history and letters is an advantage in business as well."

Clarissa sniffled into her handkerchief, her fingers knotted. "Why would you discuss business matters with Mr. Bradley-West?"

"He once brought me news of my father, Clarissa, before the war broke out. He still has conduits to information that I find important. Some of it, most of it actually, is personal."

"So you've already begun to keep things from me. Memories of my mother, who died when I was still tiny, are all I have to comfort me. I have no women in my family to mold myself after, to turn to for advice, other than distant cousins, and some of my late mother's relatives, who live mostly in the country. She was of Dutch and Huguenot descent, as you know. They still live the lives of patroons, and seldom venture into the city. If I spend more time at Yellowfields I may have to cultivate closer relations with them. I've been warned that men often take their wives for granted, after a while."

"We aren't even married yet. How could I take you for granted?"

"Oh, don't let's fuss. It's such a fine day. Look at that forsythia. And the tulips. It's almost prettier than Yellowfields."

"You don't even know how much I think about you. If only I could bring myself to say it, how I feel. You're so beautiful. I see your face before me every night, and I wake up sometimes, with your image in my mind. It makes me … Clarissa, I desire you so much. I'd never fail to give you the attention you crave. I wish we could be alone somewhere right now, all barriers gone.

In other cultures, there's more leniency towards the passions of youth. Do you not feel something like this for me?"

"You know I can't talk about that aspect of our love without compromising myself in your eyes. I wouldn't have you think me without virtue. Of course, your image is in my mind and of course I've got strong feelings. Why else would I have consented to marry you? But men and women are different. It's difficult for me to admit the surge of my feelings and harder still for me to imagine how you, a man, must feel. At finishing school there were titters at night when girls talked of these things. I'm the only female left in the Renfield line. I must conduct myself with the utmost virtue. More than most girls! More than any of those girls downtown where you went that day with Mr. Bradley-West. You had a strange look in your eye when you saw me after that excursion. I hardly recognized it."

"Do you think you have any reason whatsoever to fear me? Don't you realize that your virtue is enshrined in my heart and could never be lessened by anything we might do together? Most of all, especially in my case, do you think I'd shrink from you if you were more candid about what it is exactly you feel for me, physically, I mean"

"Physically! Oh Chad, we mustn't do anything that would embarrass us later. We're taking a chance right now, driving through the park like this. Did you know there's never been a divorce in my family?"

"What's that got to do with us? What are people saying?" Chad sat back in his seat, glancing at the passing trees and bushes as the coach clipped-clopped at a brisk pace around the curved and crowded drives of Central Park. "Why would anybody discuss divorce with reference to us? We aren't even married yet."

Clarissa looked to the right and left and then planted a solid kiss on Chad's lips.

"Clarissa! What will people think?"

"What people?"

"I don't know. The coachman."

"I can vouch that he doesn't have eyes in the back of his head." She snuggled closer to him, put her arm inside his elbow, and pressed her knees against his. "Tell me how it feels, to be a man."

"You mean, in general?"

"Of course not, silly. I know how men feel in general. I grew up with Schuyler, you know."

"I don't know if he would be the example you're looking for."

"What do you mean by that?"

"I mean nothing, dear, except to say that how men feel, well, in general, is often the same but from one to another it could be different."

"I don't understand."

"Neither do I."

"Then explain it to me."

"I just told you I don't understand it either. What are we talking about?"

"Not how men feel generally. What difference does that make? I mean, how do you feel, you know, as men?"

"It all depends."

"Depends on what?"

"People feel differently about different things."

"But how do you feel about me? Precisely, I mean …"

"Precisely? I don't understand."

"Well, exactly, then. Tell me how you feel. Exactly. About me, in a man and woman sense." Clarissa's voice was husky now, almost in a whisper.

"The first time we took a ride in this park I held you close to me and said things you thought were bold."

"But I told you I wanted you to be bold. We're betrothed now. Tell me exactly, precisely how you feel."

"Clarissa, men get excited."

"So do women."

"Yes, but it's more obvious with men. Don't you remember, we dismounted, we walked over by the pond. There weren't any people there. We went behind that big tree, and I kissed you and then I held you close to me and you …"

"I did what? Be specific."

"You indicated you were aware of the physical changes occurring at that moment under that tree on the side of that pond. You and me. My body and yours. Now there, I've said it. Please don't ask me to be more specific."

She squeezed his hand. "I know what happens. Remember, I've got a brother. We were left to our own so much of the time. I interrupted Schuyler in the bath once. You can't imagine what I saw."

"Tell me, then."

"He was in the tub, that's all."

"Clarissa, tell me precisely what you saw!"

"Precisely. Oh, I couldn't do that."

"Then tell me exactly what you saw."

"Very well then. If you promise not to lose respect for me."

"I promise."

She turned her head away then whispered in his ear. "He was aroused, Chad. He was aroused the way you were when you pressed against me under that tree. And every night I think about it. I think of what it means to you.

I want us to be married and then I never want there to be any barriers. No barriers whatsoever. And not even a rumor of divorce. Never."

* * *

A broad semicircular driveway defined the center portion of the Renfield Mansion facing W. 28th Street. The large carriage ground to a stop. Simultaneously the family's formidable housekeeper in her black dress and white apron and cap opened the front door. She gestured towards the interior and one of the stableboys appeared, opened the carriage, lowered the folding steps, and offered his arm to Clarissa. She twirled her parasol even though it was now late afternoon and the May sun was rapidly fading over the Hudson.

"It's not too late for tea, dear. The family's not dining together this evening because a number of Father's business friends are coming. Cook is preparing a light dinner for Schuyler and Marcus and me to have upstairs. I know you can't stay that long, but come into the front parlor and have a sherry or something and let's see if we might have a chance to talk with Father. We needn't be specific. Just let him know we're as determined as ever." She leaned closer to his ear. "I don't even care if he guesses how amorous we've become!"

The front parlor, however, turned out to be empty. Chad was tired and worried, but most of all aroused by Clarissa's forthright and vivid discussion of her feelings for him which made it even harder to keep his mind away from the subject. Not even the great Greek and Roman poets could keep his mind off her when she was in so flirting a mood.

"Your father isn't home yet, Miss, but he's expected. I'm to arrange for a rather large dinner party. Mr. Renfield has ordered us to set up a buffet and then leave the gentlemen alone for the rest of the evening. Apparently there's much to be decided."

"Send him into the front parlor the minute he arrives, please." Clarissa said. "Will you wait for me there, Chad darling? I want to freshen up."

Chad was now familiar with the Renfield Mansion. He'd dined or had tea or sherry or brandy in all of the major downstairs rooms and continued, on occasion, to lunch with Clarissa, usually in the company of Schuyler and Marcus, in the upstairs sitting room. Neither her brother nor his "bosom friend" had made further reference to the scene in the bedroom or the incident at Holder Pratt's. Chad's initiation into the steamy side of downtown life, after his day with Bynum, had made him more averse to bawdiness but at the same time more indifferent to whatever it was Schuyler and Marcus were up to now.

He eased himself into a large club chair with soft upholstery and leaned his head against the high back, letting his eyes slowly close and his mind drift off. It was not long before he heard Phillipse Renfield's voice, first greeting and then further instructing the housekeeper, who directed him into the front parlor.

Phillipse had changed in the last few months. He was taller than Randall, thinner and more aristocratic in his bearing. Although he could pass for a younger man his hair now seemed grayer, his face more lined, and his eyes more troubled. But he greeted his future son-in-law warmly and asked the housekeeper, who was standing in the doorway, to bring in some sherry.

"How are you, my boy," Phillipse asked after they sat down. They sipped a lustrous Spanish liquid, shining with gold in tapered glasses. "Is my brother keeping you busy with these ventures of his?"

"Yes sir, we meet frequently. I'm not aware how involved you might be."

"We lead separate lives. He's a lawyer, after all, and as such there are things he can't even admit to his family. Frankly, there are very few people around who have adequate experience in the intricacies of high finance during wartime. As far as business matters go, I allow him to act as an intermediary on these Federal loans, in those stages where underlings may negotiate details after I've ironed out the overall conditions with the Treasury Secretary or, quite often, with the President." He took a small taste of his sherry, his lips primly pressed together. It seemed to Chad he didn't really want to allow anything to pass between his lips but his own words. As if in silent agreement, Phillipse put his glass down on the old Chippendale side table next to his wing chair. "But what of you," he went on. "Is my brother keeping you from overstepping legal lines with these speculations of his?"

Chad was uneasy with the unexpected burst of candor, reinforcing his own apprehensions about Randall Renfield and Grover Appleby. "Well, Sir, he's an ambitious man and I'm flattered he's placed such confidence in me. These new companies embody an entrepreneurial spirit and it's my hope that they'll flourish. If so, they may aid the war effort, reap dividends for our investors, and add more to our own finances. I hope they'll bring honor to the names of Renfield and Laymus, which will be associated in many people's mind when Clarissa and I are wed."

"Wed? Ah, yes. Wed. But we've not set a date yet, have we? Chad, let me be frank. I'm not sure when any of us can get on with our lives with any certainty. This war is tearing the country apart in ways none of us had expected. Why, this very night, I've summoned an impressive group of financial and business leaders, and some political people, too. Both the governor and the mayor are expected, in hopes of arriving at a consensus—a position, if you will. Our financial institutions have made huge loans to Southern planters. Some of these loans are secured by their property, which includes, I'm sad to say, their slaves. We've also guaranteed their letters of credit. And of course, our commerce with them is disrupted and theirs with us. They're in a somewhat better position since they could ship all their rice and cotton and tobacco to England if they wanted to. If there were no blockade, that is. In the meantime our New England clients—and that includes the Laymus mills—are suffering. Where will they get the cotton they need without paying a higher price? And the government is borrowing more and more money, and there's even talk of an income tax! Can you imagine that? The government should run itself on tariffs, not tax the populace. Unemployment here is rising even with the heightened war effort. Speculation is rife on the Exchange. Indications are similar to the panic of '57. You may not know, Chad, of my role in helping the city recover from that calamity. So these people here, tonight, will examine the conditions—all of the conditions—and try to arrive at a meeting of the minds, so we might approach the President together and sway him. He's not inured to advice. Indeed, when he was a one-term congressman from Illinois seeking to fill the highest office in the land, he welcomed our every word. And he makes really great speeches. But where are we to take our stand? Even his own cabinet is confused and some of them, Secretary Chase, for example, are openly hostile to his policies and to him as a person. So, to wed? Clarissa wants it and you want it. And I want it too. But I don't think we should be so rash as to set a date until we see how we're going to fare in this conflict. We must avoid further bloodshed, compromise somehow on the tariff and slavery issues and get those cotton gins going again and your family's mills operating full steam ahead."

Phillipse lifted his little glass to his lips, took another tiny sip, and put it down again. He was half out of his chair when Schuyler and Marcus opened the parlor doors and walked quickly in.

"Father, there you are," Schuyler said. "I haven't seen you for days. Clarissa and I've been dining upstairs and I'm afraid I usually miss you at breakfast."

"I expect so," Phillipse said, "since you're never up when I leave for my office in the morning."

"Hello Mr. Renfield." Marcus said.

"Hello Marcus," Phillipse said. He didn't look at him and didn't proffer his hand.

"Hello Marcus," Chad said with forced gusto. "Hello Schuyler. Clarissa and I wondered what you were up to."

"In fact, Marcus has privileges at the Federal Club through his club in Cleveland. We had lunch there and then joined some of the younger folk for billiards. Then we went shopping for some clothes we'll need when we embark for Europe again. Then we visited that new art gallery on Broadway. And now we're home for a drink or two and dinner and then off to the opera."

Phillipse was openly glaring at them but said nothing. Chad sensed tension in the air, so he replied in Phillipse's stead. "What a busy life. I envy you all that, especially Europe. I may not get there for a long time, since I'm now involved in some new business ventures. And of course, since I hope Clarissa and I may wed soon. As soon as Mr. Renfield thinks it best, of course."

"We really have to hurry if we're to keep up with our schedule," Schuyler said. They both turned abruptly and left the room.

After a long silence Phillipse spoke in a weary voice. "I hope we settle things tonight. I want your wedding to happen too. After all, I'll be wanting grandchildren, and you may be my only hope."

Startled by the significance of Phillipse's comment, Chad decided not to acknowledge it. "Tell me, Sir, about this meeting. You're all private citizens, except the Governor and the Mayor. Do you think you can devise a way to influence the outcome of this terrible impasse we're in?"

"I don't know. I do know that the power of the purse has always prevailed. If we deny them money they may come to their senses. But if they decide to level some new form of taxation and to extend Federal credit in the form of bonds sold abroad, they'll have cut, in effect, their ties to those of us who put them in office in the first place. They'll possess, in short, almost unbridled power. Perhaps that's what they sought from the outset."

Late May 1862

"What is it? The new job? Clarissa? Or are you trying to avoid me?" Harriet no longer averted her eyes when she subjected her son to a rigorous interrogation. Chad no longer reacted as quickly to her moods. They were, he felt, at a stalemate.

"I have my own life to live."

"No need to keep it a secret from me, though, is there?" Her tone was conciliatory and for a moment Chad sensed a flash of their old affection for one another. But it was an intimacy that made him uncomfortable, so he deliberately allowed himself to revert to their verbal fencing matches.

"I believe you're the one who's got a secret. I've had news of my father's conversations in London concerning this big secret of yours. So you're now an international dissembler."

"Do you actually enjoy tormenting me?" She had a pained look on her face but she'd given up her fretful fist-to-the-face strategy. "All my married life I thought only of you."

"I'm trying my best to be civil. The country's in a mess, your marriage is destroyed, Phillipse thinks Clarissa and I should wait until the war is over to marry, and I'm engaged in questionable commerce with her uncle and your brother, both of whom strike me as superficial in their plans as well as their statements. My home is no longer a peaceful haven, and I've discovered aspects of the world I'd rather not know about. Other than that, Mother, I'm just fine."

"Is it possible you think too much of yourself and not enough about others?"

"I don't know and frankly I don't much care."

"Have you grown hardened so quickly? You're still young, you've got so much promise."

Chad sprang up from the dining table where they'd eaten breakfast together for the first time in weeks, turned his back to her, and stood at the sideboard slowly filling his cup from a finely wrought Georgian silver urn brought back by a Laymus from one of their seafaring expeditions years ago. He replied without facing her. "My initiation into what you call the everyday world has perhaps given me a new perspective. Is that elusive enough to torment you?"

"Would you mind pouring me another cup, too, please?" Her suppliant tone conquered Chad's resentments. He took her cup to the sideboard, filled it, and gently placed it in front of her.

"You know more than anyone that I've always tried to be forthright about my feelings. I know you've been deeply hurt. But it was not my doing, Mother, and if you persist in this mysterious game of tease and retreat every time we talk, then I'd rather not talk at all."

"Perhaps someday you'll understand what I've done for you. Maybe then you'll once again be the tender loving son I knew for twenty years."

"Someday? Next century perhaps. It's likely we'll both still be around in 1900, if we don't get killed in the war or mock each other to death."

"Sharper than a serpent's tooth. You're not the only one who can quote from ancient sources."

"Ah, but you see, I'm not as wrapped up in my books as I was. When I quote them now it's usually in irony. Uncle Caleb and Randall Renfield have set me up in a business venture that has distinctly shady overtones. Apparently they think I'm an educated idiot. My father's afraid to write me directly now because it might bring the Federal marshals to our door, so he uses an intermediary whose loyalties are ambiguous, to say the least. And the woman I love refuses to displease her father by insisting we get married at once. And here in the safety of my loving home, I play these little word games with you. Before you accuse me of being a thankless child, you might ponder this: I'm a caring man who may be a bit too intellectual but I possess a rather impressive frame of reference going back over two thousand years. You think the immediate world is the standard for decision-making and I prefer to weigh my thoughts, and my actions, against more tested, and I believe more universal, criteria. But to be compelled to discuss one's innermost thoughts in such a clinical way doesn't, I presume, auger well for continued intimacy and unqualified love for one's opponent, if that opponent also happens to be one's mother."

"Have I hurt you that much, Chad?"

"Obfuscation and secrecy aren't my favorite methods. Nor is this on-again, off-again interchange. You could, you know, simply come out with it."

"It might harm you more than me." She sipped her coffee and slumped, elbows on the table, a posture quite unlike her. But Chad said nothing and the silent interlude stretched out uneasily.

They were both relieved when their housekeeper knocked lightly at the dining room doors, and then came in. "Madam, you have a caller. The gentleman says you're expecting him."

"Is it the Reverend Mullen?"

"I believe that's what he said, Madam. It's not someone I've welcomed here before."

"Show him in, please. We'll see him in the parlor." She shifted in her seat, smoothed her skirt, and quickly brushed a stray hair from her forehead.

Chad leapt to his feet, his eyes fixed on his mother's face, which now seemed strangely serene. "You invited him here?"

"Where else would you expect me to receive him?" She was tranquil rather than defiant, which upset Chad even more.

"You intend to introduce him to me right here in the parlor of my family home?"

"Actually, it's my home. I paid for it more dearly than you know."

Harriet rose from her chair with a slow dignity and stood a moment, looking stalwart, like the women in Winslow Homer woodcuts Chad had seen in *Harper's* magazine. She seemed a stranger to him, and his curiosity lulled him into a receptive quietude. He followed her through the double doors to the parlor. When they entered, her visitor stood awkwardly in the center of the room.

"I'm so glad to see you, Tad. It's good of you to come all the way over here to meet my son. I doubted I could ever coax him to come with me to Brooklyn. Chad, please shake hands with the Reverend Thaddeus Mullen. He's a dear friend and a colleague in our fight against slavery."

"May I call you Chad? I've heard so much about you I feel I know you already."

"Reverend Mullen." Chad shook his hand and said nothing more.

"Will you have some coffee? Or tea? Something cool? It will soon be June but it's warmer than I like. Chad, ask the housekeeper to bring us some cold water and some lemonade. And some of those little cakes I brought home yesterday." Harriet was radiant now, a woman still beautiful who was, Chad realized with a troubled heart, quite comfortable with the affection of this unmarried preacher from an adjacent city who had no qualms about meeting his mother in front of her son in his family home at ten o'clock in the morning. He stepped into the hall, signaled the housekeeper, and returned to the parlor in dejection.

"Your mother has told me about your Princeton days. It's impressive to find a student ranked at the top in such a prestigious school. Your classmates must have represented the best minds of your generation." Without waiting for Chad to acknowledge the compliment, he proceeded. "I'm the product of a theological seminary. My church is Congregational in affiliation. But like you I savor the poets and philosophers of old. And I find inspiration there for many of my sermons."

Chad couldn't resist a chance to assert himself. "I doubt that you'd quote Aristotle on slavery, then."

"Are we to be at odds so early in our acquaintance? I'm familiar with the passage you refer to. We abolitionists have to refute all the justifications for enslavement that are quoted to us by those who persist in this vile and cruel practice. But Aristotle, like Plato, is not without error. You're too smart to believe anybody whole hog."

"I'm not convinced 'whole hog' is an appropriate critical summary of either Aristotle or Plato. Did you come here to pay homage to my mother or do you want to discuss slavery?"

"When a condition as sinister as this exists in one's own country, it's the moral imperative to oppose it. I do so with my sermons but I back it up with action. Your mother tells me you've had trouble in the past supporting your convictions with decisive activity."

"How considerate of my mother to inform you of my character traits before she invited you into our home. I fear she's not so enlightened me on yours."

Mullen sat quietly for a moment when the refreshments were brought in. Harriet poured a glass of lemonade and handed it to her visitor. Chad watched as they exchanged warm glances, noticing the hint of a smile on his mother's previously sullen face. He studied the man he assumed to be his mother's lover, trying to suppress the echoes of Aeschylus in his mind as he accepted his predicament. The Reverend Dr. Mullen seemed to be perfectly at ease. He had a roundish, beaming face, full lips, and surprisingly dark, melancholy eyes. His hair, still a light brown, was receding noticeably. There was a cord around his neck, attached to what appeared to be a silver-rimmed *pince-nez* thrust into his vest pocket. He reminded Chad of the chaplain at Princeton, the only man of religion he had any respect for until he met Father Flaherty. Dr. Mullen returned Chad's studious gaze and spoke again.

"My character is as imperfect as yours, my boy. I try to make up for it by serving a higher purpose. Right how, I can best serve my God and my Church by taking up this battle against the cruel subjugation and torturous treatment of dark-skinned people who are as much God's children as you or I."

"You needn't lecture me on the subject. I revile slavery perhaps as much as you."

"I'd expect it in a man of intelligence and learning, a man who has had the great fortune to grow up under the guidance of a woman of such merit and nobility as Harriet Laymus."

"Unless she's been keeping another secret from me, my mother is not as yet divorced, so I believe her legal name to be Harriet Wales."

"Have it your way then. Harriet Laymus Wales." He looked at her again with the tenderest expression and Chad slumped further down in his chair, like a petulant child.

"If you wish to pursue this issue, perhaps you might inform me of the solution you and my mother have cooked up during your long days together in the wilds of Brooklyn."

"Your mother told me you tend to be sarcastic, but I find it a humorous habit and welcome it, as long as you're sincere in debating fairly a question that troubles both of us gravely and persistently."

"He's not pro-slavery. He just has a romantic notion of the South, partly because of his father. They once had one of those stately homes down there, but it was lost through financial carelessness long before the war. Chad's father hoped to get it back, but the Union forces in the Shenandoah recently occupied it. Think of it, Chad. Yankees in Cedar Crest Hall!"

"The papers yesterday had news of a Confederate General named Stonewall Jackson. He's advancing rapidly through the Shenandoah, and I suppose by now he's liberated my ancestral seat. Reverend Mullen, you mustn't be misled by my coquettish mother. I've never seen the estate, but as a child I looked at drawings and watercolors of the land down there, and the house. My father, on those rare occasions when he felt comfortable being at home, used to spread them out on the library table and we would look at them together. I've no illusions about life on a slave plantation. But there were no slaves on my father's farm. It looked to be a serene and happy home, one that

I longed for as I grew up. I suspect it was family circumstances that inspired my romantic reverie."

"You're privileged to have been given a dream like that. And to have in addition this handsome home in a great city. I'm sure you realize how many Americans aren't so blessed."

"Chad has enjoyed a sheltered life but he's now taking his place in the business world. I'm confident that he'll marry Clarissa Renfield and build a fine home for himself. I look forward to visiting my grandchildren, when I'm old."

"But dear lady, you'll not be old for such a long time!" Mullen edged forward in his chair, put his lemonade down, and settled back in comfort, as if for good. "No one would believe right now that you could possibly be a grandmother!"

Chad's mind had been racing throughout Mullen's wholly inappropriate remarks. He remembered Bynum's instructions to disguise his feelings. Hard as it was, he decided to put on a different face.

"It's regrettable that so many have so little. I suppose that's why President Lincoln has decided to give away all the Federal land in the West through this Homestead Act he signed last week. My ancestors acquired, for a price, a huge, unexplored tract near the Blue Ridge Mountains and with the sweat and toil of their bodies, carved out of the wilderness a civilized and restful home. By 1800, it was an enviable estate known up and down the Valley. Perhaps these people who are being offered free land will work as hard as we did to make something of it."

"Perhaps so," Reverend Mullen said. "They will, of course, have some of the same troubles as your ancestors did, fighting off the Indians who have this quaint notion that it's their land."

Chad was too appreciative of the minister's wit to get angry. "How true, Sir. My Southern forebears didn't have, unfortunately, the skills of my New England family, who solved the problem by inviting all the natives for a Thanksgiving turkey. As to our bloodline here in Manhattan—there's a little Dutch in most of us, you see—those patriarchs simply purchased this island for a reasonable sum. Trinkets, you might say. But one offers what the other side desires in transactions of this sort."

"Indeed, unless it's life itself that's demanded. Total subservience. Renunciation of the privileges outlined in our own revolutionary documents. Come, Chad, you don't fool me. Nor your mother. She's told me how you examined every subject that came up, since you were a toddler, and questioned her about both sides of each topic until she grew exhausted trying to keep up with your brilliant mind. You know in your heart that slavery must be done away with no matter what the cost."

"Even if it's war?"

"Even if it's war." It seemed Mullen has rested his case.

"I agree with the need to right wrongs. But I question the methods. You're a man of God. Don't you agree that war should be the last resort, not the first? This current conflict didn't initially have slavery as its primary motive. Still doesn't, if we're to believe the President. This war started because one part of the country wished to prosper at the expense of another, and because the less powerful worried that new states being carved out of the West would undo the balance of influence in Congress, which has been one of our nation's strengths. I'm not naive enough to believe the tariffs are solely responsible for what's happened. If we're to fight a war against slavery, if it's to be the only solution, then I'd support it. But let us not confuse principles with the methods of power-hungry rulers. They'll cousin any cause that contributes to their domination."

"I wish you'd come to Brooklyn with your mother, Chad, and listen to the discussions that go on there. I believe you've met one of our congregants. A fine black man named Holder Pratt."

"Did Mother tell you I knew Holder Pratt? And under what circumstances?"

"She merely said you were doing a good deed for some friends and that you met them at Mr. Pratt's workshop. But he's an eloquent spokesman for abolition, being black himself but also a freedman. He has among his cousins and his ancestors many who have worked secretly and tirelessly for liberation. We're engaged in a bitter struggle but we'll prevail. In the meantime, we should offer help to those who must wend their way northwards to escape the cruel vise of bondage. And we must act on a political level to coerce our elected representatives to rid us of this curse at once. Otherwise, it will destroy our democracy."

"The Republic has weathered other storms and I trust it will weather this one. I believe we might follow the example of the British in dealing with this problem without butchering an entire generation—for that's what I think we'll do. New Orleans fell to the Union last week, on the same day Lincoln signed the Homestead Act. They think the South will be split in half and will surrender. But my sources tell me they'll never surrender. Right or wrong, there'll be a long and bloody conflict and everybody, including the slaves, will suffer. Let's solve the tariff problem and the industrialization issue. Let's restore constitutional government, make overtures of peace to the South, and present it in a fashion that mandates a swift abolition, with financial recompense. It would be much cheaper that way, in dollars. It would be more compassionate that way, in human lives."

"We're both idealists. I'm older than you, and as a minister have witnessed both contrite and stubborn sinners, caught up in the throes of painful and anguished lives. You take the long, reasoned view, and I applaud it. I know from your mother's conversation that your heart is in the right place. I wish we could do it your way. But alas, I've lost my faith in human reason. Perhaps that's why I'm so successful as a preacher. Now let us compromise, along rational lines. Will you consent to a visit to Brooklyn? You and your mother may cross together. I'll make sure Holder Pratt is there to join in our discussions of this primal issue. He remembers you, Mr. Pratt does, and he says he was impressed even during such a brief encounter, with your demeanor and your attitude. If you really believe in reason as a path to progress, you could at least sit down with us and give us the benefit of your keen intellect. Perhaps we'll convert you or you'll convert us. It would be a small conversion, perhaps, since fundamentally we're in agreement. Slavery must go and go soon!"

Chad glanced at his mother who was in rapt attention to the Reverend Mullen's every word. She thought her son to be a man of words and not action, and didn't know his secrets any more than he knew hers. But he was not afraid, any longer, of entering the fray.

"Very well then," he said quietly, "I'll come to Brooklyn."

June 1862

Since he first occupied his office, Chad made several changes. First he found a small bookcase to hold a dozen of his favorite volumes, despite Randall Renfield's advice to keep the door shut when he read. Growing more assertive by the day, he'd stood his ground on the book issue. He also found a pillow for his wooden swivel chair, attractively embroidered, in an antique shop on upper Broadway. Then he was presented, one evening at a Phillipse Renfield dinner, with a Matthew Brady photograph of Clarissa, in an old silver frame. Clarissa boldly kissed him on the cheek in front of the entire family when she ceremoniously presented it to him, decrying his hours away from her in "the hub of American finance," as she termed it, and avowing that her portrait on his desk would keep his mind on more important things, namely their impending marriage.

He spent one or two days a week in the office, but as he explained to his mother, he had other important duties as well. Once he met with a group of newspaper reporters upon the initial offering of shares in the Eureka Mine Exploration Company, the latest product of the Randall Renfield-Grover Appleby collective mind. He was introduced as "our dynamic young President, educated at Princeton, and descended from a proud textile dynasty in Massachusetts and a noted agrarian family in Virginia," making him,

Appleby informed the group, "ideally suited to oversee our rapid expansion into markets north and south, and positioning us for growth with the western railroads when the war is over." In the ensuing discussion, all the questions were addressed to Grover Appleby.

Still he maintained a heightened sense of self-worth, since he viewed the new business endeavors as peripheral to his long-range plans. Doubtless, should one of the companies actually begin operations, he might be called upon to do something, or else resign so they could hire a professional manager. His self-esteem, in fact, was daily growing. He made money on each of the offerings and deposited it in different bank accounts, and invested, as well, in old time stocks with proven records and in what he felt were gilt-edged bonds. He kept up his courtship of his bride-to-be, and he expanded his reading.

Schuyler gave him a copy of poems by the new poet from Brooklyn who was gaining more and more attention, and who was reported to be leaving for the battlefield soon to comfort the soldiers. He read Walt Whitman's poems with hesitation, not so much for their "questionable content," as one reviewer called it, but because of his loquacious style, which seemed to Chad to be formless. He especially decried the lack of a rigid metrical structure, and found the versification to be, as he told Clarissa when she quizzed him about Schuyler's gift, chaotic at best. "What the man requires is a good editor," he told her. "One need merely to read Sextus Propertius, especially Book Two, to discover how a careless style, even in the classics, can undermine structural integrity. In short," he told his beloved, "poets went on and on even back then, and sometimes touch, as Whitman seems to do, on unsuitable erotic implications." But he was surprised to learn that his betrothed actually admired the poems, saying they contained a new vision of America that was freely expressive of a love for one's fellow man. He decided not to debate that issue with her, but quoted for her some verses from an ode by Horace and a few lines from Catullus, pointing out that the latter wrote about racy enough subject matter, but didn't find it necessary to spill over the edge of the page like a raging river capping its banks. Later on, he wondered if it might be a suitable task for himself, as a scholar with poetic aspirations, to render a tightly structured, perhaps even a rhyming, version of Ovid. But he discarded the idea, since he was very busy with the three main interests in his life, Clarissa, the Renfield enterprise, and the subject he couldn't discuss, his work with Bynum Bradley-West. Although he'd consented to visit Reverend Mullen in Brooklyn in late June or early July, he resisted a one-sided viewpoint that seemed to accept without reservation the wartime mentality as the best way to solve the nation's problems. So he gathered data, discussed shipping movements, and informed his collaborator about imminent financial deals involving the government or its many suppliers, termed by Bynum to be "as avaricious a band of cronies to be seen since Caesar's days."

And today, one of those splendid New York mornings in June, he was preparing for another three-way conference. But this one was different and in many ways more intimidating, for he'd agreed that today his mother could visit the office for a discussion with him and Randall about "a number of serious concerns."

He heard a bell ring down the hall but when he peeked out the door, saw only the sweep of his mother's skirts and the tip of her parasol disappear into the law offices. He told himself that either she couldn't find his suite, or else she wanted a word in advance with Randall Renfield. He couldn't convince himself that the former, rather than the latter, was true. So he sat in his swivel chair and fidgeted, then got up and raised one of the window sashes slightly to provide fresh air, or air as fresh as one could get downtown. In a while he heard her chirping away at Randall as they approached the offices of Financial and Industrial Enterprises, as it now said in gold letters on the door, and under it, in black script, Chadwick L. Wales, President.

Randall opened the door and with his hand on her back, ushered Harriet into the reception room. Chad brushed her cheek with a kiss, more to keep up appearances than to express any spontaneous warmth, and gestured to the conference table where he had, once again, carefully placed notepaper and pencils and a pitcher with water glasses for each.

"What is the source of that water, Chad?"

"Dear Harriet," Randall responded, "our law offices provided the water and it's as pure as anything you'd get in the Renfield Mansion."

"It's not from the Croton Reservoir?"

"No, my dear, it's not from the Croton Reservoir." Randall filled her glass, brushing his hand against his mother's arm as he did so.

Chad realized as he watched the improper familiarity between the two that the water interchange was a private jocular routine of some sort. His suspicions grew darker and more complicated as he watched Randall pull back a chair and hold it while his mother sat down, once again placing his hand on her back.

"You may remember that it was Randall here who was retained by my father to assist in drawing up the original trust instruments, some of which bear your name as well. I needn't go into the difficulties we experienced when you were about eight. The terms were modified when your Grandfather Bartleby came down from Boston and explained the revisions. I believe you still maintain some recollection of that event, although, as I recall, your interpretation of it was askew, to say the least." As she finished speaking, she glanced at Randall conspiratorially and they both attempted to hide what appeared to Chad to be smug smiles.

"I'm pleased to welcome you to my office, Mother. This is where I work, as you know. Uncle Randall and Uncle Caleb have said they value my efforts highly and I'm paid handsomely for my performance. I'm happy to aid you as much as you wish in the discussion of the financial and administrative elements of our trusts and to offer you any other assistance you feel desirable."

"This is a family matter, Chad, so we can all relax." Randall took off his dressy coat and loosened his collar, which seemed even more inappropriate for a serious business discussion with his mother. "It's a little hot in here, Harriet, so I hope you don't mind if I get comfortable."

"Not in the least. I've always wanted to see you comfortable," his mother said and they both laughed loudly at a joke Chad didn't fathom. Whatever was going on, Chad knew he understood his mother better than anybody else and kept himself on guard for the glacial ice that would form around her when her warmth had softened everybody up.

"You men of affairs are busy enough so I'll get to the point. Randall, you know as well as I do that my father reduced my dowry at the time of my marriage for wholly unjustified reasons. I accepted that, but when the trusts were later frozen and the income lessened, for reasons we needn't go into now, it was cruel and perhaps actionable. I shouldn't say 'actionable' since you're the lawyer here. But because of our long and respectful friendship, and because it was I who brought my father to you in the first place, I now call upon you to exert all your influence and legal know-how to restore these trusts—which have grown considerably—to a more traditional structure. This means, first, more income from them, and secondly, the ability to invade the corpus in times of special needs, with your personal oversight of course."

"You surely realize, Harriet, that I'm merely your father's legal representative in New York. The Boston lawyers would have to draft such amendments. Indeed, most of the trusts are in Boston banks."

"I'm quite aware where the trusts are and the exact amounts that are in them. I learned long ago I couldn't depend solely on you." With that she laughed forcibly again and Randall joined in, as if they were circus clowns unwinding an elaborate pantomime.

"Mother, I'm glad you've seen fit to make these consultations in my presence but I fail to see what authority or influence I'd have in any of this."

"Just learn to listen patiently and you may increase your influence, Chadwick."

"Yes, Mother."

"As you know, Randall, I've worked with you over the years for a dual purpose—first to provide an income appropriate for a family of our station so that my son could grow up to be the educated, able, handsome and loving son that he mostly is. The second of my goals, and this is the one Chad is ignorant of, was to exert all pressures possible that when he did grow up he would have the best of opportunities, a chance to make some money on his own and perhaps to test the waters of the financial sea around us, and also to marry well. I was delighted that he fell in love with Clarissa, he's known her since childhood and you and I have watched with keen interest and barely suppressed hope that they'd decide to marry, which they have. This cements the relationship of Renfield and Laymus and together will create, in a few years, one of the greatest fortunes on the Eastern Seaboard. There's been nothing clandestine about my motives, my methods or my goals."

"Yes, dear Harriet, we've planned this for such a long time."

"Well the time is approaching fast when we must make certain it's all irrevocably in place. Phillipse Renfield has been lagging a bit on the marriage date. He believes the war has made circumstances too uncertain. But my son and your niece are passionately in love—I can see it and so can you, since we're not unfamiliar with the syndrome. You must exert all your powers to see that the engagement proceeds steadily and that the marriage, which will be a major event for all New York, is on schedule."

Chad sensed that Randall now saw his mother's two layers and that their little private jokes did nothing to dispel the iron will that exuded from her very pores.

"As you know, I can only advise. Like many investment bankers, Phillipse thinks he's above influence. They've got such grandiose notions of themselves. And some of them have been openly involved with Drew and Gould and the Commodore. Look at this street railway thing. First the City Council is bamboozled into approving a rail line down Broadway to the Battery, and then Vanderbilt gets Drew involved and then Drew tries to pull a fast one, selling short on the rumor that the Council is planning to revoke the charter. But Vanderbilt kept the price up by purchasing the shares himself, got the charter reinstated and Drew and his cronies in the government now have to pay three times the amount they sold the shares for in order to honor their futures contracts or else go to jail!"

"Thank you, Randall, for explaining that to me. But it's beside the point."

Chad didn't think it was beside the point, but with all his experience as a financial executive he still couldn't understand what had gone on in the New York and Harlem Railway controversy. It had a certain comic drama about it, not unlike Aristophanes. Or better yet, if it could be laughed at, it would have been ideal for Juvenal.

"Chad, are you listening? Randall has just displayed his knowledge of the way these people operate, smugly sitting in their book-lined offices and buying art right and left and sailing their yachts and racing their trotting horses and starting more clubs. Pretending they're without blemish while people like you and me, Randall, see through it all. But we're maligned behind our backs and threatened with censure and deprivation for doing something of little concern to anybody."

"What are you talking about, Mother?"

"The point is Phillipse Renfield and his crew cannot tolerate even the whiff of personal scandal. It's all they can do to fend off lawsuits while parading around the ballroom and hobnobbing with princes. Randall, there's nothing I won't do to achieve these goals. That means, dear Sir, that there is, perforce, nothing that you won't do."

"I surrender, Harriet, as I've so often surrendered in the past. God, I admire you! Permit me to say that I've often wished I could have married a woman like you. What a team we would have made."

"Perhaps. And there's another thing. Chad already knows that these new corporations you're reaping a bundle on may or may not survive. You're making him party to rank speculation, perhaps even to criminal deceit. I'm sure you'll protect him, and yourself, from any scandal. Nevertheless, it's obvious that his compensation for taking such a risk must be significantly increased immediately. And there may be other ways of helping him."

"What do you mean?"

"Are you not counsel to several of the biggest insurance companies in town?"

"You already know that I am."

"And isn't it true that these insurance companies have enjoyed a phenomenal growth since the war started? Writing all those life insurance policies for hundreds of thousands marching off to do battle. Their dividends are higher than ever. I want you to make sure my portfolio includes some of that stock, but not at market price. They're floating new issues and I assume we could get in on the ground floor. See that it's done. By the way, do you think it would be appropriate to get Chad a seat on the Board of Directors of one of those companies? Insurance always seems to be so respectable. At least until you file a claim."

"Well, I don't know, Harriet. This is surprising. It's ambitious. As far as the insurance profits go, it's true they're making money now. But what happens if the war goes on for a few years and a lot of those boys are killed? Look at Shiloh, 24,000 in a single day. If we have to pay out death benefits like that over five years or so—should the war last that long—these companies may have to endure a period of austerity."

"You know as well as I that their premiums are already invested and by the time the soldiers get shot the principal will have doubled or tripled."

"That's more or less true. But the casualties are mounting exponentially. The problem is, I think, in the way they wage this war. Chad, did you not tell me your Southern family was related to Francis Marion, the Swamp Fox, during the War of Independence?"

"Yes, I did." Chad, totally lost now, couldn't even recall a line of Latin or Greek, which was full of warlike references, to apply to what he believed he was hearing.

"This Francis Marion, he'd hide in a swamp, sneak out and shoot some British, and then disappear into the swamp again. These soldiers today, they line up on either side of a field and march forward shooting at each other. They're such a mass you don't even have to be a marksman to get your man. There's got to be a better way of killing people than that!" As was his habit when overexcited, Randall poured himself glass of water and drank swiftly.

"I'll leave the art of war to you, Randall. In the meantime, take care of Chad. Get those trusts freed up and reinvested. And see what you can do with the insurance idea. It's a thoughtful business, in a way, people sitting in their little offices trying to figure out the odds of somebody dying. It's more or less a mathematical issue, I suppose. Chad was tops in mathematics at Princeton."

Harriet's face beamed, like a Renaissance painting of some Greek goddess. Chad couldn't help but admire her—or fear her. She smiled at him and went on.

"There's one more thing. As you know I'm involved, deeply involved, in the abolitionist cause. It's a generous gesture on my part that more than makes up for my severity in other matters. I work with a parson in Brooklyn who helps slaves, and promulgates a number of initiatives relating to emancipation. He works hard at it and together we've managed to ship over two hundred of these poor tormented people to Halifax and St. John. But he needs money. You administer trusts for the deceased, do you not? I mean when somebody dies and leaves a lot of money with no relatives to speak of you set up a fund and donate the income to worthy causes. Isn't that how it works?"

"More or less, I suppose."

"I thought so. I'd like you to funnel some funds to that church. The Reverend Thaddeus Mullen. Here's a card with his address. Randall, I'll be so much in your debt if you could see to it that grants are made to them on a regular basis from the trusts for which you have discretionary powers. I'm sure that's not too much to ask, as a gesture of friendship and gratitude for the years we've known each other."

Harriet got up, straightened her hat, and put her gloves back on "Now I must leave you two gentlemen to your chores. I'm so grateful you've found time for a poor defenseless woman like myself, inexperienced in the ways of high finance and the manly challenges of Wall Street. But I hope, in my clumsy way, I've made myself clear."

"You were clearer than ever, Harriet. I'll do what I can." Randall looked like a defeated candidate for a men's club office that, while prestigious, would be known only to the members. "Let me walk out with you."

"Don't get up, Son," Harriet said, and bent over and kissed him on his ear.

* * *

A brief note from Bynum arrived at Chad's East 10th Street door early in the day. His mother, talking in the front hall with the housekeeper, stood back from the door when the messenger rang, and allowed her chief assistant to collect the envelope, which she promptly handed over to Harriet, after thanking the courier and closing and bolting the door.

All entries were kept locked now, and several families on the block had pooled their resources to engage a Pinkerton man to patrol the neighborhood at night. There'd been no incidents, but there were reports of increasing disorder and fears that the South, having lost two of its key ports already, might make a desperate stab at the North's citadel of commerce, with its great harbor and its swift rivers offering a highway into the heart of the Northeast, and via the canal to Ohio. But Bynum had privately informed Chad that such an action was highly unlikely, since many New Yorkers continued to do business with the rebel states, and since the financial institutions, in particular, were trying to effect some sort of truce, even if it was simply a monetary one, to allow them to continue their trade as before, lest the banks, the Exchange, and perhaps the currency itself should suffer crippling losses.

Harriet stood by the front door and scrutinized the envelope as Chad descended from his bedroom in search of breakfast. He surmised immediately, noting his mother's expression, that the message was for him, and that it was probably from Bynum Bradley-West. Having witnessed his formidable mother in action at the conference with Randall Renfield, he knew she would stoop to any device, including opening his mail, in order to increase her knowledge, and hence her power, concerning the current state of affairs with her son. She heard him on the stairs and looked up guiltily.

"Would that be for me, Mother?"

"It seems to be addressed to you."

"Well, then, I think we can assume that the letter is in fact intended for me." He walked quickly towards her and snatched the envelope from her hand.

"You really have grown quite rude, Chad. I'd think after our meeting with

Randall you'd have at least some inkling of how far I've gone—and will go—to protect your interests." She turned her back to him and stalked through the hall towards the rear of their home, her housekeeper behind her.

The note was short and confusing, and was signed only "*B*". There was no letterhead and no return address on the outside. It was a simple command. *"Meet me around noon at 235 Prince Street. Just ring the bell. Take the omnibus or a cab and watch yourself."*

The breakfast buffet was still warm, so he downed fruit juice and smeared a large biscuit with fresh butter and jam, and drank his steaming coffee so quickly he feared he'd burned his tongue and throat. Harriet came back into the front of the house and eyed him inquisitively.

"Well, dear mother, I must be quickly off. Pressing affairs await me downtown. I'm not at all sure if I shall be able to make it back for dinner. But I hope you have a pleasant and productive day. If you make any significant changes in my life while I'm out, perhaps you could leave instructions for me prior to my return. Just slide them under my door. I keep the room locked now, to protect me from perils both without and within." He took his summer hat from the rack by the door and extracted from a large porcelain barrel his sturdiest walking stick, which he felt could be used in defense against the dangers of the outside world, and perhaps, if worse came to worst, fend off his mother if she became crazed and turned her wrath on him, like one of those female Greek demigods he read about with an increasingly apprehensive sense of recognition.

It was still early in the day, so he decided to walk down Fifth Avenue to Washington Square and then proceed East to Broadway, where he would feel safer as he continued on to Prince Street. There would be time, he realized as he ambled off at a leisurely pace, to stop in a bookstore for a while before keeping his mysterious appointment.

Late June sunlight warmed his face, but there was little humidity and a light, gentle breeze. He could remember playing in the grassy areas surrounding the Square, a treed rectangle rimmed with town houses grander than his own. It had seemed so safe back then. Until he was in his teens, a servant would always accompany him on these outings, usually a maid or even the housekeeper, who'd sit with a knitting box on a bench while he rolled his hoop or mounted the swings. Dogs were allowed, and he'd sometimes toss balls to them, delighted by their spontaneous joy, tails wagging, and heart and soul immersed in the moment, without thought of danger or competition or rewards other than a pat on the head and maybe a piece of bread or cheese or a bone. It had been such an orderly world, with broad stoops flanked by carved wooden doorways painted white, the tall windows reflecting the sun, the women in hoop skirts and big bonnets and parasols, baby carriages, an occasional peddler hawking his wares, the Italian man who had a cart filled with ices, and the portly policeman with his pointed cap and copper badge, swinging a nightstick, rarely needed on a bright summer day in this idyllic haven.

But he no longer felt safe, and the facades of the great houses ringing the Square didn't comfort him. He knew from first hand experience now that within each of them, intrigues, separations, even death, awaited. And with a pang he realized that it would always be like that. If they built their love nest at Yellowfields, they'd sleep during the night with knowledge that even that well-guarded fortress could be breached. And what of those people of the South, his kinsmen whom he hardly knew? Was Cedar Crest Hall shelled? Was New Orleans turned into a police state by Federal troops? Would they bombard Norfolk again? Would his father be there when they did? He walked faster as his anxiety swelled, relieved to spot a colorfully incised bookstore sign, luring him through a portal to a cool musty sanctuary. He leafed through several new collections of essays and poems, ran his hands lovingly over leather-bound copies of French and German philosophers, and flipped through a few volumes of engravings and woodblock prints. But a glance at his pocket watch reminded him that he could no longer hide out among these reassuring volumes with names long familiar to him. He considered himself a man of the world now, engaged in bitter controversies and plotting actions of historic proportions.

He'd written down the address because the neighborhood, though actually close, was yet unknown to him. His mother had awkwardly warned him about "those destinations above Canal Street." He'd often walked or rode down Broadway to the financial district or to City Hall and sometimes to Trinity Church, where he was probably to be married. But these side streets with their panoply of inhabitants hadn't beckoned to him before. There were boarding houses and shops and a few offices, some buildings given over to quieter modes of manufacture. There were plentiful street lamps whose gassy flame would provide little security during dark nights, and it filled him with unease mixed with a tempting sense of adventure. He was changing, that was for sure.

When he found the house he was unimpressed. It was an old three-story dwelling with dormers on the top floor, not as wide as the mansions of Washington Square or his own previously cozy home on East 10th Street. The door was painted red, and there was a large brass knocker, which he struck heavily while waiting in expectation.

The door was opened by a crisply attired and very young Negro woman with a scarf tied around her profuse black hair. Her face, though, revealed nothing. She simply stared at him as they stood facing each other.

"I was told I might find Mr. Bradley-West here."

"Please wait, Sir." She gave a slight curtsy and closed the door in his face.

He looked at the paper on which he'd scrawled the address and checked it against the numbers above the door. It was the right place. Finally the door opened again and another woman stood solidly in front of the bright red door. She was bright red herself, with burgundy hair, scarlet lips, and clothed in rich taffeta of pink and crimson. She'd choked herself with pearls, stuck a jeweled barrette in her hair, and forced a goodly supply of rings onto her plump fingers.

"What are you looking for here, young man?" Her words and her pose suggested to him that she might be a character from one of the early English novels. Fielding, he thought, or better yet, Richardson. He remembered the first time he'd read *Clarissa* with his young girlfriend with the same name. The lady in red continued to stare at him with curiosity as he kept her waiting while his mind wandered.

"I'm sorry, Madam. I was told I might find a friend here."

"There's no doubt you might find several friends here, Sir. But what is your purpose?"

"I'm seeking a Mr. Bynum Bradley-West."

"Surely you've found him, then," she said, her voice revealing for the first time an Irish lilt. She motioned for him to enter, then stuck her head out again and looked up and down the street before closing and bolting the door. "Just follow me, Sir. You must be Mr. Wales."

"How'd you know that, Madam?"

"Surely, lad, it's not that big a house. And we've only got one gentleman waiting in our parlor. All our other guests are upstairs in rosier pursuits." She beckoned to him and opened a double door to what seemed to be a sitting room. There were armchairs and love seats, and sofas, heavy drapes, shutters tightly closed but still ringed with narrow bands of noon sunshine, and a few lamps providing additional light. When his eyes adjusted he spied Bynum, sitting nonchalantly on the centerpiece of the room, a circular sofa under a sparkling chandelier.

"Come on in here, Chad. Say hello to Madam Maureen. She's the owner and the manager of this excellent establishment."

Chad nodded at Maureen, who gave him a lascivious smile and then left the room. Bynum looked amused as it dawned on his young accomplice that he was in one of those "destinations" his mother so feared he would find.

"Let's go into the library," Bynum said. "We can talk there." He led him into an adjacent room with leather chairs and a desk, but nothing to read other than copies of magazines on the desk and tables. It resembled a waiting room at the station or a doctor's office.

"Bynum, why are we here? Is this house what I think it is?"

"It's high time you saw the inside of a whore house. Don't blanch. Some of the most prominent men in New York come here. The girls are clean and healthy, quite fetching, and Madam Maureen is the soul of discretion. But the reason I wanted to meet you here is perhaps grave. As I had expected they're watching my rooms. If we met there their eyes would be turned on you immediately. You'd be followed. I wouldn't be surprised if they watched me visit Marilyn Blaine's, but at least you have legitimate reasons to be there since she's a relative. But for you and me to be seen together at my lodgings, or even in a public restaurant, is far too dangerous now. And I've much to tell you."

"Ever since Norfolk fell last month I've been worried about my father. He sent his latest letters from there but I've had no word for such a long time."

"Be assured your father is safe in London, at least for now. My correspondents there forwarded letters to me. They're again in code when they refer to you, as your father doesn't want to endanger you. Lee took command of the Army of Northern Virginia on the first of this month. I've just had a dispatch telling me your father has decided to make one more run, from Bristol to Brunswick, Georgia. He thinks he can more easily infiltrate the blockade there. But when that's over he intends to make his way north and join up with Lee. He already holds the rank of Colonel as a result of his bravado in penetrating the blockade. Doubtless he'll become a major adjutant to General Lee."

Chad's heart sank. "So he's going into battle. He orders me not to fight and then he gives up an important and probably somewhat safer role as blockade-runner to join the army. There are such high casualties. The way the battles are fought, it's nothing but a blood bath."

"What would any man do if his homeland is invaded, if his loved ones are threatened and his property attacked? He'll join with other insurgents and fight to the death, if necessary. At that point it no longer makes any difference who's right, or what the reason is, or who's principled and who isn't. The people who run things want more power. Even if a cause is just, they'll use it for unjust purposes. Waving flags and chanting slogans and beating drums, they'll cross a border with hostile goals. Once the border is crossed, the people will rise up. Even the pacifists. Your father cannot fulfill his role as a patriot at a distance. Now he sees the soil of Virginia as his home, and they've invaded it. He'll fight. I'm sorry to say that, yes, as you fear, he may die. Hundreds of thousands may die. That's the woeful tragedy of this war. There'll be no end until one side has destroyed the other. But the victor won't long enjoy his spoils. Of course, the people at the top, like Phillipse Renfield and Bartleby Laymus, will prosper. They've been playing both sides all along. And some of the other war profiteers will become rich over night. But for the common man, even the victorious one, war brings death and destruction and disease and poverty. It also brings poverty of the spirit, because many people will eventually decide it wasn't really worth it. They'll make speeches and build monuments and have parades to celebrate this or that landmark day. But their hearts will be desperate and their minds in conflict. And of course, the unprincipled will always triumph over the principled."

"You make me feel hopeless when you talk like that. How can you say such cynical things?"

"It's not cynicism, it's logic. The unprincipled will always win because the principled cannot even imagine what depths the unprincipled will sink to. They don't possess the depraved imagination and hunger for power that allow tyrants and despots to win the day. So don't disparage your father and his choice. His heart now rules his head. Maybe he'll survive and maybe, just maybe, so will I. And of course you must proceed carefully now. There's talk of a draft but there are usually ways for men of your social class to escape it. But you're in more danger right here at home. You're putting your life on the line by your decision to help me in my subversion. Are you sure you want to go on?"

"If my father is willing to sacrifice his life on the battlefield, I'm willing to do my part working with you. I'll obey his request not to fight either for or against Virginia. But I'll continue to aid anyone who wants to bring this monstrous war to an end, no matter what their politics."

"You'll soon have even more reason to work for an early peace. The costs of this war are unsustainable under current policies. There's talk of an income tax, which will inflame the conservatives. They want tax cuts, not tax increases, even in wartime. But the tariffs will soon be mostly lost at our Southern ports, even the ones under Union domination. What foreign supplier wants to sail into an occupied city with goods that will simply be subjected to higher and higher import fees? The stock market is rising and falling like the tide. Unemployment is up, wages down. All this while the arms factories and the suppliers of clothing and food and transportation are working around the clock."

"People scoff at me for my bookworm 'fixation', as they call it. Somehow it all seems less threatening in Greek." Chad's voice faded out and the room seemed to darken.

Bynum's voice sounded eager, as if he'd been searching for an opening in his young colleague's mind, to deliver another blow. "Have you heard about this German fellow living in England? I think he's a disciple of your Hegel.

He's published articles and is writing a big book. He's foretelling the death of capitalism. A man named Marx, I believe. You're influenced, I think, by the romantic aura of Hegel's statism. You think he offers a haven for your ideals, held together in a stable though changing society. But many people dwell only on Hegel's obsession with a centralized political power. When I was in Germany I went to a beer hall one evening with a group of young men from Heidelberg. They all had dueling scars. They boasted about the growing German coalition. In between their drinking songs they prattled on and on about Hegel. They've been indoctrinated, at Heidelberg, Leipzig and everywhere else. But in the future I believe people like this Marx and others like my beer-drinking companions will concentrate on the power aspect. People respond to power. Many people, I fear, prefer to be told what is right and what they should do."

"You paint so bleak a picture."

"I regret the necessity to do so. But the bleakest is yet to come. Both sides continue to add to their armies. The butchery at Shiloh is just the beginning. Look at the war like a flood. It's fed by rising waters, and by more and more tributaries flowing into the swell. And when it gains a momentum of its own, it's impossible to control. These mighty tides will swamp our land with unprecedented destruction. There were 24,000 casualties in three days at Shiloh. I predict we'll soon see that many losses in a single day. An entire generation will be wiped out and the land and villages and farms will be burned to a crisp. Attilla and Hannibal couldn't accomplish devastation on the scale we'll see here in America."

"Nothing but bad news."

"On the contrary, my agents in Washington tell me that there's talk of some kind of emancipation about to be declared. A Presidential executive order. Word is it will guarantee freedom to all the slaves in rebellious states. It will encourage them to desert the plantations and the army camps where they labor, and head north. But the North, you see, is hypocritical. They'd like to free the slaves in somebody else's hometown but they don't welcome them here. There's already a network of armed resisters who vow that they'll protect their homes and their jobs from the inflow of blacks, if it comes. That's likely to reduce the will of the Federal troops, or at least of the merchants and brokers who supply goods and funds for the effort."

"So it might help end the war?"

"Perhaps. The problem is the meeting of two irreconcilable forces. The lust for power on one hand, and the irresistible urge to defend one's home and family on the other."

"I'll see what I can find out from Randall and Appleby about the financial movements. I can easily discover shipping news from my familial contacts. But I want to do more, Bynum, really I do."

"There's more to be done and when the time comes I'll ask you to do it. But it will involve direct action. We'll more than likely have to wreak violence within in order to end violence without. A band of sympathizers plans to attack the Northern cities surreptitiously. You'll be needed and you'll have to make a hard decision when that time comes."

"I can see why you wanted to meet me in a place like this."

"Frankly, Chad, I think it's time you got used to places like this. Didn't you boys at Princeton have recourse to certain satisfactions? In the South, fathers consider it to be part of their son's education."

"It's difficult to speak of these things. You see, I'm betrothed and I very much love Clarissa. I desire her strongly but respect her as well."

"All the more reason to seek an alternative. Men have needs. Nature set it up that way. The girls here are clean and attractive and pleasurable. They know how to satisfy their clients. And as I said, the cream of New York society comes here, some of them on a daily basis. I don't wish to corrupt you, but it's time you took your mind off all this death and destruction. It will perhaps strengthen you for what lies ahead. Let me show you the way, Chad. I've arranged for you to meet a very special girl, well known to me. Her name is Rosie. She's waiting for you upstairs right now. All you need to do is go up there and indulge yourself. After all, neither of us knows what tomorrow may bring."

FIVE

July 1862

"Higgens, go down the Second Avenue. Leave the top up so we can keep the sun out of our eyes." Harriet fanned herself energetically, facing away from Chad, who removed his jacket and hat and sprawled against the corner of the carriage, his legs stretched out in front of him, resting his feet against the side of the coach as it lurched across 10th Street. "And Higgens," his mother went on, "you must be certain to meet us when we return. We'll have lunch in Brooklyn and should be back in time for tea. Plan to meet us by 3:30."

Higgens tipped his hat but kept his eyes on the street. After they crossed Broadway, he slowed the horses and turned into Second Avenue, heading south.

"It's so hot," Harriet continued. "But Reverend Mullen's parlor will be pleasant. He's got an old house near his church, and the street's well shaded. Brooklyn's growing fast but I think it still has a country feel to it. You should come with me more often, Chad, especially if you decide not to spend the hot months upriver. Clarissa was adamant, when we last talked, about your promise to join her at Yellowfields."

"How long is all this going to take, Mother?" Chad tried to keep his voice well modulated. When he brushed his thick dark hair in front of the mirror in his room that morning, he promised himself that he'd be neither sullen nor truculent.

"I certainly hope you'll hold your tongue. I think it's your schooling, that's what it is. We sacrifice to send you to a prestigious college and you become more and more isolated. The world's large and you have much to learn about it. Including Brooklyn."

"Father took me to Brooklyn when I was eight or so. Right after ..." Chad

128

saw his mother stiffen and spread her ebony fan across her face. "He hired a special boat. We coasted down the East River first and then back up to the dock. We walked along the streets near the water. It's not all that different from 10th Street. Some of the houses are even bigger than ours. There's a great view from that hill." Chad's voice wound down, but he couldn't resist one final sally. "It doesn't take all that long to learn about Brooklyn."

"In the meantime, we've got an agreement. You'll reserve your sarcasm until you meet with my friends and learn more about our work. In spite of your attitude and your acid tongue, you've got a big heart. When you witness first hand what we're doing, you'll change your mind about it all. And about me. That's all I'll say now, but you must honor your promise."

"Are we going to talk about the war?"

"We shall see."

Chad glanced towards the stream of pedestrians along the street, shading his eyes from the reflected glare of mid-morning sun against the windows of office buildings and stores, more numerous as they headed towards the South Street Ferry. He rubbed his fingers inside his collar, and smoothed his moist black hair back from his forehead. He'd dressed in his lightest clothes, but he'd been careful to be as formal as possible, without drawing undue attention, for his lunch with his mother's "friend."

"If we're going to discuss the war, don't expect me to keep my viewpoints to myself. Did you see *Harper's* this week? They've sent that artist, Winslow Homer, to draw scenes from the front. Some of them are very disturbing."

"Not so disturbing, dear, as Mr. Brady's photographs. Of course, you'd prefer scenes pictured by an artist rather than the stark reality of the camera."

"What's that supposed to mean?"

"Do you still try to write verse?"

"Try? I was awarded first prize in Latin composition. When my Greek ode was read in our upper division language classes I wrote you about it and you've never even mentioned it. The literary magazine published my essay on Catullus, and one of my professors urged me to devote all my time to writing poetry. In English."

"In anguish, is more like it. Perhaps you'll meet this Whitman. He's from Brooklyn. Some people say he's a champion of our values. The New World. The American Spirit. Love and Fellowship."

"What Whitman needs is a good editor," Chad mumbled.as their carriage approached the ferry.

"Three-thirty, Higgens, don't forget," Harriet said.

On board the ferry, she sat primly, keeping her fan in motion. She glanced around at the other passengers. "You see, my dear, these people are perfectly respectable and you needn't insinuate anymore about my solitary journeys."

Once out on the river the breeze freshened them. There were swells in the swift current and in the distance, as the water widened into New York Harbor, he could see an occasional white cap, most likely the result of a passing ship. The wind was light, the heat rising by the minute.

"There's Tad's carriage," Harriet said, not even trying to hide the excitement in her voice as they floated alongside the Brooklyn dock. "Here we are," she shouted, waving her fan at the driver. "Over here, Jeremy."

"Jeremy? Are you on first name basis with his servants, too?"

"Reverend Mullen discourages condescension to those whose lot it is to serve us. You might want to review your own position, in light of your apparent refusal to acknowledge how much I and others have helped you solidify your rank in this world."

"Very well, then." A malicious mood was overtaking him fast and he felt it best to indulge himself now rather than later, in the presence of the almighty Mullen. "What's Higgens' first name, Mother?"

"Why it's, you know as well as I do. It's …"

"You see. It will take more than a ferry ride to Brooklyn to make a democrat out of you."

Jeremy clucked at his horse and brought them quickly to a brownstone townhouse, four stories high. They paused in the shade before mounting the front stairs. A black woman in a plain gray dress opened the door. She wore neither apron nor cap but was, he surmised from his mother's demeanor, one of the servants.

"Good morning Melanie, how's your sister?"

"Thank you ma'am, she's feeling better. Reverend Mullen said she should stay inside and rest until we're ready for the next stage."

"It's okay to speak about it, Melanie. This is my son Chad. He's here to join us. Chad, this is Melanie, who works for Reverend Mullen. Her sister's staying here temporarily on her way north."

Chad realized his mother was willing to risk discovery in order to impress him, for it was obvious that the sister, hidden from view, wasn't free to move about openly. A simple discovery, but it made him uneasy. He'd agreed to aid the South in order to end the war. He didn't want to confront the slavery issue, since it pained him, and was a dark blight on his dreams of an idyllic life in the Shenandoah, after the war, like one of those English scholars spending languid days in literary endeavors in Surrey, or a Roman poet, periodically expelled from Rome to a villa on an Italian lake. All he could do now, as he faced the ugly plight of these desperate fugitives, was to be kind to this young black woman who seemed energetic, capable, and friendly. "I hope your sister has a safe and successful journey," he said, with obvious enthusiasm.

Chad placed his hat on the rack in the front hall as they were led into the parlor, where Reverend Mullen stood, a cup in his hand, talking intently with a trio of his guests. Chad recognized Holder Pratt, who nodded at him, and beside him, the woman he'd first seen in Pratt's carpentry shop. Mullen made the introductions.

"Welcome, Chad. I believe you know Holder Pratt. This is his bride-to-be Mary Malloy."

Chad shook Holder's hand and nodded at Mary Malloy. But his eyes were fixed on the third guest, a man in his early forties, he presumed, with a flushed complexion and wavy red hair. There was something familiar about his face but he couldn't place it.

Harriet intervened. "Chad, you've never met your cousin from Maine. This is Corbin Chadwick. I should say Corbin Chadwick the Third. He's the grandson of the man we named you for."

Chad resented the surprise. He'd steeled himself for this visit, which he considered to be an ordeal undertaken only to soothe his frenzied mother and perhaps to gather more information he could pass on to Bynum "Am I to call you Cousin Corbin, then? Mother has never spoken of you."

"I wouldn't expect her to," Corbin replied. "I've lived quietly in Searsport for the last few years, having earned an independent life long ago by my work in the China Trade."

"You see, Chad, Corbin refused to come down from Maine for Harvard, and went to sea instead. He sailed from the Penobscot Bay on a clipper ship bound for China, and in a few years he was made captain, and then he bought the ship. Corbin, you remember my letters about Chad. He's distinguished himself at Princeton, but he's also getting his feet wet in the financial world. And he's to marry Clarissa Renfield."

"Ah yes, Renfield," Corbin said, a twinkle in his eye. "I've heard so much about that family." He looked at Harriet as he spoke.

"Did you run away to sea just to escape Harvard? You could have come down to Princeton instead."

"No, my boy, that's not the life for me. Our clipper ships were once the fastest afloat, and were to be found in every corner of the world. Ten percent of clipper ship captains came from Searsport, Maine! The China Trade made many of us rich, and I managed to get into it just before it all changed. And now I'm free to pursue activities that may bring meaning to my life."

"Are you going to write about your life at sea, like Melville?"

"I found whaling to be messy and besides, it won't be long before it's no longer profitable. Out in Cleveland, they've built refineries using lard to render oil. A man named Rockefeller, I believe. But that won't last long, either, since there's talk now about the possibility of using petroleum. Besides, I wanted to make fast journeys to China and bring back goods to sell in Boston and New York. The Chinese are very industrious. Pity their country is so divided with all those potentates and dozens of dialects. But they turn out the best dinnerware, and they can copy an oil painting of a ship in less than an hour. We bring all these things back here and sell them to eager customers who couldn't otherwise afford to have nice teacups and tureens and paintings on the wall. It won't last forever, this China Trade, but for now, I'm retired as a result of it, and can engage in other pursuits."

"Do you intend to be an artist, then?" Chad was growing impatient with his cousin's boasting and air of superiority.

"The life of the artist is not for me. In China, they were lined up in sheds like factory workers, turning out the stuff."

"Politics, then?"

"In a sense it's politics." Corbin put his cup down and turned to his host. "Might we get on with our meeting?"

"By all means," the Reverend said. The group shuffled around to form a circle, with Chad between his mother and Mullen. Then, to his consternation, they all held hands. Reverend Mullen bowed his head, and after a moment of silence, began to pray.

"Heavenly Father, bless us as we meet here today to discuss our obligations as your servants, to combat evil and sin in the world and to be fearless and decisive in our actions. Our brothers and sisters are in chains in this land and we're Thy servants who'll work tirelessly to carry out Thy will."

Everybody but Chad said "Amen."

Then, to Chad's discomfort, they all began to sing. "John Brown's body lies a moldering in his grave but his truth is marching on," they chanted.

"Hallelujah!" Mullen exclaimed. Corbin's face glowed red, Mullen's eyes flamed, Harriet smugly compressed her lips, and Mary Malloy's eyes turned modestly towards the floor. Holder looked inquisitively at Chad.

"Let's be seated," Mullen said. Harriet quickly took the chair next to the Reverend, and Holder and Mary sat on the sofa. Corbin seated himself on an ottoman, and Chad took the only remaining upholstered chair.

"Melanie, please sit with us," Mullen said, gesturing to a small slipper chair near the window. "You should hear what we have to say. Brothers and sisters in Christ, I'm pleased that Corbin Chadwick is here today, for it's he who has done the most for some of our enslaved brethren who courageously endanger their lives in their furtive journey to safety and human dignity. His ships have helped dozens of fugitives whose only crime was to have been born black, for it's viewed as a crime, in attitude if not in fact, by those who would install chains about human ankles and wrists. The Good Book says a rich man may not pass easily into heaven, but Corbin Chadwick, already wealthy before he was twenty-five, has chosen to use his money and his skill in the service of faith, and is personally responsible for the delivery of copious human cargo to the safety of Halifax and St. John. God bless you, Corbin."

Everybody applauded so Chad joined in.

"Chad, we wanted you to be here today because your mother has spoken often of your keen intelligence and your deeply held principles. We know that you, like all of us here, are sickened by slavery. But Harriet also fears you're unwilling to commit yourself to action. Lately, she tells us, you've been successful in business enterprises involving her family and the family of your intended. Now we beseech you to take another step out into the world and to open your eyes to this outrage and to join us in our battle to remove the fetters and to strike a blow for God!"

All eyes were upon him and no one spoke. Chad fidgeted in his chair. "I'm of course vehemently opposed to slavery and have repeatedly made it clear to everybody. Even my Southern forebears freed their slaves generations ago. I'd rejoice to see this curse lifted from us. Right now, I'm focusing my energies on establishing my own independence, much as my cousin from Maine did before taking up his cause. And I feel a similar motivation. This war is killing and maiming thousands every day and can have no outcome but devastation. Material devastation on the losing side and moral devastation for the victor."

"You see, my son's confused. He thinks war is immoral. But we know that we're soldiers of God and will fight until death to eradicate the enslavement of human beings for profit. And the dozens of evils that come with it—broken families, for example. Young women made to perform the vilest of services to the lust of their owners. And torture. It cannot be permitted." Harriet looked towards Reverend Mullen as she finished her speech and then lowered her eyes coquettishly.

"No, no, Mother. You mustn't choose to speak for me all the time. I'm weighing one evil against another, and as bad as slavery is, we must stop the killing first and then turn our eyes to abolition. There's a peaceful way and we must pursue it. The British did, why can't we?"

"Is it not said somewhere that to delay justice is to deny it?" Mullen looked smugly at Harriet.

"If you wish, Chad, you could serve your desires to end this war by joining up with me. After I've deposited my human cargo in a free land, I work with my colleagues in New England ports to combat the Northern traitors who plead the cause of the South, which actually makes the Confederacy better able to withstand our blockades and our revenue cutters, not to mention our ironclads. I understand the iron ships are built right here in Brooklyn." Corbin stood up as he finished speaking, looking as if he expected more applause.

"Chad, you're wise," Mullen said. "You don't welcome injustice. Help us wipe out these sympathizers who would replace the moral issue here, namely that of enslavement, with a political disagreement that's hardly significant in the long term. Let's rid ourselves of those who utilize treason in the guise of right, and who would rather flee righteous combat than to march forward to liberate slaves. Indeed, the rumor is that our President is now drafting a proclamation that will emancipate them by executive order."

"I've heard," Chad said, "that it frees them only in the rebel states, not in those border states where slavery is still legal."

"A trivial matter overall. In time slavery will be abolished in those states too," Mullen said.

"In time it will be abolished in the South, whether or not it wins the war." Chad was uneasy with this statement, since it made him seem to be an apologist for servitude, rather than a zealot for peace, which he considered himself to be.

Holder Pratt had been silent, gazing out the window at the thick green leaves against the sparkling panes, and the occasional flicker of a redbird on the sill. He looked around the room, cleared his throat, and spoke for the first time. "My ancestors back in Newport were free even before the Revolution. There were slaves in New England then but we didn't mingle with them. We thought our freedom conferred upon us a special status. So we weren't likely to join in any causes. We were artisans, and some of us were educated. I came to New York City because I thought I could make more money here, and lead a free life, raise a family. But there's discrimination here and all over the North. Speaking as a black man I say any war is preferable to the hell of slavery. But now this President wants to free slaves in the Southern states only. He has no effective rights there now. Nevertheless, there may be a mass movement of my colored brethren northwards. But they, and by inference, me, won't be welcome. The European immigrants are especially vehement on this issue. And some states, Illinois among them, are considering laws—specific laws—to prohibit the migration of black people to Northern cities. I see Chad's point. The war must end, too, along with servitude. The longer it goes on, the worse will be the attitude of the South when it's conquered, as it will surely be. And when the North is faced with the other side of its moral dilemma, to welcome these fellow human beings into their cities and villages, what then? Will this president decree that we'll all love each other as ourselves?"

Chad was cheered by Holder's declaration. "I repeatedly proclaim my opposition to slavery. But first I'm opposed to a war that's suicidal for both parties. It started primarily over economic and political concerns, not moral ones. If all of us stood together, like Mr. Pratt and me, for example, we could force the powers that be to reach equitable decisions about tariffs, industrialization, and abolition. That's what I've been trying to say. The politicians are supposed to answer to us, not vice versa."

"But, my boy, you can help us in this. To bring the war to an end is your avowed desire. Mine too. I need more information, and I need a trusted conduit, if I'm to do more than ferry human beings to safe haven." Corbin was still standing. "You, Chad, bear a name well known in the South. I understand you're on friendly terms with people here in New York who are suspected of being enemy agents. You can keep up your work with the Renfield-Laymus schemes, you can continue to socialize with all kinds of people at your Aunt Marilyn's house, you could even play cards with that man, Bradley-West, I think he's called. You could do all this and still serve the cause of freedom. You could help us hunt down and eradicate these turncoats, spies, and conspirators. When the war is finished, and the North has won, which it surely will, you'll be regarded as a hero."

"Since you know whom I play cards with, perhaps you could tell me what specifically I could do for you, Cousin," Chad said.

"Tell us who's plotting against the Union. Tell us what they're going to do next. There are pockets of them, all over the Northeast, and in Washington and Baltimore and Philadelphia as well. You're free to move in circles we can't breech. You could continue to play the innocent intellectual with your abstract principles and your literary fixation. But in the end, you can aid our cause."

Harriet spoke in support of her cousin's invective. "That's why I wanted to bring you here. Never forget that I'm your mother and I have your best interests in mind. I want you to be highly regarded when the war is over and you and Clarissa are the foremost young couple in New York."

"So that's it, then! You want me to spy for you and perhaps reveal information I've received from my father. You want me to put his cause and his life in danger. You want me to declare war on Virginia in the name of your abolitionist goals. I've told you over and over again, Mother, I'll not support this war, because two wrongs don't make a right. Is that plain enough for you?"

August 1862

"She came right out and asked me to be a spy," Chad said. He eyed Bynum with a distraught look but Bynum only laughed.

"You're already a spy!" Bynum's shoulders shook as he chuckled. He leaned forward and poured more wine into his glass. "Would you like another?"

They were seated on facing chairs in the house on Prince Street. Madam Maureen had closed the library doors so they could have privacy, though the house was nearly empty. They'd already lunched, separately, and the house, Bynum assured him, was a safe place to talk. There was a bottle of port and some fruit and cheese on the table between them. It was late August and many of the more affluent regulars had gone upriver or off to Maine or Newport to escape the simmering heat. Even the girls were given short vacations, scheduled to overlap so the house was not at any time unstaffed. Madam Maureen had made sure to retain Rosie, the girl favored by Bynum, who had now become Chad's favorite too.

"You don't think your mother knows about us, do you?"

"My cousin Corbin Chadwick mentioned your name. Does that mean they suspect something?"

"It could be a result of your Aunt Marilyn's salon. That's been a useful ruse for us. Certainly they don't know enough to arrest me yet. Or else they're waiting, baiting the trap, in hopes of capturing others. If that's true, you could be in danger. Who's this Corbin Chadwick? I never heard of him."

"He's a distant cousin. I didn't much like him. Blustery and self-righteous. He says he made a lot of money in the China Trade, owns some ships."

"Probably bought them from the same shipbuilders up in Maine who supplied the vessels they used to get molasses from Jamaica to make rum to transport to Africa where they traded the rum for slaves and took them back to Jamaica. Are you aware of your family's complicity in that outrage?"

"It's ironic, isn't it? While my Southern relatives in the Virginia Piedmont were freeing their slaves, some of my New England ancestors were transporting them."

"Of course, we're not absolutely sure that's what they did with the rum."

"Sure enough to know that my grandfather Bartleby Laymus ordered me to shut up one time when I was little and quizzed him over and over about it. It worries me, what they've been capable of in the past. They can think conflicting thoughts at the same time and still come out making a profit. Good old Yankee ingenuity, I guess. Do you actually think they'd turn on me if they ever found out?"

"It's not likely they'd trace us here. But we can't be too careful now. It's not just the weather that's heating up. There's pressure on my agents for more intelligence, as well as for a plan for action. The Union government is stirring things up and there are rumors of a purge. Anybody who's a suspect is being taken in and questioned. Some have been detained, without charges or access to counsel. You must watch what you say and where you go. In fact, your mother's suggestion that you spy for them might be a blessing in disguise. You can feed them information I give you—which will be false—and that way keep them from suspecting you too much. I've invited a Detective Hartigan to join us a little later. He's a high-ranking police officer who's on our payroll too. He's Irish and has political connections. He's totally corrupt, of course, otherwise we couldn't have recruited him. We'll ask him how you might best play your game."

"I don't think of it as a game."

"Ease up, my boy. The Union is clamping down now, but at the same time they're making more enemies right here in New York. Last month they passed a new Internal Revenue Act, an income tax, I believe. At the same time they demanded all Congressional representatives take an "Oath of Loyalty." Independent thinkers, and that includes most of the New York delegation, didn't look favorably on that. Then they issued thirty-five million greenback dollars to help pay for the war and already they're worth only ninety-eight cents on the currency markets. They raised tariffs again, pleasing the Northern factory owners but offering Southern sympathizers another reason to keep on fighting."

"I'm less certain now that tariffs alone started this war," Chad said. "Surely the economic burden of customs duties was the most apparent precipitating factor. But ever since the Revolution there's been a long and furious debate about the keeping of slaves, and much violence, on both sides, has ensued."

"I agree," Bynum said, a puzzled look on his face, as if he were a teacher whose best student was about to go off track. "There's also pressure to keep a political balance in Congress. The addition of new states offers a convenient conflict to further the goals of abolitionists—which in fact I support. Moreover, the agrarian nation has always had a love-hate relationship with the manufacturing nation, all the way back to tapestry makers, farm tools, porcelain suppliers and above all, armaments. Look what Madame Pompadour fomented when she got France to rival the German states in making little figurines and tableware and other costly trinkets. From Meissen to Sevres! The attitudes of common ordinary people also played a role. Sometimes there's what we call folk wisdom behind political movements. Alas, the common consensus is often justified in purpose but deadly in method. And not always fit to be called real wisdom. The people who run things are the hidden commanders behind the mob. Look how the *sans culottes* marched on Versailles and forced the King to come back to Paris. Their mounting passions cost him his head. It's said the Duc d'Orleans was calling the shots, so one of the Princes of the Blood could mount the throne. He was considered a candidate himself. No, I don't want you to be simplistic about what we're trying to do here."

Chad tugged at his collar in the August heat, turned his head away from Bynum, took a sip of water. He sighed as if he were about to make a decisive announcement. "I'm supposed to be a visionary. That's the definition my professors pushed on me and I accepted it. But I can't act against everything that's wrong."

Bynum sat erect, his face like a debater who's seen his opening. "We're concerned here not with the sweep of history but the broom that sets it off. And the tariff conflict, the increase of Federal troops at Fort Sumter, aimed at ensuring the furtherance of customs income, was surely the spark that started the fire."

"And now we must put it out." Chad exhaled with a sense of finality as he spoke.

"Everybody's confused, I guess, even the diplomats. The Confederate ambassador, Slidell, has the ear of Napoleon III. There's fear France may recognize the Confederacy and perhaps provide warships to break the blockade. France needs cotton too, after all. The Union has authorized the confiscation of Southern property, which some of them call 'sanctions,' and now this Emancipation Proclamation has been submitted to the Cabinet. At the same time they've got an Indian uprising on their hands, the Sioux out in Minnesota. I'd not be comfortable in Lincoln's shoes right now."

"I just want to end this war. I fear for my father. You've not heard anything since he joined up with General Lee. And I fear for my own future. It looks like my desire to do one thing will in fact accomplish the opposite."

"I recently heard from your father. It was a very brief note but he was in a good frame of mind. He alluded to you, always in code. He wrote me on August 10, the day after Stonewall Jackson routed the Union forces at Cedar Mountain. Cedar Crest Hall is once again in Confederate hands."

"But he wasn't there when he wrote you, was he?"

"He felt it unwise to indicate precisely where he was at the time. He's apparently a key intelligence advisor to Lee. Like father, like son."

"Do you think he'd approve of what I'm doing?"

"No doubt about it, as long as you play it safe and don't get caught. A man his age, when he's in battle, thinks of his only son more than ever. I'm sure you're his reason for living now, not just his love of Virginia."

"It's all so duplicitous. Horace Greeley used his newspaper to urge Lincoln to wage war on slavery everywhere. Free them all, North and South. But Lincoln responded, you read it I guess, that the purpose of the war was to preserve the Union, not to protect or to destroy slavery. How long can these people straddle the fence?"

"Well at least you've got a name now."

"What do you mean?"

"Newspapers have described Northern sympathizers with the South as

'Copperheads.' There's a big movement in Indiana, and you know already about Vallandigham in Ohio."

"Am I one too?"

"Absolutely. 'Copperhead Wales'."

Chad leaned forward from his chair and poured himself another glass of port, snapped off a grape, and nibbled a piece of cheese. He'd removed his jacket, unbuttoned his vest, and loosened his collar. "I got here before you did."

"I suspected you would. Was she here?"

"She told me it was all right, anytime, that you had made an arrangement in my behalf."

"That's true."

"It makes me feel cheap."

"Does she make you feel cheap?"

"I don't feel dirty or sordid. Rosie's very sweet and affectionate. Guilt, maybe. I love Clarissa so."

"You've got this insatiable hunger for truth, but take my word in this case, my boy. Don't tell anybody in your family about it, and don't let Clarissa know under any circumstances. Even if you managed to placate your conscience, you'd only hurt her."

"I reckon that's so."

The outside heat stifled street noises and there was only a faint movement of air in the shadowy room. After a while they heard a distant crack of thunder.

"Ah, we'll have rain soon. That will cool us down. It must've been hot upstairs for you."

"I didn't mind." Chad shifted in his seat. "One thing bothered me a little. Rosie said her brother is in the Union army. Did you know that?"

"Yes."

"What if she turned us in?"

"She doesn't know anything unless you told her and I'm sure you didn't. She doesn't even know your name. And the person she'd likely turn us in to is Detective Hartigan and he's working for us."

They sat quietly in the silent house. Thunderclaps grew louder, then they heard the splatter of rain against the windowpanes. There was a loud knock at the front door, an interchange of voices, followed by footsteps. The door to the library opened, and a tall, heavy man wearing rumpled summer clothes entered, dismissing the woman behind him and closing the door.

"Bynum, I'm sorry to be late. I was held up on urgent police business at City Hall."

"Sit down and have a glass of port. This is Chadwick Wales."

Chad extended his hand with reluctance at Bynum's disclosure of his identity, thinking he might as well have said "I'd like you to meet Copperhead Wales."

"Let me get right to the point, Detective. I have two things to settle. The first is to enlist your aid with a series of actions we're planning throughout Northern cities. The second is a more personal matter, one we should dispense with at the outset."

"I checked my account. The deposit was made, just as you said."

"As it always will be, unless the South falls altogether, God forbid. The personal issue is this. It's highly possible I'll be discovered. If so, I may be tortured before they hang me. I have a lot of co-conspirators but no names will pass my lips. If I'm taken, you mustn't admit you know me. To do so would endanger others working with me. Above all, you mustn't implicate Mr. Wales here in any of this. I hereby authorize you to help him in any way possible should he be compromised. I've got funds in London that, upon my death, will be distributed according to strict instructions. Should my death result from my service to the South, part of the money will go to Chad with instructions on how he's to pay it out to those who helped us. There'll be adequate rewards for you if I'm taken and they go after Chad. He's young, idealistic, and right now very useful. But I'm a friend of his father's and I've got an obligation. You must vow, here and now, that you'll always be on his side. I hardly need remind you that I also have a trove of documents which Mr. Wales will have recourse to in an emergency, and some of those documents could be embarrassing to you if he should make them known. I trust you, Detective, but I must make sure that my friend's son will be given all the assistance he needs to escape, if he's discovered. Are you prepared to make that guaranty?"

"I assured you earlier that I'm resolute and faithful in that regard, Sir. I'm an Irish man whose countrymen are demeaned and mistreated. But I've worked my way up and I've made many connections. I've got the ear of the people who run things, from Tammany Hall to Washington. I need money for my starving relatives in Ireland. They've got hardly anything to eat, and scores of them arrive here every day on foreign ships. So I'm not a good candidate for betrayal." Hartigan sat down and poured himself another drink. He was slightly overweight, had a round face with bright blue eyes, and sported, under his summer jacket, now agape, a revolver thrust into his belt. "Now, what's the other thing?"

"The Union army hasn't behaved with much humanity in some of its so-called victories in my homeland. My goal, and the goal of my young friend here, is to terminate this war. We believe it would end more swiftly if they were to receive a taste of their own medicine in some Northern centers, like

Boston and New York and Philadelphia. Maybe even Washington. We intend to firebomb key buildings and stockpiles in these cities. Every effort will be employed to keep civilian casualties to a minimum. But in the long run, if we succeed, we'll save lives. Both North and South. This war must end, the South must be treated justly, and there must be a negotiated peace. For that I need your help."

"You know you can count on me."

"Very well then. Here's an extra envelope for you, so you don't have to disturb your secret accounts. Good day to you, Detective. We'll continue to communicate through this establishment, which is deeply obligated to me."

Bynum rose to his feet, shook the detective's hand, and guided him towards the door. Chad heard a muffled conversation outside the library doors but couldn't understand the content. It was lengthy, and he heard the detective, at one point, cry out loud enough to be heard.

"My God, they'll hang all of you if this gets out! All of you!"

September 1862

Chad was reluctant to visit Aunt Marilyn Blaine, but was encouraged to do so by his mother, who seemed subdued since their outing to Brooklyn. Faced with her determination to work for abolition, he had no choice but to admire her for her principles. He even allowed himself to doubt that there was anything improper in her feelings for Reverend Mullen. Clarissa, pouting for the last two weeks because he hadn't visited her at Yellowfields in August, was eager to make up and be seen again with her dashing fiancé, now regarded as a budding financier, a reputation further enhanced by his growing air of mystery. There'd been rumors, his mother said, that he was engaged in monetary initiatives of vital interest to the Union, gossip he did nothing to dispel. He assumed Aunt Marilyn's coterie would be duly impressed.

There'd been no word from Bynum for over two weeks, and hence no further news of his father. He'd spent late August and early September working on several new ventures at his office, and grudgingly admitted that Randall seemed to value his opinions and efforts, after all. There were high commissions for his personal accounts and significant financial gains for a few of their investors, offsetting a larger number of calamitous failures that incensed the more vulnerable speculators. But his office time was brief, and he used his freedom to visit the house on Prince Street, ostensibly to see if Bynum were there, but in truth, because he craved the satisfaction he now felt indispensable to his peace of mind. Underneath it all, he had to admit, he was worried and uncomfortable about the direction his life was taking.

By the third week of September, as the weather cooled and the days became sparkling and dry, his spirits rallied a bit, despite the heavy toll of war casualties and troubling unrest in his hometown as workers protested their plummeting wages and walkouts became common. Civic leaders were agitated about the mass meeting in late August of the city's black population, protesting President Lincoln's publicized suggestion that the solution to the "Negro Problem" was to deport them to Africa or Central America. He considered the income tax authorized earlier in the year to be an insult to people like himself who opposed the war, in full knowledge that these new revenues were necessitated both by the loss of customs duties in the South and the disturbing acceleration of the war, costing more each day in both dollars and lives.

He consoled himself with his standard refuge, reading several of Cicero's *Philippics* about political maneuvering, written by the famed orator after the assassination of Julius Caesar resulted in an ongoing struggle for power. He'd read much Cicero before but now it seemed strangely relevant to his own circumstances. He also reread Milton's *Lycidas*, which soothed his distraction and fear with its lyrical lament for a dead youth. For it was death itself that troubled his young mind as he continued to file his covert dispatches, left for Bynum at the Prince Street rendezvous or with Detective Hartigan, with whom he lunched one day, and with whom he felt a surprising rapport. Death and destruction were in the daily papers, and wounded veterans could be seen outside Bellevue Hospital, walking on crutches, pushed in wheel chairs, and sometimes sitting quietly on a bench with white bandages covering their blinded eyes. Orphans and widows begged on the public thoroughfares, despite the efforts of charity workers like Clarissa and Susan Steinmann, who headed fund-raising events to provide subsistence for those left helpless and hopeless by a war that had already stretched out longer than anyone, on either side, had predicted. After the troops had clashed again August 31 and September 1 at Bull Run and at nearby Chantilly, Stonewall Jackson had to withdraw. The casualties for the two-day fracas exceeded 19,000 killed and wounded. Then both Lee and Jackson had crossed into Maryland, Jackson camped on the Maryland side of the Potomac across from Harper's Ferry, Virginia, and Lee in Fredericksburg.

The protracted duration of the war convinced him he was justified in his subversive activities and gave credence to his unqualified opposition to the conflict, a credo he now kept mostly to himself, but a conviction he needed to voice, if only to the inner circle of artists and intellectuals he'd meet once again on East 25th Street.

Growing in self-confidence but troubled by the changes in his character, he welcomed the ride from the Renfield Mansion to Marilyn Blaine's house.

It was a short distance but the big carriage moved slowly, and gave him time to relax with his beloved, and with Schuyler and Marcus, who sat opposite them in the luxurious coach.

"What have you been up to, old boy," Marcus asked, glancing conspiratorially at Schuyler and winking an eye. "Did you give up those dusty old books and find more lively pursuits in wartime New York? Schuyler and I can't keep up with it all, troops marching in and out, scandals on Wall Street, immigrants rioting. We're just counting days until we can get back to France. Of course, with these overtures to Napoleon III from the Confederacy, and virtual piracy on the high seas by these blockade-runners, we just don't feel brave enough to go. What's your secret? You seem ready to take on the world." He laughed again and squeezed Schuyler's knee. But Schuyler didn't respond, failing to gaze with his usual admiration at his friend's deep blue eyes and golden hair. He too, Chad sensed, was troubled.

"Clarissa has complained and I don't blame her. But the truth is, my companies are taking up more and more of my time. I don't even bother to read much any more."

"I find that hard to believe," Marcus continued. His gaze seemed to pierce through Chad's eyes and into his brain, making him wonder what, if anything, this maverick from Ohio knew about him. Had he been seen on the doorstep of the house on Prince Street? Or lunching with an Irish detective at a downtown saloon?

"We've been engaged now for eighteen months," Clarissa lamented, twirling her parasol and clutching Chad's hand.

"At least we know it was a voluntary engagement!" Marcus threw back his head with a loud laugh, but Schuyler glared at him.

"Really, Marcus, that's no way to talk to my sister."

"Dear boy, we're all friends here. The same generation. Times are changing, especially with this war. People can be more natural with each other now. You and me included. Maybe we won't have to move to Paris after all, although I think your father will be disappointed if we don't."

Chad was still unaware how much Clarissa really knew about her brother, and he'd been embarrassed to answer her questions that day in Central Park. Who was he to criticize, he realized with a pang. He sat beside the woman he loved, properly engaged and chaperoned by her brother, while less than twenty-four hours had passed since he lay naked, sweaty and exhausted in his usual room in a house on Prince Street. He squeezed Clarissa's hand.

"Yes, Marcus. Please don't be too free in your remarks. Clarissa and I are frank with each other, but I respect her. And I'm as eager as she is to get married and live together. Whatever you and Schuyler intend to do is your business and none of ours."

An awkward silence ensued, broken conveniently by their arrival at Marilyn Blaine's. "Isn't that Dr. Forrest's coach out front," Clarissa asked. "I've seen it often at the hospital when Susan Steinmann and I are working with the wounded and the bereaved."

They scrambled out of the coach and up the steps. The front door was ajar so they knocked first and then crossed into the foyer. Chad was relieved to hear his aunt's familiar cackle.

"Who's tending the door," Marilyn shouted, "Do I have to do it myself?" To everyone's astonishment she stood up from her chaise and walked across the room to greet her four new guests. She was almost as thin as Clarissa, and had managed to get herself outfitted in the latest style. Her eyes had a frenzied look and her cheeks were flushed with color. She walked quickly, with only slight evidence of a falter in her gait. She kissed Clarissa on the cheek, did the same to Chad, and grabbed Schuyler and Marcus by the hand, then weaved her way back to her usual position and leaned back with a deep sigh. Troubled expressions could be seen on all her acolytes. Dr. Forrest broke the silence.

"Marilyn has succeed in losing weight at the expense of her chocolates and cordials," Dr. Forrest said merrily. "But we mustn't let her overdo it." As he spoke he looked directly into Chad's eyes, conveying sadness, resignation, and pity simultaneously. Chad was spurred to keep up the deceit.

"Aunt Marilyn, you look so fine. I can't wait to take you out on the town."

"Would you take me shopping or would you men be too bored by that," she said, slowly recovering her breath after the walk across the room. "I want to see A. T. Stewart's new store on Astor Place. I've heard they've got everything. It's eight stories tall and you can take an elevator. It's supposed to be the biggest department store in the world!"

"If I have you for company I'll surely take you shopping, dear Aunt," Chad replied. Several guests murmured enthusiastically, but faces were mostly grim.

"Schuyler and I will take you to the opera, now that the season's just getting started," Marcus said.

"You must dine with my father and me," Susan Steinmann said.

"God bless you, dear lady, all I've got to offer you is the pageantry of my church," Father Fineas said. He appeared more at ease with the game than others, a fact that sent chills over Chad's body, for the priest, with his clerical garb, lent a somber aura to the scene.

"Enough about me," Marilyn chirped. She took a sip from a cup, apparently containing tea. Her hands shook a little as she swallowed, and the saucer rattled when she replaced the cup. "Let's talk of more important things. No doubt, Chad, you'll bring up the war so we must get it out and over with."

"Several months ago in this room I spoke frankly of my opposition to this war," Chad began. "In our discussion there was much lamentation about the high casualties at that time. Twenty thousand, I believe, in two or three days. But in the papers this morning there's news of Antietam. In a single day, in a little town in Maryland, the dead and wounded on both sides surpassed 23,000. Am I the only one to feel outrage at this barbarous and unnecessary waste of human life? And the infliction of suffering and hardship on at least three times that number, since these fallen soldiers have wives and children and parents and friends. In God's name, Father, we must stop it."

Chad knew he was venting his frustration on the cleric. Although he himself had little interest and less faith in religion, he longed for some comforting explanation. But Father Fineas, probably accustomed to such outbursts, spoke calmly and without political motivation.

"My Church and others outside my faith speak of the inescapable nature of human suffering. Indeed, suffering is the central symbol of our shared belief, Catholic or Protestant. We have no palliative or remedy or excuse. God's ways are mysterious and they must seem cruel. I can offer you only the example of the Cross. But if we're to suffer, as we all do and shall, then I say let us suffer with meaning and breathe compassion. I hope we can transform our anguish into actions which will help us humans prevent these things in the future, if it be God's will."

"Father, I respect your agility in moving the responsibility from people to God, but this war is of human origin and will be ended only by human effort. Chad is right." Marcus was visibly agitated. "We persecute each other. We discriminate against each other. And when our petty little values conflict, we kill each other. It's unusual in any species, save our own, to wantonly kill. I say we need to address the politics of the matter and let God attend to the cosmos, or whatever he does while this suffering—universal as you say it is, Father—decimates our population and destroys our resources. We look to the West and see more land than we'll ever need. We pin our hopes on a new technique or a new discovery or a new enterprise, like this Rockefeller and his refineries. We say 'progress' will solve all our problems. I say we'll never solve them. We're the enemy, all of us in this room."

"Surely not all of us, Marcus," Schuyler said. "These gentle ladies, surely they're above reproach."

Susan Steinmann leapt from her seat alongside Eliza Van Der Venner. "If you men are to deny us the vote, you shouldn't also deny us our fair share of suffering and responsibility. There are no acceptable reasons for waging this war. My father bridles to hear me say it. Like other powerful and successful men he'll detail for you the economic and social ramifications of such conflict. Slavery is an issue, taxation is an issue, congressional balance, factory workers against farmers, the will to power, fear of those different from us. Even Anti-Semitism raises its ugly head from time to time. But if I believed war is in fact truly inevitable, I'd despair of life altogether. Chad, I think you're the only one here who refuses to abandon cold reason and, what was it Father—the breath of compassion."

"You young people have such energy!" Marilyn spoke hoarsely, then fell silent, the flush gone from her cheeks and her eyelids heavy. Dr. Forrest held up his hand as if to silence further talk. His patient lay back on her chaise and slowly closed her eyes. He took her wrist in his hands and pulled out his pocket watch. After a while, he spoke, "Our friend is resting now; I suggest we listen to the piano for a while and then leave her to her slumber. As you see she's grown weak. In the future, these wonderful receptions of hers will grow shorter, but I hope all of you will continue to come. She often says you're her family, and she needs her family with her now. I've engaged a nurse for her, who's preparing her bed as we speak. I'll stay until she's soundly asleep. It's probably better if the rest of you left now."

A quiet murmur of protest and concern spread around the room, and various guests spoke in low voices to each other. Chad fetched Clarissa's big hat and parasol. In the hall he encountered Father Fineas, gesturing towards Schuyler in a fevered conversation. He could make out only one sentence, which was issued by Schuyler. "Father, I must see you. Privately. I must have your guidance in a most urgent matter."

* * *

"They told me down the hall that you'd be in here today," Schuyler said. He'd entered without knocking and leaned on the doorway, one hand against the frame, the other curled in a fist. Chad, who had his back to the outer room when he first heard noises, quickly closed his copy of Heraclitus, covered it with a stack of files, and rushed into the reception area. Schuyler's suit was soiled, his collar stained, his hair spilling onto his forehead, and his eyes afire with anxiety. "Chad, you've got to help me. I don't know who else to turn to."

"What on earth's the matter? Is Clarissa all right?"

"It's not the family, it's me. I think my life is ruined."

"Come now. Sit down." Chad held Schuyler's elbow and guided him to the conference table, easing him into a chair. He looked up and down the hall, then closed the door firmly. Schuyler was slumped over the table, holding his head in both hands. Chad returned to his inner office and brought back a water pitcher and a glass. He filled it to the brim and then went to the window, raising the sash higher. The day was balmy and bright, with hardly a wind to fill his rooms with the smoke and dust of the downtown streets.

"Is it Marcus?"

"I couldn't go to Marcus. He'd drop me for sure."

"Schuyler, out with it."

"You know more about me—about Marcus and me—than anybody in the family. You've never spoken of it, the time you came into my room, and I've not dared to bring it up. I think I must disgust you."

"It's none of my business so I've tried to put it out of my mind."

"But you can't put something like that out of your mind. I have to talk to you about it. I'll be your brother-in-law. You may reveal it to my sister or to my father. I was willing to live with that, at least for now since I thought Marcus and I'd be safe in Paris by September. And now this, God, what am I to do?"

"Schuyler, I'm well schooled in the Greek and Roman world but I know about these things, you must realize, only from books. I hear rumors. But it's mostly hidden from view. I went downtown on a wild spree once with Bynum and we saw some things in a bar down there, you know the type, I suppose, where men like you …"

"Men like me? They weren't like me at all. Otherwise I wouldn't be in this mess. If I tell you what happened, will you promise not to pass it on? Will you try not to detest me?"

"I'm uneasy with it but I'd never detest you. You'll be like a brother to me. Now, please, out with it."

"Marcus and I had an argument. I stalked out of the house and went downtown. I guess I wanted to get even or something. I went to one of those bars you mentioned and there was a young fellow there, about my age. He was a sailor from one of the foreign ships on the waterfront. We drank some beer and talked and then he said he was staying at a rooming house, down near the Seamen's Church Institute. He asked me to go there with him and I did."

Images of the Prince Street house and the room upstairs clouded Chad's mind. He felt a swell of sympathy.

"Wild oats, that's all. You needn't tell anybody about it."

"It's not that simple. We were in the room, you know, the way you saw Marcus and me. And then the door burst open and it was a policeman. He roughed me up and sat me down and closed the door. He handed the sailor some money and sent him away and then he started in on me. He told me I could be imprisoned, maybe put to death, for what I was doing. He said my family would be ruined."

"But he let you go, didn't he?"

"That's just it. He let me go for now but he wants money. A lot of it. Ten thousand dollars!"

"Ten thousand! Do you have it?"

"I guess I could get it. But you know, people like that, they'd be back for more. It would go on forever. And all my funds come through Father's bank. A sum that large, he'd be notified and he'd demand an explanation."

"You could tell him you invested it with me."

"I thought of that. But I don't think it would work. Uncle Randall, you see. He doesn't really like my father. And he doesn't like me. Otherwise I'd be sitting where you are. I always presumed I'd take over the new companies. I'm the only son."

"Schuyler, it's never occurred to me that my position would be a threat to you. I apologize."

"It's not, anymore. I really do want to go abroad with Marcus. We belong together. We're like you and Clarissa. Don't be offended, please, but what we feel for each other, there's no evil in it. We don't hurt anybody. We're solid citizens …"

"At least until now."

"It was a mistake, a simple mistake. If it had been a woman there wouldn't be a problem. I've long suspected my father would be proud if he found me with some girl in a whorehouse."

The reference deepened Chad's sympathies. "There's got to be a way out. Do you know the man's name?"

"He said he was a police officer but I don't think he's much more than a patrolman. Dietrich Mueller, he said. His parents came over from Germany, they're watchmakers."

"How'd you know that?"

"He took my watch as a down payment, then got to talking. He finagled his way onto the police force and now he's blackmailing people like me. I think he means business."

"Blackmail is a crime, too."

"But if he turned me in he'd deny it."

"The sailor, did he set you up?"

"I think so."

"Even so, he'd be equally guilty if they called him to testify. He'd get the same penalty."

"It turns out he was younger than I thought. He said he was seventeen when we got back to his room. It's his first time at sea, they'd go easy on him and hard on me. It wouldn't make any difference anyway. If there's a trial and publicity, I'm ruined, maybe dead, and so is the House of Renfield. You know how those bankers are, one whiff of scandal and they start politely turning their backs on you."

"Do you know how to get in touch with this blackmailer?"

"He gave me an address. He said he's not married and lives there alone. He gave me a month to show up with the money. Otherwise he intends to file his report. They'd come to our house, the Renfield house! They'd arrest me and take me away in chains. What am I to do?"

Chad couldn't resist the surge of power he suddenly felt. He'd already demonstrated his ability to succeed in the financial world, he was sought after as a clandestine agent by both Northern and Southern activists, and now the son of New York's most prominent banker was pleading for his help. He wished he could tell his mother about it.

"If you can get me out of this, Oh, Chad, I'd be grateful for the rest of my life. I'd do anything for you, anything at all. Most of all I wouldn't reveal how you helped me. That in itself would destroy me forever in my family's eyes."

"I'm involved in negotiations with Bynum Bradley-West. Do you remember him? One of our partners is a high-ranking police officer, a detective. I suspect he could stop this. But you'll have to meet with us in a neutral place where we won't be watched. In fact, it's a brothel on Prince Street."

"My God, you've been in a brothel?" Schuyler stifled his indignation as he recognized his own position in the pecking order of sexual disgrace. "Whatever you say."

"You're sure nobody else knows?"

"About the incident? No."

"Is there something else?"

"There's another person who knows. Not about the incident, just about me. It's Father Fineas."

"How would Father Flaherty know?"

"I haven't been as accepting of myself as Marcus has. I watch you and Clarissa planning your marriage and you, taking over some of the family business, and I see the look in my father's eyes on the few occasions he talks with me now. I felt guilty. Father Fineas knows all about confession."

"But you're not a Catholic! Wait a minute, you made an assignation with him at Aunt Marilyn's last week."

"Not an assignation. An appointment."

"Did you keep it?"

"I went down to his parish. In fact, it was after I left him that I wandered into that bar where I met the sailor."

"What did you do, confess, receive a penance, and then go out looking for a sailor?"

"I wish you wouldn't put it that way, Chad. It sounds so sordid."

"It is sordid."

"Father Fineas wouldn't let me confess anyway. He said since I'm not a Catholic it wouldn't do any good. He said he didn't have any authority to absolve a Protestant."

"Did you tell him about your situation?"

"I told him about me and Marcus, and some others, too, up at Yale, and asked him to absolve me. He said he couldn't do that but he'd give me some advice."

"What was that?"

"He said I should read Walt Whitman and move to France."

October 1862

"Maybe he should just go to France now," Bynum said.

"He fears he'll be intercepted. Or that they might get a story out, here and in Ohio. It could involve Marcus too, and maybe his family. They're important in Ohio and some of them are members of the Peace Party so the war supporters would try to make it even worse." Chad leaned forward in his chair, his knees spread, his hands clasped in front of him as he stared at the floor. "I find this difficult to talk about."

"Remember when you brought them to my place that time they were assaulted downtown? I was sure they'd antagonized some of the burly boys in Five Points. I told you then that I don't share their tastes but I don't condemn them either. It's not my business and hardly yours."

"But I'm to be married into the family. That makes it my business."

"To avoid disgrace, but not to condemn either of them for being whatever God made them. If you believe in God."

The house on Prince Street was dry and cool in a brilliant October. Some of the shutters had been partly opened to let in the light and air, but the lower sashes were obscured for privacy. Madam Maureen had brought them a bowl of nuts, a bottle of wine, and pretzels. It was early in the afternoon, a busy midweek working day, so the customers were few. As was his habit, Chad had arrived early and visited for a while with his favorite in her upstairs chamber. "It makes me feel better, somehow, about this Schuyler business," he explained sheepishly to Bynum, who merely laughed.

"You'll wear the poor girl out. What time is Schuyler coming?"

"He said about two." Chad munched on a pretzel. "You're sure Detective Hartigan will show up?"

"He does what I tell him. He relies on the money we give him and he knows we've got the goods on him if he turns on us. Best kind of cohort."

"Do you think he can stop it?"

"He's not likely to be very tolerant of a blackmailing policeman. That imposes on his own arena and invites possible scrutiny from outside. There are so many newspapers competing for readers now, they'll print just about anything to increase their circulation."

"I appreciate your help. And I'm grateful for your friendship with my father, and the news you bring me of him. Sometimes I'm convinced I'll never see him again. We didn't have enough time together when I was growing up. But the moments I spent with him are precious to me and I hunger for more. So I'll continue to work with you, but ..."

"But you're not sure you're doing the right thing?"

"It's your attitude sometimes. You're more cynical than I'd ever want to be."

"About the war?"

"About everything."

Bynum shook his head incredulously and quietly laughed. "You're a piece of work, lad. You can't stop fucking that girl upstairs, you're raking in commissions from shady business deals with your uncle and your future in-laws, you're working with me as a spy, and now you're trying to get a pervert out of a blackmail plot. I'd say a little cynicism would be in order right now."

"I didn't intend to offend you."

"Hard to offend me, my boy. I'm reconciled to what you'd call the human predicament. The Greeks made it seem noble, the Romans were more tawdry, and now you can buy novels in Paris that make Sappho and Catullus read like scripture. You'll have to abandon your naive and idealistic posture sooner or later. I've already ceased to regard you as innocent." Bynum's voice was steady, his gaze unwavering. Chad's heart sank as he realized Bynum's analysis coincided very closely with his own recent self-assessment. They sat in silence, both of them relieved to hear a voice they recognized when the parlor maid opened the front door to an insistent knock. Detective Hartigan stood in the hallway outside the parlor, looking in, his face flushed and his expression inquisitive.

"Gentlemen," he said, crossing the room with his hand extended. Chad stood up and greeted him.

Bynum remained seated. "Detective, please close those doors. We've got a matter to discuss that might titillate even this jaded ensemble."

Hartigan closed the parlor doors and sat down. He eyed the nuts and pretzels and wine. Chad shifted awkwardly in his chair, then filled a glass and handed him a saucer for his snacks.

"This is not a good time for me, there's trouble all over with the Irish and the black people and now the Germans are acting up."

"It's a German policeman we want to talk about. Dietrich Mueller. Do you know him?

"I do. A recent recruit, he seems a little standoffish. I don't much like him, to tell the truth. How'd you know him?"

"I'll let Chad explain. In a sense it's his problem."

"You may remember that I'm soon to be married into a prominent family. My fiancée's brother, about my age, is involved in some kind of ... behavior that's against the law and would bring disaster to my future in-laws."

"You mean he's got a girl squirreled away somewhere?" Hartigan's hacking laugh made Chad uneasy.

"No," Bynum said. "It seems he's got a boy somewhere."

"Oh, one of those," Hartigan said.

"Yes," Bynum said. "One of those. But the problem is your Mueller. He caught them together, the boy is seventeen, a sailor, and he's trying to blackmail Chad's future brother-in-law."

"Well we can't have that, can we," Hartigan snickered.

"I don't know, Detective," Bynum said, "Can we?"

"I gather you want me to do something about it."

Chad sat up straight in his chair. "I've asked him to meet us here to explain what Mueller's up to. Detective, I find this most difficult, but I'm put in a position ..."

"Mr. Wales ... Chad ... nothing shocks me. Here in this house I've seen the cream of New York society cavorting with prostitutes and I know there are other places around here where members of the best families do the same with boys. We raid them occasionally but it's for show mostly. Frankly, the people down here would just as soon look the other way. They've got more immediate problems, like trying to put bread on the table. But some of them, a crooked policeman for example, will resort to tactics like this. Problem is, if it goes too far, there are severe penalties for the guilty. Death, even."

"Well, Detective Hartigan, we can't have someone put to death because of a crooked policeman, now, can we?" Chad was disappointed at Bynum's tone, which indicated he was, on the whole, rather enjoying himself. He started to speak when they heard muffled voices, and then the scratch of the sliding doors opening. There stood Schuyler, hat in hand, an agonized look on his face. This time it was Bynum who stood up.

"There you are, Schuyler. Sit down and have some wine. Care for a pretzel?" Bynum looked like a cat with a newly trapped mouse.

Schuyler held his hat in both hands above his waist as if he were shielding his lower torso from view. He looked at Chad and then at Detective Hartigan.

"Sit down, lad, and have a drink. We're here to help you." Hartigan's demeanor and voice convinced Chad he was sincere in his tolerance and his eagerness to help. He renewed his initial sense of comradeship with this unlikely associate and felt himself relaxing. He looked at Schuyler directly.

"Sit down and take it easy, Schuyler. I've approached the Detective and he's willing to help you. Tell him what happened." Chad was anxious to let someone else relay the facts.

"I was drinking downtown and I got into a conversation with somebody and we went back," Schuyler paused sheepishly, "back to his room and then this policeman forced his way in and made accusations and demanded I give him ten thousand dollars."

"Ten thousand! Why, that bastard. He's only been on the force for a year or so."

"If I gave him the money my family would find out and if I don't he'll turn me in. And I have a friend, a friend who ... " Schuyler's voice trailed off in desperation.

Bynum chuckled again. "He's got a friend of his own age and social class and they're very cozy with each other and hope to leave the country soon and live in France." Bynum smacked his lips and poured another glass of wine.

"France, eh? Never traveled abroad myself. Never found it necessary." Both Hartigan and Bynum laughed, Schuyler looked mortified.

Chad blushed with embarrassment and a swell of pity. "Hold on, gentlemen. We know that blackmail's a felony and that anybody can make a mistake. Schuyler's a decent man, I respect him and I think we should try to help him."

"Five thousand," Hartigan said.

"Oh surely not," Bynum commented. "I should think three would do it."

"Four, then" Hartigan replied.

"Very well, four." Bynum smiled at Chad but didn't look at Schuyler, then stared directly at the Captain.

"Cash, though," Hartigan said.

"What else?" Bynum said, "Do you think he'd give you a personal check?" At this both Hartigan and Bynum broke into loud and lengthy laughter while Schuyler twisted in his chair and Chad looked away towards the windows. Then there was a prolonged silence.

"What do I have to do?" Schuyler said. "How will you settle it? Do you think Officer Mueller will settle for four thousand?"

"Oh, the four thousand is not for him," Hartigan said. Then he and Bynum started laughing again, as if they were watching a downtown vaudeville act.

"Can you shut him up?" Schuyler couldn't look any of them in the eye.

"That would be a way of putting it," Detective Hartigan said. He now displayed a very serious face. "The money's not for me. I'm being compensated in a far more significant and much more discreet way, and Chad here, and Bynum, are my colleagues in weightier matters. No, the money is for a ..." he paused, "for an assistant who'll 'shut him up' safely."

"It will be hard for me to get that much in cash right away, my father watches my expenses, but I have a legacy that pays me quarterly ..." Schuyler was interrupted by Bynum, who had stood up, put down his glass, and assumed a patrician air.

"One of the things I learned growing up in the South was that there's a certain code by which men of our class should live. If we stray, we'll be disciplined by our peers. But we don't approve of scum like this blackmailing policeman. It was obviously a set-up, and what you are, or do, is nobody's business. I'll pay the cash out of my current funds. You, Schuyler, can pay me back someday. What we all need is assurance that no goddamned German copper with a greedy and salacious sideline is going to presume he can mess with people like us. That's all you need to know about it, this discussion is over, and I've got more important things to do." Bynum removed a leather wallet from his coat pocket and counted out a sheaf of bills. "Here you are Detective. Thank you for handling this. We'll meet again soon over more critical issues. Now I suggest we disband, and leave, one at a time and in opposite directions.

"Let me go first, if I may," Chad said, "I'm late for a meeting at my office. With Randall Renfield and my Uncle Caleb, down from Boston. Schuyler, let's put this behind us."

"Chad, I'll do anything for you in the future. Anything you ask." Schuyler picked up his hat and shook Detective Hartigan's hand.

"We appreciate your gratitude, Schuyler," Bynum said. "And we very well might take you up on your promise, should we need you to help us out anytime soon. This is wartime and an action like the one you were subjected to is small potatoes, indeed. Yesterday Gladstone—he's a longtime member of the British Parliament—proclaimed that the Confederacy is legitimate and should be recognized. Disraeli will try to silence him. But the gesture has cheered the Confederate government. This war is not about to end. No siree, nowhere near about to end."

* * *

Chad decided to walk from Prince Street to his office. It was a clear dry day and he didn't feel like sitting on an omnibus or in a carriage. He wasn't due to meet Randall and Caleb until four o'clock, so the walk would help him clear his mind. Bynum's comments had unleashed a fulsome tide of self-criticism. Since he got back from Princeton, the pace of his life had grown more bewildering with each passing day, but now, criticism from someone like Bynum, whom he liked but considered basically immoral, forced him to take stock.

What would his epitaph look like, if he were to die soon and tombstones told the truth? *"Here lies Chadwick Wales, 1839-1862, Princeton '60, Greek and Latin scholar, beloved but unfaithful fiancée of Clarissa Renfield, son of the Southern traitor Franklin Wales and Harriet Laymus Wales, rumored mistress of the Rev. Thaddeus Mullen of Brooklyn. He was an ineffectual spy, a Wall Street conspirator, a frequenter of whorehouses, and a rescuer of perverts. Requiescat in pace."* He stared into the dusty street as if it were his final resting place.

Lost in his musings, he was almost run down by a speeding omnibus when he crossed Broadway. Noises were louder, the dust thicker and the crowds bigger, all of which he welcomed as an antidote to his soul-sickness. For in truth, he, accused of being unable to make up his mind, had equivocated himself into a sinkhole and he saw no way out of it.

He climbed the stairs to Financial and Industrial Enterprises, avoided the law office in the event they had mail or messages for him, and opened the door to his reception room with relief. But he drew in his breath involuntarily when he saw both Randall and Caleb sitting at his conference table, twiddling their thumbs.

"You're late, my boy, and there's much to talk about," Caleb said. "When you're president of a dozen different companies, the time is sure to come when you'll be asked to testify in court." Caleb spoke as if the matter were too routine to bother with.

"What am I to testify about?"

"It's a fairly ordinary lawsuit, on the whole," Randall said, adopting his lawyerly look. "You know how greed drives these speculators to take chances. When it goes wrong they turn on us."

"These are the kind of people who spend principal and then when they run out of money because of their risky investments want to blame it on others," Caleb said. "Occasionally a crazed stockholder becomes violent, takes a shot at somebody. They went after Appleby once, but they missed. Drew and Gould have bodyguards with them constantly now. From time to time we've even encountered this sort of thing in Boston." Caleb sighed deeply and stared out the window.

"Chad, our iron company in Ohio is being sued for mismanagement and securities fraud." Randall's monotonous voice sounded rehearsed. "Now, there's hardly any set of regulations that would apply to this ridiculous charge. We formed the company in good faith, Appleby found eager investors, and you, as president, will be asked what went wrong."

"How do I know what went wrong?"

"Don't worry, we'll prepare your statements in advance. They'll try to get you to come to Ohio to testify but we can put them off there. We'll have the case transferred to Federal court here in Manhattan. I'll find you a good Wall Street lawyer."

"You're a Wall Street lawyer!" Chad tried to conceal his irritation by following Caleb's gaze out the window. He remembered characters in Shakespeare who, seeming comic to the audience, shielded plots simultaneously ominous and far-fetched.

"Yes, but I'm involved as a Board member. And you're the chairman of this one, Caleb."

"We'll simply have to get the case deferred then," Caleb said.

"I suppose it might die out anyway, with the war intensifying so rapidly. Besides, there's a backlog of pending cases. Uniforms that fall apart. Rifles that won't fire. Spoiled meat and rotten vegetables. Just like any other war. And those who aren't in on it want to label all of us as insiders. Cronyism, one of the papers said today. As if I'd put myself on the same level as that rabble in Washington." Randall paused, wiped his spectacles, which he used for reading, and glanced through the documents in front of him. "Everybody's trying to blame somebody else. A member of the Federal Club is selling arms to the South and they're going to bring up charges. Some of the radical clubmen want to throw the man out."

"Why would they do that?" Caleb leafed through some of the papers in Randall's stack.

"For selling arms to the South when we're at war with them."

"My mills need cotton and the slaves need clothes," Caleb said. "It's been that way for years."

"Just hope it doesn't get back to that bunch of fanatics at the Federal Club that your mills, and some of FIE's companies, are engaging in similar commerce."

Caleb slammed his fist down on the table. "This is a free country."

"Still, if the inquiry gets outside the Club, it might lead them to us," Randall said. "I'm not so much worried about Ohio, but what if they investigate us in New Jersey, too?"

"Chad's got credibility in New Jersey," Caleb said. "He went to Princeton. I know several lawyers and three judges who went to Princeton. What else are connections for?"

November 1862

The Renfield Mansion was fully staffed and various servants came and went constantly, on the upper floors as well as the main one. It was deemed proper for Clarissa and Chad to be alone together, now that they were engaged, as long as doors were kept open. Chad didn't wish to offend Phillipse or Randall Renfield. Heretofore he lumped Schuyler among those likely to object but now, having received a promise to "do anything you want me to do," Chad couldn't repress the scheme floating almost constantly in his mind. Having grown experienced in the delights of intimacy, he now wanted Clarissa so much it was difficult for him to think of other things when she was in his sight.

"Father's quite angry," Clarissa said. "He says Uncle Randall will disgrace the House of Renfield."

"Only one of the lawsuits is likely to survive the first hearing. The one in Ohio, which will be referred to the New York Federal Court. I suppose I might have to testify, if it ever comes to trial."

"I'm so proud that you've taken over these daring initiatives with such competence. But I shouldn't want you to compromise our honor."

"Honor's not involved here. The initial stock offerings were handled by Grover Appleby. All of it according to strict regulations."

"Father says Mr. Appleby is a scoundrel. He says somebody tried to kill him last year."

"Some people have such greed they invest in anything new and when it doesn't pay off, they wail and moan. If they can't handle the risk they shouldn't invest."

"Father wishes you hadn't become involved."

"Perhaps I should explain it to him, then." The largest and softest sofa in the room allowed them to sink close together into the cushions. The high back shielded them from view from the rear, and nobody could surprise them from the front. They held hands and Chad began to run his fingers up and down Clarissa's neck.

"You'd be wise not to bring it up at all. He's got so much on his mind these days he'll probably soon forget it, as long as the papers don't continue to print all those lies." Chad moved his face closer and breathed into her ear. "Stop that, Chad," she said softly, but squeezed his hand and leaned her head closer.

"Remember what we talked about, when we were in the carriage that day."

Clarissa's free hand toyed with a button on Chad's vest. "It seems so long ago now."

He brushed his lips against her cheek." Remember what you said that day about men and women, how men, you know, react."

"Women too, I said." Chad pressed his mouth against her cheek and she seemed to move closer as she spoke.

"I know it, but you said you saw Schuyler in the bath."

"I was just a little girl, hardly thirteen."

"But you remember what you saw."

"Schuyler's all grown up now. Father won't speak to me about it but I think he's very close to disciplining him or sending him away."

"Schuyler's on our side now."

"What do you mean?"

Chad took Clarissa's free hand from his chest and placed it lower. "Remember when we kissed under that tree. What you felt."

"Chad …" She shivered but didn't withdraw her hand. After a moment she moved her palm closer into the inside of his thigh. Chad placed his hands on her shoulder and kissed her quickly. He brushed her bosom with his palm, twirling her thin gold necklace in his fingers, tracing a line from her throat downwards into her low-cut dress.

"Chad, you should stop."

"I don't want to and neither do you."

"I wish this war would end and you and I could be married and living at Yellowfields. I'd satisfy you, I know what you want."

Chad could feel her skin warming his fingers and her hand on his thigh. "What're we to do? Your father's adamant about postponing the wedding. I don't believe it's the war. I think he's waiting to see how I turn out."

"You're the most beautiful man I've ever seen. When I look at you sometimes I get almost dizzy. Do you know those gray striped pants, with the buttons and loops around the waist? The pants you wore to dinner last time."

"What about my pants?"

"They're very revealing. I look at you and I have such thoughts …"

"I want you so desperately I can hardly concentrate on my work. Even when I'm reading, my mind wanders, thinking of you. Sometimes it's almost unbearable." He kissed her again, this time on the lips, quickly lest they be discovered. He breathed into her ear again. "I want to be in bed with you, Clarissa, naked and free to do what lovers do."

"When you talk like that I lose my mind. I'd do it with you. It's our right. But I'm watched here. I can't do anything to worry Father more."

"If we did it and something happened, what could he do? Wouldn't he have to let us marry then?"

"Yes but we would be under a cloud in his mind. Remember my position. I'm already rich. Now it looks like we'll be richer than we could ever imagine. Father dotes on me. Schuyler seems to have lost favor and I'm sure Father means to make him financially independent on the condition that he live abroad."

"What makes you so sure?"

"Little things. His expression when Schuyler and Marcus come into the room together."

"It would be wrong for me to describe unnatural passions to you, darling, but if what we think is true, you know there are precedents in history for it. You should not discredit your brother too much."

"I'd never abandon him."

"Think about it. Marcus and Schuyler come and go as they please. How is it we can't be as free as two men are, who can't even reveal how they feel to anyone except themselves."

"It's distasteful. I prefer to think about us."

"Think about this then," Chad said, kissing her on the lips and placing her hand between his legs.

"Chad!" She drew her hand back suddenly, and then returned it and began to rub him. "Oh Chad, what're we to do?"

"You know what we must do."

"But not here, not in this house."

"My house then."

"But how?"

"My mother goes to Brooklyn three times a week. She's gone from ten until four. You could come to my house, we could go up to my room."

"What about the servants?"

"I could send the housekeeper to market and Higgens will be out anyway. I can get the parlor maid and the upstairs woman to clean the silver or something."

"But people here would see me come and go. That's enough to anger Father. He says I shouldn't go out alone these days. Even for my charity work, I always go with Susan Steinmann."

"Schuyler can be our chaperon."

"Schuyler? No matter what he's up to with Marcus, he still thinks of himself as my older brother. I don't believe he'd be party to some scheme to allow us to do what you want to do."

"I'm telling you, Schuyler's on our side. I can invite him and you for an early lunch. You can come right after mother leaves for Brooklyn. The three of us will be at table in the dining room and when Cook has cleared the dishes, we'll go into the drawing room. I'll then say goodbye loudly at the front floor but only Schuyler will leave. You can come upstairs to my bedroom. We'll have a couple of hours together. Then Schuyler can pick you up at the corner of Fifth Avenue and take you home. Nobody on the Renfield staff will suspect anything." As he spoke Chad thrust his finger into her bodice. His other hand massaged her leg. Her dress of slick silk and her thin underskirts were all that separated his hand from her skin. He knew she'd dressed that way for him, for this moment. He advanced his hand upwards on her leg. She began to tremble.

"Chad, you must talk to Schuyler. If he agrees, I agree. When? When can we do it."

"The day after tomorrow. I'll go to Schuyler's room now and discuss it. He's home, isn't he?"

"They're both home."

"Then I'd best knock several times before I barge in again."

* * *

The Renfield housekeeper eyed him disapprovingly as he climbed the stairs, but seemed relieved when she peeked into the front parlor and saw Clarissa sitting alone, a demure image with her carefully arranged hair and conservative but fashionable dress. Chad looked over the railing upstairs to make sure no one was pursuing him. He knocked lightly on Schuyler's door. There was no answer so he knocked again. Finally, he heard movements inside and the door cracked slightly. All he could see was one of Schuyler's eyes.

"Chad? Is something the matter?" Schuyler kept the door open slightly, still revealing only one eye, fixed on Chad's.

"I need to speak with you."

"Couldn't we do it later? I'm sort of busy right now."

"It has to be now, Schuyler. Right now." He pressed on the door and walked into the room. It was becoming a familiar scene. Marcus was under the bed covers, his unclothed chest showing and his ample blond hair in disarray. He waved a bare arm in greeting but said nothing.

"This is awkward, Chad. I've strained your tolerance already and now you're here again."

"I've discussed the situation with your sister and she's as accepting as I am. But we need your help."

"You've discussed matters like this with Clarissa?" His voice revealed indignation and curiosity combined.

"Schuyler, dear, what would you expect them to do?" Marcus said with a shameless lilt. "Chad's already caught us in here and I can tell he knows the whole story and doesn't care. It's nobody's business but ours. You really ought to put on your dressing gown, though. I don't think Chad's quite ready for that."

Neither of them had acknowledged that Schuyler was standing in the middle of the room, completely naked and in obvious excitement. He grabbed a silken bathrobe from a chair and hastily covered himself.

"What is it you and my sister expect of me?"

"We feel as strongly as you two do and your father keeps postponing our wedding. We're eager to be together. We need you to chaperon her when she visits my house and then to leave us alone."

"Leave you and my sister alone in your house? Chad ..." He was interrupted by his lover, still abed and naked and with a big smile on his face.

"For God's sake, Schuyler, we're in no position to criticize."

"But what would people think?"

"Nobody is to know about it," Chad said. "We've planned it carefully."

"You've already planned it? What if my father finds out? He's contemptuous of me already and I know he's just waiting for the war to wind down so he can ship me and Marcus off to Paris, never to return. I'm in agreement with that. But if he finds out I've made arrangements for his only daughter to ..."

"Nobody will know. And if he does find out, what could he do but permit us to marry at once?"

"He's right, Schuyler." Marcus had pulled a nightshirt over his shoulders, slowly extricating himself from the tangle of sheets and quilts. November had turned cold and even with the fireplace going it was cool in the room. He went to a sideboard and poured himself a glass of water. "In our eyes, you're already married," Marcus said, lifting his glass as if in a toast. "In fact, would it not arouse suspicion if Schuyler left and then returned? Why doesn't he stay? You've got a spare bedroom or two, do you not?"

"Several, down the hall from mine."

"Then let Schuyler and me be chaperons. And when the help's not looking, we'll all go upstairs. To our separate chambers." Marcus fell backwards on the bed and kicked his legs into the air in anticipation. "This is going to be really fine!"

* * *

Chad locked his bedroom door. Clarissa stood ill at ease in the center of the room.

"I'd have preferred it the way we planned. It embarrasses me that both of them know about us now."

"But Marcus was right. There's far less chance of our being discovered if they stay."

"But they're right down the hall. Doesn't this concern you?"

"Why?"

"Whatever it is they do it cannot be acceptable in polite society."

"We're not in polite society. We're alone in my bedroom."

"I've dreamed of this moment. I don't want it soiled by a situation that's never talked about, except in vague language, and then usually before somebody is hauled up on charges."

"Clarissa, I've seen them together twice now. It no longer shocks me and frankly I don't care. I like your brother, and wish him happiness. He understands what it means to desire somebody so much you'll do anything to be with them. Turn your thoughts from them and focus on me." He walked over to her and took her in his arms and kissed her on the lips and ran his hands up and down her back.

"I'm scared."

"So am I, but I'll be gentle and we'll experience the love we feel for each other in a different way. It will lock our futures together forever. Now I think you should undress."

"You first."

"I want to watch you, sweetheart. I've dreamed about it for years."

"Women have dreams too. You first, please." She sat down on the end of the bed facing him, her jaw resolute.

Chad took off his outer jacket, then his vest, and his waistband. He bent over and removed his shoes. Then he paused and looked longingly into her eyes. He removed his shirt and undershirt and Clarissa gazed, for the first time, on his bare chest. He was muscular, with a wisp of soft black hair running down to his naval. She clasped her hands tightly together, intently watching him.

Chad took his socks off and unbuttoned his trousers. They were tight fitting so he had to bend over and force them downwards. He extracted both his legs and tossed the pants on a chair. Only his underwear remained. Clarissa let her eyes move slowly down his chest. She looked openly at his midriff and below. "Chad … please. Go on."

Chad removed his shorts and stood completely naked before her, fully aroused. "Now you, Clarissa, now you. I want to watch."

She undressed slowly, casting her dress and petticoats and stockings on the settee. Her thighs and her breasts were still covered. Chad removed first one and then the other of the two remaining garments. He pressed himself hard against her and kissed her and moved her back towards the bed.

She was soft and smooth under him but she breathed hard and her legs and arms rubbed against him. He kissed her throat and the crevice between her breasts and put his tongue in her naval and continued downward. She gave a small cry, and began to thrust up and down with her thighs. He rolled over on his side and she began to kiss his chest and arms and stomach, disdainful now of any restraint, and eager to taste the love they'd both felt for so long a time. Chad cried out as she delighted him in ways he didn't think she knew about, then pulled her face up to his, kissed her moist lips and spread himself on top of her, moving her legs apart and forcing himself upwards and inwards, as she cried softly and shuddered when he completed his advance.

"Nothing will ever separate us now, Clarissa," Chad said. "Nothing."

SIX

February 1863

Dr. Forrest rested his elbow on the headboard as he wiped Marilyn's brow. Seated across from his mother, Chad anxiously rubbed his hand back and forth on a red, blue and green geometrical quilt, made at a Laymus quilting party over a hundred years ago.

"You Laymus's must excuse me for a minute, I need something from my bag." Chad's anxious eyes followed the doctor's every move as he closed the bedroom door behind him.

"Chad, listen to your old aunt. Your mother has much to be displeased about when it comes to me. But she's been steadfast in her loyalty. Her foremost concern has always been for you. They tried to control us, because we were women with independent minds, and when I married Mr. Blaine and moved to New York, they stopped writing to me. I introduced your mother to Franklin Wales."

"Maybe you can tell me Mother's big secret." Chad hesitated and was silenced by his mother.

"Not now, Chad." Harriet's voice was low and gentle, but firm.

"Such a beautiful boy," the invalid said. "You're a Laymus through and through, that's for sure."

"Please don't strain yourself, Aunt Marilyn. You're going to get better." Chad's voice cracked and he squeezed her hand.

"It's your love of truth that made me so proud of you. Don't spoil it now." She expelled a deep breath and lay silent for a while. Then she turned her head towards Harriet. "Chad, would you leave us for a moment?"

"Only for a moment, Aunt Marilyn." He turned his back on the two women, afraid they'd see tears in his eyes. Downstairs in the parlor, Dr.

164

Forrest sorted through bottles and medical tools from his bag, spreading them on the card table, lifting up each vial and looking through it at the pale winter light from the tall windows. The shutters were open, the fire was bright and warm, but the gloom was inescapable.

"Is she going to die?" Chad gulped his words and turned his eyes away from the doctor.

"I'm surprised she's lasted this long. Don't be selfish now. Let her go. The pain is agonizing but I've given her all the drugs I dare to. She's remarkably strong and courageous." Dr. Forrest put his hand on Chad's shoulder. "You're the only male relative here. You must play your role bravely and with great pity for this woman. She loves you more than you'll ever know."

"Where's her husband at a time like this?"

"Drinking at his club, I suppose. He lives there now. You should be glad your engagement is a long one. Hasty marriages are rarely happy."

"Whenever I'm at a dinner party or a ball, there you are, calm and confident and full of humor. You delivered half the people I know and have tended to their families for years. You watch them grow old and get sick, and suffer and die." Chad drew a deep breath. "I don't see how you do it."

"I always wanted to be a good doctor. But medicine has too few solutions. I knew when we diagnosed her cancer it would end like this. If you admire the way I go from the deathbed to the banquet table, perhaps you can learn from it. You're eager and intense and you're blessed with a brilliant mind. I know how hard you've studied, just as I did in my field. But philosophy and literature don't offer many remedies either. For every question answered a bigger question is raised. So I just slog along day by day, trying to bring healing when I can and solace when I can't."

"My Clarissa works with the wounded at Bellevue Hospital. Takes them books, the ones who still have eyes to read. The ones who know how to read. She and Susan Steinmann distribute food and money to the widows and orphans. They sit with them when a soldier dies despite all medical know-how. Doctor Forrest, they're so strong. They don't preach or rant like me. But they keep on doing the right thing."

"Your Clarissa—and you're right, I delivered her too—she's a fountain of affection and warmth. She's strong enough, but she'll need your support as time goes on. Susan Steinmann is another matter. She has those virtues we men usually think of as feminine but she also has a razor-sharp mind, like you. Her father Solomon, a fine and unusual man whom I know quite well, has no sons, you see. And there's so much money there, and such a long tradition of accomplishment since his ancestors came here from Portugal. They helped finance the Revolution, you know."

"You can't have a war without money."

"Surely you'll not dispute the necessity of our war for independence?"

"It's so much easier to accept past wars than present ones."

"Yes," Dr. Forrest said, "and hard to conclude present ones without the fear of future ones."

"What do you mean?"

"You've made much of your knowledge of Hegel. Surely you see in his philosophy the cycles we're blessed, and cursed, with."

"I'm surprised you know Hegel, Doctor. Do you read German?"

"I do, as a matter of fact. And it's helped me a lot with my work in the German community here. I spend one day a week at a clinic downtown. There are fine people among these immigrants, Chad, don't forget it. They're fired with faith and ambition and energy and many of them, the Germans and the Irish and all the rest, will eventually contribute much to our infant nation. For in fact, we're still a young country. I read philosophers like Hegel because I see their work as similar to mine. They are, in effect, trying to diagnose the ills of the world, and they begin by ruling out one possibility after another. Medicine has limited knowledge but it grows slowly and steadily. I start by ruling out whatever can be proved to be absent. Eventually, there are only a few alternatives left. Sometimes I can then make a diagnosis, and in fewer cases, I can treat it. You may want to apply that method to your obsession with Hegel. Simply put, I believe disillusionment is just one more step towards wisdom."

They were interrupted by an outcry from the second floor landing. Chad followed Dr. Forrest up the staircase and into the sickroom. Harriet stood with her hand over her mouth. Marilyn Laymus Blaine was motionless. After holding her wrist for a moment, the weary doctor folded her arms over her chest and covered her face with a sheet.

* * *

They huddled in the carriage, lap robes hugged to the midriff, hands in mittens, necks wrapped in scarves, their breath forming white haloes around them. Higgens wore his coachman's hat and clucked at the horses. The streets were uncrowded in the intense cold, the sky gray but dry.

"I must take charge of the funeral," Harriet said.

"What about her husband?" Chad regretted the question the minute it was out of his mouth.

"I doubt if he'll attend."

"That's awful."

"Not nearly so awful as the way he treated her while she was alive. He's a lot like your father."

"My father's an honorable man. A brave man, too. A hero to his countrymen."

"Don't start in with the war."

"The war's not gone away just because this wonderful crazy woman has died." For a while they swayed and shifted in the jostling carriage without speaking a word.

"Higgens, if you please, go down Fifth. You can let us off at the church on the corner of 10th Street." Harriet settled back in the leather seat, her face stern and noncommittal again. "We'll have the funeral there. It's a good solid Episcopal parish and it's half a block from home."

"She never went to church. You never go to church, and neither do I."

"Where else would we hold a funeral? Besides, I do go to church, in Brooklyn."

"I don't think of that as 'going to church' in the traditional sense, Mother dear."

"Not even the death of a beloved relative will quell your sarcastic tongue. For your information, I've asked Reverend Mullen to conduct the service."

"He's not an Episcopalian."

"It doesn't matter. Our family has given so much money to that church on Fifth they wouldn't dare to contradict my wishes."

"Have you got something on them, too? I suspect you've already learned that sometimes money isn't enough to control people. I want an answer. Aunt Marilyn's gone now. Nobody else can tell me, except perhaps Randall Renfield. I've surmised he's got something to do with it."

"Leave your future uncle-in-law out of this. Leave me out of your conjectures too while you're at it."

"How do you exercise such influence over the Renfields when you can't seem to control your fine old New England Laymus's?"

"My secret is strength of character. And courage. And determination. Aunt Marilyn spent the last thirty years of her life living alone in that house while her husband drinks himself into oblivion at his club. Your father, spouting his high principles, has left me. And abandoned you too, more or less."

"Abandoned me? Me! My father has provided for me in very special ways. And he's got the courage and loyalty to be true to Virginia. Do I have to remind you again that I'm only half Laymus? I'll not listen any longer to your invective, which is surely the standard response of a jilted wife."

"You grow more contemptible every day, and still, as Aunt Marilyn said on her deathbed, we love you more than you know. We're certain you'll eventually see the light and take your rightful place in the world to which you were born. The day will come when you'll gratefully recognize your indebtedness not only to me but to the entire Laymus 'clan' as you call it."

* * *

Chad's first encounter with the rituals of death occurred at the church at Fifth Avenue and 10th Street. Often, when he walked home from playtime in Washington Square, he'd see black-ribboned coaches lined up outside the churchyard. A small flowered space blocked by a wrought-iron fence shielded passersby from the red stone facade, emblematic of an embodied faith that was to his young eyes inscrutable. Only the brilliant stained glass appealed to him, and the flowering trees in the springtime.

But each cortege contributed to his avoidance of that dark finality, and spurred him on to his Greek and Latin studies, which revealed little of the fanciful promise of the New Testament. Majestic elegies in tight metrics, or lyrical laments for fallen comrades, became his only confrontation with the void. At an early age he tried to inure himself to contemporary death.

Still he couldn't escape the black-cloaked drivers and ebony-draped hearses, sobbing mourners behind a casket decked with lilies, the shudder of the organ when the doors opened at the close of that old, and for him, unsatisfying liturgy. The mounting anxiety of his morbid impressions was made worse when Lucifer, his flame-yellow cat with ember-red eyes, followed him into the garden one day when he was eight, and as he watched in horror, pounced upon a small black and white bird, crunching its feathered body in an instant. The snap of tiny bones and the squirts of blood from Lucifer's mouth sickened him. He tried to turn away, but it seemed the cat's eyes had transfixed him with an eternal vision.

Today the church filled steadily with mourners for his outcast aunt, who was enclosed forever now in a polished mahogany coffin, a spray of white flowers on top. They'd wheeled the container down the aisle as the organ played, lead by clerics in vestments, holding high a golden cross that marked their procession through the crowd. Aunt Marilyn, who wasn't received in polite society, had accumulated a vast entourage and they were all here today. Mostly young, mostly well dressed, mostly holding their emotions in check. They were the painters and musicians and writers Aunt Marilyn loved so well, and others like himself, immersed in history and ideas and politics, lovers of literature and the arts, a mostly privileged white upper crust who had the time to dally and made the most of it. However superficial their discussions might often seem, Chad couldn't doubt the sincerity of the grief of those mourners Marilyn Laymus Blaine had left behind.

Susan Steinmann was there with Eliza Van Der Venner, Schuyler and Marcus, of course. Clarissa sat with her Uncle Randall, having decided it more seemly for Chad to escort and comfort his black-dressed mother. And there were others he could neither recognize nor explain, officious looking men, portly, tall, more cheaply dressed, standing at various strategic positions, looking more often at the crowd than towards the altar.

Chad was discomforted by the mix of feelings inspired by this diverse assembly, and the continuing news of disaster on battlefields and at sea. Sorrowful images branded his eyes whenever he drove past Bellevue Hospital. Today, there was too much distraction from the pageantry and the quiet tears and vibrating music to allow him to review his own private mental elegies. But his mind leapt outward from the well-tended church in its privileged plot on lower Fifth Avenue, as if his thoughts were great speckled birds caught on a gust of wind, sent southward and westward towards the bloodied fields of Virginia and Maryland, and the shell-pocked ports of his father's Southern homeland.

What he struggled with, he realized finally, was his powerlessness before the resolute advance of human history and the symbolic stages of his own finite life, now pressuring him away from his bookish youth, flaunting before his eyes that inevitable terminus. His unflinching gaze was fixed upon a common unavoidable fate, fueling his rampant sense of outrage for those who lay rotting in the swamps and on the mountainsides and pasturelands of war.

To refute his mother's disdain for his preference for Winslow Homer's artistic woodcut impressions of the troops in battle, he spent a morning looking intently at the strongly contrasting photographs in Mr. Brady's studio. He knew he'd never erase them from his mind.

He saw the dead, mostly teenaged boys and men in their twenties, draped over a cannon, arms hanging down like willow branches in winter. Bodies piled up in such number and in such proximity it was difficult to see what hand belonged to which corpse. Close-ups of the slain displayed gaping mouths, bodies distended in grotesque poses by the festering gases within them as their bodies putrefied before there was time to dig a shallow grave. He saw wagonloads of bodies carted off to the railway station, for those who were deemed important enough, and fresh enough, to be transported to their native soil, from which they'd soon be indistinguishable.

He closed his eyes but the images grew more distinct. He blinked his eyelids, rubbed the moisture away, dabbed at his face with a handkerchief, sneaking a look around him to see who was watching. But all eyes were on the pulpit, except those peering visages of the anonymous officials who dotted the crowd.

Reverend Mullen had donned vestments not unlike those of his Episcopal colleagues. After a prescribed set of words and movements, which had the attendees rising and kneeling and sitting again, the Brooklyn preacher began.

"I'm unknown to most of you, having given all my responsibilities over to a small church in Brooklyn, where we pursue the Holy Task of abolition. My purpose today, having been asked to officiate by the deceased's niece, Harriet Laymus Wales, is to find solace in our shared vision of the Christ, and to extract meaning and moral purpose from every death we witness in our brief sojourn on this planet."

"I know only a little about her, but I can see from the eager young faces here today that this energetic and intelligent woman has inspired a large number of you to find your purpose in life. You're her progeny, since she had no children of her own. You're the ones who must take from her that which she's freely left you, a desire to find a common ethic, an urge to embody our scant knowledge of God's purposes in immortal forms, whether it be painting or sculpture or architecture. Whether it be song or symphony. Whether it be verse or novel or insightful prose. None of us should feel we've lived and died in vain. My plea, in honor of this woman, is that each of you examine your conscience for your personal purpose and then stick to that mission with all your will power and humility and talent. That's what she'd have wanted and that's what I'm honored to request from you."

Mullen sat down, the organ played again, and the presiding rector, whom Chad had seen at his house over the years at Harriet's few and usually small dinners, stood at the pulpit and announced a surprise speaker. "Although he's not of our faith and although his superiors frown on participation in other forms of worship, he was a friend of our departed sister and visited her often for the stimulus of creative minds and lofty aspirations referred to by Reverend Mullen. He's a Catholic priest and I acknowledge our common Book and our common Cross when I invite him to speak to you today."

Father Fineas Flaherty was simply dressed, his black suit and white collar alone testifying to his vocation, the bright gold cross missing today. He seemed awkward and embarrassed. His voice, when he finally began, was soft, but he could be heard, nonetheless, in even the furthest reaches of the sanctuary.

"There are those among you who'll mourn this woman's passing and who'll sorely miss her encouragement and her patronage. I come to speak only of her gifts to me. She included me among her guests during an age in which there's strong opposition between faiths. I'm an Irish immigrant and I work at a church near Five Points. My job is to deal on a daily basis with the downtrodden, the destitute, the hopeless and those who have known little help on life's journey. I say without hesitation that most of you here are privileged, compared to my flock. Most of you have known a sounder and safer material life, and many of you are not only well educated but also talented and creative.

I ask of you only one thing. As we share our grief at the inescapable end of each human life, and as we contemplate with hope, and in some cases doubt, the promise of a glorious resurrection, I implore you not to turn your backs on the great loss that surrounds all of us."

Chad anticipated a reference to the war and turned to look triumphantly at his mother, but her head was bowed and her face obscured by a black handkerchief. He gazed around the room and was surprised to catch the steely eyes of Bynum Bradley-West, sitting in the pew behind Schuyler and Marcus. There was a flash of recognition between them and then Bynum stared intently at Father Fineas.

"This war has already claimed more American lives than all the wars we've ever fought. Reverend Mullen is a champion of those who are enslaved and how can we not feel sympathy for that great cause? At the same time, I beg you to look into your hearts as you witness the mounting tragedy of this war. Our government has passed a conscription act, providing that names be drawn from a lottery and those chosen sent to the field of battle. Many will be maimed there, others will die there. And our government has added a codicil to this draft law, a simple provision that anybody with three hundred dollars to spare can buy his way out, by hiring a substitute or by contributing that sum to the war effort."

"For most of my parish, three hundred dollars is an unimaginable sum. Few of them have ever seen such an amount, much less earned it. In my church we've instigated a charitable fund, from which we'll try to provide the three hundred dollars for selected draftees, those who have families to support, those who have important roles to play here at home, and those—although they're few—whose conscience won't allow them to kill another human being. It was Marilyn Laymus Blaine's last will and testament that I be asked to deliver this message to you here today. She's left, in her estate, a significant sum to be used for the purposes I've described, and demanded that I speak to you today on this subject and encourage you to give as much as you can, when you can, so we may at least help young fathers and those who are the parents' only child, to enjoy the same privilege given to the rich. A way out, at least temporarily, from the bloodbath of human destiny."

A murmur raced through the crowd, like a sudden small wind in a summer field. Heads inclined towards each other in whispers. The stolid and mysterious officials peppering the room looked back and forth at each other. Then only silence ensued, to be broken by a final hymn, sung by the standing congregation, to the wall-shaking chords of the organ. Chosen by Reverend Mullen, it was the Battle Hymn of the Republic.

* * *

Sliding double doors connected Harriet's dining room, parlor and drawing room. Today they were all opened to accommodate the crowd from the church, standing solemnly about the rooms, cups in hand. Plates of sweets adorned table and mantelpiece. Voices were subdued, Harriet moved among the guests like a skiff among warships, and Mullen, Chad believed, seemed especially at home in his mothers' house. Tired of ceremony and emotion, Chad sought peace of mind with Clarissa. They squeezed closely together on a bench and a slipper chair in a corner between the front window and the fireplace. She held his hand.

"I'm so sorry for you, sweetheart. You don't have a big family so the loss of a single member of it is heartbreaking."

"It's true that I'm deeply troubled by her passing. I'm also troubled with the direction our country is going in, especially this war."

"I spoke with Father at length last night. I told him we're determined to marry, war or no war. I said you and I would build our own house at Yellowfields, and if he didn't like it I'd buy land from the Van Der Venner's and build our home there. Eliza is willing to facilitate such a sale. There are competent local architects. I can afford it."

"I'm a little uncomfortable with your paying for everything."

"Why not? A bride's dowry belongs to her husband. It's always been like that. It would be like that even if you were richer than I am. I told Father as much."

"What did he say?"

"He said that while my current forty thousand a year is a lot, I should be careful about the future. He said we're going to suffer terrible inflation, that the change in currency to greenbacks may devastate fixed incomes and I had best hearken to his wishes in order to get all the money that will come to me when he's gone."

"It's like a transaction on the Exchange, then. He looks at us as principal."

"Does it matter? We've known the joys of conjugal love. We'll no doubt know them again. I'm yours, completely. What difference does it make if we've got a piece of paper or not?"

"I wish I was as sure as you about the future?"

"Are you at least as sure as I about our love?"

"Clarissa, never doubt me. You're the one sure thing in my life. Without you, I'd sink and drown, I'm sure of it."

She lowered her gaze. "I'll pretend to be the proper young lady. We'll observe their rituals when we ourselves are observed. But when we're alone, we belong only to each other. I'll let you sneak into my bedroom at night, if you want. We could do it at Yellowfields. I'll use Schuyler and Marcus to help us meet elsewhere. I'd even spend the night in an hotel, if that should be your desire."

"I couldn't ask it of you."

"Then perhaps I'd ask it of you." She gripped his hand again, rose to her feet, and mingled with the crowd. Across the room, seemingly in conversation with Reverend Mullen, Bynum eyed him intensely, conveying with his expression a need to talk. Chad moved to the dining room buffet and pretended to be interested in the food. Bynum joined him shortly.

"Aren't you afraid to be seen with me in my own home?"

"I'm known to have been a friend of your aunt's. If I failed to show up at the funeral and the reception it might look even curiouser to those Pinkerton men."

"Pinkerton men?"

"There were at least six of them at the funeral. Lincoln has created a secret service, headed by this detective Pinkerton—I think he's from Chicago—and their agents are all around us. They watch every move I make. We should act as if we're hardly acquainted but as gentlemen, we're exchanging polite chitchat on the occasion of this solemn event. But they're closing in on me, and I in turn am making progress with our plan for insurgency. We must meet tomorrow, at the usual place. I'll tell Madam Maureen to make the usual arrangements, so you'll be fully relaxed when we talk afterwards."

March 1863

"Madam Maureen put me up for the night," Bynum said. "We can't go on meeting here during the day. I'm sure the house is watched. If you and I and Captain Hartigan are discovered here at the same time, the jig is up." Bynum wore a dressing gown and sat in the library drinking coffee and biting a biscuit between words.

"Is it the Pinkerton men?" Chad asked.

"Or ex-Pinkerton men. They're officially the Secret Service now and they'll do anything Lincoln tells them to do. I wanted to see you here early, before Hartigan arrives. I don't think they'll connect you yet with him. But this is the last time. From now on, it will have to be coded messages, mostly verbal information from my emissaries, and an occasional face-to-face in some random location."

"What am I to do?"

Bynum hesitated, looking directly into Chad's eyes, as if to anticipate his reaction. "We need more information for a plan that's months away, but which must be coordinated now, before our agents are discovered and before the Secret Service grows so large it can spy on anybody any time. I told you that my contacts are convinced we must give the Northerners a taste of their own medicine. As you know their tactics in the South have been brutal, to say the least."

"But aren't the Confederates doing the same? I hear stories of rebel raiding parties. It's disgusting. Women and children. Farms burned. Everything."

"The difference is that the raiders are more or less on their own. Renegades go on a rampage in any war. But the tactics of the North are said to be sanctioned by the military hierarchy. Look at what happened at Fredericksburg last November. Two armies lined up on either side of the Rappahannock. McClellan in charge because Lincoln likes him, and Burnside, an incompetent general if ever there was one, straining to call attention to himself. Lee was acting purely in defense. The battle went on for several days and nothing was gained. It was an idiotic repetition, every day, of war's most galling folly. They kept shelling until the town was needlessly destroyed. When the Yankee soldiers finally got across the river, the citizens had fled in terror, leaving their homes and foodstuffs and family keepsakes. They'd leveled the town without purpose, and whatever was left was destroyed by the troops. They got drunk in the wine cellars; they broke mirrors and smashed pianos and ransacked larders and burned books and clothes, even family portraits. It was wanton destruction, it was wasteful and cruel and stupid."

"I wonder if my father was with General Lee."

"No word from him as yet. But we'll demonstrate that we can strike where it hurts, in their cities. In their financial centers. In their halls of government. In public institutions. In shops and stores and trains and omnibuses." Bynum lit a cigar, blowing coils of gray smoke into the morning air. "To do this we need information. Right now I want you to start collecting details about several targets here in New York. We've got others doing the same in Boston, Philadelphia and Washington, to start with."

"What kind of information?"

"Floor plans of the buildings. Ingress and egress. How they're guarded. Visibility of the interiors from the street. Lighting. When the workers come and go. And in some cases, how the general public comes and goes, the hours, the numbers of people."

"The general public?"

"Yes. Some of our attacks will involve civilians."

"But that's unspeakable. I'm not sure I could …" Chad's voice trailed off as he looked away from Bynum's face.

"I warned you of this. You have split loyalties. I knew that when I recruited you. But you're a man of reason. You believe that we can force our citizens and our government into a negotiated peace. To do this we need to strike them where it hurts. Even the politicians who want peace fall silent on the real issues. Patriotism is in the air, flag-waving and bands playing. And now this attempt to convince the masses that slavery is the real reason they started this war. People in the limelight are afraid to take a stand. But if we launch lightening incursions in a single week in several cities, they'll be frightened. The people will clamor for some kind of settlement. Then we can bring both sides to the conference table, just as you've always wanted."

"It's very hard for me to accept the fact that these actions may result in the death of women and children."

"Women and children are already being killed. And more will fall as the troops grow bitter and undisciplined. You know better than most people, from your wide reading, that war brings out the worst in people."

"What targets do you want me to scout for you?"

"I've got a list here. There are several banks and department stores. Hotels and office buildings. City Hall, if you can make notes without drawing attention to yourself. And Barnum's Museum."

"Barnum's Museum? Why? It's just a sideshow, a carnival kind of place, a diversion for families who can't afford to go anywhere else."

"Exactly. Look, Chad, the Irish are almost in arms already. Dissension is rampant down there, especially with the new draft law. William Tweed has taken over the political machine. He finessed it with Tammany Hall. He'll try to control the Irish and maybe the Germans too. We're not sure where he stands on the war but he's started a low-interest loan fund for the poor to help them buy their way out of the draft. He can't run the city without his Irish voters. And the Irish are worried about other things too. Ever since the Emancipation Proclamation went into effect there've been rumors of unrest with the immigrant workers. They're afraid the Negroes will come north and take away their jobs."

"But there are already Negroes in the North."

"Indeed! And their lives are also endangered if there's rioting and more violence. Lincoln's a master politician. I'm not sure whether or not he's actually a thoughtful man trying any means he can to effect his goal, which he admits is the preservation of the Union. But we're now supposed to believe his purpose is the freedom of slaves. Yet his edict affects only slaves in the rebel states. He's even given the rebel states a way out. If they rejoin the Union and take oaths of loyalty, the Emancipation Proclamation won't affect them."

"That seems to me a very cynical move."

"Cynical, political—what's the difference? The truth is, not a single state has taken him up on the offer. The South feels it's an invaded land, it's fighting for its life. Issues are muddled right now. Reason is not prevailing on either side. But if we bomb some of their buildings and kill some of their civic leaders, they might come to their senses. Here's the list. Get as much information as you can on each of them. Captain Hartigan will be your new contact. He'll call at your office downtown, ostensibly to discuss finances. Tweed's boys all have investments. They're more like brokers than politicians. And since the corruption is so widespread and so lucrative, even the Secret Service won't be surprised to see a captain of police doing business with a rising young financier like yourself." Bynum ground his cigar into an ashtray and laughed quietly.

They heard Captain Hartigan's boisterous voice in the front hall. He was now familiar enough to find his own way around Madam Maureen's house, and soon poked his head through the open library door. "Ah, there you are. I had an amusing trip over. These new Pinkerton men think they can put something over on a New York City police captain with twenty years of experience. They're watching police headquarters now, can you believe it? The commissioner has protested to the mayor over the idea of federal lawmen hounding city officials. Actually, I rather enjoy it. I led them on a wild goose chase through taverns and shops and finally lost them in that big new department store on Astor Place."

"Even so, there's at least one of them watching this house right now," Bynum said. "I came in the dead of night and stayed over. This is the last time we can meet here. Things are heating up."

"Heating up is putting it mildly. Have you heard the news, about the Confederate privateers?" Captain Hartigan's words suggested reproach. "Privately owned ships have been authorized by the South to attack Northern merchant vessels on the high seas. They've destroyed several and the word on Wall Street is that if the politicians don't do something to protect them, they'll take matters into their own hands. It puts more pressure on me in a way, since I answer to Tammany Hall."

"What else would you expect?" Bynum said. "That's the way we fought the War of 1812. Besides they're talking out of both sides of their mouth as usual. I have it on good authority that over fifty New York merchant vessels have arrived at Mexican ports. The goods, including clothes and weapons and medical supplies, are simply transported to ships bound for whatever Southern port they can get into. Leave it to the merchant bankers to find a way to profit no matter who wins!"

Chad had an intense urge to press his palms against both ears, the way he did when he was a child and violent street noises disturbed his inner recitations. "Surely it will soon be over. Governor Seymour has ordered every regiment available to Pennsylvania to stem the anticipated invasion. At the same time he's publicly advocating for peace. Isn't anybody listening?"

"There's a silent core of citizens out there who see through it all and who want the killing stopped. But the political bosses, here and in Washington, have their own agenda. There's no other way but to strike them close to home. Captain Hartigan, your cooperation in this is, I know, both perilous and awkward for you personally. For that reason, we've doubled our deposits in your accounts this month and I've got a personal bonus for you right here." Bynum handed Hartigan an envelope bulging with greenbacks.

"These are greenbacks,' Hartigan said. "They've fallen to seventy-eight cents on the dollar."

"All the more reason to go out and spend your bonus right away. Your accounts are being fed specie payments, even though no New York bank has paid off in gold for almost two years. I'm being candid with you, Captain, we need your help in this endeavor. Both sides seem determined to fight to the last man. If we can get their attention with a few incidents like the ones we discussed, we'll strike terror into their hearts and it may be possible to bring this ill-advised conflict to a political end." Bynum sat quietly for a moment, shifting in his chair. "There's no joy for any of us in these monstrous initiatives. When they're both wrong, what difference does it make which side you're on?"

"It's not which side," Chad said eagerly, seeing a way to justify his own wavering commitment. "We're against the war, not the North or the South. We'll do whatever it takes to end it."

"Perhaps. Now, Captain, you should leave immediately. Chad will spend some time upstairs in pleasant diversions while I finish my breakfast and depart in a closed carriage. Gentlemen, when next we meet, let's hope we see peace on the horizon."

April 1863

Captain Hartigan looked around Chad's office, obviously impressed, but waiting for Chad to speak first. "Captain Hartigan, I need to get this over with before someone comes in. Bynum thinks I may be under surveillance."

"Relax, my boy. I recognize a plainclothesman when I see one, and there was nobody out front." Captain Hartigan had removed his military style hat and his overcoat with epaulets, and a pair of white gloves that came almost to his elbows. He looked tired. "You got anything to drink?"

"A little brandy. I don't drink much." Chad took the bottle from the small antique sideboard his mother had insisted on giving him from heirlooms stored in their crowded basement. He slid the brandy across the table to his guest, along with a small snifter, which Hartigan turned slowly with his fingers, admiring it before pouring a hefty drink for himself.

"This whole thing's supposed to be a front so you can pass me information if you want to, but to tell the truth, I'd like to know what I should invest in. I can't touch the gold in London until after the war. You grew up a rich boy, you know about these matters." There was a note of resentment in the Captain's throaty voice.

"We have some start-up endeavors, but it's risky. I suggest you stick with older companies. And the war is affecting the market. I was told by my colleagues down the hall that the New York Stock Exchange is now second only to London."

"Maybe so, but from where I sit things don't look promising. Food prices have doubled already, and some of the stuff you buy isn't any good. They're putting something into the coffee now, to stretch it out. And even the loaves of bread are smaller. Lots of carpenters downtown are out of work because construction has slowed down, and that means more poor people in the tenements. Rents are rising. My relatives in the Old Country are facing another bad potato crop so we'd best brace for an onslaught. I know you come from a different background from me but I'm in this thing strictly for the money. I intend to end up with enough gold in London to go back and buy the estate my family slaved on for generations, from the time the English occupied our land. They worked for pennies, and sure they were loyal and loved Old Ireland, but how can you stay put when your stomach's growling and the kids are crying for milk and there's no bread for the school boy's lunch? Do you think Bynum's promises are any good?"

"If Bynum tells you the money's there, then it's there." Chad felt uneasy defending his fellow conspirator.

"Gold's up again here. I read where there's over a hundred millionaires in New York now. Some of them's got more than fifteen million! All I want is my fair share. What with prices rising and the greenback falling, I need investments here and access to my gold over there. Can you help me with that?"

"I could but I shouldn't. It's too dangerous."

"I heard of this man Appleby, he wasn't born rich but he's made a lot on the stock market and I've got friends who are investing with him. Is he on the up and up?"

"Appleby? I don't know much about him, I'm afraid. I'll ask around. Right now we've got to go over this information. I've checked out some of the office buildings and banks and a government agency or two. I've clearly marked the schedules I recommend. There are times when the buildings are almost empty. I think it would be safer and more humane to have the insurgents place their bombs in such a way that innocent people aren't killed."

"I don't know any innocent people," Hartigan said.

"I'm not being philosophical about this, Captain. I'd like to think we won't stoop to the level of barbarians in attempting to end this war."

"It's Bynum's call."

"I'm quite aware it's Bynum's call. But there comes a time when you have to examine your own conscience."

"He wants you to meet with the fellows who'll be carrying the firebombs. In person. He thinks it would reassure you to know these people are professionals and that they're acting out of a sincere desire to end the war. That's what he told me to tell you."

"You saw him recently?"

"Last night. We crossed on the ferry to Brooklyn and talked on the docks and then we came back to Manhattan on different boats."

"Why would Bynum want to meet in Brooklyn? There are plenty of dark streets and unknown taverns in Manhattan."

"He's got a place over there now, Bynum has. Sure and it's a smart thing for him to do, now. His old rooms are watched around the clock. I passed by there the other day. I could spot two of Pinkerton's men from a block away. Amateurs, if you ask me."

"When you see Bynum tell him it may be possible for me to see him in Brooklyn. My mother goes to church in Brooklyn."

"Why would she do that?"

"Captain, please, let's not waste valuable time in chit chat." Chad paused and then felt obliged to explain. "My mother is active in the abolitionist movement and she works with a church over there."

"Makes it kind of difficult for you, lad, I'm saying."

"My sole purpose in collaborating in this plan is to end the war. After the two sides come together to talk, it's certain slavery will be on the docket."

"Everybody says it's Mr. Lincoln's war. And he ain't that clear, sure, of where he's standing. Fellow I know heard him give a speech in Connecticut years ago when he condemned slavery outright. Then he releases these statements, like that letter in Mr. Greeley's paper, that slavery is not the issue in this war. And his cabinet is divided, too, a friend of mine in Tammany has told me. By golly, it's a pack of leprechauns, the lot of them."

"Will you promise to take this information to Bynum, and to tell him how much I urge him to abide by it? The fewer people are hurt, the better. And tell him I'll come to Brooklyn. He can arrange it through you."

Chad's outer door burst open suddenly and Randall Renfield stuck his head in, then withdrew a moment upon seeing Captain Hartigan. After a minute he came back in, warily and with an eye on the policeman. "Sorry, lad, I didn't know you were in a meeting. "

"This is Captain Hartigan. He's a policeman."

"I can see that. How do you do, Captain."

Randall, not waiting to be asked, pulled out another chair and sat down at the table. "Is there something afoot here that might be of interest to you, Captain?"

"Surely Sir, I'll be putting aside a portion of my salary from time to time, to save for my old age, you know. I was referred to a man named Appleby. I thought perhaps I could find better advice here."

"Ah yes, Appleby. We sometimes work with him. How much would you like to invest?"

Captain Hartigan turned a skeptical eye towards Chad. "I thought you said you didn't know this Appleby."

"I said I didn't know him well. My uncle here works with him whenever there's a new offering. New stock, Captain, in start-up companies."

"Is there money to be made that way?"

"Well, Captain, it depends on how much you want to invest," Randall said. "But Chad's right. We work with Appleby the same way you would. He's an agent, and he sells our stock for us. You'd perhaps be better off dealing directly with him."

"Where can I find this Appleby?"

"I'll give you his card. If you mention my name he'll treat you fair and square."

"I'm a New York City police captain. I don't think anybody would be so bold as to treat me otherwise."

The door opened again, revealing Caleb Laymus, grown heavier since his last visit, still red faced, and out of breath. "They told me down the hall you'd be in here, Randall. They said you were conferring with the police."

"Not conferring exactly. This is my colleague and Chad's uncle, Caleb Laymus. Caleb, may I introduce Captain Hartigan? He's a long-serving officer who's managed to put a little by over the years and has sought advice from the President of our various companies. I of course told him he might be better off going directly to our agent on Wall Street."

"Better hurry then," Caleb blurted out. "Somebody's just took a shot at him."

"Again?" Randall seemed unsurprised.

"Just as he was coming out of Delmonico's. Missed him, of course. Some of these investors, Captain Hartigan, are averse to risk and shouldn't deplete their capital if they can't absorb the losses. Frankly, I'd say that goes for you as well."

"You're saying they tried to kill this man Appleby?" Captain Hartigan assumed an astonished expression but it wasn't convincing either to Caleb or Randall.

"Of course, as a preserver of the domestic tranquility you no doubt are frequently called upon to investigate these unfortunate incidents. Have you met Drew? Or Gould?"

"I know them only by name, Sir. But you can be assured that other officers are involved on a daily basis in protecting the members of the Exchange."

"Never go there myself. It's like buying a substitute for the draft. Why go into battle if you can send somebody else." Randall smirked and looked at Caleb, who was not amused.

"We mustn't treat these incidents lightly, Captain Hartigan. I suppose you were as alarmed as the general public about the murder of one of your own, down by Five Points last fall."

Chad felt tension in his chest and a fever in his imagination, even before he heard more. "What are you referring to, Uncle Caleb?"

"Wasn't it in the papers down here? This story was circulated widely in Boston, where we try not to acknowledge such breeches of decorum."

"Breeches of decorum, Sir? I believe you'll agree that this man—my fellow officer—sacrificed his life in the line of duty."

"Was that the case? The Boston stories were brief. Didn't even mention his name."

"Who was murdered?" Chad hoped there was no anxiety in his voice. He looked directly at Hartigan as he spoke.

"A new man, named Mueller. German chap. Dietrich, I think his first name was. It's a tragedy, of course, to lose one of your own. But our officers are brave and fully aware of the dangers. It's their idealism and their rigorous honesty that spurs us on. I attended the funeral myself, as a gesture of respect. We preferred to keep it out of the local papers. Such incidents discourage new recruits."

"Dietrich Mueller?" Chad asked. "How was he killed?"

"As I say, in the line of duty. He came upon a gang of ragtags in an alleyway near Five Points. They were robbing an old merchant from the area, beating the life out of him. Mueller blew his whistle for help but plunged bravely into the fray. He was stabbed to death."

"Did he live to tell you the details?" Chad turned his face away, gazing through the window at an abstract pattern of chimneys and rooftops.

"Oh no, he died almost immediately. And the gang members were of course gone when other officers arrived. But there was a cook from one of those taverns down there. He was taking a break in the alley, having a smoke. He saw it all and told our man how the sorry incident unfolded."

"You'll of course track down and apprehend the perpetrators," Randall said.

"We'll do our best. But it's not easy in that part of town. Nobody wants to come forth with descriptions and once they're hidden away we may never find them"

"But you said there was an eye witness." Chad spoke the words slowly, with his eyes downcast.

"It happened fast, so he was unable to describe the gang. Or to identify it. Most gangs have names. Some sport insignias or slogans. One or two gangs, I believe, have even paid for special flags to be designed. I'm sorry to say that many of them are Irish. They're poor uneducated immigrants who grow up under adverse circumstances and find themselves drawn into a life of crime. I'm proud to say that many of them are also attracted to law-enforcement. Our ranks are swelled by these young idealists who sacrifice everything to maintain order in our great city."

"Well, Captain, all of us here have nothing but praise for and confidence in our police force. I hope you'll be able to find Appleby to counsel you on investments. He's laying low right now, I believe that's the way they put it, but he'll be back on the floor of the Exchange before the week is out. As a uniformed officer you should be able to get in touch with him there. Tell him I said to keep you out of anything that's overly risky. We take care of our own, too, you know. Now I'm sorry to say that we must end this meeting, since Mr. Renfield and myself, and my nephew, have urgent matters to discuss."

Captain Hartigan shook hands with Chad, nodded at Randall and Caleb, put his hat and gloves on quickly, stopped again at the door to touch his hand to the brim of his headpiece and closed the door behind him.

"Caleb, really. I don't believe you should be so forthcoming in front of strangers. Especially policemen."

"In fact, Randall, I suspected he might be nosing about for information we would prefer he not have. There's been some talk of involving the police in these investigations. I've come down from Boston to examine our situation personally. In truth, I think we should get rid of some of the records we're storing in here. Especially regarding that Ohio foundry."

"Appleby just sold over five hundred thousand dollars worth of Class B stock in that company."

"Nevertheless we should close it down. We'll say the government withdrew its contracts. Blame it on cronyism. Say Lincoln wanted the contracts to go to an old time outfit run by leftover Whigs. We're all making so much money in legitimate ways now it's hardly necessary to continue with these other initiatives. We both know they were a bit speculative."

"Uncle Caleb, are you telling me you knew all along that we would end up being investigated?"

"I never feared we might be investigated because there's nobody to investigate us. The Congress is preoccupied with their own disputes, the

Governor's off on his peace-at-any-price crusade. Policemen like Hartigan are too busy finding ways to invest their surplus cash. Who would think they'd bother to look at us? But just in case, we destroy the records now, and make contingency plans."

"What kind of contingency plans," Randall asked.

"We don't know how the war will end or when it will end. Tempers are flaring. People are on the verge of anarchy here in New York. There may be riots. We'd be logical targets, to their way of thinking. And even if there's no immediate danger, think what will happen when the war is over. There'll be calls for investigations. Wartime brutality. Illegal arrests. Spies. And us, we're looked upon as money changers and the mob will want our blood."

"Money changers? We're not in the same league as those …" Randall's voice broke off as he recognized the conflict in his own view of the matter.

"Yes," Caleb said, "We must be prepared for the worst. That's always my philosophy, hope for the best but prepare for the worst."

"You've got a plan, then," Randall asked.

"We might be better off in Canada. I have some relatives there already, Tory families who fled after the Revolution. They're shippers and bankers now, in St. John and Halifax. Their currency is stable and there seems to be peace in the land. It's a vast land, like our own, and full of opportunities. Quebec's a bit of a problem. Do you speak French, Chad?"

"Fluently," Chad said with pride before he realized where the question might take him.

"I've begun to transfer some of my accounts to Canadian banks. My father, known as Brickwall Bartleby to the Boston Brahmins, disapproves of my entrepreneurial adventures and threatens to disassociate himself from me and all our initiatives. But I've trumped him on this. I've arranged to establish some textile mills up there. They'll be closer to the cotton than England or France, when the war ends. And I'm still relatively young. Perhaps I'll marry a Canadian and create a family of my own."

"My brother Phillipse has made his distaste for me known to his inner circle but such news travels fast in the banking world. He forgets I'm a skillful lawyer. I, too, have begun the transfer of some of my holdings. I thought London would be best, but perhaps you're right. Canada."

"It's right next door," Caleb urged.

"Exactly."

May 1863

"It's like a conspiracy," Clarissa said. She turned her head quickly towards her lover, her curls swirling around her neck. "The four of us, think of it!"

"But not in a negative sense," Marcus said. They were assembled in the upstairs sitting room of the Renfield Mansion. Lunch was over with, the warm spring day was more pastoral than perky, and the aura of intrigue and romance heavy in the air. Schuyler now allowed himself to squeeze the hand of his bosom friend without embarrassment, and Marcus would often pat Schuyler on the head or run his hands through his lover's hair, as if he were frolicking with a pet.

"Not negative, but frustrating even so," Chad said. "Clarissa and I want to set the date, even though we're enjoying our private moments together. You understand that we both intend to keep up at least the illusion of propriety."

"Dear boy," Marcus exclaimed, "we're all proper here."

"That's right," Schuyler said defiantly. "We're faithful. We're discreet. We don't hurt anybody else. It's nobody's business but ours."

"How about Father," Clarissa said, more as a conclusion than a question. "He evades me when I try to pin him down on a date. And he hasn't discussed your plans to move to France at all. He just scowls at both of us, brother and sister, his only children. The world's grown quite bizarre."

"It's not just the war, either," Chad said. "Our generation is facing a new and different world."

"But isn't that just perfect," Marcus asked. "Let's be honest here. All four of us are financially independent. We're all educated. We've experienced what passes for high society. All wars eventually end. And then there'll be explosive growth in this country, think of it! Lincoln's trying to get Congress to encourage more immigration. The railroads from the Pacific and from the East will eventually meet up somewhere in Kansas or Nebraska or wherever. The South will need to be rebuilt. Lincoln may finally get his central bank, the one his New York City supporters have been planning all along. They wanted a central bank and more tariffs, that's why they put him in office. So we'll see the money supply expand. Look at it this way—neither Schuyler nor I need power or social position. We'll live well but fairly cheaply in Paris. We'll have friends, go to the theater, travel on the continent and to England, enjoy each other's affection, and we'll write or paint or collect things. I can still afford some gifts to charity every year, even if my family found out and turned me away—which they dare not do anyway without raising a scandal in Cleveland."

"Were you a scandal in Cleveland," Clarissa asked.

"Don't be coy. Let's not do anything to dispel the warmth and loyalty and mutual support we've established together. Brother and sister, husband and wife, lover and friend. We all know in our hearts that we're doing no wrong, and that we'll probably have a comfortable, even a happy, future." Marcus sipped his tea and smacked his lips. "We've nothing to feel guilty about."

Chad looked away from his friends, towards the double windows opening upon the rear courtyard, devoid of bright light and made darker by heavy curtains and thick draperies. "Sin of commission, sin of omission. I'm not sure I'm as comfortable as you. This war haunts me. And my father is of course in the midst of it. The casualties are appalling, on both sides. It should end sooner rather than later. I feel we should commit ourselves to action."

"What kind of action? Do you think the war would end sooner if Marcus and I enlisted and went to the front? Or if you left Clarissa pining away at Yellowfields while you rushed off to the battlefield? I say it's Mr. Lincoln's war. Let them hash it out and let us get on with our plans. We're the new generation. We must make our own future." Schuyler was more relaxed now with his opinions. But when he looked at Chad there was a flash of recognition of their shared secret. They both knew that the blackmailer Dietrich Mueller was dead, cut to pieces in a gang fight near Five Points. But neither of them wanted to face the possibility that it could have been emissaries of Captain Hartigan, carried out with Bynum's money in expectation of their help with seditious schemes.

"I'll leave philosophy to you boys while I face the real problem, which is Father, pure and simple." Clarissa stood up and poured more tea for the men in her life. Her eyes revealed a new sense of independence. She appeared unruffled by the presence of males who knew she was intimate with her betrothed. She managed to exude confidence even with the knowledge that her brother and his friend were also engaged in an intimacy that would shock their social circle and incur legal charges if the truth were known. She bounced around the room, certain of their respect and approval, and in Chad's case, of passion. "What're we going to do about Father?"

"Do you think we should have it out with him?" Marcus smiled slyly in anticipation of such a scene.

"All of us at once?" Schuyler looked towards his sister with both glee and fear. "What if he came right out and asked about Marcus and me, the details, I mean."

"He'd never do that in my presence," Clarissa said.

"He's angry about everything, I suspect," Chad said. "Randall and he are hardly speaking, and my Uncle Caleb, who used to meet with Phillipse on financial matters, seems not to be calling anymore."

"But don't you see," Marcus went on. "We're not responsible for whatever devious financial schemes our families are concocting. You want to get married.

Schuyler and I want to live together in France. We can put it that way, without any details. If he should be so bold as to ask, we can play innocent. Schuyler and I are young, still, and want to enjoy our bachelor days abroad. You and Clarissa are deeply in love and frustrated because you can't be joined in Holy Matrimony!" Marcus threw his head back, laughing.

"He's home today," Clarissa said. "He told me he wanted to lunch here and rest before those government people arrive in the afternoon. There's to be some sort of discussion with the Treasury Department and one of Lincoln's personal aides. Something about another bond issue, he said."

"Let's go to him now, then," Marcus said. He was on his feet, smoothing his puffy white shirt and waistband, picking up his coat from the back of a chair, and casting a commanding look in Schuyler's direction.

Chad was reluctant, but also tired. He didn't want to reveal the dark nature of his own involvement in the war, or his plan to end it. Facing up to Phillipse Renfield on the question of his wedding now seemed to him to be the tamest of his alternatives. "Very well then, let's go."

They descended the broad curve of the front stairs, Clarissa and Chad in front, holding hands, and Marcus and Schuyler trailing behind them, walking so close that their shoulders rubbed together as they made the final turn at the landing in the grand foyer. But as they approached the front parlor, where the doors were tightly closed, they heard loud voices. Phillipse was in some sort of confrontation already, and Chad, his heart sinking, recognized the voice of his mother. Impelled now with a lifelong fury he opened the doors without knocking, and marched in front of his entourage directly to the center of the room.

Harriet was seated, but leapt to her feet when the young people advanced towards her. Phillipse had been facing the fireplace, unlit in the warm spring weather, his back to the door. Now he turned to confront them, eyes blazing. He said nothing at first, switching his gaze to Harriet.

"Well, Mother, my fiancée and my friends hoped to discuss our plans with Mr. Renfield, but I see you've already arrived to supplant us. Should we just sit down and hear your joint decrees?"

"Young man, you shouldn't address your mother in that tone of voice. Nor should you come bursting into a room without knocking." Phillipse glowered, spread his feet apart, clasped his hands behind his back, and looked invulnerable.

"Sir, my mother has a habit of interfering with my personal life and with my business. I believe I've a right to address her in any tone I choose, given the fact that she's faced my accusations before and failed to desist. What is it this time, Mother?"

Phillipse answered instead, with a milder tone. "Your mother has come here to explain to me certain conditions surrounding your family's investments and the future of their several companies. She's also pleaded with me to make a definite commitment, right now, concerning the date of your wedding to my daughter. Your mother's very convincing and I've conceded to her several advantageous points, but I must now defy her on her major objective, namely the imminent marriage of my daughter to a headstrong, arrogant, and perhaps disloyal young man who doesn't seem to know which side his bread is buttered upon."

"Phillipse," Harriet protested. "You were almost ready to agree when they came in."

"Ah, but I've changed my mind," Phillipse retorted. "You're a persuasive woman and you play with a loaded deck. But you can only push me so far. Despite your insinuations, I'm prepared to take my chances on this most significant of your demands. My daughter Clarissa is dearer to me than anyone else in this room." He looked at Schuyler as he spoke. "I'd fight anybody on that front, anywhere, anytime."

"Chad, why do you keep complicating things," Harriet implored. "You've committed an affront to your future father-in-law and I must concede that he's justified in delaying your marriage once again."

"Postponement is the mildest of my responses," Phillipse said ominously.

"What about me?" Schuyler said. "You've hardly spoken to me for the past twelve months."

"I can only assume you've chosen your path in life and will walk down it no matter what I say."

"Father, I don't want to irritate you. I've been a good son. I've stayed out of trouble. I've behaved well. I'm not ready to marry. Marcus and I have a wonderful friendship. We only want to go abroad and enjoy ourselves. You know I've got some money in my own right. I hope you'll continue with my additional settlements, according to the terms of my mother's will, and allow me to depart in dignity and confidence, and with your blessing."

"You may go wherever you wish whenever you wish, my boy. My blessing as you call it is wholly inappropriate at this time. I'll instead wish you Godspeed." Phillipse looked sternly around the room, meeting each pair of eyes directly and unflinchingly. "And now, if you'll excuse me, I must prepare for a visit from the highest of Washington officials. There's a war going on, in case you've forgot. And I must do my duty to preserve financial order and some sort of political harmony for my daughter and whomever she marries." He crossed the room with quick, deliberate steps, and closed the double doors behind him.

June 1863

As he searched for the address Captain Hartigan gave him, Chad was calmed by the tree-lined streets of Brooklyn, cool and quiet at the end of June. He was to look for a large corner house, with bay windows, and a garden in the back. He was to walk on by it without looking at the street number, pause on the next corner, pretend to be lost, and walk back. Then he was to go around the block and enter from the garden gate, a solid wood portal between adjoining brick walls over six feet high. If he should be stopped, he was to ask for directions to Reverend Mullen's house. Otherwise, Bynum would await him inside his new and temporary quarters across the East River from Manhattan.

The severe conflicts within him now seemed almost physical, as if he were stricken by a malignant malady, chronic but dire. He wanted assurances from Bynum that the insurgent strikes wouldn't randomly and wantonly kill and maim civilians. But he doubted he could justify that position, given his irreconcilable objections to a war that had already killed and wounded hundreds of thousands. He had a role to play, perhaps an historic one, in bringing the battles to an end. He'd prided himself on his diligent thoroughness. He tried to focus on one thing at a time, and right now, his task was to get to Bynum's rooms on Jerolemon Street undetected.

He'd have less than an hour anyway, since he'd agreed to meet Tad Mullen and his mother for another "little tea" and a discussion of the dilemma that now faced Holder Pratt and Mary Malloy, whose shop downtown had been vandalized, the windows smashed, and the interior ravaged. The couple was out at the time, and upon their return, saw the violence from a distance, rightly surmised it was part of the rising tide of anti-Negro activity, and managed to get to the ferry and across to Reverend Mullen's house. Since Chad considered Holder Pratt to be a friend and ally, he couldn't refuse to meet with them to discuss safe alternatives.

The gate creaked as he slid quickly inside the high red-brick walls. The garden itself was larger than his own, full of flowering shrubs and fruit trees, a patch of green lawn, and two white benches placed for conversation on a terrace that could be seen from the rear bay window, apparently the spot where, in peaceful times, a mother or governess might watch the household children at play. But today, standing in the window smoking a cigar, was the unmistakable form of Bynum Bradley-West.

Bynum pointed to a side door that opened as soon as he approached it and closed just as quickly. "Are you sure you weren't followed?"

Fear on his mentor's face provoked Chad's anxiety. "I was very careful. I went the usual way to Madam Maureen's. I left there by the rear entrance and walked all the way down, using the side streets. I waited until the line for the ferry was long and people were shoving each other, and bolted into the crowd at the last minute, just before the boat cleared the dock. I wandered around over here just like you said. There was no one at either end of the alley when I slipped through the garden gate."

"Well done, as always. Come into the other room, there are two people you must meet. Don't object that I'm not giving them your name nor theirs to you. The less you know about each other, the better. Hartigan gave me the information you compiled and we've been reviewing it. You must understand that there are at least two classes of Southern sympathizers. Some of them, like you, merely want to end the war and effect some kind of truce. Others, like the two men you're about to meet, have more ambitious goals. They'll not be satisfied with anything other than a Southern victory, or at least a negotiated settlement that addresses the tariff issues, and, if their new government is not viable, some kind of power brokerage in the Congress, lest the Southern states be completely overshadowed by the North and the new states about to be admitted. That would, in effect, give them little voice in government."

"I'm aware that the political disputes are confusing and ambiguous. I want the killing to stop and I want my father's life to be saved. I don't want any of the loyal sons of Virginia to be punished."

Bynum didn't reply until another door cracked slightly. "Come in, gentlemen. This is our colleague who'll answer questions about the buildings. He may not be available, when the time comes, to work directly with you. But he's rendered a great service by providing intelligence for our cause."

The two young men were dressed in passably fashionable clothes, but there was no ostentation or flamboyance about either their garb or their voices when handshakes were exchanged. One was as tall as Bynum, fair-haired, blue eyed, and slender. The other was a muscular young man whose hair was as black and thick as Chad's. "I know you to be the son of a Virginian, Sir, and that's all I need to know. But I can offer you the gratitude of all of us who want to save our homes and our families from certain destruction."

Chad neither confirmed nor denied the reference to his connections to the South. He tried very hard to focus, in the increasingly tense atmosphere, on his two principles. "Let me say that first of all I want to help bring this unlawful and diabolical war to a stand-still. And second, I've told our friend here, when I agreed to gather information, that I don't wish it to be used to harm civilians. Indeed, a demonstration of violence in the heart of the city should be sufficient to rally our supporters, even if we don't kill anyone. I hope you can abide by those wishes."

"I've seen many of my state's villages destroyed, and have personally nursed wounded women and children who were victimized by cannon fire, and in some cases by personal attacks from the soldiers. We'll try to observe your humane objectives, but I can promise you nothing but this: we'll do what it takes to strike terror into the heart of Northern cities, thereby making our position stronger when we sit down to negotiate."

Bynum interrupted the Virginian. "I've made maps, and have pinpointed key positions in the areas where you may first observe and then approach your targets. You should look these drawing over, and we'll discuss the pros and cons, including the time of an attack, and how to avoid harm to the innocent."

For the next half hour, Chad hunched around a low table with his fellow conspirators. They pointed to doorways and windows, fire escapes and basement entries, coach houses, lobbies, showrooms, and restaurants. The downtown armory was vigorously debated. The questions were quick and short and Bynum answered most of them. His heart pounding, Chad corrected them if they were interpreting his data incorrectly, and offered further opinions about the hours of use and times of closure for the selection of targets. Each minute brought more tension, his head had started to ache and his stomach was tight. Finally Bynum rolled up the maps and charts and lists, placed them within a circular tube, like those used to store documents on riverboats and merchant ships, and ushered the two visitors out the door. He came back in, brought a brandy bottle over to the table, poured a glass and offered it to Chad, who refused.

"I've got to get over to Reverend Mullen's house. I'm having tea with him and my mother, and that Negro man who helped Schuyler and Marcus that time, when I drove them over to your rooms. It seems like a century ago."

"You're under great strain. I don't believe I'll have to call on you much more, except to alert you to the attacks, when we've decided upon a time. It may not be this year, because I sense the country is going to be brought up sharply in the next few days. They've massed troops on both sides in Pennsylvania, somewhere near a town called Gettysburg, and my sources say it will perhaps turn out to be the biggest battle of the war so far. If Lee is victorious, he can make it in a short while to Philadelphia. That might make our little forays unnecessary."

"How many troops are involved?"

"Quite literally hundreds of thousands, if you count both sides."

"Is there any word of my father?

"Alas, no," Bynum said in a paternal, sorrowful voice. "He's often in the presence of General Lee and his top staff. Whether or not he'll be fighting alongside them in Pennsylvania, I don't know."

"You said there was something else."

"This city is seething. The new draft law, and the idea that you can buy your way out for $300, is the talk of every German beer hall and Irish tavern in lower Manhattan. There have already been outbursts of violence."

"Yes, it's for that reason I'm meeting with Reverend Mullen. Holder Pratt's shop and apartment were ransacked, windows broken, furniture stolen. He saw it happen from a distance and they were able to get to the ferry. The problem now is how to get them out of town. That will be my problem and not yours."

Bynum clucked sympathetically. "Don't think I'm unaware of the conflicts within you. I'm in a way more fortunate. I work solely for the money, and of course, for North Carolina. I don't expect to escape. I'm resigned to it. But you, you're an embodiment of the dilemma, with your Yankee mother and your Virginia father, with your textile mills and your banks, and your lost plantation in the Shenandoah. You're a fair-minded thinker who hasn't yet had to sacrifice principles in order to effect results."

"I suspect that's precisely what I did here today."

"You know, earlier this month, June 10th to be precise, a Federal gunboat sank the Confederate steamer *Alabama*. Near Cherbourg. Our war is now being fought off the coast of France! When the news of the so-called victory came, many New Yorkers cheered. Many didn't. You see, the different points of view escape the public mind. They can only listen to the speeches and sing the marching songs and wave the flags. Most of the soldiers, especially those who enlisted, have now forgotten why they joined up in the first place. And you can't stop a man in the street and get him to give you a clear view of what this war is about. So to stop it is an act of heroism. I hope your conscience won't trouble you unduly on that point."

"You know my position on slavery."

"And you know mine, and the actions my family took decades ago. Indeed, slave-holding families are in a minority in the South, about one fourth, but that fourth holds millions to bondage in an entrenched economic vise that permits them to rationalize their guilt. I'm convinced that once we put an end to this fighting and effect some sort of political settlement, the eradication of slavery will be the paramount condition for a peaceful and unified nation. But don't forget that the Northern merchants and bankers, the ones who brought Lincoln to power, are no more enthusiastic about emancipation than some of my colleagues in North Carolina. Lincoln's latest solution was to ship them back to Africa or to the Caribbean. And the border states, while remaining in the Union, still permit slavery. There's no simple solution other than direct action to stop the killing and start the talking."

"I hope you're not simply trying to reassure me that I've made the right choice."

"I'm of course eager to see you reconcile some of your inner conflict. And I've promised your father, as you know, that I'd try to shield you from apprehension, from military service, or from punishment of any sort. You may stay in the background, and hope that our efforts will fill New Yorkers with such a revulsion for bombs and fires that they'll make themselves heard not only in Albany but in Washington."

"And what of you? Will I see you again? When the attacks are carried out, will I still have recourse to your friendship? And to your contacts with my father?"

"That I can't say. Indeed, the increasingly deadly battles and the prospect of death and destruction right here may cause things to come to a head faster. I must tell you that I'll not betray you if I'm caught. If I'm sentenced to die I'll not utter your name. If you hear from me in person it will mean we've succeeded. If you get a scrawled note from an emissary, it may mean that I'm lost."

* * *

Chad tried to avoid looking back over his shoulder, but he couldn't. The quiet Brooklyn street was uncrowded except for deliverymen and domestics out on errands. An occasional carriage squeaked slowly by, but the overall peace was comforting, and he saw no one who might be considered suspicious. When he arrived at Mullen's doorstep, Chad nodded to a cabbie out front, standing beside his horse. When the door opened he recognized the same prim Negro house servant his mother had greeted the last time he was there. "Well, Melanie, is your sister safely embarked?" He handed her his hat and cane.

"Thank you Sir, she's already safe in Canada. Captain Chadwick, God bless him, he's here today. I should offer some refreshment to his coachman, he's been standing out there for an hour."

Chad heard voices from the parlor so he plunged ahead unannounced. The room was cool and dim, soft breezes lifting the curtains, a random gust ruffling the drapes slightly. Everyone was seated, saying nothing. Harriet's eyes focused on the floor. Holder and Mary Malloy sat side by side on a sofa, hands clasped. Tad Mullen perched regally on a damask settee, and his cousin Corbin Chadwick III slumped in a lolling chair, his legs stretched straight out in front of him, his black boots gleaming and his wide eyes glaring into his cousin's. "There you are, then," Corbin said. "We wondered if you'd keep your word."

"As both Laymus and Wales I'm known to keep my promises, Cousin," Chad retorted. Harriet looked up at him with an expression of tolerance tempered with shame.

"Testy conversation is uncalled for on a day like this." Harriet had her self-righteous look on again and sat stiffly, creasing the pleats in her skirt, a habit Chad now believed was a harbinger of censure or unwelcome demands.

"Our business is grave but we needn't strike out at each other," Mullen said. He adjusted his clerical collar and then gave Harriet a wearisome look. Harriet returned his glance with defiance.

"We're here to take action for a merciful cause and I, for one, would prefer we all leave our personal disputes on the doorstep." Harriet's voice wavered uncertainly.

"There are no personal disputes in the matter at hand, except to say I've personally rescued over two hundred slaves and transported them in my ships to a land where they'll be free to make their own future. Personal sentiments didn't enter into it then but moral convictions do."

"What are you proposing to do now?" Chad looked towards Holder and Mary as he spoke.

"You visited my shop—my home as well—to rescue a friend. Two friends. I assume you're now aware that the same kind of criminals who assaulted them nearly destroyed my home and my livelihood. If Mary and I had been there they would have surely destroyed us too."

"I'm very sorry, Holder," Chad said. "I'd do anything I could to help you both."

"I was hoping you'd say that." Corbin glanced first at Harriet and then at Holder when he spoke. "You see, my ships are endangered now, even in Northern waters. The Federal navy has been built up fast and certain commercial vessels are acting as privateers, preying on their rebel counterparts. It's not safe to transport human cargo under such circumstances. We need a different way."

"What can I do?"

"We need a river boat. The roads are beset by renegades from the city who, I'm told, grow more riotous every day. I fear New York will explode at any minute. Indeed, I've urged Cousin Harriet to leave for Boston at once, but she's refused."

"I too," Mullen said. "Perhaps you can convince your mother to leave town, Chad. Either Boston, or perhaps up to Yellowfields with your bride-to-be."

"You lure me all the way to Brooklyn to tell me I should get my mother to change her mind?" Chad feigned exasperation, but he was in fact enjoying himself. "My mother doesn't ask for my advice and if I offer it she's that much more likely to reject it."

"Don't start in on this, Chad, please."

"Harriet, you really ought not to engage in this bickering with him.

It takes both of you to sustain it." Mullen rose from his chair, cracked his knuckles, and sat down again.

Chad was offended by this totally improper tirade directed at his mother. He resisted the urge to take her part. "Is this about Mr. Pratt or Mrs. Wales?"

"I own a farm, you see. In Orange County. It's not far from the river. I could set up shop there, supply some of the big houses with furniture and maybe grow some crops. Mary and I'll be married there. We want to raise a family." Holder's voice was full of both hope and resignation.

"Will you be safe? There are bands of marauders. Of course, I suppose you could take the train." Chad saw no role for himself in this drama.

"Not the train. They'd have to cross to the Jersey side and head for Port Jervis. It's not safe. And if they take the train through Westchester, we fear there'll be danger there too. Some of the workers on the new tracks, for example." Corbin seemed resigned to the inevitable. "If you can persuade Clarissa to use the Renfield yacht and keep them at Yellowfields for a week or so, until the city calms down, then we can ferry them across at night. I can have a carriage waiting further upriver. They can get to their farm driving at night, if there's a full moon. It's sparsely populated. Pratt has guns. He has his freedman's papers. There's a good liberal clergyman there who'll marry them. They can just lay low for a while. So, will you talk to Clarissa? And then accompany them on their boat and escort them from the landing to the big house?"

"Of course I will. And I commend you, Corbin, for helping so many to escape."

"I'm not a slave!" Holder vented his accumulated resentment and rage. "We're not living in Alabama! My family has been free since before the Revolution. I'm an educated craftsman with a high-class clientele."

"Holder, I'm sorry. I don't consider you a slave. But the enslavement of blacks in the South as well as in the border states has put us all on edge. My father is a Virginian and he fights for his homeland. I love and respect him. But you must never believe I sympathize in anyway with that shameful practice. But I insist on making my point to all those who would criticize only one half of our country. Why would we be having this conversation in the first place, if there were no brutal forces in New York and Connecticut and Massachusetts? I'm tired of people who sing their marches and hold their parades and then turn their eyes away when persecution is unleashed closer to home."

"I'll not accept this attitude in you. There's no one in my family who supports violence against Negroes. We're committed to freedom and equality." Harriet sounded unconvincing.

"I hope so, Mother. I've been tortured by fears of violence since I was eight years old. And I've read widely and thought deeply on the slavery issue. I've tried to picture in my mind what it would be like to be captured and put in chains by other black men in Africa, transported to the coast and locked aboard a crowded stinking sickbay of a ship, a vessel probably built in Maine, and then, those who survive the punishment and the sickness, cleaned up and put on an auction block in Charleston or New Orleans and sent to a miserable life of subservience to a so-called master. Some of the planters rationalize and say the Negro is better off. I don't buy that. But I'd like you people to appreciate once and for all where I stand. I'll help this man and his wife to escape, because they deserve to live without threat. I'll do it because it's the right thing to do, not just because I owe Holder a favor. But I'd at least like you to allow me the same degree of moral fervor against this outrageous, inhuman, unnecessary and satanic war. For when I drop my friends off at the dock at Yellowfields, and see them secured for the night, I'll get up the following morning and return to New York and continue to do whatever I can to stop the flow of blood, whether it's Virginia blood or Massachusetts blood. Whether it's my father's blood or the blood of a poor Irish lad who's been recruited to march into the South, kill as many people as he can, and then be blown to bits at Shiloh or Antietam or Chancellorsville."

Interlude: "Bellum omnium contre omnes"
(July 1863: Gettysburg and New York)

Chad sat on his favorite bench in the garden. Filled with conflict, he let his thoughts drift back to the first time he'd retreated, as an eight-year old boy, to the seclusion of his oasis, hands over his ears. With cheek pressed against the hallway floor, one eye straining to peer under the sliding parlor doors, he couldn't comprehend his ranting grandfather and defiant mother

His dangling legs were too short to reach the red brick terrace as he thumbed through his third-grade reader and put it down in anxiety and defeat. He couldn't turn to a father for comfort, since Franklin Wales was rarely home. His playmates, mostly children who had larger families and lived in grander houses, were rarely told about disgrace or discomfort or despair.

He had only himself, his books, and Lucifer.

Lucifer, a stray kitten when he discovered him in an alleyway as he walked home from Washington Square, didn't remain little very long. Leaping up and down the stairways, chasing birds in the garden, and pouncing on anything that moved, Lucifer soon became more threat than comfort. He stared down on his human family from mantels or dressers or landings, red eyes aglow, yellow hair fluffed out. He'd rise up on his hind legs and rest his front paws against the big windows, watching the birds outside.

Chad defended Lucifer against all suggestions that he be allowed to "escape." On that summer day when he was eight, brooding on a bench behind his home, he watched his cat stalk a black and white bird, perched nervously on the rim of a small fountain, dipping its beak into the water, fluttering its wings. Lucifer remained motionless until the bird turned its back upon him, then attacked so suddenly Chad had no time to avert his eyes. Lucifer clamped his jaws on the bird's head. Snapping bones cracked like hailstones in the quiet garden. Blood spurted from Lucifer's mouth; animal fury filled the cat's red eyes. Chad ran back into his house and up the stairs to his bedroom. He scooped up Lucifer's pallet bed, threw it out into the hallway, closed and locked his door, and spread himself on the coverlet. When his mother suggested the cat was needed as a "mouser" at a charity home for unwed mothers, he quickly agreed.

Now, fifteen years later, he sat outside in the wet summer heat. Newspapers lay folded in his lap. He looked around the garden, half expecting Lucifer to return, grown large as a lion now, poised astride the garden wall, waiting to attack. He leafed through the papers, intending to absorb any useful information before he returned to his volume of Horace, where he underlined the phrase "bella detesta matribus," intending to show Harriet how a Latin author, himself a witness to civil strife following Caesar's murder, expresed war as "a mother's horror." But a chain had snapped, separating him forever from the ancient past he loved, where violence became myth and battles were sparked by vengeful gods. There was nothing abstract, now, about the Hobbesian war of all against all.

For three long days, at Gettysburg, the opposing sides murdered each other. Artillery with canister and grape rained down on both armies. Cavalrymen with swords drawn rode ahead of foot soldiers in lines eight or ten ranks deep, bayonets fixed, marching steadily into certain death. Bugles blared and flags fluttered. Drummer boys beat a tattoo until cannon fire shredded both their drums and their flesh. It was the Confederate leaders' decision to cross the Mason-Dixon line and invade Pennsylvania, ostensibly in search of shoes in the listless little town. Miscalculation on both sides had prolonged the battle, and now 53,000 had fallen.

In his history books the description of armed conflict was precise and calm, as if the writer were describing a chess match or a card game. Casualties were accounted for in orderly rows of statistics. But for Chad, the armies were like two giant beasts, snapping bones and dripping blood as they rushed into mutual destruction.

That bloodthirsty cat had tainted the privileged isolation he'd enjoyed in his books. Now his mind was besieged by decomposing bodies left on the field, tattered flags and smoking guns and the imagined cries of the fallen. It was past argument.

It was out of reach of logic. It was animal instinct alone that drove the nation now, freed of restraint, of judgment, of purpose and of gain.

A few days later, still trying to absorb the news of this "great battle", as the papers called it, he was warned by a messenger from Phillipse Renfield that death and destruction had now overtaken New York City. The conscription act had been implemented and almost immediately insurgency flared. The draft riots raged up and down the island for five days. Many blamed the Irish and German immigrants who didn't have $300 to buy their way out. So they'd turned their fury against the rich white people and the poor blacks. At least a thousand had been killed or maimed. Negroes had been lynched from lampposts and set afire, and the Colored Orphanage on upper Fifth had been burned to the ground. People were pushed out of windows on the top floors of flaming buildings. Policemen were beaten, store windows broken, offices set afire, homes invaded. Rumors said rape and torture were common. Gangs chanting slogans and carrying placards raged from the draft office in the East Forties, up and down Broadway, and westward across Sixth Avenue to the homes and workshops, taverns and brothels, churches and schoolrooms of the predominantly black citizens living there. Mixed race couples were especially vulnerable to mutilation and death.

They attacked newspaper offices and fire stations. They drank and brawled and cursed and killed. Chad and his mother had been asked to seek refuge at Yellowfields, but Harriet refused, closing the shutters, sending the servants to their homes. She sat in the front hall with a pair of pistols. When martial law was declared and the troops sent in, Chad walked about the neighboring streets. The heat was unbearable. Trash and garbage and animal excrement coated the side streets east of Third Avenue. The stench was impossible to tolerate. Bloodstains, baked into the ground by the blaring sun, became crimson reminders of the world he lived in.

What difference did it make, now, what he did? Both sides were wrong. He'd been impressed with the ancient Greeks' ability to characterize the human situation in terms of what is "possible" and what is "necessary". Unavoidable fate and a pittance of free will. It was neat and reassuring and simultaneously tantalizing, an exhilarating excursion into the realm of conflicting thoughts in an otherwise rational world.

But such journeys of the mind no longer availed. It was the killer incarnate he confronted now. Once the red-eyed beast of battle was set free, it couldn't be easily coaxed back into its cage. Seated in the familiar shadows of his leafy childhood sanctuary, he decided that if he had to risk his life and chance killing others, he'd do it. If he might be jailed or hanged or beaten senseless, he'd try. No matter what Clarissa or his mother might offer in solace or comfort, he knew now that if he had to blow up the armory to end this wretched war, he'd gladly do so.

SEVEN

Late July 1863

Red and white flags fluttered from the rigging of the Renfield yacht, safely anchored near the Brooklyn side of the East River, its glossy black paint, gilded trim and copper fittings bright in the afternoon sun. A two-masted schooner eighty feet long, the swift and versatile *Winged Victory* could be easily identified by its small but rakish smokestack jutting backwards at a slight angle, evidence of an auxiliary steam engine that gave the sleek vessel added speed and versatility.

"Father named it after that famous statue," Clarissa said, reaching her hand to Mary Malloy, who was the first to board from the cramped, narrow skiff bobbing beside the great vessel's hull.

Mary skittishly climbed the lateral gangway, followed closely by her husband-to-be, with Chad immediately behind them.

The gangway squeaked again as Corbin Chadwick stepped gingerly upon the deck, turning to survey the nautical details with his experienced eyes. "She's a fine package indeed," he said, not without envy.

"Father rarely uses it," Clarissa said. "But he thought we'd all be safer, after the riots, if we sailed up to Yellowfields. There are bands of renegades on the roads and the trains we used to take are not secure. Despite the instigation of martial law, most of us fear to venture upon the streets, even in our own neighborhood."

"I'm not a fugitive," Holder protested. "While I appreciate your generosity it seems to me to be excessive. I'm a free black man with adequate identification and more than enough money to avert a vagrancy charge."

"The roads are unsafe, Holder," Chad said. "The trains could be attacked. If you traveled alone you could be set upon by bandits or thugs."

"We'll probably be stopped by a Federal gunboat, anyway," Corbin said. "Perhaps I can be of service in that event. When I turned my big ships over to the transport of the enslaved, I had to negotiate my way out of numerous threats, even on the high seas."

"We're not really safe in New York harbor anymore. There's always the threat of Confederate ships breaking through," Clarissa said. "Father and I agreed we should bring the *Winged Victory* over from the Long Island Sound where she usually lies. He thought the thrill of a voyage up the Hudson would entice me to leave the city and stay upriver. He was upset when I came back to town after the riots. He thinks we'll be safer making the trip on board, and once at Yellowfields, we can all sleep easier."

"I'd feel safer at Holder's farm," Mary Malloy said. "I believe there are fewer renegades in Orange County."

"Father has employed additional guards to protect us while you're at Yellowfields. He thinks of them as his own private army." Clarissa nodded to a crewman, who loosened the lines from the skiff and closed the railing around the deck. The hiss of the steam engine drowned out the chirp of circling water birds as the ship headed south, where it would glide gracefully around the Battery and then edge them steadily northwards towards the Tappan Zee.

When the other passengers went below, Chad and Corbin remained on deck. "I have very little experience with ships," Chad said, "although I rowed with the Princeton crew."

"I was born to it," Corbin said as he walked along the deck, adroitly balancing himself while the gentle waves swayed the yacht from side to side. "Some of us are more at home on the ocean."

"It's our ship of state that seems to be in danger of foundering now," Chad said.

"Have you so little faith in the leadership of Mr. Lincoln and his generals?"

"You're aware of my mixed loyalties, Cousin. And I worry about my father."

"Even war itself seems easier at sea," Corbin said. "Not that we don't see victims blown apart and tumbled overboard to be finished off by sharks. No, at sea, each side maneuvers. You try to get a good shot and then quickly tack to avoid presenting your enemy with an easy target. In these land battles, it seems all they do is line up on either side of somebody's pasture and shoot each other all day. I've never heard of such causalities."

"If you'd help me try to end this war, I'd willingly help you in your efforts to free the slaves."

"Alas, lad, I'm still tied up with the Laymus family. Part of my fortune is in their hands, just like you. If their mills go under, I'd suffer."

"But the war is harmful to our economy in the long run, just as it is to the people who are gunned down."

"Most of these merchants and bankers and mill owners are making money hand over fist. I'm a businessman, not just a seagoing vagabond. I must leave the politics to somebody else."

"Except for slavery."

"Aye. But slavery's not politics. It's a mortal sin." They leaned silently over the rail as the stately yacht rounded the Battery and cut through the southerly flow of the majestic Hudson. Corbin lit his pipe. Chad listened to the lap of the water and creak of the masts. A loud flapping noise confirmed that the canvas had caught the breeze.

"There's a good wind," Corbin said. "These lads are real salts and they'll step lively now. We'll move against the current all the way up to Yellowfields, maybe under our own sail."

Corbin shaded his eyes against the western sun, peering intently towards the New Jersey shore. From the distance a fast moving gunboat approached them, rocking in the *Winged Victory's* considerable wake. When a series of flags signaled them to prepare to be boarded, several crewmen leaned out over the railings to secure the gunboat's lines. The lateral gangway was readied and three uniformed men, dressed as officers, pulled themselves upwards by the rope handles and stepped onto the deck. The first man, in a plumed hat, rested his right hand on the hilt of a gilded sword. He surveyed the men and saluted one of the crew.

"Please direct all your passengers to come on deck," the officer said. "We'll need to see your identification and a manifest, if you carry cargo."

Corbin faced the officer. "Sir, I'm a maritime captain from Searsport, Maine, and this is a private yacht. It belongs to the banker Phillipse Renfield. His daughter is on board with friends. We're *en route* to the family estate upriver. Yellowfields. You've no doubt noticed their private dock not far from the Tappan Zee."

"Indeed. Well, I'm Captain Shaughnesy, special officer in the Revenue Service's interim defense team. Please ask your passengers to assemble on deck for review and inspection. We're at war, Sir, a fact you must be aware of even up in Maine."

Corbin gestured to a crewman who leapt down the stairs. Agitated conversation seeped up from below. When the sailor returned, Clarissa, Holder Pratt, and Mary Malloy followed him. Holder displayed a leather document case, with papers, thick and official looking, protruding from the folder. He appeared both defiant and afraid.

"You're Miss Renfield?"

"Yes, officer. Daughter of Phillipse Renfield. This is our boat. I'm on my way home to our house upriver. This is Mr. Pratt and Miss Malloy, who are traveling to our estate to measure for furniture. Mr. Pratt is a skilled cabinetmaker and Miss Malloy is his fiancée. Now, Sir, if there's no other issue I'd like to get underway. We're already late."

"Late for what?" Captain Shaughnesy looked intently at Holder and Mary, still gripping his sword handle. He strolled about the deck, noting the sophistication and luxury of this private ship, bigger and faster than his gunboat.

"What goods do you carry?"

"We're hardly provisioned at all," Clarissa said. "A modest afternoon snack, and a store of foodstuffs for the permanent crew. They live aboard full time."

"A full time staff whether you're underway or not? Some of our boys at the front don't even have enough to eat while they're fighting for their lives."

Chad stepped between the officer and Clarissa. "Sir, I'm Chadwick Wales. I'm associated with Randall Renfield in business and I'm the fiancée of Miss Renfield. I don't believe we need to delay you because of our personal excursion. There's indeed a war on and I suppose you and your associates would prefer to secure our ports against enemy ships, rather than to dally on the Hudson River with a private and unarmed vessel, fully registered, and going about its business legally and without reason for your arbitrary interference."

"Did you say Chadwick Wales?" Captain Shaughnesy pulled a sheaf of papers from his breast pocket and ran a finger down the page, moving his lips as he read. "Ah, here it is. Chadwick Wales. Are you not an intimate friend of one Bynum Bradley-West?"

Chad steeled himself, his face blank and his voice calm, though the interlude recalled his recent nightmares. "I've met Mr. Bradley-West at my great-aunt's home on East 25th Street. She died recently and he attended her funeral. As a result he was present at a reception after the services. We held the funeral at the Episcopal Church on lower Fifth Avenue. Our house is nearby. That's all I know of the gentleman. Why do you ask?"

"Never mind why. My men are charged with securing our homeland. We're empowered to detain anyone who may pose a threat to the city or to the nation." The Captain, still with hand on sword, seemed to stiffen and grow an inch taller as he surveyed the ship and its passengers. The two officers behind him assumed identical vacant expressions. The only sounds were the lap of water on the hull, the squeak of the gunboat as it scraped against its lines, and the wind whistling in the rigging. Chad noticed a white gull with black-tipped wings perched on the halyard. He could feel his heart beating.

He let his thoughts wander back to ancient Greek narratives about sailors and their adversaries in conflict at sea.

Corbin broke the silence. "Captain Shaughnesy, we're all grateful that you and your fellow officers …"

Before he could finish his sentence, Captain Shaughnesy turned to Holder and Mary. "Are you people trying to get out of the city because of the riots?"

"In fact, Sir, my shop and home have been invaded and nearly destroyed. Miss Malloy, my bride-to-be, has agreed to accompany me to Miss Renfield's home where we'll measure for some new furniture I'll produce at my farm in Orange County, for I don't intend to return to this city. I'm glad you're so diligent in patrolling our inland rivers. I wish we had experienced similar efficiency in securing the streets of New York. Then I wouldn't be making this journey."

"Well, boy, you shouldn't take that tone with me. But I'll let you proceed. I've noted all your names, and taken down information about your ship. Should you be stopped again, give them these papers." He scribbled on a pad of printed forms and handed two of them to Corbin.

As the officials disembarked, Chad exchanged glances with his cousin from Maine. It was out in the open now, his possible connection with Bynum Bradley-West, and although Clarissa knew of Bynum's visits to Aunt Marilyn's soirées and of his friendship with a fellow Southerner, Cousin Corbin had heard only rumors. Now Corbin Chadwick, the abolitionist, stood face to face with Chadwick Wales, spy and possible collaborator with a determined and valiant enemy.

August 1863

"Well, they've all gone now," Clarissa said. "We have Yellowfields to ourselves until Schuyler and Marcus get here. They're coming up on the train."

"I was grateful to Corbin for escorting Holder and Mary across the river. He said he had a coach waiting to take them to their farm. It would be dangerous for them on the railways. The riots have disrupted everything and people are now willing to accept life in a police state."

"Don't fret, darling," Clarissa said. "We're safe here. And we're alone. There's a large staff, including Mr. Plummer, the estate manager, and Miss Cartwright, the head housekeeper. Father considers me to be well chaperoned. But they're both heavy sleepers and you can come to my bedroom this very night!"

"If Corbin gets the *Winged Victory* safely back to Long Island Sound, he intends to return to New York and visit my mother. They've devised a complicated plan about some escaped slaves from the border states, where they haven't been 'emancipated' yet. They asked me to help but I said no. I did it because of you, Clarissa. The truth is I'm weary of it all, especially my difficult situation. The slavery issue is becoming central to the conflict. Even so, I'm worried about my father and about the ongoing butchering on both sides."

"I don't want to hear a word about it for at least a week. We're here on my land, safely guarded, free to do what we please. Schuyler and Marcus will be viewed by the staff as chaperons. Somewhat ironic, isn't it?"

"Clarissa, I really don't feel comfortable with your explicit references to their relationship and the activities it implies."

"Live and let live. You know more history than I do but I read about Napoleon and his laws. In France, people can do what they please in that regard. Why can't we be more like them, our revolution came first, didn't it?"

"Don't forget that their revolution ended in a bloody reign of terror. Napoleon was a dictator. A warmonger. Because of him over a million people died. A million!"

"Will Schuyler really be safe over there? I love him so, despite everything."

"Bynum thinks there'll be another European war, a much wider war, within a few years. He said there are radical movements all over Germany and France. The Italian city-states are in arms. I was only ten in 1848 but I remember reading about street fighting and barricades, communes and subversion. There seems to be enough war to go around. Even so, I don't believe any European country has slaughtered its own populace in numbers comparable to ours."

Clarissa sat in a lawn chair, sipping lemonade. She had one of her fans beside her, although the air was crisp for early August and the soft breeze kept her cool and calm. But she turned on him suddenly, her voice cracking. "Why did you tell that awful man who boarded our yacht that you knew Bynum Bradley-West only slightly?"

"It's the truth, Clarissa."

"No it's not. Every time we talk you bring him up. You always refer to him by his first name as though you were friends. And Schuyler made a comment, I don't remember what it was exactly, about meeting him too. What's going on that I don't know about?"

"I can't speak for Schuyler. If you accuse me of lying to you, I'll simply shut up and if that doesn't do it I'll go back to New York. I've already had a lifetime supply of nattering from my mother."

"I think she's on our side. Father made a reference to something the other day, when he was so upset. He was blurting things out, right after the riots. He said I was behaving like your mother. What could he mean by that? Do you think I behave like her?"

"Sometimes."

Clarissa turned away from him, put her lemonade down, and fanned herself furiously.

Chad gave her a loving look and spoke softly. "It's not that hot, my dear. Put the fan down. It looks like a lethal weapon when you're in that mood."

Clarissa laughed. "Darling, let's not fight. Let's ride around the grounds and choose the perfect spot for our love nest. That's what it will be, a love nest."

Chad looked over her shoulders as she spoke, his eyes fixed on two figures rapidly approaching them from the main house. His anxiety subsided when he recognized the familiar gait of Schuyler and his bosom friend. "Well, my darling, at least our chaperons have arrived."

* * *

The grounds were too extensive to explore on foot, so they commandeered a large open carriage and instructed one of the stable boys to drive them slowly about, pausing whenever they chose to inspect a site, pace off some of the dimensions of a proposed new house, then climb back in the coach and ride to the next possibility. Marcus and Schuyler insisted on going along.

"We have nothing else to do except loll about in bed all day," Marcus said, inspiring a glare from Chad and lowered eyes from Clarissa. "Besides, we can fill you in on all the latest gossip."

"Oh Marcus, let's not gossip, it's so boring," Schuyler said.

"Chad will want to know what happened at the Club."

"Which club?"

"Don't you often dine at the Federal Club with your Uncle Caleb and Clarissa's Uncle Randall?"

"I've done so but not all that often."

"You should feel more at home there, after what's happened," Marcus said.

"Marcus, I really don't see any reason to bring this up. We've got more important decisions to make today, about my sister's new house."

"What are you driving at, Marcus?" Chad said.

"Well, my boy, there's a member of the Federal Club who's accused of selling arms to the South."

"While I have sympathies for the South, because of my heritage, I haven't indicated I approve of armaments, on either side."

"Yes, but this man has been accused of treason by some of his fellow members. At the Federal Club! Can you imagine? Not only that, but the man is Jewish."

"What's that got to do with it?"

"Quite a bit actually. You see, some of the members demanded that this man be expelled from the Club, because of his treasonous activity. But the majority voted not to do so."

"A minor issue, surely." Chad said.

"*Au contraire*," Marcus said. "A large number of members have renounced their connection to the Federal Club, and have gone off and started a new one. They call it The Federal League, and they plan to build a great clubhouse. Part of their charter requires members to swear allegiance to the Union."

"It's just politics, Marcus!" Schuyler was irritated, having started to sketch, on a pad of drawing paper he thoughtfully brought along, some designs for a possible new love nest for his sister.

"Call it politics if you wish, but some of the most powerful people in New York are joining," As he spoke, Marcus leaned closer to Schuyler to see what he was drawing. "They say even J. P. Morgan may become a member."

Clarissa kept her eyes on Schuyler's sketches, indicating approval and disapproval alternately. "Let these powerful men have their little tree house."

"I tell you it's more than politics," Marcus said. "The men who left their old club to found a new one have been accused of Anti-Semitism, since the arms merchant was Jewish. But they trumped their opponents by asking another Jewish banker—a prominent one, I'm told—to join. They said they were not Anti-Semites but patriots and knowing of their new candidate's considerable role in a number of national crises, they asked would he please join to discredit the allegations. And guess what?"

"What?" Clarissa stretched the short word out into a moan of *ennui*.

"The story is he said yes. And President Lincoln has been made an honorary member. And their first line of action, after they secure a clubhouse, is to muster and outfit a Black Regiment, and march them off to war, flags waving and drums beating. Thus do they show their allegiance to and fervor for the Union."

"But my father's sticking with the Federal Club. Perhaps I should join the new one just to spite him." Schuyler put his sketchpad down in Clarissa's lap. "I've never spoken publicly about this. But Chad once surmised that I harbor a certain resentment. Father now casts a disapproving eye on everything Marcus and I do. But he forgets that I was driven away by his own indifference. I should've been groomed for a key position in the Renfield bank. Uncle Randall should've chosen me to head up his new endeavors. They've paid no attention to me all my life, and now when I assert myself, my plan to move to France with my friend, they pretend I've always been a weakling."

"Schuyler, I wouldn't have been inclined to work with them if I'd thought it an offense to you. You are, after all, like a brother to me. And I felt that way long before you made public your desires."

"My desires?"

"Your plans, I mean. To move to France."

Marcus watched this interchange with amusement. "Well, we're on the verge of pulling it off. That new French Line steamer has published its schedule and its fares. It's a luxurious vessel, and many of the best people will be traveling on it. It's just a matter of time, a very short time, until Schuyler and I'll embark on it too. And if there's any financial pressure from the House of Renfield, we'll use my money. It's from Ohio, but it's good money and there's a lot of it." Marcus sat back in the carriage as it halted at another potential site. "Schuyler, let me see what you've been sketching. I'm the visual artist, remember? You're supposed to write something."

"Clarissa's my sister and I want to help her decide on a house."

"But what have you drawn here? Are these more of your Georgian exercises?"

"You know I don't like excessive ornamentation."

"I agree, dear boy. But let's be more imaginative." Marcus took the pad from Schuyler's lap and rapidly sketched the outline of an imposing structure. It was square, but with sparse decoration in a vaguely Italian style.

"Let me see," Schuyler said, tearing the sketchpad from his friend's hands. "This will do, I suppose. Of all the new Victorian styles, I prefer the Italianate."

"As well you should, my dear. We saw some villas in Italy which tempted us to stop our tour and settle down right there."

Schuyler looked more closely at his friend's drawing. "I'm not sure I'd choose this style of fenestration."

"What's wrong with the fenestration?"

"Don't you think it's a bit, you know, *de trop?*"

"How *de trop?*" Marcus closed his sketched pad and glared at his friend.

"*Tres de trop.*" Schuyler sat up in the carriage and inched away from Marcus.

"I don't mean how much *de trop,*" Marcus said. "I mean in what way *de trop.*"

"The windows are too large. More like French doors."

"No they aren't. Remember that villa outside Firenze? Our bedroom had a balcony looking into the garden. The windows were just like this."

"Maybe so, but how will they look from the inside? I suggest, Marcus dear, that it will be difficult to treat windows of that size in a drawing room or dining room, and still retain proper proportions and a sense of the *intime.*"

"Shades and fabrics, that's all. Nothing too showy, and nothing ornate. Except for the grand entrance hall."

"The grand entrance hall?" Clarissa sighed with a touch of resentment. Chad had grown tired of the interchange and gazed lazily across the meadow at a group of swirling birds, circling their way downwards to an ornamental pool flashing in the sunlight.

"To set the Italianate mood indoors. You should have seen the entries to those houses in Venice, from the canal. They were so atmospheric inside."

"God, Marcus, that's far too fancy for Clarissa. Or my father. He wouldn't want a Venetian palazzo on the grounds of Yellowfields. He'd be furious."

"Nonsense. Ornamentation, if it's in good taste, is not to be dismissed. I'll make up a few more sketches, in greater detail."

"I too will make up some sketches, then," Schuyler said.

"I really think your sister would be better served if you took my sketches and then wrote up a description of them for her to use with the architects and designers. Then it will be a true collaboration. The first of many times we'll work together, especially when we get to France."

"I don't want big windows and I don't want a big entry. I'd like a front door that's secure, and a library that's ample." Chad felt he might be more convincing in his austerity if he used a little French. "Perhaps a modest *porte cochere.*"

"You men," Clarissa said. "You persist in thinking you can make up women's minds for them. In fact, I've produced a ream of sketches in my bedroom. I'll show them to Chad tonight and let him pick out his favorites." She did a variation on her fan routine and called to the stableboy, who had seated himself on the grass, under a tree, and fallen asleep. "We must go back now, Susan Steinmann and Eliza Van Der Venner are coming for tea."

* * *

Susan Steinmann, standing cup in hand in the Yellowfields conservatory, kept her back to her friends as she spoke softly in the warm air of the plant-filled and glassed-in room. There seemed to be an unspoken agreement, when she arrived with Eliza Van Der Venner, that their conversation not be shared with staff or unexpected visitors. Seated in his bamboo chair, Chad watched an exchange of mysterious looks between Susan and Schuyler. Holding but not drinking cool lemonade, he stared at the blue-tiled floor, in a design much like his mother's Delft. He'd vowed to himself that he wouldn't start one of his lectures about the war. He'd be amiable, quiet, and pensive. At the same time, since Clarissa always acted as hostess, he considered himself to be the "man of the house," even though Schuyler had been walking possessively around the large room, inspecting the plants, before he spread himself seductively on his pillowed chair.

"If you take the French Line to France you'll be in good company," Susan said. "Some of my cousins are going, and of course my father has banking offices in Paris and London, and an agent in Berlin."

"Why don't you and Eliza join us," Marcus said. "We'd make a dashing and inscrutable quartet."

"Why inscrutable," Clarissa asked.

"People are gossipy enough on land. On an ocean voyage, even on a ship as sumptuous as this new French liner, people tend to become familiar. They talk and talk. We could have a spot all to ourselves, just the four of us. Then who'd know what to think?" Marcus stood behind Schuyler, who sat in a wicker armchair padded with plush cushions and a pillowed back. He seemed to be sinking deeper into his pillowy perch, and his eyes, after that first mysterious interchange with Susan, were tightly focused on his lap, where he held a copy of *Harper's Weekly.*

"I no longer care what people think," Schuyler said sullenly.

"I never did care what people think," Susan retorted, "and my poor father finds me disconcerting."

"Yes, but you have your father's respect and confidence." Schuyler now displayed a childish pout, before sitting up quickly and rubbing his face, as if to erase any clue to his thoughts.

"You're a Renfield," Eliza said. "That name alone opens doors for you. I've managed to use the same tool in my personal and social life. Perhaps you think me arrogant. But a Van Der Venner is fawned upon, so I've simply allowed it. It's so tiring to have to explain oneself."

"It's tiring but necessary," Schuyler said, getting up so quickly he almost struck his head on the tea cup Marcus was balancing as he stood behind his friend.

"Schuyler, don't do this," Marcus said, pouring spilled tea from saucer back to cup.

"It's time for me to take a closer look at myself. I'm here with my intimate companion and my sister and her future husband and two ladies who are among my family's oldest friends. If I can't speak out here, and now, where or when can I?"

"But we're leaving for France. You needn't explain anything else."

"I told Chad I was hurt when my father excluded me from a family sinecure. And when the war started I actually considered joining up. Father bought my way out without even asking me. I could be a soldier. Marcus, don't look at me like that. I could. I know I could. I might have been an officer and returned a hero."

"You might have been shot dead," Clarissa said. "Don't fret about what Father thinks, please. All of us in this room love and respect you."

"We're all against this war, I believe," Susan said. "I admire Chad for his strong position against it, and I wouldn't want you, Schuyler, to fall into the trap of accepting all the rhetoric and flag waving and the deadly games these grown-up generals play with the lives of their troops. Most of the time they keep far back, on a hill or in a clump of trees, admiring their strategies through a telescope."

Chad felt he was being drawn into it again but couldn't stop himself. "General Lee seems to be at the front. And one of the best generals, Stonewall Jackson, gave up his life at Chancellorsville."

Susan flipped her head and patted one of her curls. It was a new fashion for her. Her straight black hair was usually swept close to her neck and head. Today she seemed somehow softer, more approachable. "Chad, you know as well as I do that Jackson was shot in the back by one of his own men and then died of pneumonia. They say it was a mistake. But who knows?"

Clarissa turned to Eliza with a determined look. "Eliza dear, we rode around the grounds this morning and looked for a place to build our house when we're married. I think Father will consent. But I wanted to remind you that we appreciate your kindness and may take you up on your offer if he's recalcitrant. A few acres of Van Der Venner land would add luster to our reputation when we become a young couple entertaining our peers. I certainly hope you and Susan will be among our frequent guests."

"You're deliberately changing the subject," Chad said. "You ask me not to talk about the war but somebody else always brings it up."

"Clarissa, I'm afraid I agree with Chad," Susan said. "There's no aspect of our lives left unaffected by this conflict. Not just the death and suffering and the riots and hardships; even the map is being redrawn. Back in June we got a new state, carved out of Chad's beloved Virginia. Now West Virginia is aligned with the North in this war that's supposed to be against slavery. But this new Northern ally was deeply divided, so deeply their proposed constitution equivocates on the issue. Abolition is gradual and under the terms my father told me about, it would be twenty-five years before the last slave is freed. How can people be so two-faced?"

"Precisely," Chad said. He checked himself quickly, still hoping to keep his promise not to "get into it."

"Each of us must make choices, as Schuyler and Marcus are doing. I'm pleased Susan has been able to spend so much time with me at Kuyperkill Farm. Schuyler visited me recently too, and persuaded me that it might be fun if Susan and I joined them in Paris. Why not? I'm really quite alone most of the time and I don't even get into town for the opera very much. And I really don't like dancing."

"Schuyler, you didn't tell me of this visit. Although I'd be pleased to have you girls as our guests in that great city." Marcus glared at Schuyler, who was thumbing through a sheaf of house designs.

Eliza continued, her measured pace indicating she had something more important to say. "I had a chance recently to visit with my cousin Pietr Ten Eyck. He's got a shipping line, so he's always sitting on the edge of his chair, worrying about the war. And it seems he has regular interaction with people from both sides. I don't know how to do this, Chad, but a messenger from one of my cousin's Southern friends gave me a letter for you. I suspect I should have handed it over at once, and perhaps privately, but to tell the truth, I forgot. It was Schuyler who reminded me."

Eliza pulled a small envelope from her purse and held the letter in the air with her delicate fingers, almost as if she were teasing the recipient. Chad leapt up quickly from his chair, snatched the letter, and stood motionless in one of the bay windows. The warm light glittered on beveled glass topped with delicate Tiffany edging, framing the view of wide peaceful lawns and the mirror-like calm of the Hudson in the distance. Chad hesitated a moment, soothed by the opulence and grandeur around him. Then with a trembling hand he ripped the envelope and pulled out a small folded ivory-colored sheet.

There was only one sentence, and no signature, though Chad recognized Bynum's handwriting at once. *"I wanted you to know that your father is with Lee at Chickamauga"* was all it said.

September 1863

"Your husband's in the thick of battle," Phillipse said. "The city's in peril. Our ports are threatened. There's financial turmoil. The sick and wounded line the roads, the dead pile up on the battlefield. My son and his 'bosom friend' are about to run away to France. Still you insist on setting a wedding date? No, I can't permit it."

Harriet stood by the window in the family parlor of the Renfield mansion, her back to Phillipse, a covert glance cast towards Clarissa, demure and prim on an old side chair with a floral seat and sharply chiseled back in the shape of a lyre. Chad stood behind his beloved, rubbing his hands on the old wood surface, allowing a finger to trace the back of her neck. Schuyler and Marcus sat side by side on a love seat. The room was stuffy, even though a window had been opened. It was a humid September, leading both women to display their fannery. Clarissa, after a long silence, folded her fan with a thump and stood up, facing her father.

"Father, you know I love and respect you. I'm grateful for your kindness. After Mother died when I was so young, you became all the world to me. I don't wish to defy you. But can't you see that Chad and I love each other? We want to be together, we want to start a family."

"A family," Phillipse growled, bitterness dripping from every vowel. "I once wanted grandchildren but I'm no longer sure I want to bring another descendent into this world. Everything I believe in is collapsing all around me."

"Sir, surely you exaggerate," Marcus said. "This war is a vile charade and we're all guilty of it, my family as well as yours. They're making outlandish profits on the conflict. We, like you and your peers, are playing both sides. It's always been this way, I suppose. And I bought my way out of the draft. I'm not ashamed of it. I've got a lot of money at my disposal, none of which I've actually earned. So what? Every generation has its destiny. And every individual has a right to the life he was pre-ordained for. Schuyler and I'll live in France in peace and with dignity. If necessary we'll live on my money."

"I won't have my son living off somebody else like a kept woman." Phillipse glared at Marcus and both Harriet and Clarissa gasped audibly at Phillipse's openness.

"Are you calling me a whore, Father?" Schuyler put his hand on Marcus's shoulder. "What would you expect me to do? I wasn't trained to take my place in the House of Renfield. I wasn't invited by my uncle to join in his new endeavors. If you want to cut off my funds, I'll devote my life to Marcus and he'll support me if necessary. If that happens I'll never set foot in this house again."

"Wait, wait," Chad said. "The country is falling apart. Our peers are showing both deceit and greed in this war. There are people dying everyday. Let's not tear our family asunder too, Mr. Renfield. What else do we have but each other?"

"I should think with your schooling in the classics you'd not expect anything else from a family." Phillipse sighed and picked up a leather-bound book from the oval table beside him.

"All of you have the wrong idea about me," Chad said, "All of you! I love my books but don't think I mistake literature or myth or history for present day fact. I've taken a dangerous stand on this war—everybody knows it. Clarissa supports me even if she doesn't agree with me. And I've made money on my own. Clarissa has her own funds, too. Please, Sir, don't force us to defy you and further rupture this great family."

Phillipse looked towards Harriet, who maintained an uncharacteristic silence during the exchange. Finally she stood up and walked around the room, skirts swirling. It was her habit, Chad knew, to do this before delivering a lecture. But she seemed more agitated, this time, than she'd ever been outside the sanctity of their East 10th Street parlor.

"There's much innuendo in our conversations these days. I myself have been maligned. As if my purpose in Brooklyn were anything but a moral one, to work for the eradication of this great sinful blight on our country. And Chad sides with his father so people call him a traitor behind his back. And my brother and yours, together, have stirred up a hornet's nest on Wall Street with their questionable endeavors. Rave on if you wish, but my family, and yours, Phillipse, created this country. We fought in the French and Indian War, we fomented the Revolution. We built ships and planted fields and brought factories to full production. We provided jobs for immigrants and we gave our own money to the poor. I'll not engage in this masochistic flagellation. Nobody in this room is personally responsible for this war. And the shenanigans of Randall Renfield and Caleb Laymus pale beside the dubious exploits of Mr. Drew and Mr. Gould and their ilk. And what of morality itself? I know what it means to be sneered at. Love triumphs, it's a cliché but it's true. And for that reason I'll say in this room what I'd never say outside of it. I hope Clarissa and my son discover the fulfillment only physical love can bring, whatever the circumstances and whatever the cost. And I might add, to your great horror, Phillipse, that I wish Marcus and Schuyler *bon voyage* and a long and happy life in France."

Phillipse clinched his fists, his mouth tight, his jowls red. He surveyed each face in the room, one at a time, as if they were aligned against him and he had no recourse but surrender. He started to speak, then moistened his lips, relaxed his hands, turned awkwardly towards the double doors, and stalked out. Extending both arms simultaneously, he closed the sliding doors firmly but without a sound.

"Really, Mother, I think this time you've gone too far," Chad muttered. No one else spoke. Clarissa took Chad's hand in hers. Marcus squeezed Schuyler's knee.

Drawing a deep breath, Harriet glared at her son. "If you think I've gone too far today, wait until you see how far I'm able and willing to go to give you the life you deserve." She looked into a gilt oval mirror, picking at her hair. "Higgens is outside. I'm going home. Are you coming?"

"No, Mother, not this time. I think my place is here now."

* * *

Clarissa was still asleep when Chad finished dressing. The Renfield house, vast and secretive, provided both pairs of lovers with ample opportunity to be alone together, now that Phillipse had retreated to his private chambers. Marcus and Schuyler retired early. The only sounds were the domestic frivolities of the wealthy home: the squeak of a window washer, the mumble of cook and scullery maid in the kitchen, the clip and sweep of the gardener outside their second story room, one window open to the cool September morning.

Chad sat on the edge of the bed, pulling the coverlet down, and kissing Clarissa on the concave valley of her elegant neck. She stirred, then opened her eyes. Her face brightened spontaneously when their eyes met, and she reached her hand out, palm against his cheek. "You don't have to leave so early, do you? There are few secrets left in this house now."

"My mother has something up her sleeve. It's time I had it out with her, whatever it is she's hiding. I'm going home now and I'll be kind and understanding. I'll tell her I don't mind if she continues to see her Reverend Mullen. I'll thank her for her efforts on our behalf. I'll make it clear that we welcome her support in bringing us to a speedy wedding. But I'll not leave her until she confesses what power she seems to hold over Laymus and Wales and Renfield alike."

"Have the coachman drive you, darling. It's early and the streets may be deserted. It's still not safe in New York anymore."

"I've got my stick. I've even got a little pistol, now, in my pocket. Bynum gave it to me."

"I'm so fearful of guns. Especially now."

"What do you mean?"

"Dearest Chad, haven't you heard? I was going to discuss it with you, when Father started in on us."

"Discuss what?"

"It was in the late edition of the paper last night. Didn't you see it?"

"See what, Clarissa?" Chad was bent over, adjusting his shoelaces, deliberately avoiding her eyes. Each and every day now he feared he'd be discovered, his role publicized, and officers sent to knock on his door and speed him away to a dark dank cell.

"That man you work with. That awful man. The one on Wall Street, what's his name?"

"You mean Appleby?" He couldn't resist the weak old joke. "Grover Appleby of the apple grove Appleby's?"

"Don't tease about it. He's been shot."

Chad straightened up in his chair, hands on each knee, watching her face for a clue about how much she knew, the news of Appleby clamping down on his heart, his arms stiffening. "Will he recover?"

"Chad, he's dead. They said it was instantaneous, a bullet in his face. From a little gun like yours."

"Where did this happen?"

"It was outside your building, where your office is. The paper said it was a crazed investor who'd lost all his money on one of Appleby's schemes. He's a farmer from New Jersey who started buying stock in these new companies. One of them, I think they said it was in Ohio, failed and the man was ruined. He'd bought futures or something."

"Dearest, you shouldn't worry about these things."

"But my father told me a year ago this Appleby was involved with Uncle Randall. Did you know him personally?"

"Once or twice, I guess, we talked. I rarely dealt with him directly."

"But there may be others like him, people who speculate and can't take their losses. I know you wouldn't do anything wrong. I was worried about this Bynum Bradley-West because, frankly, darling, I think he's some kind of spy or something. And Appleby, well, we knew he was a scoundrel but none of us thought it would be connected to Uncle Randall. He even made a statement."

"Before he was shot?"

"Uncle Randall made a statement. It was in the paper. He said he was shocked and disappointed in the man. He said his relationship was a routine one. He was just a broker only peripherally involved in your companies. But it didn't sound convincing."

"I'm going to see my mother and have it out. Then I'm going to see your Uncle Randall and have it out with him, too. They hinted already there would be trouble. If I have to, I'll resign. I have a little money of my own and when the trusts are settled I'll have enough to marry."

"You don't need any money to marry me. I'm more than rich enough for both of us."

"Please, Clarissa, not now." He brushed her cheek with his lips. "Go back to sleep. Nothing's going to stop us now."

Completely comfortable in the Renfield house, Chad descended the ornate staircase with a jaunty gait. Even if Phillipse suddenly emerged from his study and bedroom, where he'd fled the previous night, with a loud clank when he locked his door, it would instill no fear. But the foyer was quiet, and the starched Renfield housekeeper was nowhere to be seen. Chad took his hat and stick from the hall closet, checked to see that his pistol was securely hidden, and then twisted the end of his cane. He drew upwards on the handle, revealing a stiletto blade. He flexed his muscles and breathed deeply. He opened the front door, stepping out towards Fifth Avenue, ready for the world.

*   *   *

The day was warming, but still cool enough for a brisk walk. He followed Fifth all the way to the church where he'd said goodbye to his Aunt Marilyn, and turned towards his doorstep on 10th. There were few people on the street, except a vendor with a cart, and two maids sweeping steps, including one of those nice Irish girls his mother referred to, well shaped, a white cap on her thick red hair. She gave him a pert, and impertinent, stare as he passed by her and crossed to his house.

Inside it was dark and cool. All the shutters were closed and there was only a dim light in the hall. He stowed his hat and cane and opened the parlor doors. The gaslights were flaring in the shuttered gloom, and his first glimpse, as his eyes adjusted, was of his mother, sitting on her settee, sobbing.

He started across the room towards her, his arms outstretched, when he saw another dark form standing in front of the windows. It was too dim to see the face but he recognized the posture.

"Bynum? What are you doing here?" Without waiting for an answer he sat down beside his mother, putting his arm around her shoulder. All his childhood tenderness returned, rekindled by the sight of a frail woman in tears. "Mother, what's going on?"

Harriet leaned her sobbing head on his shoulder but said nothing. Chad looked at Bynum accusingly. "What are you doing here? You know it's not safe."

Bynum came closer, put a hand on Chad's other shoulder, then sat in a chair facing the two of them. "I had to come. I lost the Pinkerton men in Union Square. I managed to squeeze through that house on 11th, the one they're remodeling. I climbed over your garden wall."

"Whatever for?"

"Chad, I have news. Very bad news. I felt I had to deliver it in person. I couldn't think of any other way to tell you and your mother."

"Has something happened to my father?" As Chad spoke his mother sobbed more violently and let out a slow anguished moan. Chad knew what it all meant before Bynum spoke again.

"Your father has sacrificed his life for the Confederacy, Chad. I warned you he was with Lee at Chickamauga. The fact is, he's been killed. It was quick and he didn't suffer, my source told me. A bullet in the forehead. It was instantaneous. He was defending the command post. They're awarding him the highest honors."

"Honors? What difference does that make now?"

"It would've made a difference to him. He fought for what he believed in. He never betrayed his principles. And his thoughts were with you. My contact sent me this letter, along with the formal notice of his death." Bynum handed the letter to Chad, looking him carefully in the eye. Chad put the letter, unopened, into his breast pocket, rubbing his hands against his pistol as he did so.

"Honors? Doesn't anybody understand? Some wars may be unavoidable, maybe; but at least we could stop glorifying them. Speeches and drummers and medals and flags. I tell you the word 'great' and the word 'battle' shouldn't be used in the same sentence. The word 'glory' and the word 'war' shouldn't be used in the same paragraph. This war wasn't necessary in the first place and now it's taken my father from me forever." At these words, Harriet howled again, bending her body forward until her face was buried in her lap.

"Mother, try to control yourself. We can't let this destroy us."

"Your philosophical insights into the nature of war are acute and accurate but also, I'm afraid, meaningless," Bynum said. "Your father was gunned down by an army of fellow Americans who invaded his home state and then marched on to Georgia. The dirt there is red, red as blood, and now the blood of your father has made it redder. They buried him in a makeshift cemetery. He said if he fell he wanted to be interred with his men."

Harriet howled again. "He told me when we were first married he wanted us to live in Virginia. He wanted to be buried at Cedar Crest Hall."

"Mother, what difference does it make where he's buried? He's gone now, taken from us, not by some stupid cause, not by some noble devotion, but in fact from a wasteful and unneeded war. It's got to stop. I'll do anything to stop it now. Anything."

"Mrs. Wales, is there someone we can get to stay with you? You need to lie down and rest." Bynum's courtly tone seemed to soothe her. She raised her head and looked at her son beside her. Chad held her hand and looked accusingly at Bynum.

"I apologize for my histrionics," Harriet said, her old flinty resolve in evidence again. "I'll go upstairs and rest. Chad, tell the housekeeper to bring me some juice and tea and a little cake or something. I've prepared myself for this and I'll not capitulate to it now. Thank you, Mr. Bradley-West, for your kindness. I can only assume my husband was a valued friend of yours and I expect that you're of a respectable Southern family. Our values are different but our emotions are the same. I'll endure my grief. And as my husband chose to die for his cause, I'll work even harder now for mine." She stood up and faced her son. When he embraced her, Harriet's face brightened.

Both men sat quietly after she left, closing the hallway doors behind her. Finally, Chad broke the silence. "I'm sorry, Bynum, if I lashed out at you. I know you did what you thought was best. You risked your own safety to deliver my father's last letter to me. We don't see eye to eye on everything but as my mother observed, I know you're a respectable man of sincere purpose and gentlemanly attitude."

"You needn't sound so formal with me, Chad. I'm truly your friend and I take no umbrage at your anger, born as it is of grief. Indeed, if I may take advantage of this meeting, though instigated by grievous purpose, it might provide us with a chance to assess our situation. Afterwards, I'll steal away the same way I came in and on up to Union Square where the Pinkerton fellows are still going around in circles looking for me."

"Yes. I want to take action swiftly now."

"We'll use something called Greek fire. It's a pasty substance. Once it's opened to the air and left behind, a reaction starts and in a few minutes it will burst into flame. We'll place these incendiary devices in the various places we've chosen, based on your research and recommendations. It may not be possible or even useful to do it now. But after the year-end holidays, we'll strike."

"I'm now prepared to take a more active role. Something significant. The armory, for example."

"The armory? It's carefully guarded. Even the most daring of my agents wouldn't try to attack them there."

"But it's the armory—all armories, perhaps—that we must destroy. I'm not without credibility. I can say I want to enlist. I can talk myself in."

"They might search you."

"Can these incendiary devices be hidden, let us say, in a book bag, among some of my treasured volumes about the Trojan War? And the Punic War. And Caesar, Alexander, the whole rotten lot of them."

"If we could destroy the armory, it would surely send a shock wave throughout the Northern cities. The anti-war people here could use it to force a reconciliation. At least a high-level conference for peace. Yes, let's do it."

"I abhor violence in any form but now I walk the street with knife and gun."

"It's too bad we couldn't meet at Madam Maureen's. You need to have your nerves calmed."

"No, Bynum, I'll no longer sully my beloved Clarissa's passion for me with betrayal. We're often together now and everybody knows it. She'll marry me when I say so. Her father has no power over us now. My mother ... well, hers is still the big secret."

October 1863

For almost a week Chad remained in his East 10th Street room and read, or sat dejectedly in his garden sanctuary. His father's last letter remained in his vest pocket, where he could feel the paper against his chest. It had been a noncommittal letter, citing reasons for fighting for Virginia, admonishing Chad to stay out of it, and providing more details about the London accounts.

Messengers brought him a daily pouch of papers from his downtown office. Clarissa, powerless to ease the pain of his bereavement, sent her coachman with perfumed notes and chocolates and copies of new books from Boston. She herself, though, remained at Yellowfields. Her last missive reminded him of autumn colors and crisp breezes, and urged him, once again, to come to her at her family's upriver estate.

Today he stood in the hall outside the front parlor. A slender slash of light squeezed under the closed double doors. Undecipherable voices, muffled by the heavy wood, rumbled ominously. His reflexes, numbed by sadness, still reacted to his experience, seventeen years ago, when he eavesdropped outside those same inscrutable doors. This time, he opened the barriers without knocking and stepped immediately into the room. His mother, her eyes downcast, sat in her usual spot on the old striped settee. The man in front of the window, his back to her, spun around abruptly at the sound of the sliding doors, and raised his *pince nez* to afford him a better view. It was the Reverend Thaddeus Mullen, fresh from Brooklyn.

"Chad, I've come personally to express my condolences for your great loss," Mullen said portentously. He lowered his *pince nez* but Harriet didn't look up. "Regardless of how I feel about this war to end slavery I'm still filled with sympathy for your loss of a father."

"Really," Chad said. "I hardly need remind you that this war didn't commence over slavery, nor has it made any inroads in abolition in those border states still loyal to the Union, where black people remain in chains. And I suspect it would be disingenuous, or perhaps indelicate, to remark that my tragic loss may offer you new opportunities for support from the Laymus clan. Especially from that ill-fated daughter whose every move, ostensibly made on my behalf, has brought you to this darkened house with black strips of crepe on our doors and on our carriage."

"Chad, please. No melodrama. Not now." Harriet's voice cracked and she pressed her handkerchief over her mouth.

"Mother, I'm not naive. Indeed, all of us in this room, and other New York rooms like it, have become excessively 'modern" it seems." Chad sat in his old wing chair, his eyes on Mullen. "It doesn't embarrass me to allude to my mother's feelings for you. And since my father had already announced his plans to divorce her, when I saw him for the last time in this very room, I don't wish to continue this mockery about your real motives."

"You're bitter, my son. I don't blame you. But your father has gone to a better world and in time you'll heal, and be grateful for the years you were given with him, and for his great love for you."

"I don't call the red dirt of Chickamauga a better world. It's my intention, after this stupid war is finished, to exhume his body and bury it at Cedar Crest Hall. I intend to use every cent of my money, and Clarissa's too, if I must, to regain him his home."

Harriet straightened up quickly at this announcement and stared directly at her son, her old composure returning, that ancient green fire in her eyes. "Chad, is that wise? Who'll want to live in the South after the war? It's ravaged. The war's not winding down, it's winding up. The news is of more conflict, not less. And what of those renegades, like Quantrill? He's supposed to represent the Southern view. But he and his men killed almost two hundred civilians out in Kansas. There's the real evidence of your 'noble' cause."

"Quantrill was a criminal before he weaseled his way into the Confederacy. He doesn't represent my views or those of my late father. Certainly not those of General Lee. If you wish to cite atrocities, you only have to look at Fredericksburg, and other Southern towns where Lincoln's generals are behaving like Hannibal or Attila the Hun."

"This war has already destroyed your father, and half of your heritage. Would you allow it to destroy your feelings for your mother and for your bride and all your friends?" Mullen sat down opposite Chad. He reached his hand out, squeezing his shoulder. "Please, let's try to make things better, not worse. It's the least we can do."

"It's surely the *very* least we can do. But I intend to do more. In the meantime, I suppose I should be careful to schedule my wedding so it doesn't coincide with yours."

"What wedding?" Mullen mumbled.

Chad turned towards his mother, but she'd once again cast her eyes to the floor. Her expression revealed more than grief, he suddenly realized. She was hurt, yes, but angry and defiant, too.

"Since we're being so modern as you put it let me tell you that Reverend Mullen has no plans for marriage. And therefore neither do I." She looked directly at Chad as she spoke, then glanced furtively around the room.

"But I thought you had some kind of agreement ..." Chad's attitude reversed itself in an instant. He now gazed upon a sad and aging widow, doubly bereaved.

"I've explained to your mother that any hint of some kind of agreement was counter to my intentions, my actions, my beliefs and indeed my statements." Mullen put his *pince nez* back on to emphasize his point. His voice was cold and unapologetic. His gaze, fixed on Harriet, was unflinching.

"Sir, if you've misled my mother or if you've willfully brought her further pain, I'll demand an answer for it. You should be warned that although I'm a man of peace I was known at Princeton for my skill with both rapier and pistol."

"Don't be hysterical, Chad. We've had enough killing in the family for now."

"Yes, Mother, but don't you see the logic of it? While my father was away at war, you consorted with a false priest who then abandons you. I'm the son who must avenge. It's right out of Aeschylus."

"Nothing is 'right out of' anything. Reverend Mullen claims I've mistaken his purposes. Perhaps he sought only financial support for his cause. Such a motive doesn't dishonor him. Despite my pitiable situation, I won't abandon such a compelling challenge. I'll continue to work for abolition. Perhaps it's time I joined forces with a broader range of collaborators, however. I have cousins in Boston who were running the Underground Railway long before this preacher ever set foot in Brooklyn."

"Dear lady, in your grief do not forget how much you're needed in Brooklyn."

"Don't worry, I'll dispatch Higgens with the checks."

"Mother, you mustn't let this man rile you. We can work together, once this war is ended, to bring justice to all of the states. I'm made richer by my father's accounts abroad, and I believe I can prevail upon your family to be less constraining about your trust funds. I promise you this, once Clarissa and I are married and this war is over, I'll help you achieve emancipation. Real emancipation. For all the slaves. Not just those whose sorry fate it is to reside in states Lincoln considers disloyal."

"If I'm to continue to increase my flock, to draw attention to my work, and to allow for a continuation of my principles and influence after the war, we must implement our plans. Harriet, think of what it will mean in the long run. Our group will be recognized throughout the land. We'll enter the history books. Please. Let's not fragment ourselves for personal motives."

"Personal motives? Reverend Mullen, your little speech sounds to me more political than principled. If our goal is to free the enslaved, what difference does it make who gets the credit? Unless you have more personal goals. Goals that are hardly likely to include my mother."

As if waiting for words from the chorus, the participants in the unfolding Greek drama sat mute and awkward. Presently there came a knock at the doors and the housekeeper entered.

"Madam, there's a caller in the vestibule. I told him we're in mourning, but he insists. He's a priest, a Catholic, I believe. I think he may have been here after your Aunt Marilyn's funeral. He calls himself Father Fineas Flaherty."

Harriet said nothing, glancing first to Mullen and then to Chad, who replied. "By all means show him in. He's a friend to me and to my future brother-in-law, and Aunt Marilyn specifically requested that he speak at her services."

The housekeeper bowed, left the room, and came back with Father Fineas, whose Roman collar and black attire suggested a formality, Chad thought, more appropriate than Reverend Mullen's bald personal disclosures.

"Forgive me for intruding. I heard of your great loss from a Captain Hartigan, who's apparently in communication with Mr. Bradley-West. I can see by your demeanor that you've already been informed. I wasn't sure, since Mr. Bradley-West is seldom seen in society these days, so I thought it best to visit you. I confess I'm relieved not to be the one who was burdened with being the messenger. But that doesn't mean I'm without sympathy for you in this dark hour. Our churches have different rituals and different points of view, but we're united in Christ in our desire to ease suffering and sorrow."

"Well, Father Fineas, Mrs. Wales is a member of my congregation and I've made it my priestly duty to console her."

"Father, we need all the consolation we can get. Please come in. Sit down here, and talk to my mother while I fetch you something to drink."

"Just a glass of water, please."

Chad watched Mullen squirming as Father Fineas, exuding warmth and sincerity, sat beside Harriet and took her hand in his. At least, Chad thought, there could be no mistaking the motives of this celibate priest of Rome. Mullen's eyes followed Chad out of the room. When he returned with water for Father Fineas, Mullen had moved towards the door, turning to face them.

"Don't mistake the depth of my feelings. Don't abandon those who would console you, and work with you, to achieve our common purpose. My followers and I stand ready to assist. My congregation grows every day and our work broadens with each passing week. We'll surely make our mark on these critical issues and I hope you'll be with me when we do." He nodded perfunctorily at Father Fineas and left the room.

"I hope my presence didn't seem intrusive to this Protestant preacher," Father Fineas said.

"Not at all," Chad said, his spirits improving a bit as he relished the wry, petty and ineradicable friction between faiths, even in a time of sorrow. "You're most welcome here. Tell me, how is Captain Hartigan?"

"He continues to bring order to our area. He seems to have prospered also. I take it he's invested with your organization. He spoke to me recently of buying himself a house and finding a wife. I encouraged him to do so."

"He's not actually a client of mine," Chad said.

"My son is the head of a number of companies but he doesn't himself engage in any of these speculative practices you read about in the yellow press." Harriet's statement was aimed, Chad realized, not at Father Fineas but at him.

"Yes, but my work with my mother's brother and my fiancée's uncle brings me into contact with the most significant financial activities. I've been pleased to offer Captain Hartigan certain options."

"I take it that the options are not confined to the world of finance."

"Father, what do you know of these intricate maneuvers? My son is young but he's talented and disciplined. He didn't engage in anything untoward."

"Surely not, Madam, I didn't intend to be saying it. My mission here is one of sympathy and comfort. For you, Chad, I hold a pronounced and personal identification. Did I tell you that my father was a fighter for Ireland in one of the uprisings against our conquerors? He loved Ireland and he fought for her and he died, leaving me an orphan when I was but eight years old. I ended up in an orphanage run by Jesuits and so decided to be a priest, even before I arrived a mere teenager on these shores."

"You're a good role model, Father. And it's important now that I'm widowed that my son be given increased respect and guidance as he takes his place as leader of our family. And since his bride is a Renfield, he'll doubtless play a major role there as well."

"I'm acquainted with her brother, Schuyler Renfield," Father Fineas said. "Is he to have no position in his family's enterprise?"

"Father, I believe you know that Schuyler intends to leave America for France as soon as possible. He'll likely wait until I'm married to his sister before he and his friend depart. They're interested in the arts and plan to reside in Paris, to paint and write and such."

"Ah yes, the arts," Father Fineas said. "They unite so many of us in such unexpected ways."

"Farther Fineas, don't think me rude if I tell you that I must discuss with my son some personal matters regarding his stewardship of our family. May I, by way of an apology, invite you to dine with us next week? Thursday, perhaps. It will be a small and quiet dinner, since we're in mourning, but I think your presence will be comforting, and useful. I had intended to invite Reverend Mullen but now I've changed my mind."

* * *

Harriet seemed more like her old self after their visitors left. She noted the time, summoned the housekeeper, and ordered a late lunch. "We'll eat in the dining room like we did in the old days. My courage is coming back. I'll not let the black garb of widowhood deter me from my true purpose, which is you."

"Are we back to that, then?"

"Absolutely. Here's the situation: my brother and Clarissa's uncle are incompetent scalawags. I have it on good authority that they're about to be exposed. Both have made plans for escape, to Canada, I believe."

"How would you know such things?"

"I've had further news from your Grandfather Bartleby, who for some reason seems conciliatory. He dreads the possible shame it would bring on him in Boston if Caleb were arrested or even indicted, even though his Brahmin friends rarely read anything about New York society. Indeed, they're known to say that there's no such thing as 'society' in New York."

"Mother, what are you up to now?"

"I'm restoring my prominence as the sole honorable offspring of Bartleby Laymus, which in turn means that not only will my trusts be unlocked, but that there will be more. More for you, since you'll now be the lone banner bearer for the Laymus family, for the House of Renfield, and whatever is left of the Southern aristocrats known as Wales."

"But what if I don't wish to bear any banners? What if I merely want to end this war, then retire to my new house at Yellowfields with my wife and spend the rest of my days reading Greek?"

"Why do you persist in that fixation? You're a man of the world now."

"I persist because it's only in Greek tragedy that I've been able to find parallels with my own family history. Perhaps if you want me to quell my fixation you'll reveal all your secrets and then I'll embrace you lovingly and admit I've been wrong."

"You and I will be the only ones left. Along with Clarissa. Even Phillipse may not survive, at least not as head of the House of Renfield. In fact, the House of Renfield may not survive."

"For the last time, Mother, what are you up to now?"

"I've met with Clarissa and we're of a single mind. You must resign your position with Caleb and Randall, now, before it blows up on us. And she and I have agreed to put pressure on her father, pressure he'll be unable to resist, for a wedding early next year. You and your beautiful bride can live in your new house and wait out the war. You can read Greek every day if you want, as long as you find time to produce heirs. And not just daughters. There must be a son. My grandson! It's my grandson who'll embody the Renfield-Laymus-Wales legacy. It's he who'll be the most powerful man on the Eastern Seaboard. And I'll live to see it. Yes, I'm in good health and I'm determined. You're too much like your father to bond with me. Go ahead and read Greek and Latin for the rest of your life. Take up Farsi and Sanskrit for all I care. As long as you keep a low profile, marry Clarissa, and produce heirs. That's the future and there's my reason for living."

"Poor Mother, I know how you've suffered."

"You have absolutely no idea how much I suffered. How much I've been abused. Humiliated. Left like a discarded piece of furniture on the trash heap of society. But you don't know about my power either. You've consistently questioned me about it and I've evaded you. I'll soon be ready to reveal all. Not yet, since it would weaken my strategies. Make no mistake about it, you'll prevail, and through you I'll prevail. We'll name him Renfield Laymus Wales, and people in years to come will pronounce his name with reverence and awe. He'll arrive at power and riches at a very young age, and he'll need me beside him to point the way. I'll outlive them all and I'll outwit them all. For now, we must keep up our appearance of mourning. I know that you're genuinely distraught about your father's death in this war."

"It wasn't just my father who fell at Chickamauga. There were 34,000 casualties in two days. Two days! You've got your grand scheme and I've got mine. Perhaps it's not so far-reaching as yours. Go ahead and create your dynasty. I'll give you a grandson. But in the meantime, I'll do whatever I have to do to end this war!"

November 1863

Chad was up all night, unable to sleep after reading the President's short speech at Gettysburg. He admitted the prose was excellent. The meter reminded him of Latin elegaics, or the hard beat of Anglo-Saxon verse. And he accepted the fact that the cadence quickened the pulse and prodded the mind.

At first, alone in his room with a dim lamp at his right elbow, he tried to dismiss the five paragraphs as one more example of cynical propaganda, replete with obvious devices. First, the resounding biblical echoes to fix the date, then the reference to collective "fathers," the grandiose sweep of the first person plural pronoun coupled with "great" and "civil" war.

By the time the President made his speech, thousands upon thousands of bodies were already rotting in the soil of Pennsylvania. This master politician would have his audience endorse the comforting idea that the war was "great", that it was of "civil" origin, and that it was fought to make men free and equal. But the actions of this same tall thin man in frock coat and hat belied his sparse and powerful rhetoric.

He argued that nothing less was at stake than the endurance of a nation conceived, managed, and financed for the people. But as he spoke, citizens wasted away in prisons without trial. Others were paraded before tribunals and threatened to be shot at dawn, legislators had been hauled off to jail, and a Supreme Court Justice had been threatened with arrest.

Still, the words reverberated in his mind. When he spread himself on top of his coverlet as dawn broke, hoping to find a short respite in sleep, he couldn't relinquish the idea that perhaps there might, indeed, be a "rebirth of freedom". Was this an intended irony? That the freedoms taken away by the war would be restored by the war? And what of the other dead bodies in the cemetery? Did they also give their "last full measure of devotion" for an idea of freedom, for their hope to preserve their homeland, to acknowledge the independence of states and the right of each one to decide its own destiny?

Was there true honor for these dead and if so, did it make any difference? His father lay putrefying in Georgia clay. He'd been neither slave owner nor slave trader. He'd not wished to take arms against anyone. But when the troops began to destroy the towns and villages of Virginia, when the Federal generals torched barns and farmhouses and granaries, slaughtered cattle, robbed private homes and, reportedly, raped and abused the women, where, then, is honor? Where then, his tortured mind beseeched, is a cause that's "nobly advanced."

He tossed in irritation as the morning light spread across his carpets and climbed up his walls. He was proud of his ability to see "the whole thing." Was he deluded? Was it his unusually deep knowledge of languages and literary styles that offered him a skeptical perspective on these admittedly powerful words? Was the President right? Would it be better, in later times, that all these people had been killed, and millions of others impoverished, so the nation might expand its power, raise its tariffs, and create a central bank, freeing the slaves as an afterthought or as a political expedient?

Where was truth?

*   *   *

Chad, who'd never before entered a Catholic church, advised Father Fineas by messenger that he'd come in the forenoon. He sat in the front pew, studying the intricate altar, abloom with marble and gold and huge paintings in colorful oils. A sparkling rose window in red and blue and green surmounted the nave. Candles flickered and a trace of incense tickled his nostrils. People came and quickly went, genuflecting, lighting a taper, leaving coin and greenback in the poor box, parading up and down the gloomy aisles, exiting silently on their way back to work or family or office or more dubious enterprises.

Father Fineas approached him from the right, wearing a long gown with a sash around his waist and pausing to kneel as he passed before the cross. He stood at the end of the pew, offering his hand without any words.

Chad gripped his palm and eagerly shook it as the cleric smiled and gestured towards a door on the other side of the altar. Chad followed him, tempted to stop and bow before the cross, but thinking better of it. He didn't wish to be a hypocrite.

Allowing the priest to open the door for him, he passed through a deserted anteroom off the main church and then entered, at Father Fineas's behest, a small office. He sat down facing a simple oak desk. Father Fineas took his place behind the desk. "I'm both surprised and pleased to see you here," he said.

"I feel somewhat awkward. You know that despite my Protestant upbringing I'm not a religious person. Indeed, I'm suspicious of doctrine of any sort. I've been privileged to gain a good background in literature and philosophy and history and languages. You're already aware of that. I'm now in my mid-twenties. I come from a wealthy background and am engaged to one of the richest and most beautiful women in New York. It would seem I have an enviable future. But the truth is, Father Fineas, I'm torn apart now by conflicting ideas and I don't know where to turn. Schuyler told me you had been helpful to him and I beg your indulgence, now, to treat me as you might one of your parishioners who comes to you in anguish and in hope for a word of wisdom or a grain of insight."

"I've been most impressed by your comments. As a follower of Christ I too hate the idea and practice of war. I too have sleepless nights when I can't justify my faith. I walk in darkness one minute and in hope the next. But it's in trying to offer peace to supplicants like you, to help sort through the tortured dialectic of history, that I find some small reason for my own existence. If I can help you in any way, any way I deem proper and moral, I'll do so."

"I think I need to confess a few things to you first."

"You must be aware that as a Protestant seeking my advice, you'll not necessarily be protected by the bond of the confessional. It's possible a priest in my position might listen to your words and then, should he find a wrongful intention, alert those who might be harmed by what you may say or do."

"I'm fully aware of that but I trust you to do the right thing."

"Very well then."

Father Fineas sat silent and motionless in expectation. A mantel clock on a cupboard ticked. Chad stared at it. Someone had begun to play the organ in the adjoining church, and the rumble of the bass shook the windows. It was cold in the little room. Chad felt a constriction in his throat. He was afraid to go on. He waited, hoping for encouragement, but none came. The silence prevailed until, squirming in his chair, Chad began his confession.

"You must understand first of all, that I and everybody in my family are revolted by slavery. My mother and relatives have worked for years to help escaped slaves. My father, the late Franklin Wales, was a died-in-the-wool Southerner, but he neither practiced nor approved of the bondage of others in servitude."

"You've often made this point. So often, in fact, that I've been teased by it, sometimes wondering if you do not 'protest too much'."

"I'm aware of that impression. My repetitiveness is partly because I've taken no specific action to aid the abolitionist cause. There I must plead guilty as charged. But I intend to be more active in the future. All my education, all my eagerness for principles, convince me that it's not enough simply to talk. Action is needed. But there must be a balance. It's not right to perpetrate monstrous evil to cure another monstrous evil. England corrected itself, throughout the Empire, without such butchery as we now experience on a daily basis. I want to make that point clear, realizing as I do so that there are those who would advocate any form of violence to eradicate so gross an evil."

"I'll take you at your word."

"This war has been politically inspired and only later morally justified. In the process we find some of our most treasured constitutional guarantees compromised. And the bloodshed, on both sides, is unimaginable unless one is there on the battlefield with them. Even Mr. Brady's photographs or Mr. Homer's drawings or Mr. Whitman's verse cannot portray it in all its horror."

"We're certainly in agreement on that."

"You see, I feel I must do something to stop it."

"You feel personally impelled to stop a war?"

"Yes. Is that grandiose?"

"I'm not sure." Father Fineas picked up a rosary from his desk and rubbed in between his thumb and index finger. He avoided Chad's eyes as he continued. "There once was a man who took on his entire government, an occupying government, and his own people, his fellow religionists, to make a point. He died for it, in agony. Some of us believe He still lives because of it."

"Please, Father, I'm not deluded. I'm not possessed with a belief that I've got spectacular powers or particularly brilliant insights. The actions I've committed myself to were arrived at by reason, pure and simple."

"Pure, simple reason?"

"Yes."

"I've found reason to be as puzzling as faith. I've found thought to be as mysterious as feeling. I've found that the more questions I ask, the more go unanswered. Do you still think I can offer you anything useful in this crisis?"

"Crisis?"

"Only crisis would bring a rich young man like yourself to a poor Catholic church in this wretched part of town."

"I've had a privileged life and a fine education, but for the last three years I've been tested in the world, I've met challenges, I've demonstrated my grasp of the quotidian."

"The quotidian?"

"Yes, the issues of daily life."

"I know what quotidian means. I'm inquiring about your version of it, how you pass your days."

"I read. I go to my office. I spend time with my betrothed."

"Are you behaving properly with her?"

"What do you mean?"

"You know what I mean."

"We have the greatest love for each other and we don't feel wrong in consummating that love."

"Outside the bonds of marriage?"

"At this point, yes. It's her father's fault, mostly."

"Her father is to blame for your behavior?"

Chad squirmed again. The clock ticked. It was still cold in the cramped little room. He began to wish he hadn't come in the first place. "It sounds juvenile, I suppose, to a man like you. I don't understand celibacy."

"Neither do I. I only practice it."

"We'll be married as soon as we can convince her father of it. He's resisting. There's so much going on in the world."

"But marriages are viewed by some as a protection against the threats of the world."

"Not by Phillipse Renfield. To him marriage is a bilateral treaty. Or a break-proof contract with lots of codicils."

"You're growing cynical and it makes you uncomfortable."

The accuracy of the priest's diagnosis was inescapable but it troubled Chad to admit it. "May I have a glass of water?"

"Certainly." Father Fineas stepped outside the room and quickly returned with a water pitcher and two glasses. He ceremoniously poured for each of them, sat down again, took a long drink, folded his hands in his lap, and looked expectantly but silently at his guest.

"I was unfaithful for a while. In a brothel." Chad cleared his throat. "I don't know why I told you that."

"You told me because you feel guilty about it. I can't absolve a non-Catholic, but I can say that it's attractive in you to feel such guilt and that it's understandable for a healthy male your age, and that if you stop betraying your beloved, you'll feel better."

"Thank you."

"You're welcome."

Chad wondered if he could now thank the priest again and leave. But he knew Father Fineas was too smart for that. He'd have to go on, to the real moral dilemma he could neither quell nor escape.

"I'm engaging in treasonous activities aimed at stopping this war."

Father Fineas stood up suddenly, smoothed his clerical cloth, turned towards the window, then sat down again just as abruptly. "We're both on dangerous ground now."

"I know it. But I still trust you."

"I hear all kinds of things in the confessional. Most of them don't personally affect my behavior or my beliefs. But this is a mutual issue of the gravest significance."

"I so consider it. That's why I'm here."

"I'll stop you if I sense your revelations will force me to betray you."

"I was confident you would."

"Go on, then."

"I intend to blow up the armory. It's just a few blocks from here."

"I know where it is. When do you intend to blow it up?"

"I'm not sure. Probably next year. After my wedding."

"You've decided to postpone blowing up the armory until after you're married?"

"Yes but not for that reason only. You see, I have co-conspirators."

"Including Bynum Bradley-West I presume."

"I'll not betray my colleagues."

"Then I'll make no assumptions."

"I only hope there's nobody in it."

"In what?"

"The armory. When I blow it up."

"That's thoughtful of you."

"Don't patronize me."

"I'm not patronizing you. If you've decided to commit a violent act in the name of your beliefs, just as my sainted father did back in the old country, it's comforting to know that you don't wish to harm others needlessly. Not all enemy combatants have such scruples."

"Do you think my position to be a laudable one, then?"

"You're pressing me for a sermon, so I'll deliver it. I can't make up your mind. I endorse nonviolence as part of my faith, yet my Church has fostered death and destruction on a grand scale. It has oppressed some while favoring others. It's been wracked by scandals, abuse, greed, and coercion. But it survived and it helps me to survive too. I have faith. But I also know that faith is often a product of fear, and that faith, when it comes, is aimed at overcoming the fear of death. Few of us really believe, in our hearts, that the soul is immortal. But it's nice to think so."

"I'm not concerned now with theology."

"Neither am I. I'm concerned about you. You're in a moral crisis and you've sought my help. Why? You're uncommonly intelligent and supremely educated. But you can't find comfort in that. You're one of those men with the mixed blessing of deep rational thought. You see the whole thing. Few of us do. But you can't act on the whole thing. You can only act on a small part of whatever's there. And you know as well as I do that the causes of this war are more complex than the tariff issue you keep harping on. There's jockeying for power in Congress, the central bank controversy, and the very sincere indignation of most of us here about the horror of slavery. I'll grant you that the political impetus at the very start was the burden of customs duties placed on your Southern homeland. So you'll debate in your mind forever—I've heard you do so in public—the dialectic of Hegel, failing to realize that Hegel is as mortal as the rest of us. And you ignore the fact that Hegel is the object of Kierkegaard's scorn—have you read him yet? He's Danish but available in German. Don't you know that power-hungry misfits can and will use Hegel's statism as a basis for total tyranny, now and in the future? No, you'll weigh every option and argue every opinion. You'll end up in a quandary. You want me to get you out of it and I can't. Who among us knows the answer? Should I commit a small evil to stop a larger one? Will my small evil lead to larger evils? Does evil exist? Does it matter or not? What can I tell you? I cling to my faith in desperation for I find life without it to be unlivable. You've got more courage than I, yet you seek my help. You must do whatever your conscience tells you, and you had best not tell me any more about it. What you've said won't be revealed. But if you tell me more, I might be forced to stop you. Frankly, in my heart, I don't want to stop you. I suspect you're right. But I can't give you my blessing, nor the blessing of Him I serve, nor the blessing of my embattled and vulnerable Church. You say you're not religious but I advise you to pray anyway. Humble yourself enough to know you need guidance. Look to your heart and perhaps, if you believe in one, your soul. Now I must leave you, to attend to my poor and suffering parishioners. Tell your mother once again how much I appreciated having dinner at your house. I enjoy your company as well, and hope we can speak again, in happier times, and on happier subjects."

Father Fineas rose quickly, stood by his desk, started towards the door, then turned, and with tightly pressed lips, looked at his seated guest. Then he offered a blessing after all, making in the cold still air before him the sign of the cross. Then he closed the door.

December 1863

Harriet insisted that the black wreath of mourning shouldn't be retained any longer. Instead, she'd searched the basement storage room for the wire frame she used each Christmas to make her own festive adornment for the front door. This year would be no different, she vowed to Clarissa and Chad, who joined her for tea on a cold bleak Saturday in early December.

But it was, of course, different. The fact of his father's death had settled in and left a calm but absent expression on Chad's face. Clarissa, also subdued, shared her belief that her family now was marked for strife, the atmosphere in the big house strained. Phillipse rarely left his private rooms once he was home from the bank.

Schuyler and Marcus kept up a front of jollity and dashed around town to this party or that. They went shopping almost every day, and colorfully wrapped packages piled up in their bedroom.

And the war ravaged on, no end in sight.

"Clarissa, I wouldn't embarrass you by sharing what I know about your Uncle Randall, but be prepared for a shock. My brother Caleb, too. I fear they've overstepped the bounds of proper practice and will be found out. The financial markets have been in a whirlwind for months. I'm pleased to say my insurance portfolio, the one I insisted upon when I visited your uncle in Chad's office, is doing well. But we must all review our investments, get out of the finicky ones, and above all, distance ourselves from what seems to me unavoidable, a financial scandal of momentous proportion."

"I know Father's worried, although he shares nothing with the rest of us," Clarissa said. "Solomon Steinmann is with him almost every day, and my intuition tells me they're plotting some kind of merger. Susan told me Father's at her house as much as Solomon is at ours."

"It would make sense, wouldn't it," Harriet said. "The war will end eventually and then, like all wars, there'll be an aftermath. The South will have to be rebuilt. Mr. Steinmann has offices in New Orleans. He's done a lot of business with the planters. It would be easy for him to buy up real estate for a pittance and hold it, if need be, until the turn of the century, leaving his daughter a handsome and invulnerable legacy."

"Mr. Steinmann may not truly understand the South," Chad said defensively.

"What will it matter? The South as we knew it, or thought we knew it, never really existed anyway. Now even the myth will be lost. But the real estate will remain and eventually the prices will go up. I'll discuss this with Phillipse when I inform him of my plan." Without asking, Harriet poured tea in Chad's cup, picked up his plate and refilled it with small sandwiches and cakes. She then turned her attention to Clarissa, who gestured negatively. "What about your brother? Why hasn't he left for France with his friend?"

"I think they want to be here for the wedding." Clarissa took Chad's hand in hers. "I want it to be in the spring, as soon as it's warm enough. I'd like to have the reception at Yellowfields. It's too depressing in the city right now, and our big old house is like a mausoleum."

"Are you making progress with plans for your New Year's party?" Harriet's tone suggested she already knew the answer.

"There will be no party this year, I'm afraid. Father says nobody would come and if they did they wouldn't enjoy themselves."

"I don't agree," Chad said firmly. "You've had that party since we were children. We used to sit on the balcony upstairs with our legs through the railing and watch the best people in New York dance all night. I'm the one who's most concerned about this war, it seems. And even I recognize the need to hold on to our old way of life."

"It's useless," Clarissa said. "I've never seen Father like this. It scares me. He's aged ten years in the last two months. His hair is all white now and the lines on his face look like they've been chiseled in Vermont marble. I fear for his health."

"But you're healthy my dear. And so is Chad. And soon you'll be married. You can build your house. You can avoid the rumble and strain of a post-war flurry of failures and accusations and indictments. Live on your estate upriver, enjoy each other, and produce a family of your own. I foresee good things for the Laymus-Renfield alliance. You'll be the cause of it. All New York will be at your feet."

"I've told you time and again, Mother, I don't want anybody at my feet," Chad said. He punctuated his words with waving hands, then rose from his chair and walked to the window. Outside there were small grains of snow sifting lightly onto the sills. The street wasn't yet covered so the passing carriages bounced and clattered on the pavement. Workmen had erected a scaffold across the street, where they assiduously repaired the patch of roof above a well-proportioned bay window. It all seemed so ordinary to him, but there was no longer any comfort in the familiar. He spent his nights thinking of the New Year and what it would bring. He'd not relented in his plan to take action, and he felt pity and fear, now, for his beloved and for his mother, both of whom seemed to think the future would be bountiful if they planned it that way.

"Don't fret about Chad's moods, my dear. He's far easier to live with than people think. I'll prepare him well prior to your wedding. I've kept some important things from him over the years, because I felt he wasn't yet ready to hear them. But I'll soon share my proposition with him, and the powers I can use to bring prosperity and status to you and your children once they start to arrive. He thinks I'm secretive but I'll be so no more"

"I really don't think we should make many plans right now," Chad said finally, turning from the window and standing behind Clarissa, his hand placed gently on her bare shoulder. "The war's not over yet. We still don't know who'll win. But we know that nobody's really safe, even us, even here. My kinsmen in the South have learned to live with bombs and fires and devastation. Perhaps it will be our turn next."

EIGHT

January 1864

On a cold January morning two weeks after the holidays, Chad was directed to the front parlor, and then left there by his mother to confront his florid New England grandfather.

At 69, Bartleby Laymus still spoke with a powerful voice and walked with an authoritative stride. His marble-green eyes intimidated everybody, including his family. Because Chad had no surviving grandparents on his father's side, he'd hoped, when he was in his teens, to turn to Grandfather Laymus for encouragement and counsel. But there seemed to be a wall between them, and neither made an effort to scale it.

For the first few moments after Harriet left, Bartleby sipped his coffee without speaking, holding the cup and saucer delicately, in seeming opposition to the personality Chad had learned to expect.

"It's time we got to know each other, son," Bartleby said. "I fear I've been lax in attending to my grandfatherly duties."

"Many was the time, when I was a frustrated and confused boy, that I wanted to turn to you." Chad feared his tone might be interpreted as censure. "I know you've been occupied all your life with the mills. And Boston to New York is a long journey for a busy man. Even before the war."

"Let's not talk of the war just yet. I know you have strong views and I suspect I don't agree with all of them. But I'm here to talk to you of matters I should have explained to you long ago."

"My life in New York has grown complicated since I left Princeton. I've made some money, gained exposure to commerce, kept up on my reading and my languages, and have engaged myself to be married to a fine and beautiful woman."

"You needn't justify yourself to me, Chad. I haven't come here to criticize you. I've come to explain family situations that have long confused you. Matters that are sensitive, to say the least."

"I hope you intend to shed some light on my mother's behavior."

"It's time we faced the truth. We need to close ranks as a family when pressures are against us and our position and our fortune may be imperiled."

"If you're concerned about my future, let me reassure you. I've made a significant amount on the endeavors initiated by your son and Clarissa's uncle. My profits have been invested in sounder, more traditional, instruments. My late father has also left me handsome sums in his London accounts."

"It's not money I wish to speak of. Our capital is secure and the trusts your mother lives on have actually grown larger and will eventually come to you. We must reunite after this war, and we must put past incidents behind us. Women behave much differently in New York now, and there may be less reason for me to continue to ostracize my daughter and to upbraid her for what I perceived to be …" The old man hesitated, put his cup down, and wiped his lips with his napkin. He coughed quietly, his head turned aside. "What I perceived, shall we say, to be questionable conduct for a young woman of quality."

"I'm not unaware that my mother has attracted disdain, if not outright rejection, from those she holds most dear. When I was about eight, I spread myself on the floor outside these doors and tried to understand what you were saying to her in such a loud and threatening voice."

"You remember it that well, after all these years?"

"Sir, I've never forgotten it and regardless of our conversation today, I expect I never shall."

"You must put aside your childhood fears now and look at things in a more, well, let's say a more enlightened way."

"I invite you to assist me in such an attempt."

"You're a well spoken and confident young man. A little too well spoken, perhaps. Let's hope these worries have strengthened you."

"Perhaps so. I've made certain decisions about what it is I must do and I'm prepared to honor them."

"Nothing, I assume, that would exacerbate our family problems."

"That will have to be decided later. And not by you only."

"Chad, I know you think I was cruel to your mother. I suspect you believe I've held a grudge against her. But the truth is, she was a very difficult child."

"Maybe difficult children need even firmer guidance and kinder aid."

"You might not have found it that easy to dismiss. You see, she was headstrong. Her behavior, in Boston, was … was inconsistent with the standards of our social circle."

Chad wanted to offer another rejoinder, but he feared he'd already been too defiant with his formal language and his angry curiosity. "I'm eager to hear what you've come to tell me at last."

"It was partly my fault. Your mother was more mature than others her age. She possessed a precocious mind that unfortunately was matched by a premature interest in … in physical matters, shall we say."

"Was she indiscreet with men at that early age?"

"Let's not get ahead of ourselves, here." Bartleby stood up and walked around the room, hands clasped behind his back. He wore a knee-length jacket and a vest stretched tightly about his chest, which bulged in a semicircle from his otherwise bony frame. "Your mother was discovered in an indelicate situation with a distant relative of ours from Maine. There was nothing seriously wrong about it, but the Boston ladies who came upon them in the stable, from whence they were to be driven to their home in the Back Bay, were nevertheless shocked and began to share this discovery with other families considered to be our peers."

"You're certain nothing actually happened between them," Chad said, more as a statement than a question, since he feared Bartleby would name the Maine family member who had participated in this indiscretion. Right now he didn't want to have his suspicions confirmed.

"She was only sixteen. She was mature for her age. And curious. And her mother had died. So there was only me and her older brother, Caleb, to watch out for her. And a governess, too, of course. We had to fire her later and ship her off to New Hampshire. We already had some mills there." Bartleby paused, as if he were musing on the importance of his Concord and Portsmouth mills rather than the unraveling fate of his only daughter. "Alas, I fear I failed. Failed dismally."

"But you say there was nothing wayward in her actions."

"True, but perceptions can ruin you in our circle, even in New York. I felt I had to do something. I fear I simply made matters worse."

"You punished her too extremely?"

"I didn't consider it punishment at the time. After her mother died, unexpectedly and still young, I thought she'd be better off with an older female in the family, somebody who could be at the same time sympathetic and strict, encouraging but forceful. I sent her to live with her Aunt Marilyn Blaine. Here in New York."

"She came to New York alone at sixteen?"

"Alas, yes. Of course we knew my sister was a lot like her niece. Harriet and Marilyn, well, they just seemed to understand each other. Mind my word,

I thought it was the right thing to do. It never occurred of me then how things would turn out. The disaster ..."

"Disaster?" Chad shifted in his chair, his eyes following his grandfather around the parlor. The flames flickered in the fireplace as a strong gust of wind whistled through the windows. Tree limbs coated in ice crackled outside the panes and the smell of smoke penetrated his nostrils briefly. He reached for his coffee and put it down again, and used his handkerchief to cover his nose. It was his eyes, however, that were beginning to well with moisture.

"Perhaps that's too strong a word for what actually happened, I don't know. You're a learned man, far more so than I. I know that your field of study, the immoral behavior of those ancient figures in Greece and Rome, is full of references to distasteful conduct. Even their gods were likely to run off with defenseless maidens."

"And defenseless lads," Chad blurted out, thinking of Schuyler and hoping to shock his grandfather. But Bartleby didn't miss a beat in his proclamation.

"Your mother found a fast crowd, women mostly her own age with whom she attended questionable gatherings. Her Aunt Marilyn, who was drinking a bit and having trouble with her rascal of a husband, failed to fulfill her responsibilities, I'm afraid. She allowed Harriet to do as she pleased. As you may have surmised already, Harriet was never easy to please."

"So you're saying Aunt Marilyn's to blame for it all?"

"That might be a cruel summation. You see, Marilyn's first and only child didn't survive. She'd married quickly, if you receive my meaning. The child was born in the seventh month. It was stillborn, perhaps fortunately in the long run. But word was given out that she had a miscarriage. The father, Blaine—he's still alive and still drinking, I hear—wasn't worth much, but we set them up in a decent house and an adequate income. We figured that in New York society nobody would notice, and word wouldn't get back to Boston of another crisis in the Laymus reputation."

"I was never told Aunt Marilyn had a child."

"None of us ever spoke of it again."

"But what of my mother?"

"She consoled Marilyn and further ingratiated herself, in order to do as she pleased. She is, as I said, surpassingly willful."

"What did she do to earn your scorn?"

"We thought it to be more compassion than scorn. Her friends, you see, weren't of our class, for the most part. Oh, I mean they were schooled and had good manners, dressed well, and were for the most part exceptionally attractive. But they didn't come from the generations of influence and position our family is accustomed to. They were, in short, *nouveau riche*."

"My God!" Chad exclaimed, not expecting his grandfather to sense his tone.

"Your mother has warned me that your character is often marred by impertinence and sarcasm. I'll not address your various faults today, since our purpose is an older one. Later on, if we're to become closer, I may help you sort out some of these unfortunate habits you seem to have acquired."

"Thank you."

"You're welcome. Harriet and her friends began to frequent a house on West 26th Street, not exactly a club, but a place where wealthy men could socialize with and entertain women of education and charm, without stooping to more sordid activities."

Chad's heart skipped a beat as he remembered Madam Maureen and her welcoming house on Prince Street. "A house of ill repute," he gasped.

"Oh, nothing as bad as that. At least it was so claimed. Everything seemed to be quite proper and the most important men in New York went there. Hunter Collins, for example, have you heard of him?"

"The man who built all those railroads out west?"

"The one and the same."

"He was rumored to be richer than any of us. And gave fortunes to charity. Had a son I believe, just a little older than me."

"I never met the gentlemen and don't regret it, however much I admired his business acumen. But your mother met him. Along with Randall Renfield. And later, Phillipse Renfield as well, as we shall see."

"My mother met Clarissa's family in a place like that? How can this be?"

"You shouldn't say 'a place like that.' You see, there are differing degrees of proper behavior here in New York and we must learn to adapt to their looser code if we're to increase our resources and stabilize connections for, shall we say, the dangerous but promising future we're facing. I know now that I reacted too strongly when I found out your mother had been seen there. As soon as I learned about it, I hopped aboard a steamer, one of our own actually, and made my way to this immoral metropolis on the Hudson. I was of course driven by paternal concern. I knew I had to stop it, to nip it, as it were, in the bud."

"That's why you shouted at her when I overheard you?"

"Not quite. You must put it in the proper time frame. This episode occurred long before your mother married none other than your father, with alacrity I might point out. The incident you refer to, the one implanted in that fertile brain of yours, occurred when you were, what did you say, eight?"

"Eight."

"I fear I overreacted then, too. I had heard that your father was spending less and less time here and that there was an impending rupture in their marriage. I also knew that your mother was frequently at the Renfield mansion, ostensibly on your behalf. I felt it was time to remind her that once before, her behavior had brought us to the brink of scandal."

"That was all?"

"Remember, we had to watch her like a hawk after we disrupted her little circle of friends, extricated her from their society and the house on 26th Street, and ascertained through Dr. Forrest, who was already in practice at the time, a young doctor looking to establish himself with the upper classes, what was I saying, oh yes we ascertained that your mother was intact."

"Intact?"

"Surely you realize what I mean?"

"But you said the house was a social gathering place, nothing seamy or steamy or sordid or scandalous." Chad was losing his composure by the minute, made worse by his growing fear that Bartleby would tell him something that would jeopardize his marriage.

"We were mostly men in the family after my wife died, you see, and we couldn't trust my sister. So we had young Dr. Forrest examine her. She was as pure as the day she was born."

"Pure?"

"Well, yes, in that sense."

"So when you learned years later that she was likely to alienate her husband through a friendship with one or more Renfields, you came down here and accosted her?"

"Not just the Renfields. Remember we were already solidifying our alliance with them. No, there were other issues I came down to resolve, rumors that proved to be mostly unfounded—except for her trouble with her husband. So it worked out. I didn't know my eight-year-old grandson was in the audience during that later confrontation." For the first time that day, Bartleby laughed.

"That's the whole story?"

"Lock, stock and barrel."

"So why didn't you restore her regular income and free up the trusts, as she wanted you to do?"

"Call it sound management. Call it blackmail if you wish. We wanted to make sure she didn't stray again."

"Again?"

"We told her to mind her manners and restrain her headstrong will and when you were out of school we'd talk again and see if she deserved to assume her rightful place as a Laymus. One who could be introduced to our family friends in Boston."

"And has she fulfilled your mandate?"

"More or less. She's still both cunning and resolute but the war has changed people's attitudes so we think it's okay for her to be welcomed back."

"What about the Renfields," Chad asked. "Are they not doubtful of me now after all this?"

"Don't you see, my boy, they dare not contradict her. She knows too much. I've only told you the parts that affect you directly. She's an observant woman, it's part of her controlling nature. To put it in the words of an unpleasant stockbroker I met a few months ago during a meeting on Wall Street, a man named Appleby, as I recall. He said, 'Once you've got the goods on them they have no choice but to buy your apples.'"

Chad considered these revelations to be incomplete. His mother was more like a wronged and angry Greek goddess than a willful teenager sent to New York to hide out, and who wandered into indelicate situations, but was still "intact."

"There must be more," Chad said.

"We needn't worry about it any longer. We're a strong family and when you marry we'll be one of the richest families on the Eastern Seaboard."

Chad found the familiar phrase even more disconcerting now. "Will we talk again?"

"Eventually, and of other things. Now I fear I've taken too long in my discourse and must get back to business. There's a major new bond offering today. $200,000,000 at 6% due in forty and redeemable in ten years. The '1040's' they're called. And I'm meeting the representatives of this new Bessemer process. Steel will be bigger than cotton after this war. And we need to sort out our Southern cash flow problems. There's over a billion dollars of confederate currency in circulation and it's bringing only $4.60 in gold to the hundred. And the greenback dollar is now worth sixty-four cents. These are challenging times, my boy. Let's work together to make sure we stay on top. That's what it's all about in the long run, isn't it? Staying on top?"

* * *

Chad sat dejectedly in his old wing chair, eavesdropping as Harriet and Bartleby exchanged words in the hallway. The solid thump of the front door closed them in once again and warded off a world, Chad now believed, full of invaders eager to overthrow his personal principality. He walked to the window and watched his grandfather climb into a carriage. With a rap of his walking stick, Bartleby signaled the coachman, and made his escape from the stifling atmosphere of his daughter's foreboding house on East 10th Street, in "that immoral metropolis on the Hudson."

He was still standing at the window, gazing uneasily into the snow-swept street, when he heard his mother's voice behind him.

"I'm unaware of what he told you but I can only hope it's sufficient to soothe your troublesome nature and to restore our respect for each other."

"Mother, are we going to keep this up forever? You must know perfectly well what Grandfather said. And you know me well enough to assume I'm not satisfied with a story that is, at best, both sketchy and unconvincing."

"I'm the victim in all this."

"So you say."

"Even as a young girl I knew I was born before my time. And to tell the truth, women in Boston have, in a sense, more leeway than those in New York. At least those of our class. All this talk of freedom. I was only sixteen and I knew I had to be free. Free as any man."

"Do you think so simple a sin would lead to estrangement in our family?"

"So he told you about Corbin and me, in the stable."

"Then it was Cousin Corbin." Chad was embarrassed with his mother's offhand reference to a young girl and her cousin alone in a stable on Beacon Hill.

"It was indeed Corbin and it was completely innocent. I was sixteen, he was somewhat older. He'd already been away at sea for a while so it was titillating for me to hear his stories. We started out in the hayloft, just talking. Children—I was a mere child, you see—are curious. I had no mother to guide me and the governess, the one they had to get rid of later, hardly ever spoke to me after lessons and our daily walks on the Common."

"I find it most unnerving to discuss such an event with my own mother."

"One would think your broad background in the antics of Greeks and Romans would assuage any discomfort you may feel in so trivial a misdeed as our, what did Corbin call it, our 'lark.'"

"Mother, really."

"That's what it was. We started daring each other to do this or that and eventually it turned into a more dangerous game. We disrobed, piece by piece. Neither of us had seen the opposite sex before. At least I hadn't. Not as grown-ups. It was a simple lark and nothing else happened. I didn't see anything you don't look at every day in those etchings in your Greek art books."

"Such an innocent pastime was enough to practically ruin our lives?"

"Father had guests, two maiden ladies from Back Bay who had invested in our mills. They were stern and cold and unforgiving. They came to the stable to get their carriage and saw us in the hayloft. We were so startled and so bold we turned our backs on them and gave them a sort of salute."

If it hadn't been his mother talking, Chad was sure he'd have laughed. "*Morituri te salutamus.*"

"What?"

"We who are about to die salute you," he finally chuckled. "It's an old Latin phrase, from those who are in mortal danger in the arena. Like we are, it seems."

"It was a childish prank and if it hadn't been those particular old hens nothing would have come of it."

"Grandfather made reference to other questionable behavior. After he exiled you to Aunt Marilyn's."

"All that's grossly exaggerated too."

"Exaggerated? That you frequented a questionable house on 26th Street where men—many of them married I'm sure—sought the company of, how did he put it, attractive, intelligent well-educated women?"

"I was all of that and then some."

"Mother, I'm not a prude. I've had worldly experience of my own, perhaps far beyond anything you might expect of me, since you think I'm an impractical bookworm. The problem is—and remember I'm both tolerant and forgiving—the problem is my marriage. You were in the company of the Renfields in that questionable establishment."

"That's true."

"You met Randall there. And Phillipse as well."

"That's true."

"What must they think of you now?"

"They have very little choice in the matter. Frankly, Chad, I don't care a whit what they think as long as they do what I say."

"What went on between you and the father and uncle of my fiancée?"

"You're the expert on Greek literature. But I'm not illiterate, you know. You must realize you're on dangerous ground here." Harriet anxiously studied her son's taut face. "Perhaps you'd like to bow out now before you learn things that will distress you for the rest of your life."

"I pride myself on facing the truth and I'll not leave this room, nor allow you to, until I have answers. Complete answers. Were you intimate with them?"

"Yes and no."

"Stop this! I demand you to be honest."

"Yes, with Randall. No, with Phillipse."

"Does Phillipse know what went on between you and Randall?"

"Of course."

"Have you no shame?"

"I have purpose, not shame."

"He'll surely find a way to stop us from being married."

"I doubt that. You see, Phillipse was involved in similar behavior. Not with me. A pretty little girl from the Midwest somewhere. Pert and smart and utterly charming. All the men were crazy over her. She'd come East to go to school and ran away from it all just as I wanted to do. Phillipse was attracted to her and they had an affair. Since I know about it, he's unlikely to disobey my orders concerning your future."

"He could deny it."

"Hardly."

"He's strong and well connected. He could convince people you're lying or even mad."

"He could deny the affair but not the outcome."

"Outcome?"

"There was a child. A daughter."

"Phillipse had another daughter? Did she survive?"

"Chad, I beg of you to stop this now. There can be no possible result but grief for you and Clarissa."

"I fear these revelations as much as you're reluctant to impart them. But there can be no peace between us until the truth is out. All of it."

"Are you aware that Schuyler's birth was a difficult one for Phillipse's wife? She was from old Dutch stock, you know. They intermarried so much their blood would hardly clot. When Schuyler was born she was stricken ill. She was forbidden to have marital relations thereafter. Phillipse was devastated but he was also a man. So he sought what all men want, including you, Chad. I'm aware of your sensual nature, though you've spared me the details while insisting I reveal every little misdeed to you."

"Schuyler's over a year older than Clarissa. How could they not have had relations afterwards? There's no doubt in anybody's mind that Clarissa is the true daughter of Phillipse Renfield."

"Oh, she's his daughter all right." Harriet looked, for the first time, smug, as if her old sense of power and control was uncompromised.

"They were even brought up together. Schuyler and Clarissa have memories dating back to early childhood."

"To be precise, their memories date back to the year when Schuyler turned two."

"What is the significance of these revelations, Mother?"

"You demand the truth. I'm telling it to you. Clarissa is indeed Phillipse's daughter. But not by his wife."

"Good God!"

"I wish you wouldn't be so melodramatic all the time."

Chad waited in stunned silence as he pieced it all together. The light was dimming as the snow thickened. He lit the gas lamps and stirred the glowing logs. Harriet sat still as a statue, eyes unwavering, hands folded, face stony. Waiting, Chad thought, like a sibyl.

"Clarissa is the daughter of the woman in the house on 26th Street, is that it?"

"You're such a clever boy."

"Mother, don't use the sarcasm you accuse me of, not at a time like this."

"I begged you not to go on. What is to be served by this?"

"I must know what kind of woman she was, Clarissa's real mother. How will it affect our children?"

"She was a fair-haired, blue-eyed, healthy woman from a good family. With a vigorous mind. You don't have to worry. Your son, my grandson Renfield Laymus Wales, when he's born, will be of good stock."

"What happened to her?"

"Phillipse had to get rid of her, of course. He called in Dr. Forrest again, the young medic who examined me. Phillipse ordered Dr. Forrest to forge birth documents claiming his wife was the mother. She'd been sick in bed for months, nobody had seen her, so it was given out that she'd suffered a painful pregnancy. She died shortly afterwards and the enfant, your own Clarissa, was brought home late at night and smuggled in through the back garden gate into the nursery. The next day Schuyler was told to embrace his baby sister. Of course he was only a year or two old so he doesn't remember any of it. Indeed, Clarissa was told so many stories when she was a toddler she's imagined she can actually remember her mother."

"He 'got rid' of her? Do you realize what you're saying? He got rid of her!"

"You really ought to learn to hold your delusions in check, Chad. It was nothing so terrible. He gave her money and sent her off to live in Ohio. All sorts of people have disappeared in Ohio, when it was in their own best interests."

"Did Phillipse and Randall continue to frequent the house on 26th Street?"

"Many of the more prominent men gave it up after the Hunter Collins business."

"What Hunter Collins business?"

"Surely you know Parker Collins. Wasn't he at Princeton?"

"I never actually met him. He was several years ahead of me. But people on the campus still talked about him,"

"Hunter had a child by a woman who visited 26th Street. He later married her and adopted the child she gave birth to. Of course, the child was actually his own. It was Parker, in fact. Everybody knew the story but they mostly kept quiet, in self-defense, I suppose. Of course, it turned out all right for Parker. When Hunter died his mother married Hunter's brother. Then he died too, so she, and now Parker, inherited just about every railroad in California. They've got houses in New York and Newport and Charleston and give fortunes away to charity every year."

"We've not addressed the most shameful part of this story. You and Randall Renfield."

"I was lonely, so was he. To tell you the truth, I felt sorry for him. He's not all that bright, you know. We went our separate ways after a while."

"But you were pronounced 'intact'."

"By this time Dr. Forrest was on my side."

"And my father?"

"Marilyn introduced us, after I had to give up my little adventures and stay home with her. He liked me and I liked him and the inevitable happened. I think Aunt Marilyn wanted it to happen. When it became clear that I was with child, my family prevailed upon your father to do the right thing. Your father complained at first that I was not intact when we first met. But you're legitimate and even if you weren't, there's nobody left in town who'd dare to contradict me. I've got the goods on the lot of them!"

"It's all so sordid."

"My dear boy, no more sordid than visits to a certain house on Prince Street."

"How can you possibly know anything about that?"

"I had you followed one day. I gather it's none other than Bynum Bradley-West who lured you to such practices. Never fear, I won't use this data to your disadvantage. After all, it's I who've sacrificed personal happiness in order to guarantee your future, and the future of your son, who'll be the standard bearer for a great new dynasty. And there'll be not one shred of historical evidence to blacken his name!"

"How did you know I'd want to marry Clarissa?"

"I made them promise me that you'd be treated as a social equal and that you and she would spend a lot of time together as children. She was a lovely child and you were a strapping boy, if a bit too pensive, I might add. I made them promise that they'd encourage your friendship and if it blossomed into love, they'd facilitate the marriage without obstruction. They try to wiggle out of it occasionally, but whenever they do I simply confront them with the evidence."

"Evidence?"

"Chad, don't underestimate me. I've kept duplicates of all the documents drawn up by Dr. Forrest and some other certificates as well. And some letters from Ohio. They'd survive scrutiny in the highest courts. Randall and Phillipse know this. So they do as they're told."

February 1864

"My mother was of Dutch descent like you," Clarissa said. She poured tea for Eliza Van Der Venner and Susan Steinmann, who'd been invited to the Renfield Mansion to discuss wedding plans. "I can hardly remember her, for she died less than two years after I was born. But I think we always remember our mothers, even if they're taken away while we're babes-in-arms. Little things, a special scent, the feel of their satin and lace, the sound of their voice, lulling you to sleep."

Chad squirmed in his chair. As his mother had warned, he now knew more than he wanted to know and he must, at all costs, conceal it from the woman he loved lest he erase her fabricated memories and drive her from him forever. "My darling, I'd love you whether you were Dutch or English or even Irish. I'd love you whether you were rich or poor."

Marcus, who sat beside Schuyler on the love seat, raised an eyebrow. "What's this? Our scholar-in-residence has turned into a hopeless romantic."

"Not only that," Schuyler said, "but he now voices his sentiments in public. What do you think of that, Marcus?"

"These traditional lovers are prone to exaggerate, that's all."

"Exaggerate? Do you believe genuine affection can be simulated, at will?" Schuyler turned his bright eyes on Marcus, who adjusted his posture, putting a little more distance between him and his seatmate. "Well, do you, Marcus? Do you think a person of intelligence and integrity could merely pretend to possess dedication like that?"

Susan laughed, more loudly than usual. She sipped her tea, raising the cup to her lips and looking over the rim at Eliza, who smiled back, as if there were some kind of secret between them. Chad watched the tableau uneasily. Susan put her cup down and reached forward to take Clarissa's hand. "We all love you regardless of anything, and we're overjoyed that your father has finally consented to set the date. When will it be?

"I thought June at first and then decided, no, we've waited this long, let it be in the fall. At Yellowfields, not in the city. My father is so harried with business matters and Chad is dashing around solving problems for my Uncle Randall's business ventures. Early October. The trees will be ablaze and the air will be cool enough for a garden party. A grand country reception. On the very site of our new home. We'll string ribbons around the footprint of our new house and set up chairs and tables and invite the guests to review the drawings. Marcus has done a great job and both Chad and I are happy with the result. Schuyler helped, of course."

"More than helped. Some of the ideas Marcus used were originally mine. And the whole concept of those big windows, well, Marcus gets carried away all the time. Over just about everything. I had to make him try to be more subtle."

"Don't forget me," Chad said. "Without me there might have been no *porte cochere.*"

"Schuyler, why are you so excitable today," Marcus asked. Susan flashed her mysterious grin as he spoke. "Are you worried about who gets the credit for designing your sister's new house? Neither of us is an architect. All I did was provide some renderings, concepts if you will, which need to be finished by a professional. Your role, however, needn't be discounted at a later phase by the expertise of a professional. You need only capture our ideas in words, so the architect won't ruin what I think to be an imaginative structure."

"I suppose I could write something up while you're off in Ohio." Schuyler inched away from Marcus and scowled. "God knows you'll be gone long enough. I'll have time to write *Pilgrim's Progress.*"

"I'm no pilgrim and there'll be little progress as a result of my journey," Marcus said, putting his cup down, his face clouding as he watched Susan Steinmann's patronizing grin.

"When are you going to Ohio," Eliza asked.

"Why are you going to Ohio," Susan added. She seemed about to burst into titters.

"Tell them, Marcus, all the reasons you've got to go out there in time of war and spend a whole month while I stay here by myself. I could make such a trip. We were together all the time in Europe."

"But London and Paris were safe at the time, dear boy. And besides, I'll be busy with political and financial matters. You'd best remember that I'll settle my affairs once and for all and we'll leave for France without a worry in the world."

"What political matters," Chad asked.

"I thought that would get your attention. A radical wing of former Republicans is holding a convention in Cleveland in May. Word is they'll nominate John Fremont for president and General Cochrane for vice president. As you know my family is prominent in Ohio politics so they got me named as a delegate. I'll support them both. Of course, Fremont's a military man who was once convicted of mutiny. But maybe a little mutiny's just what we need right now."

"Fremont and Cochrane instead of Lincoln?" Chad sat up straight and put his cup down. He removed his hand from Clarissa's and put both palms on his knee. "Do you think they have a chance?"

"I don't know, but they're well regarded in Ohio. There's a big anti-war movement there. Vallandigham himself is called a Copperhead now. The Federal authorities hounded him out of the country but he still ran for office and won substantial votes, although he was forced to remain in Canada. Regardless of what you may think of them personally, Chad, with your pronounced views, I suspect you'd welcome such a ticket."

"So you've got two reasons for going to Ohio but not enough to convince me I should just stay home and do nothing for a month." Schuyler slid down the love seat and turned to face Marcus, who only smiled at him, thus provoking a ringing laugh from Susan Steinmann.

"You two," she said. "I hope we can cross to France with you, just for our amusement. You do bicker."

"Like an old married couple," Eliza said, also laughing.

Her words and her mirth were totally out of character, Chad thought. He didn't mind the obvious tension between his brother-in-law and his friend when they were alone. But with others, even Susan and Eliza, he felt embarrassed. "Well, friends need to have time on their own, to better appreciate why they're friends," he said stiffly. "Tell me more about this convention."

"Oh let's not start in on politics," Clarissa moaned. "We were discussing our wedding plans."

"How did you ever get your father to come around after his long resistance," Susan asked.

"Chad's mother came over to see him, with her father, Bartleby Laymus, in tow. They met behind closed doors and when they left Father called me into the drawing room and said—rather bluntly, I thought—that it was all right with him if I started to plan my wedding. He didn't seem pleased. He just huffed and puffed and went to his room. I'm worried about his health. He's under such strain."

"My father, too," Susan said. "These are such tragic times for our soldiers and here in New York our men folks, the ones who don't have to go to battle, run around making more and more money."

"Since you'll eventually get much of the money, you ought to be glad on that score," Marcus said. Chad surmised it was a comment made in revenge for Susan's teasing laughter.

"Your mother seems to possess a most convincing character," Marcus said. "Maybe I should take her to Ohio and let her address the convention."

"Marcus, don't make jokes about a woman's role in political life. Chad's mother has deep convictions and she, like me, is not pleased with the inferior position we're forced to occupy in what you think of as the manly pursuit of political reform." Susan was no longer teasing, and her eyes stabbed into Marcus, like rapiers.

"Wait a minute, don't blame me. I was sincere in my invitation. We need all the help we can get."

"I seem to be left out of this discussion altogether," Clarissa said. "Like an orphan allowed to sit with the grown-ups for a little while if she remains silent. I'm the one to marry Chadwick Wales. We'll be the ones with power and influence. Then, after this war, I'll help you address the place of women in this world. But not until after I'm safely married."

March 1864

Chad took Clarissa to see the new Winslow Homer painting, *Prisoners from the Front*. The crowd was sparse in mid-week, and the breeze light and warm for March. "Aunt Marilyn used to arrange special visits to the galleries," Chad said. "My mother would study the latest works by Cole and that young painter Church, and stop afterwards to discuss them over tea and cakes with her friends."

"What friends," Clarissa asked. "I've never seen her with anybody other than my family or yours."

"She doesn't, of course, occupy herself with casual acquaintances now that I'm home and she's active in so many causes. She's obsessed with abolition. Although I feel the issue is more complicated than she makes it out to be, I'm proud she can devote her energies to a moral purpose." Chad was certain his words sounded artificial and that Clarissa would sooner or later sense his difficulty in talking about subjects that brought to mind the secrets he now carried with him every day.

Indeed, the revelations thrust upon him by Grandfather Laymus and then his mother served only to agitate his already desperate frame of mind. Nor did he know how to extricate himself from his commitments to Bynum, although the continued news of bloodshed on the battlefield rendered their plot more urgent than ever. He slept little, tossing in his 10th Street bedroom all night long, getting up frequently to sit at his *escritoire* and make meaningless lists, dividing his opinions on every subject into two columns, opposing each element against another, then scrapping the entire page and starting all over again.

His business activities brought him little satisfaction. Since Appleby's murder on a public downtown street, a stream of letters from disgruntled investors had accumulated in his office, many of them as yet unopened. He informed Randall of the onslaught but was hushed up with vague assurances that the controversies would resolve themselves. Having been trained as a lawyer, Randall easily lapsed into pallid jargon when confronted on testy issues. "We'll monitor the progress of activities until such time as specific initiatives may seem proper in effecting our desired resolution," he answered during their last encounter. After one such terse discussion, he scooped all the mail into a gunnysack and toted it off to his law firm's suite, slung over his back like a Santa Claus visiting an orphanage.

But business worries were soon to take priority. "Clarissa, my dear, you must forgive me if I drop you off at home now and get to work downtown. Grandfather Laymus has set a meeting there with Randall and my Uncle Caleb. I sense he wishes to deliver some strong advice to both of them."

"I wish this war were done with and everything was like it used to be and you'd not just rush off without me at the drop of a hat when I want to spend time with you. I want to be alone with you more often. It's my right."

"And mine. But I've no choice in this case. There's been trouble surrounding some of the transactions in which I'm involved and Grandfather Bartleby thinks he must step in and straighten it all out. I wouldn't be surprised if he orders me out of it, after all. In that case, my dear, I'll have more time to spend with you. That's indeed my foremost desire. Never doubt it."

"What did you think of Mr. Homer's painting? He's such a fine artist, his technique is so subtle but so accurate. But it was a sad picture."

"War is sadder than any painting could ever be, by Homer or anybody else." Chad was surprised with the vehemence of his outburst, and felt Clarissa's tension beside him in the Renfield carriage.

"You have such strong feelings on everything except our wedding date."

"That's not true. And it's not fair either. We're living in a time of war. Your family and mine are players in it whether we admit it or not. Our financial status alone makes us key participants. My grandfather, who's an honorable man, nevertheless is devoting his time right now to saving our family position and fortune. Your father's doubtless doing the same. I'm preoccupied, as you know, by the war and feel I should try to do something to stop it."

"But what could you do, darling? You're only one person, and you're mostly a scholar turned businessman. Leave the war, at least, to others."

"There'll soon be plenty of 'others,'" Chad said. "Lincoln just called for 200,000 more draftees. 200,000! And they'll all soon be dead or maimed or sick with disease."

"I've read nothing of this new development." Clarissa had long since grown defensive when he brought up the war.

"It was yesterday. And last week he made Grant head of all the Union armies. He doesn't plan to let up until every Confederate or every Yankee soldier is dead or wounded or imprisoned. Last month the South took thousands of Union prisoners off to Andersonville. I'm sure conditions are wretched there, but what else are they to do? They don't have enough food and clothing for their troops and the civilians live from hand to mouth. Somebody's got to stop this outrage."

"I suppose you think you're destined to stop it because of your heritage."

"Clarissa, please. My father has already been killed in this war. How do you expect me to feel?"

"I don't understand it at all. I'm not like Susan Steinmann and those other women who want to engage in politics. I've read widely, you know that. I speak French almost as well as you do. And perhaps one day I shall travel. But I don't fool myself into thinking my vote, or my paltry actions, could change history. I'll continue to make bandages and visit the wounded, and I'll give to charities and try to help the widows and orphans."

"Nobody could question your compassion or generosity. Please let me go ahead and do what I must."

"Just as long as it doesn't threaten to tear you away from me." She squeezed his hand as the coach circled into the Renfield Mansion drive.

"Clarissa, allow me to continue on to my office. You don't need your driver right away, do you?"

"What I need right away is you," Clarissa said, rubbing his hand warmly but giving him a petulant frown.

* * *

"Let's not bother with all these papers and pencils, Chad. The less written down the better, after what I have to say to you this morning." It was Bartleby Laymus's first visit to Financial and Industrial Enterprises. Since Chad was never given a secretary, he'd arranged for the meeting by placing four chairs around the table, bringing out the water pitcher and glasses, and distributing writing materials.

"Father, it's kind of you to come here but we could have discussed this back home in Boston." Caleb shifted his eyes and broke the point of his pencil as he drew criss-cross lines on the paper Chad provided.

"Caleb, if I felt you'd ever be received in Boston again, I'd have done so. News of your shenanigans has permeated the Massachusetts financial world and hence, dowagers and dottering old retirees whisper of you all day long."

"My business affairs are my own. Would you intend to ruin my life the way you botched up my sister's?"

Chad bristled at this comment, as Bartleby's flushed face grew redder. "Since my grandson intends to marry your partner's niece, we're all one family here. But I urge you, Caleb, to show not merely discretion, but consideration for those who'll be disturbed by such an utterance."

"I'm my own man and I'll do what I think is in my best interest."

"It's hard being a father," Bartleby said. "But before you make extravagant threats, let me fill you in on my purposes. I've had several of my most trusted clerks and lawyers scan all the records we could obtain of your business activities here in New York. Over half the new companies you sold stock in aren't producing any revenue whatsoever. Some of them exist only to decorate a letterhead. The remaining ones either operate at a loss or are under attack for selling faulty goods, missing deadlines, or engaging in unfair employment practices, such as this new immigration act Mr. Lincoln has seen fit to sign— an ill-conceived policy which allows a new hoard of desperate people to arrive on our shores, only to find out they're little more than indentured servants, lured by false promises and exploited by cronies of this administration."

"That immigration bill was enacted under pressure from industrialists like yourself, Mr. Laymus," Randall said. "I'm merely a lawyer and investor. It's people like you who know how to exploit labor."

"I won't react to your insult since it's beneath me. It's true that we've made grievous mistakes in our employment policies in the past, but I hope to see improvements in that regard. As for you, Mr. Renfield, I regret my son ever joined forces with you. It's likely you'll both be shot dead on the street like that Appleby, or else find yourself so deep in lawsuits you won't be able to make it over to Delmonico's for lunch."

"Father, you're too severe."

"I have a severe purpose and I'll not waste words. First, you've euchred my grandson into your schemes and he's to wed the flower of New York society in the fall. I want that wedding to go forth without blemish so I'm submitting his resignation for him, here and now."

"Surely you realize that Chad has prospered greatly through his work with us," Randall said.

"Yes, and I'm proud he had the good sense to invest his profits in sounder and more proper enterprises."

"Why do you think it necessary for you to speak for me in this matter? Did my mother get to you too, just to make sure things work out her way?" Chad was afraid he was turning as red as his grandfather. "I've made myself clear on this point, once and for all. I'm my own man and I can handle my career without interference."

"No, you can't," Bartleby said. "You've let them draw you ever deeper into their schemes and your name appears on this prospectus and that contract or some other warrant. I intend to remove your name and the papers you've affixed it thereunto, to paraphrase our counselor-at-law here."

"This is an outrage," Randall said.

"You've no right," Caleb said.

"Let me continue. Number two, I want you, Caleb, to sell all your shares immediately."

"But who'll buy them?"

"Randall will see to it that somebody buys them, at whatever price, along with his own stocks. You can give them to charity, if any respectable charity would take them. Otherwise just dump them with Appleby's successors."

Randall grew as red as his antagonist. "What makes you think I'd agree to that?"

"Your desire neither to be shot nor hanged should prove an adequate motivation," Bartleby said.

"You'd best guarantee your threats prior to dictating any actions to me or to your son."

"There's a grand jury assembled just three blocks from here. They'll study information that one of my colleagues has inspected beforehand. It will cite grave malfeasance and actionable behavior. It will name names and cite dates and list amounts. In short, Randall, you need to get out of town as fast as you can. I can arrange that for you as soon as you and Caleb disgorge all outstanding interests in these companies."

"You'd ruin your own son?"

"Yes, if it would save him from a jail cell or an assassin. I've prepared two documents here, one for each of you. It turns over your power of attorney relative to Financial and Industrial Enterprises, documents I'll provide to a legal representative here who can act on them without revealing my role in the matter and without sending the Black Maria to wait at your door, eager to convey you through the public streets to prison. Although if the mob finds out who's inside, they'll do you in themselves."

Caleb and Randall fell silent, exchanging glances with each other that seemed to grow more resentful by the second.

"I confess, Father, that Randall here has anticipated trouble of this nature. We didn't expect you to be the messenger."

"You shouldn't be tempted to shoot the messenger. Indeed, I've got your salvation in my hands."

Caleb looked hopeful but Randall shifted uneasily in his chair.

"As for you, my son, you've always liked your summers in New Brunswick. There's a fine old colony of traitorous Americans there, descended from the Tories who fled to Canada when the Revolution started. You may join them. I've arranged for an income for you, an ample but unostentatious residence, and a small role in some of our Canadian mills. You'll not, naturally, be trusted with much authority."

"What of me?" Randall said, almost screaming. "It was I who told Caleb we might eventually end up in Canada. I had rather looked forward to it. I may marry there."

"If you're still alive when my ship docks in St Andrews, I wish you a speedy courtship and a hasty marriage. Too bad you couldn't take your bride's name after the ceremony. You'd be safer."

"Sir, you go too far. I shall speak to my brother Phillipse."

"I think not. You know as well as I how much my daughter Harriet influences his actions, as well as yours, by certain documented knowledge she possesses. She and I have already discussed this solution, and she embraces it even more fervently than I, because she doesn't want anything, anything whatsoever, to darken her son's future when he marries your niece and produces an heir who'll unite the Laymus and Renfield lines. She expects a grandson as soon as possible and Clarissa and Chad will more than likely give her one. She wouldn't take kindly to any recalcitrance on either of your parts. And as I say, I've arranged for a ship to slip out of the harbor tomorrow night. That will give you enough time. I trust, Randall, since you've already anticipated such a move yourself, that you've smuggled enough money into Canada to allow you to buy yourself a wife and live quietly for your remaining years."

Bartleby shoved the papers, in two batches, to Randall and Caleb, and set a smaller set of documents before Chad. "Now let's everybody sign. Secretary Chase is due in New York shortly to grumble about the soaring price of gold. It's likely he'll try to salvage what's left of the greenback. I'm to meet with his advance men this afternoon to tell them where we New Englanders stand on the plunging currency issue. So sign, gentlemen, sign!"

May 1864

Clarissa's skirts and stockings hung over the back of an armchair in Chad's East 10th Street bedroom. Clarissa herself, unclothed, lay on top of him, teasing his hair with one hand and nibbling candy with the other.

"Thanks for the sweets, my darling. I've not had anything else to eat all afternoon." She moved her free hand from his temple and placed it on his chest, tracing an invisible line downwards to his naval and further still. Chad was on his back, also nude. Although their vigorous lovemaking had pacified him, he sighed occasionally and averted her gaze. "What's troubling you, sweetheart? We've got a clear path now. Nobody can stop us. And when we're wed we'll answer to no one but ourselves."

"The thought of our happiness together, in a peaceful country, and with all these financial schemes over and done with, that thought, Clarissa, is all that sustains me. I don't wish to cast shadows on your happy face. I love you so."

"I'm confident that you do, but I fear your mind. It's always wandering and you see things others don't. Things that always seem probable to you but half the time do not materialize."

"It's my personality. I'm afraid you're stuck with it."

"I want you just the way you are. My opinionated, visionary poet of a spouse, who can also show his business side if he wants to."

"Opinionated?"

"You've got the courage of your convictions."

"It's not the same thing."

"Don't blame me for bringing it up. We're here in the most intimate of circumstances and your face has that faraway look. I want all your attention when we're together."

"I'll do my best."

"Is it your mother?"

"Is what my mother?"

"The way you are."

"You just said you like the way I am."

"But not all the time. I want you to be my mirror. I want to see myself in your eyes and my happiness on your face."

"I'm happy when I'm with you, but the world won't go away and I'm involved in troublesome activities."

"Your mother, God bless her, will settle most of that. My father had no recourse when she and your grandfather laid down the law. My father's troubled too but he goes about his business. He has fears about the future. You and he are alike in that regard. They say a girl often looks for her father in her husband. Perhaps you aren't all that much unalike."

"I respect your father and wouldn't be grieved to be compared with him. But my troubles are my own. I must extricate myself from the rumors surrounding Uncle Caleb's business dealings. And your Uncle Randall as well."

"I thought all that was settled."

"More or less, although my name was mentioned in the financial pages more than once. Nobody really knows me that well so I suppose some poor mad investor won't gun me down like old Appleby."

"Appleby was a scoundrel. Uncle Randall said so."

"He's hardly in a position to feel superior."

"Darling, I don't care a whit about all this. We're together in your house like man and wife and neither of us cares if the housekeeper storms in or if people talk. When we're wed and this war is over, nobody will have the nerve to malign us. We'll be too powerful for that."

"It was never power that I sought."

"Yes it was. If we were that powerful you wouldn't worry about business or even the war."

"You do me a disservice if you think I wouldn't still oppose this war. It's a matter of deepest principle with me."

"I shouldn't even mention it, I guess. I don't want to act like your mother, you'd just end up hating me. I understand you better than you think. I do wish you'd just try to keep your mind on me and the future. The war will end one way or another no matter what you or I do about it." She twisted his curls again and placed the candy box on the nightstand. "Thanks for the candies but I'm hungry for something else. Want to do it again?"

"Do what again?" Chad mumbled.

"How do you think that makes me feel?"

Chad interrupted her words with a long deep kiss, rolled her over on her back, and lay gently on top of her. "We'll do it all day if you want."

"Well not all day, Chad."

"Why not?"

"We have a date with the Aspinwalls. We shouldn't be late."

"It's just at the end of the block."

"I know where it is and I'm surprised you haven't been there before. Their Old Masters are the talk of the town and not everybody gets invited inside to see them. They say some of the pictures, the Dutch ones, are even better than the Italian collection. How did they make their money?"

"The Aspinwalls?"

"Yes. I never heard father mention them and they live right here on the same block and you never said a word before."

"I have my dreams, too, Clarissa. Do you think I enjoy all this worry about the war and the fact that I feel I must take action soon, something personal? Or lie awake at three in the morning wondering what my mother is up to, or lamenting the loss of my father? Or afraid I may be tainted by the financial *legerdemain* of your and my relatives? I read and I write a little and I pace the room and I dream of a better life ahead, peaceful and gentle and refined and meaningful."

"What's all that got to do with the Aspinwalls?"

"I've taken more interest in the visual arts. Everybody teases me about being a bookworm and I don't mind it. But I think an art collection, when we're living at Yellowfields, might be comforting as well."

"Then I shall buy you one. Now kiss me."

A loud knock at the door was followed by a louder voice. It was Higgens.

"Mr. Chad, are you in there? A messenger just left a letter for you. He says it's most urgent, a matter of life and death, he said. The housekeeper said it would be better if I brought it to you."

Chad donned his dressing gown and Clarissa inched down under the coverlet. When he opened the door a crack he saw one of Higgens' eyes, gleaming in the half light, and then, as he pulled the door slowly forward, was treated to his coachman's full visage, that noncommittal look on his face, but somehow, Chad was sure, a sparkle of understanding in his eyes. He now assumed all the servants knew what went on in his bedroom.

"Did you recognize the messenger?"

"No, Sir. There was no carriage outside and when he handed me the envelope he repeated how urgent it is and fled afoot down the street towards Fifth Avenue. He seemed quite afraid."

Chad felt the now familiar fear in his stomach—anxiety that repeatedly woke him up at three in the morning. He struggled to maintain his composure. "Very well then, Higgens. Let me have it."

He closed the door tightly and turned up the gas. The message was once again in a familiar handwriting, but the paper was a cheap brand and was soiled by water and ink. But it was Bynum's handwriting, that was for sure. He ripped it open and gazed, transfixed, on the brief inscription. *"You must guard your every action now. I'm taken."*

* * *

Captain Hartigan was almost unrecognizable in the gloom of the tavern, more so since he hadn't worn his uniform with the long white gloves and the white banded hat. He was a tall man, though, so Chad discerned his plainly clad form, familiar even from a distance. The tavern, not far from Madam Maureen's, was boisterous on a Saturday afternoon, laughter reverberating from the mirrored walls hung with advertising broadsides, a lamp or two, and the mounted heads of elk and bison. As he snaked his way across the crowded room, barely able to squeeze between tables, Chad felt the sawdust under his feet, making the floor as slippery, he thought, as his own current position in the disordered wartime world of his once-happy hometown.

Captain Hartigan nodded but said nothing when Chad sat down. There was a pitcher of beer on the table and two glasses, one already filled. White foam rimmed the captain's lips as he swallowed. He wiped his face and then spoke softly.

"I thought it best to meet somewhere like this. Can't be too careful now. It's my day off and nobody much knows me here, out of uniform. Were you followed?"

"I don't think so. I went to my favorite bookstore on Broadway and browsed for a long time, keeping my eye on the other customers. I slipped out the back way."

"Let's not take more time than necessary. The situation is this: my sources tell me they're going to let Bynum go after keeping him overnight. They grilled him but didn't use any of the methods we sometimes employ to gain a speedy response."

"You mean torture?"

"We call it 'special interrogation'. It's not pleasant. There are those who are more forthright and call it torture."

"Why would they let him go?"

"Obviously, they want to see where he'll lead them. Remember, Bynum's clever. He's operated here for several years. He has access to high society. He's never been observed in an unlawful act. He makes no public statements. And he's not in cahoots with any movement, as far as our men can tell."

"He was arrested by your men?"

"Oh, no. It was the Secret Service. Pinkerton's men. We have no choice but to cooperate with them. In fact, in many cases they're doing us a favor, getting some of these rowdies and spies and perverts and God knows what off the streets. Sometimes Lincoln's men use our precinct headquarters for their 'interviews'. Of course, you and I and Bynum have an agreement, so you know you can always count on me."

"But you're growing in prestige and power. You may be asked by the government and by the newspapers where you stand."

"I'm used to that. They came to me when Appleby was shot. Found out he sold me some stock. I told them I'd sold it shortly afterwards and therefore had no further motive for shooting him." Hartigan threw his head back in laughter, reminiscent of what Chad now thought of as the 'old days.'

"I hope you don't blame me for that."

"Oh no, I'm grateful. When you introduced me to Randall Renfield I immediately decided I should make investment decisions on my own. He struck me as phony and pretentious. I'm sticking mostly to real estate now. And a few war-related enterprises that are actually making money and serving the cause."

"You know I'm opposed to the 'cause' as it's defined by our government."

"I have a hard time with it too. Especially with my Irish and German constituents. They get news every day that another son or nephew or husband has been killed. I've never heard of casualties in this magnitude. So I'll not grieve if the war is brought to a halt, by whatever means and by whichever side."

"Captain Hartigan, the slaughter is unimaginable. Ten days ago in

Virginia, in the Wilderness campaign, there were 27,000 casualties in two days. Two days! Now Sherman has left Chattanooga with a vow to take Atlanta and then march across Georgia to the sea. If his past performance is any indication, he'll devastate the countryside beyond any necessity, even by the rules of war."

"There are no rules of war, not really. Even my patrolmen know that. Just a string of platitudes peddled by fence-straddlers to allow them to advance their own purposes at any cost. When the chips are down, either side will do whatever it wants to. Individual soldiers, hungry and scared and away from home, many of them drunk, will rape. They'll burn. They'll steal. Outraged with grief for their fallen comrades they'll kill the innocent in revenge. You're a well-read man. Surely you know such things already."

"The historians tend to gloss over that aspect, even the Greeks. For the most part they tell their war stories in an atmosphere of glory and courage and righteousness."

"You persevere in your conspiracy?"

"Yes. You have some indication of our purposes, Bynum and I. I thought at one point that one side or the other would run out of money. The Confederate currency is sinking like a stone and inflation here is rampant. But responsible people, otherwise decent people like Steinmann and Phillipse Renfield, keep the cash flowing. They've helped the Federal cause and they're selling our bonds abroad."

"Investigated a burglary at his house once, Mr. Steinmann. A small man with black eyes and an expressionless face. Couldn't for the life of me tell what he was thinking. But I gather he's a very rich man. The house looked like a castle, full of pictures and fine rugs. What does he do, actually".

"He's a prominent investment banker, like my future father-in-law. Like Mr. Morgan."

"Investment banker. What an interesting term."

"They're for the most part bound by rigid rules of propriety. They have a culture all their own. They avoid the limelight and abhor bad publicity. For a while I aspired to be a part of that."

"But you don't trust them any longer. You see, I never did trust them, and I'm just a simple policeman."

"I want to be married and settled down in the country. We'll build a house on the Renfield estate. I want to pursue the things I'm comfortable with. My books. Some writing. And pictures, too. I've grown interested, lately, in art, since it seems relatively free of propaganda and rhetoric. Even Winslow Homer, though he has a message, seems to hew to the truth."

"I've seen his drawings in *Harper's Weekly*. Truth? I'll leave that to you and your philosophers."

"Will you let Bynum know the truth, then? That we've met. That I'm glad he'll be released. And that it will be up to him to arrange a time and place for us to meet so we can make our final decisions?"

"I will. Don't forget that I continue to receive deposits into my account. And that you also have access to funds set aside by Bynum to compensate me for my assistance and to use in my behalf should I be compromised in any way. I'll hold you to that as a young man of honor."

"Be assured, Captain, I won't shirk from my duties, either towards you or to my greater cause, which is to stop this legalized murder and to restore sanity to our nation."

"I have confidence in you, lad, in all but the last of your goals."

* * *

"Schuyler, this is outrageous! How can you ask me, face to face, to help you arrange such a tawdry assignation? In my own home? And with Marcus gone off to Ohio? How tolerant do you suppose me to be?"

"If we go to an hotel, it would look odd, because of his social position."

"You're worried about social position in a matter such as this?"

"Put yourself in my place."

"I'm unable even to imagine doing that, Schuyler!"

"Well, then, think of your reading. What about Zeus?"

"Zeus?"

"Zeus and that boy. The one who's in all those etchings and picture books. Runnymede or something."

"Ganymede. I thought you went to Yale."

"I wasn't all that interested in the pictures since we had so much going on in real life. But wasn't this Ganymede, in the pictures at least, just a young man? A boy, even?"

"Schuyler, it's a myth. If you want to be realistic in your portrayal of them you'll have to believe their gods really existed. Besides, the youth in question here today is a stableboy."

"That's why I can't do anything around our house or go to an hotel."

"Good God, how far do I have to go to be a good brother-in-law to you!"

"I've assisted you in achieving premarital relations with my only sister."

"It's not the same thing."

"Chad, I disagree. When Marcus and I were in London we went to a house where young men were available for all the upper classes. We had an escort, a friend from Yale who had settled in London. He introduced us to the other patrons. There were people there with titles. Lord this or that. Sir this or that. And members of Parliament. And merchant princes, as our papers call them. Even investment bankers."

"Investment bankers in a male whorehouse?"

"You really shouldn't use such terminology. You're a wise and tolerant man. You have a wider worldview than most. Why should you be offended?"

"Most of my experience comes from reading Greek and Latin."

"How about poetry? English poetry?"

"Very little reference to that subject, and it's usually well disguised."

"No, I mean how about the poets themselves?"

"Who?"

"George Gordon Lord Byron, that's who."

"Come now, Schuyler, Lord Byron was an idealist. He used his humor to satirize social ills and ridicule the unjust. He was thoughtful, like me. He even went to Greece to fight for freedom there. Lost his life in a truly noble cause."

"No he didn't."

"Didn't what?"

"Go to Greece to fight for ideals. In that house in London, I think it was on Cleveland Street, which struck Marcus as ironic. It was in that house that I met this very old man, an Oxford don, who came there regularly to appreciate what he referred to as 'the Greek ideal.' He told us Byron had to get out of the country because he was about to be arrested for having sexual relationships with a choirboy from his parish. The very parish he was 'Lord' of."

"Is there nothing to limit you in justifying your practices? I've tried to be understanding. I like you. I like Marcus. And now he's off in Ohio with those radical ex-Republicans who may, I hope, nominate a suitable alternative to Lincoln. And he's facing up to his family and making arrangements for you to live with him in France. And you repay him by sleeping with a stableboy!"

"I haven't actually slept with him yet."

"Please, spare me the details."

"It's the details that matter. He's been eyeing me ever since he grew up. He's almost twenty, you know. He started looking after our horses three or four years ago. But whenever I summon a carriage, there he is. And he gives me these looks. There's no mistaking his intent. So I caught him alone in the stable one day and we talked. He agreed we couldn't do anything on the grounds. Too risky, for both of us. I told him I have a friend who might let us spend some time in his house because I did him a similar favor once."

"Similar? Damn you, Schuyler."

"Don't get angry with me, Chad. I'm lonely with Marcus away. I've nothing to do. Father hardly speaks to me. I don't want to frequent those taverns downtown, where we got in trouble that time. But I'm flesh and blood and I need affection and tenderness and companionship. I know you and Clarissa are frequently together and I can tell because both of you, well, you glow, you absolutely glow. I want to glow too."

"Well, you can't glow here, Schuyler. Look, I'll do this one thing. Let me give you a note to a woman I know on Prince Street. It's the place you visited me and Captain Hartigan and Bynum, when you were being blackmailed. I'll tell her to let you and your friend occupy a room there. You'll have to pay her. And for God's sake don't let anybody see you and don't let there be any evidence. I feel awful doing this because I like Marcus."

"And what do you think he's doing in Cleveland besides casting his vote? I know for a fact that one of the sons of a very prominent member of Cleveland's wealthy upper class is just like me and Marcus. He even went to Yale. And Marcus will no doubt look him up and they'll go carousing. We're young, Chad. We want to experience life while we can."

Chad wrote a few words on a piece of paper and handed it to Schuyler, who now looked sheepish.

"I'm sure you can't understand this, Chad, but this boy, he's all right. He's handsome and wholesome and trustworthy and he just wants to be given some affection and friendship like any other human being. Regardless of social class."

"If anything gets out and I'm linked to this I'll deny I ever met you at Madam Maureen's or made arrangements for you and your stableboy."

Schuyler folded the note and put it in his pocket. "Please don't think less of me. I'm as good as you and I'm your friend and your relative. I'll not bring public disgrace on our families and I'll not, I'll absolutely not, ever do anything to harm you and my sister." He picked up his summer hat and a pearl-handled walking stick and closed the parlor doors behind him.

June 1864

Chad found his way to Reverend Mullen's house without difficulty, although he'd almost decided on the ferry to forego the invitation and then changed his mind again when he sat foot on the dock, where Jeremy waited with Mullen's carriage. He knew that his mother was already there, and suspected Cousin Corbin would be too. More than once he asked himself why he went on with these relationships, when he could simply firebomb a few buildings and escape, undetected, to Yellowfields and settle down, alone with his Clarissa, and without daily contact with the lot of them.

Melissa opened the door and welcomed him enthusiastically. She seemed more animated this time and he knew the reason—the only reason, in fact, he'd accepted their request for a meeting, although he couldn't foresee any way he could serve their immediate need, which was to rescue Melissa's family from Virginia, transport them to Baltimore where they'd board one of Corbin's ships, and sail for Nova Scotia.

Harriet, Tad, Corbin and Melissa sat in a semi-circle facing him, as if he were a prisoner in the dock. Chad tried to engage his mother's eyes but she stared only at the floor. Tad looked embarrassed, as did Corbin, who perhaps already knew that his playful teenage behavior in a Boston stable had been shared and therefore was forever to be a barrier between them.

"What can I do," Chad said in response to their silent gaze. "The war, that's my first goal. Afterwards, we'll address the slavery issue and eradicate it from our country once and for all."

"Ah, yes," Mullen said. "You're as idealistic as ever but it seems to me one is more likely to change things on a small rather than large scale. Our problem is this: despite Federal victories in Virginia, we still lack the means to smuggle Melissa's family out of there. Only last week Grant defeated Lee at Cold Harbor, as you must know. He'll surely continue until the whole state is under his command and the war will then be almost over. But we can't delay, since there are reports of slaves being sent further south in hopes that the war will be settled before a total military victory is achieved. Even with Sherman advancing towards Atlanta, we can't take that chance. Melissa is in suspense and all of us here want to take a smaller action, rather than the grander deed you seem to be contemplating."

"Grant lost 12,000 men in three days at Cold Harbor," Chad said. "You call this issue second to any other? Dead and maimed! Twelve thousand! And that doesn't include the Southern losses."

"Nonetheless we must follow our conscience," Corbin said. "Chad, it's quite simple. We know you're in contact with Bynum Bradley-West. We know he was recently arrested and then released. Doubtless you'll meet with him again. All we ask of you is to enlist him in our cause. He's stated that his family held no slaves and he is himself opposed to servitude. He's confided that his primary loyalty is to his home state of North Carolina. For that reason we want you to seek his help in making connections in Virginia, connections that will allow us to get Melissa's family out now before the entire Confederacy collapses into anarchy in the final days of this war you're so opposed to." Corbin glanced first at Harriet and then at Mullen as he finished his speech. The room was hot for early June and the air still. Corbin wiped his forehead with a spotless white cloth from his vest pocket, glanced at his watch, and shifted uneasily in his armchair.

Harriet finally lifted her eyes from the floor and looked at her son with a pleading expression. "You know this is an awkward time for me, for reasons that most people in this room know about. Despite the affronts I've suffered from all of you, including you, Chad, I'll not abandon my work to abolish the supreme evil in our land today. And that's slavery."

"Evil yes, but no more 'supreme' than this murderous war." Chad felt the hair on his neck crawling in the unexpected heat. He wanted to scratch himself but felt it unseemly, since all eyes were focused on him and he, apparently, held the key to their strategy. "While I understand your sense of urgency, I'd beg you to put things in perspective. Rapid developments internationally may affect the course of this conflict. Maximillian, a man described as a pawn of Napoleon III, landed last month in Vera Cruz to rule Mexico. The French would like this war to end just as the English do. And on May 31, in Cleveland, a group of disaffected former Republicans offered a substitute ticket for the election, Fremont and Cochrane. They want to seek a speedy resolution to the fighting and negotiate a truce. The Democrats have nominated McClellan, who's unlikely to defeat either Lincoln or Fremont. Here at home I hear rumors of insurgencies that may force the people who run things to end this obstinate and futile bloodshed and address the slavery issue forthwith, for once and for all. I'm just a young man only four years out of college, labeled a bookworm by most of you, and considered to be somehow outside the mainstream of business and politics. I'm not flattered that you've decided to seek my help, which seems to me unworthy of all your efforts."

"But politics is most affected by dramatic actions close to home, deeds that make the newspapers, and will thus remind the populace that the slavery issue hasn't been solved by Mr. Lincoln's proclamation." Mullen paused, as if suddenly aware he was revealing his motivations, which weren't altogether aimed at Melissa's dilemma. "We must show our compassion for our fellow humans one by one, but we must also realize that sometimes a single action, a small event, can have momentous impact on the public mind."

"If there is a public mind," Chad said. He viewed Mullen's words as a threat, as if the Reverend knew that the examples advanced were very much like his own agenda, an effort to disrupt Northern morale by a series of deadly attacks in its major cities. Did his face reveal too much? Had they somehow guessed he was himself plotting "smaller" actions in an attempt to change public opinion? It was too close for comfort and he knew he must find a way out. "I hope to hear from Bynum now that he's been cleared of any seditious endeavors, and will propose to him that he provide a conduit to Virginians who may assist you. But that's the extent of my compliance and now I must go, for I've a multitude of other demands upon me. As you may know my Uncle Caleb and my Clarissa's Uncle Randall have closed down their business ventures and are leaving this very night for St. John. I believe on one of your ships, Corbin."

"It's true that I've offered to help them relocate in view of the largely unfounded rumors of irregularity in their commercial enterprises."

"There seems to be no end, Cousin, to your compassion in aiding the downtrodden."

Harriet laughed loudly, piercing the warm tense air and surprising everybody, most of all her son. "All of you know how devoted I am to my son and his future. Indeed his offspring will carry the day sooner or later. In the meantime, I've learned to admit that sarcasm will always be his most telling trait."

* * *

"I took the usual precautions," Chad said. Although he no longer wished to betray Clarissa with Madam Maureen's girls, he felt strangely peaceful to be back in her house on Prince Street. When Madam Maureen opened the front door, he expected a comment about Schuyler's visit, but all he got was a conspiratorial smile as she ushered him into the library. Bynum was smoking his large curved pipe, which spewed gunmetal gray wisps of smoke across the room, warm and dim, although it was a brilliant late June day.

"It's obvious they know about us. Your name was on that officer's list when they came aboard the Renfield yacht. The only reason I'm sitting here, more or less free, is they think they can catch larger fish, or perhaps foil our plot."

"Can they?"

"I don't think so. Our agents from the South, the ones who'll carry out most of the attacks in at least five Northern cities, are unknown to them. They have no mailing address, no other contacts, no relatives or close associates. Some are themselves of Northern descent, and a few are old enough to sport gray hair and an elderly gait. No, the problem is you and I. I'm sure they'll arrest me again soon. The question is, how much can we get done between now and November?" Chad raised his eyebrows at this question. "We've chosen November for our actions. Election day. We'll use the incendiary devices I told you about. They're already stockpiled. We've selected the targets. All that's left, now, is for you to decide what role you want to play from here on out."

"I'm of two minds, as you know. I don't wish to harm the innocent. And selfishly, I wonder if it's worth it for me, since Clarissa and I'll soon be married and I'll be able to retire to Yellowfields and pursue my real loves."

"I wouldn't seek to restrain you, if you wanted to part ways. It would be perhaps the best thing I could do, if I let you go, to honor your father's memory."

"I said I was of two minds. I didn't say which one I favor."

"You must think carefully on this."

"I've done so."

"And you've reached a conclusion?"

"I have."

Bynum pulled on his pipe and looked towards the shuttered windows. There were distant sounds in the house, a titter, a shout, a slamming door. Chad sensed that his colleague was reluctant to ask, perhaps fearful to know, his decision.

"Don't you want to know what I've decided?"

"I suppose I must."

"Everybody patronizes me. I'm given a job, money, schooling, even a bride. My mother has disclosed that her real aim in life is to have me provide her a grandson to unite the Laymus and Renfield lines. It's like I was a stallion at stud, simply a pawn in everybody's larger schemes. But on the level of my feelings, my ideals, I can't sit by and watch, from my privileged position, as more and more people are killed, day in and day out."

"Yes, the slaughter is unprecedented and unimaginable."

"It might be different if we lost a dozen here or there. Or if there were some reason to think that the end is near and we'll be better for it. But I foresee a fight to the last man and an aftermath of hideous atrocities and punishment, from the side that wins, for the side that loses. And I suspect we both know that the South cannot endure much longer on its own."

"So you're with us to the end?"

"Yes, to the end."

"And what other role do you intend to play?"

"I'm determined to blow up the armory," Chad said.

NINE

September 1864

Clarissa's personal sitting room, connected by double doors to her boudoir, sparkled in the light of early fall. Just outside her windows a large maple flamed with scarlet. In the distance the head gardener and his crew prepared sapling and shrub and flowering bush against the imminent onset of a Yellowfields winter. Their voices, unintelligible across the dry autumn lawns, rose and fell on a gentle breeze from the river.

She'd been listless all morning, barely responding to Chad's insistent caresses. She averted her eyes suddenly when they met his. Chad never admitted any doubt of her constancy, but the moodiness was unmistakable and he felt both concern and irritation rising in his chest.

"Is there something the matter, sweetheart?"

"What could be the matter? Our wedding day is set for mid-October. You've torn yourself away from that mess in the city to spend some time with me for a change. My brother and his friend are due soon. They'll tell us all about their planned departure for France. Over and over again. Our private little army has secured the estate. We're safe. So why should I fret?" Her tone belied her words as she continued to avoid Chad's gaze.

"I've loved you since we were children. Do you think I can't tell when you're distraught?"

"I'm surprised you'd even consider it, with your burden of worries about business and the war and your friend Bynum."

"I haven't seen Bynum for weeks."

"But you want to see him. You're alike, the two of you. Even though you haven't even been down there."

"What are you talking about?"

267

"The South, that's what I'm talking about. This Bynum fellow is a loyal Southerner and you try to act like him because of your father and that big plantation with a silly name."

"Clarissa, I'm still mourning my father's death. And I'm of course loyal to his memory, and to the Virginia family I've never known. Cedar Crest Hall is no sillier a name than Yellowfields."

"My mother named it 'Yellowfields' just before she died."

"How do you know that, you can't even remember her."

"I can too. I feel her presence all the time. I remember her silks and lace and her perfumes and the tone of her voice, even though I was so very young when she died."

Chad released her hands and stood up brusquely, then crossed to the window and stared at the maple's red leaves, fluttering in the soft ripple of air. He took a deep breath and silently counted to ten, lest he hurt her with his knowledge that she couldn't have known her real mother.

"Let's not be unpleasant over such trivial matters. You know I love you more than anything else. You mustn't let your selfishness cloud your respect for me and the issues I'm concerned about. I've been out of Princeton scarcely four years and already I've proved my mettle in business, taken part in various political activities, and continued to devote all my spare time to you."

"That's what it is, alright, your spare time."

"Are you determined to force a rupture between us? You know how much I detest bickering."

"Would you allow me to 'force a rupture' as you put it?"

"I'd try to forestall such an event. But you're rather spoiled, you know. So rich. So beautiful. With a doting father and a loving brother. And a lover who wants nothing more than to marry you and settle down here to raise a family and pursue my scholarly goals."

"Which is more important, scholarship or love?"

"Darling, that's a ridiculous question."

"You always dismiss me as if I weren't on your intellectual level." Chad remained silent while she fumed. "Maybe I should just go abroad for a while. I could live in France for a year with my brother as chaperon. He could guard my honor."

"He can't even guard his own honor." Chad blurted the words out and regretted it instantly.

"What's that supposed to mean? Just because he's a little different."

"A little?"

"You said you didn't wish to discuss the particulars of their friendship. You told me to accept him for what he is, a loyal sibling and a constant friend."

"Then what the hell are we arguing about?"

"How dare you swear like that in my bedroom?"

"You call that swearing? Listen, my dear, I'm experienced in the ways of the world. I've heard and seen things you'll never encounter."

"Such as?"

"Is this what you're up to? Do you want me to reveal all I know about everybody? Your family? My friends?"

"Don't leave out your dear mother. What a piece of work! She's on some kind of crusade and you and I are caught in the middle of it."

"This is vulgar and common behavior. It's unbecoming of you."

Clarissa lifted a small lace handkerchief to her lips and lowered her eyes. "Calling me selfish!"

"What?"

"Spoiled and selfish, you said. So that's what you really think of me. No wonder you kept postponing our wedding."

"That's totally unfair. Not once ..." Chad's mind drifted back to the imagined scenes of Clarissa's birth, to the image of his father lying dead on a gruesome battlefield, of his own upcoming actions. "Do you want to call it off, is that it?"

"Chad!" Her tone had changed, she rose quickly and firmly from her seat and walked towards him, her eyes half closed in the glare from the window, perceiving him now only as a dark shadowy male form outlined against the sunlight. She reached her arms outward, found his sleeve, clutched at it, rubbed his forearms, moved closer to him, looked up at his bright green eyes. "Do you?"

"Want to call it off? Never!" He held her close and began kissing her lips and cheeks and bosom. They clawed at each other in desperation, knowing that the only end to this conflict was in wordless union, in the ecstasy of their physical love.

"Bolt the door, Chad. I want to do it in here."

* * *

"You're not having second thoughts, are you, Chad?" Bynum asked. They were seated in the rear of a dusty tavern near the South Ferry. Sailors and workmen, devouring their mid-day meal, kept up a boisterous chatter. It was dim in their corner, their nostrils tickled by strong smells of corned beef and cabbage, beer, pickles and salami, swirls of smoke from pipes and cigars.

Chad coughed, then sneezed. "I guess I got something while I was at Yellowfields. It was cooler then I expected."

"You're avoiding my question. You look glum."

"It's Clarissa," Chad said. "We've started to fuss a lot and she brought up your name."

"She suspects something?"

"She's just jealous of my time, that's all. I really don't have a lot of friends. She thinks I'm aligning myself with you and the Southern cause."

"Isn't that precisely what we're doing here?"

"I've told you often I'm not really a partisan for either side. I just want the war to stop. I feel that if it doesn't, I'd be obligated to join in somehow, but which side? I'm of two minds."

"But not two minds about stopping the war."

"Definitely not."

"It's only going to get worse. If we don't strike them in the heart with violent and widespread and unexpected attacks, they'll never come to the table. You agreed with that long ago. And now look what's happened." Bynum paused, looking straight into Chad's eyes, expecting a question from him, then went on. "Sherman. Three weeks ago he burned Atlanta. Why? He laid siege for weeks, since June. As he prepares to leave on his drive to the sea, he burns the entire city. It's like Carthage all over again. How can we ever forgive this wanton destruction? The South will have nothing left. The people, the women and children, are starving. Invaders have terrified them, assaulted them, driven them out of their homes, burned their houses, killed their livestock, scorched the fields and poisoned their wells. They've even destroyed medical supplies and set hospitals on fire."

"Is this what Lincoln wants?"

"Lincoln wants victory on his own terms and he wants to get reelected. But I don't think he's as ruthless a man as Sherman. I'm no admirer of Lincoln, but I admit he seems to have grown since he took office. It was his political ambition and his cronyism with certain Eastern conspirators that caused him to provoke the war. But he's changing. I'm inclined to think his well-articulated compassion may be genuine. Especially after that Wade-Davis business."

"Because he vetoed the Wade-Davis Bill?"

"The terms of that legislation were severe. It would have further subjugated the South, reduced them to a colony and deprived them of any rights. Lincoln saw that. I think he wants a reconstruction policy that will heal our wounds. That's what I mean about his growth in office. But no, he couldn't use an ordinary veto because the Congress would have over-ridden it. Zealots in the Senate, members of his own cabinet, and a lot of power brokers want to punish the South, to profit from their defeat. So he waited until the last minute, before they adjourned, and 'tabled it' for future action. In effect he neutralized the movement with what they call a pocket veto."

"When I met with my mother and Cousin Corbin in Brooklyn, I found it hard to defend my position. I had just read what General Forrest did somewhere near Memphis back in April. The papers called it a massacre. The rebels killed most of the black troops and many white soldiers as well. They had them outnumbered fifty to one. Neither side would surrender. But the papers said General Forrest burned the barracks to the ground with wounded soldiers inside. There seems to be enough brutality to go around."

"I too was bothered by that report. But it will be a long time before we know exactly what affected the decisions. I've already admitted that war— from any perspective—is unconscionable. Not even Hegel at his murkiest can find a way to avoid it."

"You're not so forgiving with Sherman. When he was criticized for his tactics he merely told the reporters 'war is hell'."

"A simplistic excuse for his extremism. He acts like a madman. He's drunk with bloodlust and power. And sometimes just plain drunk. Now don't you see why we must strike back, here, in their own cities?"

"They're fighting in Winchester again, for the third time. The Shenandoah goes back and forth, from Confederates to Federals. Have you heard anything about it? Are they burning everything there too? Will my father's home be destroyed?"

"Possibly. But not so likely as the homes in Georgia. Wars are run by a hierarchy of military men. Some of them are insane, or drunk, or just devoid of emotions. Others, like Lee, are reluctant at first, but they've been so readied for it in the war colleges it's tempting not to try it out on the battlefield. I suspect that's true on both sides."

"I've not read any military manuals. There is, of course, a plenitude of references to battle in the Greek and Roman texts."

"*Dulce et decorum est pro patria mori.*"

"If it's ever 'sweet and honorable to die for one's homeland,' there's also a time to seek alternatives. Bynum, what can I do? I know I must act. This has got to stop. The generals and politicians plot and argue and contend for power and the soldiers die and their families are impoverished. But the idea of blowing up buildings with civilians in them, that's repellant to me."

"As well it should be. You're a sensitive and honorable lad who seeks an easy solution; but there is none. You don't have to participate in the attacks on the hotels and public buildings. We've used your information to plan these insurgencies. It was, after all, your idea to blow up the armory."

"Because it's a military site."

"Most of the soldiers on duty will have been drafted. They're not sleeping on cots in that dark and damp building because they like it."

"What's wrong with us, all of us?"

"Not even your fine Greeks have a real answer for that."

"They felt there was destiny, some form of determinism, attributed to the gods if you will or to fate. And then they believed this fate was tempered—even activated—by circumstance. But the final ingredient, the *sine qua non*, was human action. The tragic flaw."

"We seem to be in agreement on the human element. Politicians and generals have seized on a series of, for them, fortuitous events. They've found a way to expand their power and domination and increase their wealth. You're a privileged man who won't have to work a day for the rest of your life if you don't want to. But your heart is torn by the anguish you see, the pain of losing your father, your indignation at the lies and hypocrisy—on both sides, I'm sure—that brought about this catastrophe."

"Clarissa is right. She says we're so much alike."

"I harbor for you the same feelings your father did. When he spoke of his love for you, his hope that you might escape some of the horror, he made me part of it. A pact. So now I'm allowing you to join in an action that may endanger your life, perhaps lead you to the gallows. All because of your muddled integrity."

"*Dulce et decorum est pro patria mori.* If I have to die for my country it will be to end war, not to start it."

"Well said. We're completing our plans. We'll strike in November, on Election Day. If you wish to proceed with your attack on the armory, it would be good if you did it at the same time."

October 1864

It was unnerving to see Father Fineas in the Renfield Mansion on such a dreaded occasion. When the messenger knocked at his door on East 10th Street, Chad had intuitively known the news would be very bad. Clarissa had voiced to him, over and over, her concerns for her father's health, his demanding schedule, the stress and strain of momentous responsibilities. But the news of his soon-to-be father-in-law's heart trouble was no less disturbing because he was forewarned.

Higgens drove him as rapidly as possible through the wet streets. It was a chilly fall and the leaves still clogged the gutters and lay limply on the sidewalks. Seated tensely erect in the carriage, Chad noticed how the soggy air and glistening streets seemed to muffle all sounds, as if the great city itself were hushed in apprehension at the serious illness of one of its leaders.

Schuyler greeted him and introduced him once again to the Catholic priest, whom he'd not seen for many months. "Father Fineas and I've been working together on an athletic program for the youth of Five Points," Schuyler said. "I asked him to come back here with me because I find his manner comforting. Our family clergyman was just here, and now Clarissa is in Father's bedroom with Dr. Forrest."

"What's the news?"

"It's his heart, the doctor said. But my father's strong and there's hope he may survive. If he does, we may not know him. Dr. Forrest says events of this gravity will compromise him in the future, his mobility, perhaps his spirit, even his mind. I can't imagine Father subdued in any way. Even though we argue, he's been the most important man in my life."

Marcus, standing beside his friend, smiled faintly at Chad, conveying an intimacy that seemed, at this point, inappropriate. "I must go to Clarissa," he said, nodding to Schuyler, Marcus and the priest and pressing by them to the sick room.

Clarissa sat beside the huge bed, an Elizabethan antique purchased in England and carefully crated and shipped back when the mansion was first completed. Surrounded by pillows and blankets and a white, embroidered spread, Phillipse Renfield looked, for the first time, vulnerable and afraid. His skin was ashen and his eyes half closed. Clarissa stroked her father's palm while the proud man raised his free hand feebly in a wave to his daughter's young lover. Chad stood behind Clarissa, put his hands on her shoulders, bent to kiss her cheek, and then reached across and squeezed the invalid's other hand.

"So you've come so quickly, then," Phillipse said.

"Sir, I came as soon as I could. You're part of my family now and I wanted to be here. To see if I can help. To pray if it's your wish."

"Prayer? Ah, yes. We can all pray. Most of all pray that I shall recover soon, since I can't bear to miss the wedding of my only daughter. The plans have progressed so far already and I know you two are eager. I fear my illness will delay things and simply contribute to your frustration at so long a wait." The sick man's yellowed eyes pierced the gray gloom of the large chamber, focused on Chad, waiting, it seemed, for a response.

"Sir, we must think now of nothing but your recovery. We won't do anything to strain you further. I'm sure my mother will share in this sentiment."

"Your mother, as you well know, will make up her own mind."

"I'm aware of the conflict between you, but I'm sure I speak for her when I say that your health surmounts all other concerns."

"Clarissa, my dear child, what do you think of that? Will you want to wait until I'm better? Would you risk that?"

"I can't walk down the aisle without you, Father. You've placed me above all in your love. You've indulged me. And you've guided me. Now let's concentrate on your speedy return to your old self."

Dr. Forrest clutched his patient's wrist and drew a large watch from his pocket. "I think there's cause to be hopeful. But now, dear friends, you must let him rest. I've engaged nurses to be with him round the clock and I'll stop in every day." He glanced in Chad's direction as he took up his medical bag and started towards the door. Clarissa kissed her father on the forehead, and put her arm around Chad's as they left the room, stopping at the door to watch the large, intimidating nurse, in a starched uniform, fluff pillows, pour water, and smooth covers.

In the hallway, after the doors were closed, Dr. Forrest took Clarissa's hand. With his other hand on Chad's shoulder, he spoke softly but in an even tone. "It's serious, but there's hope. It's essential now that he not have any disturbance—no bad news, no business visitors, no noise, no surprises. I know how eagerly you've planned for your imminent nuptials but I strongly recommend you postpone them until we see how he progresses."

"Doctor Forrest, we'll do anything we can to help him get better," Chad said.

"I want him at my wedding, so I'll wait if I have to," Clarissa added.

The doctor gave them an approving look and left them together in the hall, bewildered, torn, and impassioned simultaneously. Clarissa glanced towards the second floor, as if in invitation. Chad was roused, partly because of his usual passion for her and partly because the aura of mortality had quickened his blood and piqued his desire. He was about to suggest to his beloved that they spend some time alone upstairs, when he felt Father Flaherty's hand on his shoulder.

"Forgive me," Father Fineas said, "but I need to speak with you, Chad, privately, about a matter unrelated to this sad occasion or to this family. Is there some place we can be alone for a while?"

* * *

"I'm surprised to see you here, Father." Chad waited expectantly in the Renfield library. As his eyes crept across the leather-bound books, he couldn't resist the urge to run his fingers along the spine of one of the larger volumes, an illustrated copy of Dante. He removed it from the shelf and opened it on the massive library table.

"Schuyler has visited with me often in the last few weeks. As he prepares to forsake us for the temptations of France, he's had some attacks of conscience and piety. I've directed his energies, and frankly, some of his money, into a program for boys in my parish, who otherwise wouldn't have access to athletic facilities."

"You'll not think me cynical, then, if I raise an eyebrow, given what we both know about Schuyler's inclinations."

"He's to be your brother-in-law. I hope you'll have more faith in him and me than to think I'd urge, or even permit, activities which would shame either him or me or our Holy Church."

"I take you at your word, since you've been forthright with me and helped me examine my own conscience in a matter of personal, perhaps national, importance."

"It's that matter I wish to speak to you about."

"Indeed?" Chad turned a few pages of the *Inferno*, feeling the fine old paper under his fingertips and leaning closer to squint at the engravings of scenes of imagined suffering in an unlikely afterlife.

"I've not violated your confidence, even though your remarks weren't made in the sanctity of a Catholic confessional. I've since heard hundreds of confessions. I won't violate them, either, except to say that one young man, in particular, passed on news of what I fear will be a disastrous and evil consequence."

"And how does that affect me?"

"I'm not sure and I'll draw no conclusions. The truth is, one young man, a Southern Catholic, told me in confession of a macabre plot to bring the violence of this war into our Northern cities. I've not shared this information with anyone else, lest I be coerced into disclosing the truth, a truth that might lead to the apprehension of the confessor. Of course, I can't do that. So I turn to you."

"I'm one of those deemed by many, including Dante here, to be among the heathen."

"I don't believe that. I find you to be an earnest young man struggling with a difficult moral and philosophical problem. A political dilemma as well."

"I'm involved in these issues, as I told you."

"But this plot, if executed, would bring death and destruction to the innocent."

"War tends to do that. Even wars fought in the name of your Church. Wars raged in the name of this god or that. It's always been that way, do you not agree?"

"It's not for me to pass judgment on the past actions of my Church, nor to idle away my time at this crucial moment speculating on the role of religion in war."

"At least you admit there is such a role, then?"

"Please, let me come to the point. If you or any of your colleagues are involved in these plots, which I gather involve explosions in public buildings here and in several cities, please try to encourage forbearance. It can only bring more trouble and more suffering."

"Do you follow the war news, Father?"

"I've no choice but to do so, since so many young men of my parish have been drafted into the Union army and carried away to the battlefield to die. I've conducted funerals, counseled the grieving families, and tried to comfort those who've returned home alive, but maimed for life."

"Is your concept of good and evil so rigorous you'll not even consider a middle ground somewhere, an effort to take actions which may bring violence in the first instant in order to prevent a greater violence later on?"

"Do you believe that violence is a remedy for violence?"

"You're evading my question."

"If we return for every aggression another aggression, whether equal in scope or not, we perpetuate a cycle that escalates the war rather than bringing it to a close. Those who engage in such chicanery are represented in that book you're thumbing through. Warmongering comes in many guises, including those who spout self-righteous rhetoric about a war fought for peace."

"You're a Jesuit, Father, and I have no defense against such penetrating logic."

"Your mother has spoken to me of your sarcastic tongue."

"And what further business would you have with my mother?"

"She's enlisted my aid in her efforts to rescue those who suffer in servitude in your, what shall I call it, your other homeland."

"Your own gift for the ironic has not escaped me."

"We're dancing around the point, so to peak."

"Like angels on the head of a pin, engaging in sophistry about trivia?"

"Blowing up buildings in New York, buildings in which women and children are certain to be present, is hardly trivial."

"Massacre on the field of battle continues. Men of the cloth like you serve as chaplains while they hang back of the lines, safe from a bullet. Is this bloodletting less trivial than the supposed violence you speak of to me, a non-Catholic emboldened to do what I must do to stop this outrage? I also suggest you not become too enchanted with my mother's causes. She's a woman whose sense of right and wrong rests securely on her own needs and indeed her own plans."

"You do her a disservice if you don't recognize both her sincerity of motive and her devotion to your future."

"Ah, how well she enlists support from the most unexpected places."

"I'll not dwell on this further. It's for you to decide. A dead child, a murdered mother, the suffering of a crowd of shoppers or a family on their way to church—any church—will sit sorely on your conscience and will accomplish little in ending a war like this, that has raged for years, and is embedded so deeply in the nation's politics."

"They say I have a good mind for the abstract. But in this case, Father, I'm thinking of the particular."

"I'll pray for you. Promise me you'll give my remarks some thought. You're a brilliant young man with most fortunate prospects. Pray, if you will, for guidance. Come to see me again. Let's talk in confidence about other ways to achieve your goals. Join with me and your mother to help the enslaved. Work, as even Schuyler has done, to help ease the torments of poverty and despair here at home. That's as particular as any of us need get."

"We shall see, Father. We shall see."

*   *   *

"I admire the old man, actually," Bynum said. He turned his collar up against the wind, looking out over the water at intermittent whitecaps, and the swollen sails crossing the harbor from the Narrows to the inlets and quiet estuaries of New Jersey. Chad sat beside him on a small bench in the Battery. The day had been bright with late October sunlight, but the clouds were gathering low in the southern sky. Neither of them spoke for a long interval.

"I never said he's not to be admired," Chad said. "It's puzzling, that's all. Where he stands. He pretends to disapprove of his brother and the shenanigans he got into with my Uncle Caleb. He says he's reluctant to cause a delay in our wedding but something in his eyes tells me he's really glad."

"But he's getting better?"

"Seems to be. Clarissa's with him most of the time."

"Is everything all right with the two of you?"

"I think so. She's stopped fussing with me. Of course, I've been busy setting up my schedule. The plans we've made."

"Plans for your wedding?"

"I meant my plans. Our plans."

"So you'll go through with it, after all."

"People are ganging up on me. Do you remember that Catholic priest?"

"Father Fineas? I rather liked sparring with him at your Aunt Marilyn's parties. He seems remarkably intelligent for a clergyman."

"He called me aside right after Mr. Renfield's heart trouble worsened. I was surprised to see him there. He said he'd been working with Schuyler on some kind of athletic program for boys in the Five Points."

"I'm not so sure that comes under the heading of philanthropy."

"No, I think he's sincere on that issue. He works hard for his parishioners. He was helpful to Schuyler, as you know, and Schuyler, before he sails for

France, wanted to do something useful. He's got quite a bit of money of his own already, you know, even if his father should choose to disinherit him."

"Does he plan to?"

"I don't think so. He's mellowed after his brush with death. He's up and about a little bit already, not much, but for a few hours at a time. Clarissa tells me he now receives messengers from the bank and he met once in private with Schuyler. Clarissa said Schuyler seemed quite happy after the meeting but he refused to discuss it with her."

"Not a good sign."

"What do you mean?"

"Doesn't it seem like he's cleaning up after himself? Making amends. Getting ready, you know, to meet his maker or whatever."

"I don't believe Phillipse Renfield is a religious man."

"Doesn't matter. Everybody's afraid to die. Some people find it easier to seek refuge in the highly speculative idea of an afterlife. It helps them get through the day."

"You don't believe in anything do you?"

"Whoa! Why the sudden vitriol at me? You know I believe in myself, in trying to protect the values I've inherited, and a commitment to living by my principles."

"But you're not afraid to die?"

"I didn't say that. Who wants to? An occasional suicidal malcontent. But I long ago accepted the obvious fact that life is a mystery. You've accepted it too. Your Greek erudition has steeled you for tragedy. My learning and my experience have rather leaned me towards comedy."

"For a comedian you're taking very serious actions."

"Yes. I should tell you now that our agents from the Confederacy have been in town. The Copperheads here and in Ohio are somewhat less convinced now about the attacks and a few of them have dropped out. There's a growing feeling that the South is vanquished, that Lincoln and his generals will prevail. So like the proverbial rats they're deserting our vessel in order to escape punishment when it's over. That's why I wanted to see you again. To let you know that we still intend to strike on November 8, Election Day, but there may be some problems with a few of our more timid conspirators. I want to make sure of your commitment."

"That I intend to blow up the armory?"

"More importantly, whether or not you may abandon us altogether. Turn us in. Warn the authorities. Perhaps even spell out the plans in such detail that I and my compatriots will be taken even before we've planted our firebombs."

"My mother's been seeing Father Fineas as well. That's what I wanted to tell you. When I saw him at the Renfield's he called me aside and said he'd learned from a confession that there were insurgencies afoot. He inferred from one of my remarks weeks ago that I might be somehow involved."

"Surely you didn't discuss our plans with a clergyman!"

"He's an educated man, a Jesuit. I sought to explore with him some of the moral and spiritual issues that confront me."

"That sounds very evasive, coming from you." Bynum looked around the crowded waterfront. The trees were nearly bare, leaves blowing across the lawns, the walkways crowded with sailors and longshoremen and business men in top hats and cloaks to resist the unseasonal chill. Across the railings, farther out in the harbor, the masts and smokestacks of gunboats pierced the cold sky. "You mentioned your mother. What's she got to do with it? And with him?"

"He said he's helping with her abolitionist work. Then when I got home and asked her about it she railed and howled and scolded me like she used to. She's upset that Phillipse has taken ill and delayed the wedding. She urged me to elope! When that failed she insisted I go to Brooklyn again to meet with Reverend Mullen and Cousin Corbin. She said she'd ask Father Fineas to attend as well."

"Did you agree to go?"

"Of course not!"

"That was a mistake, my boy."

"How so?"

"You must keep yourself close to all of them to find out what they know. I advise you to go home and tell her you've reconsidered and that you'll be happy to join her with her Brooklyn entourage of abolitionists and their new Jesuit ally. You can then determine how much they really know. And we'll meet again, the final time perhaps, to adjust our plans if need be. That is, if you're still with me."

"They've opened that new zoo in the Central Park."

"What?"

"I went up there with Clarissa to take her mind off her father. To reassure her we would continue our life as before. There were people from different classes and races, different languages, trying to throw pieces of bread or nuts into the cages. Of course it's forbidden to do that. It was a cloudy day and suddenly the sun came out and a beam of light spread through the bars on the windows, landing right in front of me, on the floor. I felt a stab of pity for the animals in the cages. I felt nausea when I thought about the slaves on those ships, and the auction blocks in the South. Then I thought of all of us in our own separate cages. And the Southern and Northern jails. And the hospitals, and asylums. I wondered if I was going to make any difference at all. Whatever happens is going to happen anyway. I felt so powerless, Bynum."

"When a scholar like you has an epiphany, practical people like me are in trouble."

"Don't get me wrong. I still want to do my part to stop the war. But I'm doubtful of my efficacy. And I thought of myself, wasting away behind bars if I'm caught. And whether or not I could withstand torture."

"I've already warned you that if we're caught we'll not long languish behind bars. The gallows if we're lucky, a worse fate if we're not."

"And you're resigned to that?"

"I tell myself I am. In truth, I'm not sure. But every time I waver, I find incidents in current affairs that convince me all over again. Did you read about that Confederate raid up in Vermont? St. Albans? They came in from Canada, held the townsfolk at gunpoint and robbed the banks. But they fled back into Canada and the government there failed to permit extradition."

"What's the point?"

"The point is they made a military incursion into the northernmost part of Federal territory. They needed money so they robbed banks. But look what they didn't do."

"I still don't understand."

"They didn't kill women and children. They didn't assault civilians. They didn't burn the town or destroy their medical supplies or lay waste to their foodstuffs. That's the point. It's very likely we shall lose this war. But after what's been done in the so-called name of freedom to the people of my state and all the states in the South, don't think that I shall waver ever again in my conviction. Even if I have to mount the gallows because of it."

November 1864

"It's good of you to come, my son." Reverend Mullen locked Chad's hand in a tight grip and pumped his arm up and down like a small steam engine. Chad felt embarrassed. Harriet looked on without expression and Corbin stood with his back to the room, looking off into the gray Brooklyn streetscape.

"Yes," Father Fineas said. "It's possible we can help you avoid a grave mistake and find another way to give you respite from the inner turmoil we all know you to suffer."

"How do you know what I'm suffering or not suffering," Chad said, unable to keep the irritation out of his voice. "I'm a grown man with much experience now to add to my considerable learning. Forgive my vanity but I'm tired of being patronized by the lot of you."

"Chad, put aside your anger—and your sarcasm, if you can—and let us tell you what we know and what we're planning." Harriet rose and walked to the window, clutched Corbin's elbow, and guided him firmly back to the settee where she pushed him down with hands on his shoulders, and then seated herself with a swirl of her skirts and with metal in her eyes. "Before you protest, Father Fineas here has told us nothing of your conversations. We've learned through other sources, Corbin has, I should say, that there are plots afoot to implement traitorous and murderous acts right here in New York. This cannot be permitted. You're to be a leader of this great city when our families merge to create a dynasty that will influence American history for a hundred years or more. I can't stay silent when I suspect, as many of us here do, that you might possibly have certain involvements in these plots through your friend and co-conspirator Bynum Bradley-West."

"I don't feel even remotely compelled to respond to such accusations."

"We thought you'd not," Corbin said. "That's why I'm here. It's likely that trouble is brewing throughout the Northern cities. The election is upon us and it's certain, I believe, that Lincoln will win. Support for him here in New York is scant, a mere third of the electorate, the experts predict, and there's a likelihood of further 'civil disobedience' as it's now called, right here at home. Worse, there will likely be violence."

"Yes," Father Fineas said. "My parish is embroiled in political dissent. There's a reformist consensus that seeks to abolish the privileged classes, some of it coming from Germans who were involved in the European revolutions of 1848. They advocate actions that could bring commerce to a standstill and disrupt our plans for an orderly post-war environment. We must prepare for the migration of former slaves who'll find life in the South, even the postwar South, to be intolerable. That's why I'm here today."

"I'm aware of your devotion to your father's memory," Harriet interjected. "I want to set up an endowment, perhaps some sort of facility, to help Southern families after the war. I also want to make such an effort more acceptable to others who may join with us in funding such an initiative. I've also suggested efforts to improve the life of immigrants in the Five Points, and to provide a stabilizing source of advice and funds for those freedmen like Holder Pratt who've already proved their industry, their loyalty, and their integrity."

"I thought I was the idealist, Mother. Have you suddenly repented or are you simply using rhetoric to influence me in what you imagine to be my dastardly plots?"

"Your sarcasm no longer affects me. Everyone in this room knows my will and my ability in achieving my personal goals. My work with abolition has emanated from a moral sense, but I'm not without awareness that in a postwar New York, when our family ascends to pre-eminence here and in Boston, we'll need evidence of our self-effacing love for our fellow citizens."

"Self-effacing? Really, Mother. It would take a regiment of sharpshooters, or some of Pinkerton's torturers, to eliminate your sense of self."

"As I said I'm no longer troubled by your effrontery, nor even embarrassed by it. The others in this room share my goals. We want the war to go on until the South has accepted our terms. Primary among them is that slavery must be ended forever. Secondly, we must use our financial, military and moral leadership to help the South rebuild, providing it abides by our sentiments regarding racial issues. And thirdly, for my sake and yours, you must proceed with the wedding, father a son, and let us get on with our long-term strategy. Since the child won't reach his majority for over two decades, you'll have to take the lead."

"How so take the lead?" Chad was once again amazed at his mother's combined gall, impertinence, vision, will, and ruthlessness.

"You'll head up the organizations I'm founding, with the help of Reverend Mullen, Father Fineas, and dear Cousin Corbin."

For a moment there flashed in Chad's mental eyes the vision of young Corbin and young Harriet, bare backsides gleaming at a pair of Boston spinsters, in a carriage house on Beacon Hill. He couldn't suppress a grin.

"Ah, well, Chad, your smile indicates you've at least understood both our rationale and our resources." Reverend Mullen's face, frozen in a perpetual attitude of condescension, beamed first at Harriet and then at Chad. "As Executive Director of our organizations you'll be honored throughout the nation, and you'll have considerable authority. However, as Chairman of the Board of the entity—whatever it turns out of be—I'll help relieve the pressure on you so that you may have adequate time for your scholarly pursuits, which all of us recognize are so dear to you."

"Most reverend Sir, your spiritual powers do not facilitate a clear glimpse inside my soul, nor into the sources of my merriment. I'm simply amazed at all of you. I'll make up my own mind about the future. Clarissa and I'll decide when we'll marry, after her father has recovered. And God, or destiny, or chance will determine whether or not our considerable passion for each other will produce a Prince for my ambitious mother to stand Regent to."

"Don't underestimate our seriousness of purpose," Harriet said, quietly.

"Don't think that we speak impetuously, or without evidence," Corbin said.

"My respect and concern for you impel me to cooperate in this intervention," Father Fineas said.

"Good day to you all," Chad said.

* * *

"This may be the last time we meet so I thought it worth the risk to come here," Bynum said. They were sipping hot tea in Madam Maureen's library. The house was quiet, the day cold, their mood somber. "By the way, Madam Maureen has been forced to discharge that perky little lass we both enjoyed."

"I've not thought of Rosie since I've been intimate with Clarissa."

"Just as well. You told me her brother was in the Union army, remember?" He handed Chad a platter of cakes. "Poor lad's been killed. Maureen says the girl was distraught and threatened to make a scene. She knows a lot of Southern sympathizers frequent this house."

Chad bit into a puffy cinnamon roll, but found it unpalatable. He gulped at his hot tea, but there was no satisfaction in it. Wind shook the windows, an orange fire sputtered in the grate, a vase full of flowers was ringed with fallen petals. He breathed deeply at Bynum's remark, but said nothing.

Bynum eyed him craftily and spoke again. "You see, I was right in urging you to go to Brooklyn. They not only suspect you, they must also know something. Perhaps details of our plan. Even Father Fineas, if he wanted to, could rationalize his way out of the sanctity of the confessional. He could tell them or the police what we're doing."

"You're concerned, then."

"At first I was. The original date was November 8, Election Day. But we had to delay, so that event came and went. Perhaps they'll rest more comfortably, thinking we've abandoned our plans, or else are powerless to carry them out."

"Are we?"

"Of course not. We've simply changed the date. It will be next week. On the 25th."

"Next week."

"You don't sound very enthusiastic."

"I'm troubled. What do you think of this election?"

"Oddly enough, I'm glad Lincoln won. I'm now convinced the man has changed in office. I think he's still a master politician and that he stays up all night scheming. But I think he realizes that lenient terms for the South will be better for all of us. McClellan was not a really appealing opponent. I think he's now where Lincoln was five years ago."

"Meaning what?"

"Meaning he's a tool."

"But he carried New York City. Lincoln got barely thirty percent of the vote. That must mean something."

"It means the antiwar sentiment is strong. It means the merchants and bankers are still divided. It means the Irish and German immigrants and other working classes who vote want a change."

"But you don't?"

"Of course I do. Our actions will be effective if they force negotiations to start sooner rather than later. If Lincoln and Grant push for an unconditional surrender and they succeed, which I'm afraid they'll do, then it will be more difficult for Lincoln to show compassion in his reconstruction plans. We've discussed the hostility in Congress and the Cabinet to Lincoln's possible leniency with the South. They want to pour salt in our wounds. They want to whip us into political impotence. We cannot let that happen. We must press on with our agenda."

"I confess I'm ill at ease with it."

"Your information was key in our preparations. You don't have to do anything else. The armory was your idea and it's up to you to decide what to do about it."

"My entire family and everybody they know spend most of their time analyzing my behavior and then making demands. My mother, most of all."

"Yes, she'd not be a good person to have for an enemy."

"She isn't my enemy, on the face of it. There's concern for me there, I know. But I'm such a pawn in her hands."

"Her devotion could be useful if you're taken."

"Taken?"

"It's likely that she could pull strings. You should leave something around in your room with Captain Hartigan's name on it. If you're held without access to counsel, unable to communicate with anybody, she could alert him. He's still obligated to do whatever he can to help us."

"You're making me fearful."

"I've always warned you of possible consequences. I suspect there may be evidence out there somewhere. A note. A map. Even a confession, somebody apprehended and tortured. The most loyal Southerner, and I'm one of them, would prefer to die rather than to betray you or anybody else."

"The election did little to soothe people's nerves." Chad said. "News from the front is still mixed, the body count rises every day, the hospitals are full of the wounded. And the draft goes on."

"Lincoln is shrewd in his management of information. And I suspect he's got agents planting stories. Like the one about the snakes in the post office."

"What was that all about?"

"Rather silly, actually. But it did instill fear. Because they call people like you 'Copperheads,' somebody started the rumor that Southern agents had released copperhead snakes in the post office. And that they could somehow attack anybody who came in for a postage stamp."

"That's ridiculous."

"Of course it is. But it helps dramatize the fear. Fear's a weapon during wartime. Sometimes even in peacetime. Governments that are rather shaky anyway, as Lincoln is in the extent of his electorate, and in the support from his enemies in the Congress, will use fear as a weapon. Frightened people are more likely to want their leaders to stay the course."

"You'll strike next week. I'm left on my own to decide what to do. I'm worried that I may not see you again until the war is over."

"If we're successful in our attacks there'll be panic and a distinct reaction. The government will try to calm the populace by making speeches and arresting a lot of people. Many of those arrested will be completely innocent but since they use military tribunals, or deny *habeas corpus*, it means the guiltless will be detained and their families will know nothing about it. Under such circumstances, some of them will tell what they know and if they do not know anything, they'll make it up. There are Secret Service agents everywhere, they were at your aunt's funeral. Even your closest family has suspicions. No, I think we'll not be able to meet for a long, long time."

"Where will you be?"

"I'll try to get away on a foreign ship. Bound for England, if possible. Like you, I have accounts there, enough to live well on."

"And if you don't escape?"

"Let's not think about it anymore. Each day will reveal something about our destiny. We've chosen a path that many would criticize. Others may favor our motivations, but deem us foolish to sacrifice ourselves for this cause or any other. 'What to do?' is an eternal question, even in daily life. War brings everything into sharper focus. You and I study history and we realize there have always been wars. It's facile to say that war is hell but nevertheless necessary. I suspect it sometimes is. But that doesn't excuse any of us from the moral imperative to question every act of government. To stop looking for a hero in which to place our blind trust and to recognize that even the best of leaders is imperfect. Hero worship is at the heart of misgovernment. The other problem, one with which you're familiar in your reading, is the tendency to glorify combat. In the abstract, it seems like a chess game. When we're brought face to face with death and suffering, we feel obligated to honor those who fight for our side. But it's still a bilateral evil. It's still a sorry way to settle disputes."

"A long time ago you mocked me for sentiments like that. You said I was assuming man is rational."

"Just because we recognize human failings doesn't mean we can't advance the principles to which people aspire. If only we would stop our idolatrous hero-worship, if we would relegate war to the position it ought to have, the very last option, one to be used only as a final resort! We would all fare better if we stopped glorifying battles. We can't live peacefully with an emotional, misguided and ultimately self-destructive adherence to an abstract patriotic mythology. In the end we destroy the very society we were fighting to preserve."

"You're your old cynical self, I see."

"No. I'm examining the truth. It's you who are cynical."

"I?

"Yes, because you debate the options forever, and eventually do nothing. That's cynical."

"I'm not cut out for politics."

"Nor I. Speaking of politics, did you hear about that theater group that's in town? They're performing *Julius Caesar*. It's my favorite Shakespeare."

"I prefer Lear."

"I expected you would, because you want to ponder the timeless issues which, because they can't be resolved, relieve you from any obligation to make a decision today."

"Perhaps I should take Clarissa to see the play, then. Is it an accomplished troupe?"

"Indeed. The Booth brothers are both in it. Edwin and his brother John Wilkes Booth. Just don't take her on the 25th. The theater is one of our targets."

Interlude: November 30, 1864
Chivington at Sand Creek, Sherman in Georgia

Chad walked the cold wet streets, fear struggling against shame inside him: fear that he'd be caught, that his work had been for nothing, that he'd be branded both traitor and coward. And shame that he was a human being, revulsion rising like acid in his throat.

His ancient texts no longer offered solace. His confidence in reason was erased. Hope drained out of him like the blood of a million victims of the war, like the crimson gush from animals slaughtered by Sherman on the last leg of his march from Atlanta to the sea, like the entrails of women and children ripped out with swords and jagged knives by Colonel Chivington and his drunken troops in an obscure Indian encampment in Colorado.

He'd failed at his chief target because he was unwilling in the end to attack a house of armaments where young soldiers slept in exhaustion within the armory walls. Because he now hated his naive embrace of the very violence he sought to end. And resentment that Bynum, suave, articulate, full of self-confidence and apparently fearless, had smoothly welcomed him into yet another circle of destruction.

But Bynum had failed as well. Their fires were set on the 25th as planned, but there was little consequence. Obviously, the militia and the police had been forewarned. Fires in hotels, in Barnum's Museum, in offices and banks, had been quickly extinguished. Although the damage was reckoned at $400,000, no injuries were reported. And the results underscored the futility of all terrorist actions: if the insurgents succeed, they kindle in their adversaries even more resolve and more reprisals, and if they fail, the result is the same, only leavened with ridicule.

Ridicule and irony. As the Booth brothers prepared to present Shakespeare's play about political assassination, armed guards had emptied the theater because of a threat of fire. Chad was reminded of the President in his box at the Academy of Music four years ago, savoring Verdi and musing on his opera of intrigue and murder among the people who run things.

Greed and indifference. The holiday season was drawing the wealthy to the huge new department stores. Prices reminded the poor, who couldn't afford $300 to avoid the battlefield, of the chasm between them and those who spent hundreds of dollars for lace and more than a thousand for a shawl. What did these wartime prices matter to those whose pockets were lined with the bounty of battle, his pockets included?

Today's papers told the story of the raid out west. Chief Black Kettle and his band of Cheyenne and Arapaho sought peaceful reconciliation. They camped outside the fort with American flags fluttering beside white banners of surrender. Colonel John Chivington, riding deceitfully into their midst, unleashed his troops in a rage of unparalleled brutality. They ripped open the bowels of children, slit the breasts and vaginas of the women, scalped the dead. Brain matter was spilled on the sandy soil, rifle butts clubbed warrior and child alike. At least half of the 250 killed were women and children. Although the Eastern papers were outraged, apparently Colonel Chivington was worshipped as a hero in his Colorado territory.

Why did he believe that lyrical descriptions of Athens and Sparta, of Rome and Carthage, made the horror any different? Sophisticated metrics and evocative metaphor couldn't disguise this eternal canker festering in the human soul.

Noble words chiseled on marble monuments. Lyrical speeches that inflamed the heart. Music and pageantry and marching hordes, urged on by the cheers of the multitude on all the occasions when that ancient falsehood could be repeated: "Dulce et decorem est pro patria mori."

December 1864

"There will be no tree this year. I don't even want a gift from you. What I want is for you to explain what you've done, if you've done it, or why these rumors persist if you haven't." Harriet was her old self, pacing around their East 10th Street parlor, a silk square clutched in her clenched fists, her lips stern, her voice strained but under control.

"It really doesn't concern you." Chad's eyes were fixed on his mother's back as she stood at the front windows, looking out on the snowy street.

"You're such an accomplished linguist, do you know what equivocate means?"

"If you want to accuse me just do so without simultaneously maligning my education."

"I've been completely and painfully honest with you. I've revealed my so-called secrets. I've admitted my determination to salvage something for this family and for myself from the wreckage of our past. Yet you persist in compromising me and Clarissa and your grandfather. You're even darkening your dead father's legacy."

"I acted on the dictates of my conscience. I met with various people across the financial and political spectrum. With your behind-the-scenes participation I made a pile of money on enterprises that are now censured. I've escaped from that little quagmire with my honor and my reputation intact. I've suffered your controlling spirit even with my engagement. And I considered a number of political alternatives that I thought might lead to a just and moral solution to this horrible war. But I took no specific actions and I committed no actual deeds. Does that satisfy you?"

"At least I've not known you ever to lie."

"I'm not lying now. I continue to commit myself to the thoughtful, self-searching life. I've made my opposition to the war well known. You've succeeded in almost all of your plots, except one. I'll not lend my name to your new foundation or whatever you're calling it since it's such a bald maneuver for power. And I especially wouldn't accept such an appointment if I had to answer to your lover."

"Tad Mullen is not my lover."

"Your beloved, then."

"Hateful! There's no other word for you."

"Have it your way, Mother. I'm no longer even remotely interested in arguing with you."

"Not even about Clarissa?"

"Leave her out of this."

"She's our leverage for the future. You and she must have a child. Even if you conceive it before the marriage."

"Phillipse may die. If he does, we'll elope."

"The child, that's what matters! The child!"

"Well, Mother, you are, as Clarissa said recently, a real piece of work. Would you like me to excuse myself now and run up to the Renfield Mansion, burst into her room, and implant my seed? Would you like to watch, just to make sure I'm performing well?"

"Horrid! Hateful and horrid at the same time."

"As much as I enjoy these warm family chats, I find the repetitiveness has begun to wear thin. Have you other questions?"

"Have you other revelations?"

"I told Bynum I'd blow up the armory. But I lost my nerve. So I've committed no seditious acts. There, is that enough to get you off my back?"

"I just want you to stay out of sight for a while. The war will end in a few months at most. The nation will be strong as never before."

"The Federal government will be strong as never before, you mean. The South is in ruins."

"They brought it on themselves with their moral abdication of humanitarianism."

"What a two-faced way to put it. I've stopped presenting my case against slavery. Nobody seems to believe me."

"Talk, talk, talk."

"Let me try to make peace. I sympathize with your fanatical attempts to make a life for yourself because of your—may I say it, Mother—your rather sordid past. And the humiliation of your abandonment by my father. I even tolerate your continued interference in my life, and my own susceptibility to being a mere tool in your assorted endeavors. Could you, in return, just leave me alone? I'll marry Clarissa, produce an heir, and retire to Yellowfields exhausted but free. I suspect I'll not even want to journey into the city while you launch your campaign to establish 'the most powerful family on the Eastern Seaboard' as you call it. Just leave me alone."

"You'll never acknowledge what I've done for you."

"I only wish you had done it with a little less self-interest."

Harriet sat down, turning her eyes on her son, her face softening a bit. "Maybe we should go ahead and have a tree. Maybe we should pile presents under it. Phillipse won't be able to celebrate, even if he continues to improve. You and Clarissa and me. Maybe Schuyler and his friend. Father Fineas, even. A good old fashioned Christmas."

Chad accepted the surge within him of his old childhood reflections. "I really don't enjoy fighting with you."

"Nor I with you."

"Truce?"

"Not just truce. A treaty." She extended her hand towards Chad's. He held it briefly, turned it over, kissed it, and sat down with a sigh. A knock at the sliding doors was a welcome end to the latest installment of their conflict.

"Is that you?" Harriet asked, then turning to Chad. "You see, I had anticipated the outcome and told the housekeeper to bring the decorations down. The tree is out back, in the garden."

The housekeeper entered but carried no wreaths or ornaments. There was a tremor in her voice. "Madam, there are two men at the door, dressed in suits, and two more in police uniforms. There are two carriages out front, waiting. They want to talk to Mister Chad."

Chad rushed to the window and looked out at the horses, lifting alternate legs and exhaling their steamy breath upwards in the still morning air. He pressed his face against the pane to get a better side view of their stoop. The two men in suits looked like Pinkerton men, and the officers, with clubs and pistols and handcuffs hanging from their belts, looked angry and eager.

"Mother, you must go upstairs now. Stay in my room. On the desk you'll find a list of names and addresses. One of them is a Captain Hartigan. I fear I must go with these officers, although I'm confident no harm will come to me. But just in case, go to Captain Hartigan. Ask him what you should do."

* * *

They ushered him briskly out the door, hands cuffed and a cloak over his shoulders. The street was nearly deserted, except for two black-and-white-clad maids from the house facing his, who stood shivering with heads together in gossipy speculation. Chad knew they'd tell their peers from neighboring houses about the young man who'd been carted away by the authorities. He didn't look directly at them, nor cast a glance backwards at the familiar tall windows of his lifelong home.

The black coach they locked him in was rectangular, like a milk wagon, but with only one small window in the rear door. Benches lined each of the three interior sides, but no other prisoners were aboard.

He sat awkwardly on the bench beside the door, leaning back to balance himself, but watching, with a sidelong glance, the orderly town houses of his youth, narrowing in perspective as the carriage sped away, tottering from side to side. The two policemen sat above him in the front, with two Pinkerton agents in a smaller carriage leading the way.

At first he felt neither fear nor embarrassment. He believed his actions, so long in planning and so summarily abandoned, seemed unlikely to land him in trouble. Never in all his ennobling fantasies about helping to stop the war did he dwell overlong on the possible consequences. Now, as he was jolted from side to side over the rough avenues leading to a downtown jail, he felt a new fear inching upwards from his stomach. Bynum's warning resounded in his brain. "We'll be lucky to get the gallows." But what could possibly be worse?

He tried to grip, with both his cuffed hands, the four iron bars in the small rear window. He twisted his body from the waist in order to watch the streets crowded with workers and holiday shoppers. Traffic noises seemed stifled by the lightly falling snow. Which of these pedestrians might he have killed? Which of them could now be lying in a mortuary, had Bynum and his conspirators succeeded?

He wanted to direct his thoughts to his beloved texts, reciting passages that touched on imprisonment and punishment and escape. But it didn't work, and he felt as if he were somehow suspended in time. He savored the view from the small opening, hoped the journey to his destiny would be long. But the policemen drove fast, and hauled him up abruptly at the station house. Throngs were gathered there, many of them bearing placards mounted on sticks. He strained to read them, but closed his eyes instead when he heard their loud, angry chants. "Death to Copperhead Wales." "Hang all Copperhead traitors now."

Struggling to keep his composure in the new world he was about to enter, he tried to evaluate his position with logic and detachment. How could these people know it was he in the coach? How could they have assembled themselves outside the station, awaiting his arrival, signs already lettered, slogans already in mind as they rushed him through the big oak doors? Surely, this was all planned. Surely they were trying to make an example of him. Who had betrayed him? And how far would they go in exacting their revenge?

* * *

There was only a cot, crammed against the corner of his cell. They'd taken his money, his belt, his watch, his handkerchief and comb, and all his clothes except a cotton shirt and brocade vest, and his trousers and socks. It was a cold December and there was no heat. The only light came from a small opening over the bed, inaccessible, and leading, Chad believed, not to the outdoors but to another, larger room. He'd asked them for a candle, which they refused, and for a blanket, which they threw at him with a surly gesture.

He stretched out on the hard cot, trying to keep warm. The blanket was not very long, so when he wrapped his feet in one end, the other reached only to his chest. He drew his knees up towards his waist, lay on his side, and clasped both arms closely around his midriff.

Ignoring his pleas for an explanation, they'd marched him quickly, between two guards, to his cell. There was no indication of a charge, and when he asked to send a message to his family, they laughed.

He shivered and twisted on his makeshift bed. From time to time, outcries of other prisoners interrupted the dull murmur of the vast detention center. He heard defiant laughter, a shouted demand, tearful pleas for food or water or warmth, chillingly interspersed, from time to time, with a loud male scream, as if someone were being tortured.

He'd lost all sense of time, but there seemed to be some regularity to the making of rounds, as guards in pairs, loudly scraping a large key against the metal bars as they walked slowly down the corridor, stopped to provide a dipper full of water from a wire-bound wooden pail. He drank eagerly, remembering as he did so his mother's worry that he should always drink "good water." Would she find a way to get to him? Would she be as brave and as determined now as she'd been in her efforts to control his future and to avenge her own abandonment?

Would Clarissa be informed? How would she take it, her privileged world collapsing around her, her brother off to France with his friend, her father most likely near death, her betrothed confined to a cold jail in lower Manhattan, perhaps isolated from her forever.

His mind raced from one imaginary event to another, a sudden release, a breakout, bail. Hartigan or Harriet or even Bynum to the rescue. But no one came, except the two grumbling guards on their periodic rounds. Finally, out of exhaustion and despair, he closed his eyes and pretended to sleep.

Barely conscious, he heard the guards approach again, but they were in conversation with another man, their chatter drifting down the passageway. He believed he recognized one of the voices but fear and pessimism wouldn't allow him to hope. But the sounds grew closer, and he was sure it was in fact a familiar accent, and he allowed himself a flicker of optimism.

The guards stopped before his cell, blocking his view, but as they turned the lock and stood aside, he saw the hefty form of a New York City Police Detective.

"That will be all, gentlemen," Hartigan said. "You can lock me in with him if you feel like it, and I'll summon you when I've finished my interrogation." The guards shuffled off, without locking the cell.

"Detective Hartigan, thank God!" Chad said.

Hartigan didn't answer, instead raising his finger to his lips in a command for silence. Chad couldn't make out the expression on his face.

Placing his hands on Chad's shoulder, Hartigan gently forced him to sit on the cot, then perched on the end, body turned to face him. When he spoke, his voice was low and measured.

"They mustn't realize you know me. This is a Federal detention center. I told them you were wanted on other charges by the New York City police and persuaded them to allow me a few minutes to question you. You must listen closely for I don't have much time."

"But I haven't been charged! And there were crowds outside the jail when I got here, chanting my name. How could they know?"

"I'm not sure what they have on you. Probably not much but hearsay. But it's likely you were set up and a crowd alerted before you were brought in. They'll try to make a statement with your case and others like you. There's no way we can help, using ordinary channels. The trial, if and when it comes, will most likely be conducted as a military tribunal."

"But I'm an American citizen."

"In the eyes of the Federal authorities you're an insurgent, a combatant for the enemy, guilty until proven innocent, and not much chance for that. Lincoln was taken to court on the *habeas corpus* issue but they continue to ignore it secretly. And don't be surprised if they threaten you with torture. Although it's unlikely they'll use it right away."

"Why not?"

"Word is they might decide to parade you before a bogus court of some kind and use the newspapers to rile up the masses. There's hysteria everywhere after the attacks on Manhattan, even though no one was hurt. But fear is their weapon, as you must surely realize. Once they've released your name and status in society, it will be hard to find a single Southern sympathizer of means who'll be brave enough to speak out. Even the Copperhead papers will ignore you."

"I'm doomed, then." He felt a lump in his throat, a raw edge in his voice, and a thumping in his heart. He was facing it now, the fruit of his actions, and couldn't find in all his languages and texts and fables and myths any gleam of comfort.

"Your mother's a most convincing advocate, and she used not only her charm but also her money. I didn't of course tell her we were already working together, so she thrust a big wad of bills upon me and said I should do whatever it takes to get you out."

"I have funds for you also, in my London accounts."

"I also know you've got certain documents carefully hidden away by Bynum to use if I fail to help you."

"How can you do it?"

"The first step is to keep them from harming you straightaway. I'll tell the commandant that I have information concerning your alliances that may affect some of our financial institutions and even the security of the harbor. That always scares them. I'll say that torture won't help because without my personal intervention it would be impossible to put two and two together.

I'll tell them to keep you alive and well-fed and warm until I bring in higher authorities."

"Will it work?"

"I'm not sure. The Federal militia does as it pleases, even in New York. But I'll try. And you must try, as well, to keep your hope up and more importantly, should they not adhere to my suggestions, don't let them know anything about me or Bynum or anybody else."

"Bynum can help me, surely."

"Alas, lad, Mr. Bradley-West can help no one now, not even himself, for he's taken and is certain to be hanged."

*   *   *

A continuous clang of keys and metal doors echoed in the darkened prison walkways. Chad stood at his cell door, hands gripping the bars, trying to press his face close enough to look in either direction. But it was futile, he couldn't gain a better view and even if he did, the light was too pale and the gloom too pervasive to allow him a predictive glimpse.

His body ached from sporadic naps cramped on the cot, a growing itchiness spurred by his lack of a bath. His clothes reeked with staleness. He tried to eat the bread and stews they brought him but could manage only a taste. He was constantly thirsty, yet drank the water with apprehension. A slop bucket in the corner was, fortunately, covered. He had no books and no writing paper. His reserve of strength—a belief he'd found a rationale for the human predicament in his Greek and Roman texts—was fading fast. He was a rogue in his mid-twenties to these people, and to himself he was nothing at all now.

He thought of his Clarissa and steeped himself in outrage about the carnage he'd fought against. He even allowed himself some awkward physical exercise in the tiny chamber, hoping to preserve both strength and dignity.

They told him nothing. When they escorted a visitor to cells farther along the block, they didn't even glance in his direction. Perhaps, he thought, it was a good sign, an indication that Captain Hartigan had succeeded in stopping them from torture or a summary execution.

He stretched out on his cot for another attempt at restorative sleep when he heard them approaching again. This time they stopped and rattled their keys. A figure behind them, with a hat and a cloak and bearing a small knapsack, waited to enter. Chad rubbed his eyes, first as a habit and then in amazement. It was Schuyler.

"You have fifteen minutes, Mr. Renfield," the guard said. "You may leave him the contents of the knapsack but you'll have to allow inspection before you leave."

"Schuyler! Thank God. How are you, Schuyler?"

Schuyler, his face unrevealing in the murky air, waited until the guards shuffled back to their posts before speaking.

"I brought you some food and a change of underwear. There's cheese and bread and some sweets. They told me they don't usually allow this but apparently somebody has put in a word for you."

"Yes, Captain Hartigan," Chad said. "Remember him? He helped us deal with your problem downtown. We've become well acquainted. But how did you get here? Aren't you afraid?"

"I told you a long time ago that I'd never forget what you did for me. Despite my father's view I'm not a weakling."

"I never thought you were."

"My boxing club days may be over but I've worked hard in the Five Points with Father Fineas, to provide those poor boys some outlet for their energies. In doing so, I've learned a little about their lives and their families. Some of them are children of police officers. The honest ones don't make much money."

"Neither of them?"

Schuyler and Chad shook hands and laughed at the little joke. They sat on the cot while Schuyler handed him a crusty loaf, an apple, and a wedge of golden cheese. "I wanted to offer you some wine but they said I couldn't bring any bottles in here. I guess they think I'll break the glass and fight my way out, in a daring rescue worthy of a cheap novel."

"Schuyler, it's so good to see you. Thank you. Thank you so much. Tell me about Clarissa. Does she know? How's she taking it?"

"Your mother visited us and tried to put a positive slant on the events. She's determined that you shall go not only free but unsullied. Clarissa is as loyal as ever. Indeed, it's of her I wish to speak."

"And your father?"

"He was getting better but he's now taken a turn for the worse, I fear."

"Not because of my arrest? I guess everybody knows about it now and even if I'm somehow released it will ruin Clarissa's hopes."

"We didn't let Father know about it at first. In fact, we've mostly kept it out of the papers. Father's sick but he's still strong, and in concert with your mother—she told him and asked him to help—they seem invulnerable, to put it mildly."

"But Clarissa, how is she taking it?"

"She's strong and fervent in her devotion. As am I."

"If only I could see her."

"She wants to visit you. I told her it wasn't a good idea but she insisted.

Since I want to help her, and you, deal with this as you helped me, I was converted. We have a plan, but it was necessary for me to visit you first."

"A plan? To get me out?"

"I'm afraid that's beyond my ability, but your mother, she is, as you know, formidable. She's working with Tad Mullen, the Brooklyn preacher you once mentioned. And with Susan Steinmann."

"What on earth can Susan do?"

"She has the ear of her father. He in turn has a network of what somebody called 'odd-job johnnies'."

"What does that mean?"

"Susan said nobody remembers that her family came here virtually penniless from Brazil, after the Jews were expelled from Portugal. In the beginning, she said, they had to foster alliances with the underbelly—that was the word she used—in order to survive and build their financial empire. After the Revolution, grateful New Yorkers welcomed them into high society, but Susan's father kept in touch with the family's former collaborators. So Susan's able to advise your mother on ways to get you through to the dock without being attacked by the gangs. I believe also that your Cousin Corbin is involved, something having to do with ships bound for Britain."

"I'd prefer not to leave."

"If you don't they'll put you on trial."

"Bynum said it might be less than a trial. A mock process used to set an example."

"Our first job is to keep you healthy. Marcus is well connected to the Ohio Copperheads. Despite their failed insurgency, there are a number of agents still working in the city. He's approaching them to see what can be done."

"Marcus, too? Thank you, Schuyler, thank you."

"Marcus is as grateful as I for your understanding and affection and assistance. After we leave for France—very soon now—we'll be unable to repay you for your kindness. Even though your mother harps on your sarcasm, that doesn't fool me. Underneath it you're the most honest, the most fair-minded man I've ever known. So I'll keep working for your release."

"Release? Do you think it possible I could get out of here?"

"Your mother has asked Captain Hartigan—you see I did remember him from our meetings at Madam Maureen's when I was being blackmailed—your mother has asked the Captain to grease some palms. We hope to get you out on bail."

"Bail? I thought Lincoln's men would keep me here until I rot or die on the scaffold."

"We've got a lot of powerful friends and we're all on your side."

"Clarissa's not the least disaffected?"

"To the contrary. She insists on visiting you here and it's up to me to find a way to facilitate such a rendezvous." Even in the half-light Chad noticed Schuyler's smile. "I'm here to arrange a clandestine intimacy for a jailbird and my revered sister!" They both laughed nervously.

"To see her would be to gain a new grip on hope."

"You see, brother, your understanding of my passion promotes me to appreciate yours. She wants to be with you as much as you want her. But I had to warn you. To let you know she might come to you in—how shall we say it—in some other guise."

"What am I to expect?"

"Frankly, I don't yet know. But you'll receive a message. Or an impromptu visit. Or whatever it takes to get her to you. And after that, our next goal is to secure your release. One way or another."

"And even my mother is complicit in all this?"

"Your mother has abandoned any semblance of subtlety. It's true she loves you. It's also true, and everybody in the family seems to know now, that she wants you to impregnate my sister!"

"Thank God I had the courage to welcome you as a brother. If I get out of this, somehow, I'll always be your champion."

"As you always have been in the past, dear friend." Schuyler stood up, embraced Chad, emptied the foodstuffs from his knapsack, and called for the guard. Then in a low voice, he whispered in Chad's ear. "Do not despair. She'll come."

* * *

Shivering through the long night, unshaven and sick at heart, Chad curled his body under the skimpy blanket. Voices in distant reaches of the prison blended with the shriek of the wind down drafty corridors. He'd eaten the fruit and cheese, but kept his clean undergarments wadded under his head, like a pillow. He wanted to be clean and fresh if indeed she came to him.

His fitful sleep was tormented with dreams. Once he found himself in the hold of a ship, tipping on a giant wave, while crewmembers shouted in panic as sailor after sailor toppled over the side. Waking in a sweat, he turned his face to the wall, drew up his legs and finally drifted off once again, only to enter an imaginary ballroom, chandeliers aglow, the Prince of Wales standing on a platform at the far end, couples whirling in a merry dance. But as they swept closer, their fine garments turned to rags, and when their faces circled around him, they were drained of color and pocked with disease. Some of the dancers appeared to be soldiers bearing arms, others with open wounds. Finally he woke with a gasp, sitting upright on his cot, shaking his head to rid himself of the dreamed image of his father, gaunt as a beggar, pale as a ghost, gesturing to him with a hand that dripped with blood.

Slowly the dark night ebbed and a weak luminescence filled his cell. The sounds grew louder, and the chatter of guards and rattle of keys grew closer. Two uniformed men waited outside his cell, one of them gripping a bundle of clothes and the other with a small basket of food.

"These clothes were left for you, and some food. You people of privilege are all alike, you stick together. But I've found myself defenseless against the pleas of tearful women. You seem to have two females on your side. They're waiting to see you, but wanted to let you dress up a bit first. Don't try to pull anything, and remember when they're gone, you'll be searched and punished, if you commit even the smallest infraction. We've got rules here. You're a traitor. If I had my way, we wouldn't bother with a trial, nor waste government money keeping you alive."

One guard opened the door and threw the bundles across his bed, while the other put a wooden pail filled with water on the floor. Chad said nothing, eyes locked on the bucket. The guards shuffled off, shouting curses at the other inmates.

He rose and washed his face and arms quickly in the cold water, drying himself with his dirty shirt, and quickly donning clean underclothes, and the shirt and sweater the guards had brought him. He tried to smooth his hair, and ran his hands over his prickly beard.

Footsteps drew closer. A tall, heavy guard blocked his view as his colleague opened the door again, and two women, wrapped in cloaks and shawls and bonnet-style headpieces, were pushed through the open door towards him. The clank of the lock was followed by the fading banter of his sentinels, talking their way down the corridor.

The first figure removed her bonnet and brought from her loose sleeves a small book. "Chad, we're with you in this and we'll save you, you mustn't worry." His mother's voice, once so infuriating, filled him with energy. "I brought you this book, I don't know if it's of use to you. It's in Latin. You may not even have enough light to read."

"And I brought you this *potpourri*," Clarissa said. "Schuyler told me the air is foul here and that you don't even get to exercise in the yard."

"It's too cold to go outside and not much warmer in here," Chad said. "How did you get them to let you in? Did they search you?"

"A female attendant examined us intrusively," his mother said. "We're willing to suffer any indignity to help you."

"Thank you for the food and for the clothes." He kissed his mother's hand. Then he drew Clarissa close to him and touched his lips to her cheek. "I've brought you both such pain and disgrace."

"Not so, Son." Harriet said. "You've never realized how much I sympathize with your beliefs. I wanted to use this horrible war as a means to advance both our abolitionist cause and your future. I've not given up."

"Nor I," Clarissa said, clinging to Chad's forearm.

"But I'm deemed a traitor, a Copperhead."

"Yes, but you didn't do anything outright. Father Fineas has been a great comfort to us. He said you were wrestling with your conscience, that you wanted to do something to end the war, and that you considered violent actions. But he doesn't think, nor do I, that you did anything really wrong."

"Even if you did I'll never cease to love you," Clarissa said.

"It's true that I conspired with Bynum in the beginning. I gave him information about a number of buildings. But it was information anybody could have had simply by walking across the lobby. My other plan, to destroy the armory, was to be an act of faith, to show that we could deprive them of their arms, and maybe draw them to the conference table. But you see, I'm a coward in that too, for I abandoned the idea of it. I couldn't allow myself to inflict death on the soldiers inside, no matter how strongly I feel about everything else. But this doesn't matter, since I'm taken. They've not charged me, though. And I gather this is a military prison. I may be hauled before a tribunal and summarily judged."

"I'll not have it," Harriet said, resolution returning to her voice. "And I've got allies who won't permit it either. Your Captain Hartigan is a motivated man, so much so I gather you—how do they say it—that you 'have something on him.'"

"It's true that Bynum set things up in such a way that I could use incriminating documents if he failed to respond. But I'm sure he'd have done it anyway."

"Perhaps," Harriet said. "Even so, I invited him to our home where I made it clear that he's to gain your release. I also sent Corbin and Tad Mullen to see certain authorities. Corbin, in particular, has influence over the harbor police and Mullen and Father Fineas know some of the lower level officials. And Schuyler has engaged a team of Five Points boys to make sure we have muscle power if we need it."

"You see, my darling, we'll get you out of this." Clarissa snuggled closer to him.

"What is the first step?"

"Bail," Harriet said. "We must get you out on bail. But I fear this will take several days. You'll have to endure this hellhole a little longer. But I'll prevail." She paused then continued in a husky, suggestive voice. "In the meantime, I know you and Clarissa have much to talk about, so I've persuaded the guards to let me leave first, and to give you some time alone together."

"Mother! Is this a good idea?"

"It's the only idea, as far as I'm concerned," she said. She pecked him quickly on his lips and went to the door, banging on the bars with her heavy rings. A guard appeared promptly, wordlessly opened the door, let her out, and locked it again. Clarissa and Chad faced each other, alone together in a prison cell.

"What's she thinking about?"

"She's thinking what I'm thinking and what you surely must be thinking. I've longed for you. I've dreamt of you, ever since you were arrested. I want to make sure you have no doubt, no doubt whatsoever, about how I feel." As she spoke Clarissa put her hands on his waist, then thrust her hand inside his waistband.

"Here? Are you sure?"

"Yes, I'm sure." She kissed him with open mouth and continued to massage his lower belly, her hands reaching deeper under his clothing.

"What will Mother think about all this?"

"The truth is, it was her idea in the first place. Hers and Schuyler's. Now I'm yours wherever we may be, whenever you want me, however you want me."

TEN

February 1865

When the cold weather broke unexpectedly in mid-February, bringing gentle breezes and sunny days, Chad sneaked out through the kitchen to his old garden sanctuary. Warmly dressed in a woolen sweater and wrapped in a scarf, he sat on a bench and looked up at the blue winter sky. Before they let him out on bail, he'd despaired of ever seeing such a sight again.

The terms of his release, negotiated by his mother with behind-the-scenes manipulation by Captain Hartigan and Father Fineas, were strict. He was not to leave his home on East 10th Street until the trial, and he was to have no concourse with "other traitors," as the jailer told him, pushing a crumbled heap of clothes and personal belongings at him in contempt.

It had been so cold in his cell he welcomed the brisk but bright winter day. When they unlocked the door to the street, Harriet was waiting in a closed cab to take them speedily home by a circuitous route, lest they be discovered and attacked by the demonstrators who gathered daily around the Federal prison, demanding that the Copperheads be hanged or shot or tortured to death.

These were the same rowdies from downtown who had the most to lose from the war, Chad mused. Few considered him a hero for wanting to end the bloodshed, and there were no longer any meetings with other conspirators to convince him his original aims were honorable.

Harriet reserved her scornful criticism for a later time. Now she was a mother comforting her endangered son, and he allowed himself to be coddled by her, satiated with food and drink, refreshed by hot baths, cozily covered in clean sheets and warm blankets. He now knew as never before the degree

301

of privilege and luxury he'd been blessed with all his life. Even his childhood memories of harsh words and mysterious desertions seemed to fade.

But his respite was not long. As the sun began to warm him enough to unfurl his scarf, the housekeeper opened the creaky garden door and summoned him once again. "Madam says you must come inside right away," she said, more at ease with her dominating tone now that he'd been publicly shamed. "She says there's urgent business with a Captain Hartigan."

When he entered the familiar parlor to find Hartigan seated in the wing chair by the fireplace—the chair he'd always thought was his alone—fear and hopelessness returned. He eased himself wearily onto the settee beside his mother, rubbing his thighs, which still ached from weeks of long sleepless nights on a hard cot in a cold cell.

"Captain Hartigan has some disturbing news and he seems unwilling to tell me the details because he thinks it unfit for a woman of quality to hear." Her tone was the old intimidating one, her words chosen for their sharpness, each one cutting him painfully.

"What do you mean?"

"The truth is, Chad, a young woman has turned up at the Federal prison. She works in a house down on Prince Street. She claims you visited her there in the company of Bynum Bradley-West."

"Captain, my son is likely to be hanged. You needn't refrain from describing the nature of this incrimination. I already know he visited one of those destinations downtown. To be honest, I had him followed because I feared he'd make the wrong decisions. He's still young, you see, and impractical, and he vacillates." She looked at him with a benign expression that failed to hide her old ruthlessness.

"Very well, then. She works for a Madam Maureen and was a favorite of numerous upper-class men who sought her favors. But she's become pregnant." Chad was impressed with Hartigan's duplicity, suavely keeping to himself that he knew the house, Madam Maureen, and the girl very well indeed. Hartigan ignored Chad's skeptical glance. "To make matters worse, her brother, who was drafted into the Union army, has been killed in the war, and she blames you."

"Me? I haven't laid eyes on her for over a year. Two years, actually."

"She's not charged you with her pregnancy. But she blames you for betraying the Union army. She feels her brother will have died in vain if the cause for which he fought, unwillingly of course, is somehow blemished."

"She didn't even know my name. Did Bynum have something to do with this?"

"Bynum's still in jail. We were unable to secure his release but we're still trying." Captain Hartigan's tone and his expression conveyed, Chad was sure, his fear that certain documents would be used against him if Bynum were not set free.

"My son is hot-blooded like his father. He's impetuous. He's easily swayed. And although he hides behind his bookishness, it comes as no surprise to me that he'd have relations with a common prostitute in a brothel on Prince Street. But that's not the point. Why is this woman threatening my son and how much influence will she have? My goal is to set him free, as you know, no matter what it costs."

"Like many poor Irish girls left without a future when the war took away the men in her family, she's in despair," Captain Hartigan said. "She doesn't know what to do about the baby, for one thing."

"An abortion, surely. They're readily available. If that's what she wants, I can arrange it, with the woman who built that big house uptown on her considerable earnings from such procedures. She's even seen at the opera with her coteries of young men. Jewels. A fancy coach. All from helping girls like this—what did you say her name is?"

"I believe she's called Rosie O'Brian."

"Yes" Chad said. "Rosie is her name." He looked defiantly at his mother whose face revealed no reaction to this bit of news. "How are you so familiar with this helpful woman with the big house uptown and seats at the opera, Mother?" He'd intended the question as a mere sarcastic sally but as he uttered it he saw a flicker in his mother's eyes and he realized, for the first time since she'd piled her revelations on him, that there might be still more to discover about her many secrets.

"We must help her, Captain. Tell her a benefactress has arranged for her to stay with this woman while the procedures are implemented. Tell her she'll be given enough money to get out of town. Perhaps to Boston. Yes, that's it, to Boston. She can find more of her kind there."

"You mean there are prostitutes in Boston! I'm shocked, Mother."

"I wonder if you'll resort to sarcasm when they ask if you have any last words." Harriet paused, then drew a sharp breath, as her remark sank in, a tacit admission to herself that his execution was indeed likely. "Tell her she'll be set up comfortably in Boston with an income and a place to live. I'll arrange it through my family."

"Most of our family, Mother dear, have deserted their homeland in disgrace and have by now become Canadian citizens."

"My father is as secure in Boston as he's ever been. Our mills are thriving and we'll join his money with Clarissa's. We'll prevail. No downtown strumpet will derail my plans for the future of this family." Harriet stood up, walking imperiously around her parlor, before settling herself down again and wiping her brow with her fine silk kerchief.

"Please calm yourself," Captain Hartigan interjected. "She's already made her charges known. If I can get her to the abortion house and then off to Boston, her testimony may not stand up. But there's also other evidence. You see, this is not a court of law. It's a military tribunal. Bynum is already slated for a hearing and we fear the worst."

"I'll not permit them to destroy our future," Harriet said, her fists tight and her lips firm. "Captain Hartigan, we have access to ample funds. You're close, I've been informed, to the political bosses. Some of them have made dubious liaisons with the military leaders. Cronyism. Contracts. War profiteers, to say the least. You must use your influence to get this over with. At least, if the prospect is dire, arrange for Chad of get out of the country."

"Are you not aware they're watching your house night and day?"

"My coachman, Higgens, watches them as much as they watch us. We'll not be defeated by these johnnie-come-latelies."

"I admire your devotion to your wayward son, Mrs. Wales. But there are limits even for people like you."

"People like me?"

"I mean people of great wealth and influence."

Chad opened his mouth to comment but was stilled by a rap at the parlor doors. "Madam, Father Fineas is here. He says you're expecting him," the housekeeper said.

"Indeed," Harriet said. She waited silently while the housekeeper returned to admit Father Flaherty. "He'll pave the way for you, Captain Hartigan. And we'll get my son out of this and we'll go on with our plans."

Father Fineas seemed relieved that Captain Hartigan was already there. "I'm not sure why you asked me to come, Mrs. Wales. I'm of course willing to do anything I can to comfort you. To attend to your spiritual needs, as it were."

"My spiritual requirements are few, Father. But I do need your help. You've advised my son. You were a confidante of my dear late and lamented Aunt Marilyn. And despite your calling you're a man of the world. Captain Hartigan here has advised me that it may not be as easy as I supposed to get my son off scot-free. Therefore, I'd like to engage your agile mind in his behalf. If all else fails, we must get him out of the country. We might even disguise him in a Roman collar. What do you think?"

"I mustn't act against my conscience."

"Father, your conscience has already been placated by the fact that my son didn't go through with his ridiculous and completely ineffectual plan to blow up the armory. Really!" She looked at Chad and then at the other two men as if to communicate her disbelief that her only son was ever competent to carry out such an action. "And I know you're grateful for the contributions to your work with those poor boys in Five Points. The ones who beat up my son's future brother-in-law."

"I was unaware you knew about Schuyler's unfortunate mishap," Father Fineas said.

"I'm not only aware of it, I'm aware of why it happened."

"My mother, you see, is omniscient as well as omnipotent."

"Chad, you should realize your position. Your mother's got you out ostensibly on bail. The truth is she's bribed Federal officers. You're subject to re-arrest at their will," Captain Hartigan said. "And without her I don't believe we could have come this far, much less go farther still."

"Ah, but we will. If we smuggle him to the docks, one of my Cousin Corbin's ships can speed him away."

"They're watching all ships sailing under Corbin Chadwick's flag, mum," Captain Hartigan muttered.

"Then we'll simply get him aboard another ship. A British one, perhaps, so he can live in England for a while. His renegade father provided well for him there, I'm told." Harriet's voice mingled triumph with humiliation.

"Bynum's London accounts may also be available," Hartigan said.

Chad scowled at his accomplice. "It's best we keep Bynum's finances to ourselves," he said.

"Perhaps. But he's told me about the arrangements. Bynum is distressed at the news from Wilmington. Another Federal victory in North Carolina and the last port in the South, lost and closed. He's resigned himself to his fate, and he spoke to me candidly about the accounts there. He cited certain previous promises."

"Captain, you'll be handsomely compensated for your services." Harriet said. "Whatever secret pacts Mr. Bradley-West made with my son or with you must remain secret. It will be hard enough to gain liberty for my son as it is. But we shall do it, I'm certain."

"Hard indeed, Madam. And I must deliver now, I'm afraid, the latest and worst news. The authorities believe the war is winding down. They're looking to their political futures. And I'm to be involved in it. There's a proposal for me to run for office, perhaps the Congress. In return I must present a patriotic face to the bosses. It's for that reason that I must take Chad with me today, back to jail."

"This is outrageous," Harriet said. "You sit there pretending to help us while I reveal my most intimate plans."

Chad shifted in his seat, his limbs still sore from confinement and his heart skipping at Hartigan's words, which struck him as both betrayal and deceit.

"You must trust me," Hartigan said. "There's no doubt that one bribe is insufficient. They'll send a team of soldiers and make a public military arrest. That'll make it harder for you to save him. Once he's publicly humiliated and the news is spread there'll be a clamor for swift retribution. A tribunal no doubt, and a likely execution."

"But the public knows already," Chad protested. "There were crowds screaming outside my cell and people carrying placards with my name on them as I was hauled in."

"That was a staged demonstration," Hartigan said. "You'll note there was nothing specific in the newspapers about it. At that point they needed to fire up their lower-class supporters and also to make you more fearful. They're afraid, now that the end of the war is likely, you could get away. Or be pardoned. Lincoln has changed in the last year. He seems determined to show compassion for the defeated. He wants to reunite us. I have to admit I admire him for it, and intend to learn from it, how a man may mature in office. He turns a deliberately provoked war that was brutally executed into a benign call for reconciliation. There are those who vehemently oppose this compassionate attitude. That's why they prefer the tribunal. If you let me take you in, quietly, right now, I'll see to it that you suffer a minimum of distress while there. That will give your mother time to complete her plans. I'll assist in these but I must first make a public appearance with you at my side, as I turn you over to your captors."

"But what about the accounts," Harriet said.

"I still expect to be compensated and I'll want those other documents handed over to me."

"Not until my son is safely at sea," Harriet said, her voice cracking in uncertainty.

March 1865

Chad's cell was larger this time, with a window opening on the street. There was a thin mattress on the cot and a water pitcher and bowl. They'd permitted him to keep his own clothes, including sweaters and a blanket. Harriet had prepared a basket of bread, fruit and cheese to be smuggled inside. There was hardly any paperwork at his readmission, and the two guards who escorted him down the cellblock were silent.

But it was nevertheless a cell, and he was still a prisoner facing a charge of treason. Hartigan didn't further confide in him on the ride back to confinement and his unusual silence further convinced Chad that he couldn't be fully trusted anymore.

He could hear the noises from a parade in the distance. He was allowed to receive newspapers, where he learned of a massive victory rally, signaling the city's attempt to disguise its ambivalent past in a rash of patriotic events and proclamations. Brass marching bands and fife and drum corps filled the March winds with music, distorted as it reverberated through the streets and alleyways, and sometimes drowned out entirely by the roar of the crowds.

He tried to see the throngs outside but his window was too high. He munched sporadically on an apple and broke off a chunk of cheese. Then he stretched out on his cot and drew his knees to his chest and tried to sleep. But there was no peace for him, not even in contemplating the worthiness of his original intentions. The war was still wrong. Bynum himself had summed it up in one of their talks: "It's possible to use a just principle to wage an unjust war." Even so, he was only another prisoner waiting to be hanged and nothing seemed likely to prevent it.

The newspapers brought further grief. Four days before New York staged this great parade for victory, the Confederate Army of the Valley had finally been destroyed. The Shenandoah was now, and perhaps forever, in the hands of the Federal government. Even if he survived, there was little chance for him to visit his father's lost estate, nor, indeed, his Chickamauga grave.

High Federal courts had recently handed down indictments of numerous Copperheads, some of whom were arrested forthwith, while others escaped to Canada, or were still at large somewhere in the vast territories west of the Mississippi.

As Phillipse Renfield would have pointed out in dismay, the markets reacted during the bitter weeks prior to this imminent victory. Gold had risen first to $149 and then to $152. This meant greenbacks had plunged to a new low. Since his initial arrest he'd not seen Phillipse and had been told only that he was still confined to his mansion with an uncertain prognosis.

Bedridden at Yellowfields with a mysterious disorder, Clarissa had been unable to visit him at the East 10th Street house during his brief respite. In a note to his mother, hastily scrawled in his bedroom upstairs, he insisted she must attend to his promised bride and, when she recovered, get her to his cell so he could once again profess his love for her and feel her comforting and exciting touch.

So he sat there, thumbing through the papers with feigned detachment, listening to the whisper of the wind and the bruised sounds of celebration. Trying to concentrate on the latest editions, he turned absently to the financial pages. A bold headline across the upper right column caught his eye and his heart sank once again at the latest evidence of deterioration in his once-privileged world: Phillipse Renfield was dead.

The great financier must have succumbed while Harriet and Hartigan and the priest discussed plans for his escape, or while he rode roughly through the chilly streets to his second confinement. Would Clarissa be able to return to the city? And what of Schuyler?

Phillipse Renfield was lauded in the article as one of the city's foremost bankers, a middle-aged man who had aided the war effort, cared for his family, and contributed generously to charity. His illness was described as "a sudden one," and his son's departure for France noticeably unmentioned.

Most of the article was given over to the financial implications. Apparently Phillipse was not confident of his survival and without a designated heir to run the bank, he'd managed to merge it, days before his death, with the House of Steinmann. There were no indications of the impact of this merger upon the family fortune. A side bar revealed that the Renfield Mansion had been sold to a developer who wanted to turn it into an hotel.

Thus the lengthening days blurred into each other, the light grew brighter, the cold less chilling. One morning, as he huddled under his blanket, refusing even to open his eyes, he heard the chirp of a bird outside his window. The stripped limbs of a tree cast a faint shadow on the sill, street noise was more distinct in the approaching spring. But the heaviness in his heart didn't lessen and the hopelessness grew with each waking hour. When would they come for him?

* * *

He awoke one morning strangely refreshed. He'd dreamed of Yellowfields and Clarissa. In the reverie of sleep he'd somehow come to believe they'd be together there again, and the world as he knew it restored, peace upon the land, love in his heart, and reconciliation among the people. But a distant clank jarred him awake. He sat up straight on his cot and listened to the approaching footsteps.

When they opened his cell door he remained rigid, his eyes turned to the window, hoping to hear at least one more time the shrill birdsong of a warming season.

"Chad? Chad, are you all right?"

It was Clarissa's voice for sure, brighter than any bird, more liquid than a song. He leapt up and approached her, only to be rebuffed by the guard, who spoke in a lowered but firm voice.

"You must try to keep quiet. It's been arranged that several visitors will come here this morning. We mustn't let other inmates know you can receive so many people at once. It's forbidden."

After the guard crept out and locked the cell again, he took her hands in his and drew her close to him. "I'd given up hope of seeing you again. Why didn't you come to me?"

"I've been ill and confined to the estate. Did they tell you my father has died?"

"I read it in the paper. Do you have people with you? Are you able to rely on anybody?"

"Your mother has been helpful. She was with me during the funeral. Afterwards, when we met with the lawyers, she was very helpful."

"Clarissa, I'm so sorry I couldn't be there by your side during your loss."

"Doctor Forrest looked after me. Father Fineas came to call. And that preacher from Brooklyn, your mother's friend."

"Reverend Mullen?"

"Yes. We spoke at length. He and your mother have a plan. I wanted to tell you about it first, before they arrive today. There's a new issue in our life."

"Issue? You mean money? The papers said your father merged with Steinmann before he died."

"It's not the money. Your mother helped me negotiate with the insurance companies and banks and brokers. Father was thorough, and Mr. Steinmann has been generous and kind. He had a letter from Susan, in Paris, and he let me read it. And I've had a letter too, from Schuyler. He doesn't want to contest any of father's arrangements." She paused, leaning her cheek against his chest. "No, it's not the money I've come to tell you about. In fact, it seems I'm even richer than before."

"So you'll be secure?"

"If my health holds, yes."

"Your illness … was it serious?"

"There's an epidemic of smallpox, but I'm safe from it, Dr. Forrest said. No, my health problems are more, how would you say it? Salubrious."

"Nothing must happen to you, Clarissa, You're all I have left to hope for."

"Not quite all."

"Whatever do you mean? Clarissa, you're everything now, more than ever. Even if I have to go to the gallows I'll hold you in my heart, believing our love is strong and you'll live a long life."

"We shall, I promise it."

"We?"

"Chad, I'm with child."

He kissed her gently on the cheek and ear and forehead and then on her lips, which parted to receive him. He felt her shiver with delight, and then sensed she was weeping. "You mustn't despair, my darling."

"I can't afford to do that now. Your mother has taken over my life, it seems. She advises me on diet, on exercise, and promises to be with me throughout. She's so concerned that I'll be healthy and that the child will be strong."

"The child! Yes, Mother will watch over you and the child."

"She seems convinced it'll be a son."

"If her prayers have any effect it will indeed be a son."

"But how can I raise him, without you? How can I even endure without you?"

"You must be strong."

"Strong, yes. But I'm determined, also. Your mother hasn't worked out the details yet, but she's met with that police captain, and she's involved Reverend Mullen and Father Fineas and your Cousin Corbin. And that nice man we transported from Manhattan on our yacht, do you remember him?"

"Holder Pratt?"

"Yes. He's back in town. It seems the country didn't appeal to his wife. They've had a child, too. It's a boy. They're opening up the shop again, downtown. They believe the war will end and that there'll be a boom in business."

"How can he help Mother with her plot?"

"I'm not sure but I think it may be something like that abolitionist thing, the underground railway. His house was a way station, your mother called it. So was the rectory in Brooklyn."

"I may be smuggled out of here, is that what you're saying? Taken to Reverend Mullen's house in Brooklyn like a runaway slave?"

"Your mother knows you better than I do, I suppose. She says you let principles interfere with your own good fortune. She thinks you may resist a clandestine escape."

"I'd want my name to be cleared in any case. Even if it's after my death. I acted on principle and I'm not ashamed of it. I like to think that maybe my actions will yet inspire them to come to the conference table and talk of peace."

"There's much talk of peace in the air. But Corbin said Lincoln is determined to elicit an unconditional surrender. Lee's on the defensive. Grant's marching towards Richmond."

"What has my mother cooked up for me this time?"

"She thinks we can sneak you out of the country. For England."

"But if I flee I'll be convicted *in absentia* and your name and our child's name will be blemished. Worse, I'll not be with you when the child comes and I may not be able to return to see you again and to hold you like this." He crushed her in his arms again.

"She thinks she can get the case dismissed, or postponed until people have forgotten it. She's even convinced the girl about it."

"Girl?"

"Oh Chad, I know all about that. I've forgiven you completely. I know you were misled and that it's long over with. And that her child is not your child. Not like our child. Of course there will be no child in her case."

"My mother's doing?"

"Harriet arranged for an abortion, at that woman's house uptown, the big house where she lives like a queen. Your mother supervised the whole thing. And then they shipped the poor girl off to Boston where members of your grandfather's company are to look after her. She'll not testify against you. But you must agree with us, you mustn't resist our plan."

"To leave you ..."

"It's the only possibility. Harriet's on her way here right now with Reverend Mullen. He's going to marry us, here in jail. Our child will be legitimate, there will be no mark on his name. Your mother has been most adamant on that point."

"As only she can be," Chad said, not without a spark of resentment, even in the face of new hope. "What about the paper work?"

"The license and all the documents have been prepared. Reverend Mullen will sign them. Father Fineas is coming, he'll be a witness. And when he goes home from here he'll leave a vest and a collar behind. You'll be able to dress as a priest and then Captain Hartigan will have you escorted out. A carriage will be waiting. The coach is unmarked, it belongs to a livery in Brooklyn. Reverend Mullen uses it for his own secret work. It will take you to Holder Pratt's."

"Every last thing she wanted."

"Your mother's a remarkable woman. Will you agree to this plan? Oh please, Chad, if you were dead there'd be no hope for me. I'd pine away at Yellowfields. Even the laughter of a child couldn't soothe my despair. Your mother has in fact anticipated that I may be distraught and has agreed to help me raise the child."

"Help you? How?"

"Our house has been sold and I don't want to furnish a new one without you here with me. I'll spend my time at Yellowfields. But after the war is over, your mother says, the child needs to experience life in the city. So she's agreed to be a surrogate mother when the need arises. It's very comforting to me to know I'll have her help. I've no family left at all, you see, except Schuyler and he's never coming back. His letter says so." She handed him a thick envelope. "He mentions you here, I wanted you to know how much he respects you." She handed Chad a crumpled envelope.

"I can't read it now."

"Just the last page."

Chad read aloud, in a low voice. *"And so I've decided never to return because I'd be scorned and persecuted there. Marcus and I found an elegant apartment in the Faubourg St. Honore, and he's also purchased a small estate on the river, easy for us to get to when we want a change. I'm writing and he's painting. So I want you to have everything coming to you after Father's death. I'm set for life here. Please tell Chad that I love him, in the most proper of ways, and that I'll always cherish his memory and his willingness to accept me as I am. And I pray that he'll be free to come to Europe with you when you start a family, so Marcus and I can act as uncles and show your children the marvels of France. I love you so, and I miss New York sometimes, but I'm French now, and Paris is my home."*

"You see, we can visit him. If you're in England, if you have to stay there a long time, I'll come to you when the child is old enough. We'll be together there and then we'll sail for the Continent. We'll live in Paris, too, if we have to."

"I'm an American and I want to take part in America's future. Clarissa, I consider myself to be a patriot. After this war there'll be even more challenges."

"Yes, dearest, but first we've to get you out of jail. And then out of the country. Until it all blows over. Will you cooperate?"

"Of course, I will. My heart is bursting with the dream that I'll live to raise our children with you. To grow old with you." Chad gripped her tightly again. They lowered themselves to the cot, and lay quietly together, perhaps, Chad's racing mind concluded, for the last time. "Do you think it's safe for you to stay this long?"

"They'll be here soon." Clarissa's soft voice in his ear was drowned out by footsteps and voices and a hasty turn of key in lock. Sitting side by side on the cot, they watched the guard swing open the door and then stand back to usher three figures into the shadowy compartment. All had cloaks and caps and mufflers, helping to hide their faces in the dim milky light.

"You've got half an hour," the guard said. "Not one minute more. And then you must exit as planned. I'll be at the side door to let you out. You must leave the first payment with me, if you expect us to risk our reputations and our lives for this traitor." He locked the door behind him.

The three figures stood without talking until the guard's footsteps could no longer be heard. Harriet removed her cloak and scarf, standing with her back to the door, obscuring the view from outside. The other two forms removed their outer garments and stood in the light.

"There's not much time," Mullen said. "Our ceremony will be brief but legal. The papers are filled out. Repeat after me."

Chad's mind, racing in conflict again, barely sensed the meaning of Mullen's almost whispered ritual. But he answered on cue, held Clarissa's hand, and then slipped a gold band on her finger, the ring thrust into his palm at the right moment by his mother. "I now pronounce you man and wife," Mullen said. "Father, would you sign these papers where I've indicated. Harriet, you too. And then the bride and groom."

Father Fineas was the last to sign, with a flourish and a deep sigh. "There's so little time but I must speak out, now, lest my own conscience be forever troubled. I'm a man of peace and an instrument of forgiveness and I've agreed to participate in this plan because I know all of you to be, at heart, decent people whose motives are inspired by familial love. But I must tell you, Mrs. Wales, that I object to your part in the abortion. That woman, who's grown rich on the bodies of the unborn, is the devil incarnate. And I was hurt and surprised that you knew her so well and were able to speed the process so efficiently. I'm also grateful to all of you for the help you've offered, through financial contributions mostly, to my work in Five Points. So I can say you're charitable and generous. But you're also privileged. None of your family, Chad's father excepted, has borne the heavy yoke of battle. You live in elegant isolation in your mansions and your estates and when your will is crossed, you summon all your powers to wiggle out of an otherwise inescapable fate. Chad confided in me, outside the holy confessional of my Church, and I tried to help him. I feel he heeded my words since he didn't, in the final days of his alignment with the insurgents, try to blow up the armory. And the other Copperheads, whose motives I consider to be questionable, failed also. No lives were lost in the fires in Manhattan and most of the conspirators have been arrested. One of them is to be hanged. All of you, when you leave here, and you especially, Chad, if you make your escape, must harbor in your hearts forevermore a gratitude for your pampered status and use it as a charge to do good works. For works, as well as faith, are essential, in my opinion and in the opinion of my Church. So I bestow my blessing on this hurried marriage and, once out of here, won't share with anyone the nature of the ceremony nor the details of your further plans. But please, pray for me after you've gone and do not forget to examine your conscience every day, to see if you're doing right with your wealth and power." Nobody responded to the priest's sermon. He stood still for a moment, then removed his collar and vest and placed it on the cot. "You'll wear this when you flee, Chad. Don't be indifferent to its significance."

"You and I are not as far apart as you may suppose, Father," Chad said.

"We thought at first Canada might be best," Harriet said. "Randall and Caleb have both settled down in St. John. Both of them married widows. Widows who also happen to be sisters, and very rich. There's been no extradition of earlier escapees, but Canada's too close for comfort in your case. It will have to be England. And not on one of Corbin's ships. They're watched around the clock. We'll have further news for you later."

"Thank you, Mother," Chad said, feeling for the first time that he really meant it.

"By the way," Harriet said, "About your friend, Bynum. They hanged him this morning."

April 1865

When he heard loud noises in the streets, starting with sporadic cheers and occasional gunshots, Chad used the promise of money to convince a guard to provide him with newspapers.

The stack of dailies covered an entire week. He forced himself to read them in order, his ambivalence growing as he absorbed the rapid rush of historic incidents. On the first of the month Sheridan had defeated the Confederates at Five Forks, considered likely to be the final major battle of the war. Richmond had fallen. Grant overpowered Lee at Petersburg. When the two battered armies mustered at Appomattox Court House, the weary but revered Southern general capitulated at last. The war was over.

Whatever justification he felt for his treachery now seemed irrelevant. The bloodshed had been stilled, not by conversation and compromise over a mahogany table, but in a ramshackle village ravaged by rifle and cannon and sword. If he were brought before the tribunal now, his protestations of just cause would be deemed false, his once-fervent belief that the war should be ended at any price judged to be cynical, and the growing demand for vengeance satisfied by a sentence of death. He could still remember voices shouting "Death to the traitors" and recalled the placards he read on a nighttime walk from the Renfield Mansion across Union Square in the days when so many New Yorkers were still suspicious of Lincoln's goals.

He spent anxious hours reading all the related stories. Gold had fallen now that the demand for provisions and military materials would decline. Speculation would be rife on Wall Street. The people who run things would reassemble in closed rooms and discuss new ways to take advantage of both victory and defeat.

Although the Yankee Congress had finally drafted a constitutional amendment outlawing slavery once and for all, the fate of the black man was still distressful. Lincoln's earlier "proclamation" had affected only states in the rebellious South, with the dubious proviso that the proclamation was not effective if their legislatures voted to rejoin the Union and agreed to loyalty oaths and exacting specifications on governance, finance and behavior.

Resentment and fear among the working classes boded ill in the North, while rancorous and ingrained attitudes would poison whatever racial compassion might still remain within the more liberal Southern aristocracy. The poor whites of Georgia and Mississippi and Alabama would choose violence as remedy for the shame of their defeat and the continuation of their impoverishment. War does, as Bynum said, bring out the worst in everybody.

Chad sat brooding on his cot, head in his hands, the papers spread about him on the floor. But one thought couldn't be banished from his mind, a vision surpassing his personal terror. Maybe Lincoln had indeed grown in office. Maybe this strange man, so untested when he assumed his high office, so ready with riposte, so easy with jest, so subtle and manipulative in speech, maybe, just maybe, Chad thought, he'd rise to authentic greatness with a policy of compassion and understanding and fairness. Knowing now the webs of deceit and self-interest among the people in power, Chad began to believe that Lincoln might be an asset to the nation after all, despite the bungling atrocities of the war and the politically expedient judgments and murky rationales for battle foisted upon the people with every change in the wind.

For the next few days, the accustomed prison sounds seemed different and the familiar routines of incarceration more flexible. There were fewer people coming and going in the corridors, the guards less attentive. The food, never good, was at least edible and regularly served. But for Chad the quiet was more ominous than comforting. His mother's callous last words to him, casually uttered as she left his cell, tortured his mind with the image of his collaborator Bynum, swinging from a rope. How bravely did he meet his death? What were his last words? Would they ship his body back to coastal North Carolina for burial in the soil he loved and died for?

An inescapably real image plagued his waking hours and troubled his sleep: a man with a hood over his head, his legs bound together, turning slowly under a wooden platform. It would be him next time. With his death, the ancient texts, the fevered aspirations, the fleshly passion, the pride of home and family—all would belong not to him but to somebody else. History deceived only the living.

Day faded into night and morning returned in painful slowness. He lost count of the calendar and no longer noticed the sounds outside his window. He waited, the Roman collar and black vest stuffed under his bed.

* * *

He woke up in the early dawn, gray gold light on the stones of his prison floor. Through the window, a wispy moon flickered. It was warm, almost humid. There was little to be heard, either in the streets or in his cell. He wiggled out of his blanket and turned on his side. Sleep was his only escape and he didn't resist it when it came.

In the distance he heard a voice, then another one. The words were unclear, but the voices were approaching. They spoke less loudly now. They were outside his door. He'd heard they did it mostly in the morning, without warning, rushing the prisoner out a side door, up the scaffold, the speed of their motion the only evidence of sympathy.

"He's in here, Captain," the voice said. The door was unlocked. Chad stood up, facing the intruder.

"Don't say anything." Hartigan's voice surged with confidence. "We must move quickly. You've got the Father's clothes?"

"A collar and a vest."

"Put them on. Listen, I can't be seen with you. I'll leave this door open and I'll engage the guard in conversation. He's in on it but none of the others are. Make sure your collar is showing, just in case you meet anybody else. If you do, make a gesture of some sort, like a benediction. They're mostly Catholics on the staff here. But you must sneak out on your own. Turn left outside the cell, go to the end of the hall. There's another door there, solid wood. It'll be open for about seven minutes. Outside, turn right. A half block away there's a closed carriage. Get in it and knock three times on the roof. The driver knows what to do. Don't get out when the carriage stops. You'll be met and payment will be made to the driver. You'll recognize the man who meets you. He'll tell you what to do. Now, I must go. Move quickly. Quickly!"

Hartigan left the door ajar. Chad focused his wandering mind on the immediate. He put the vestments on, arranged his other belongings in a heap on the cot, so it looked like a human form, and gently eased the cell door shut. He walked down the murky hallway without looking left or right. Some of the cells were empty. He heard snoring and stopped in fear when one of the inmates turned on his cot. He followed instructions like a seasoned warrior. When he stepped across the threshold into the warm morning, he couldn't resist a split second pause, to breathe deeply the sweet air of freedom. He walked deliberately towards the coach, not too fast, with his head down. He climbed into the cab, and curled his fingers into a fist, knocking three times. The horse strained and the cab moved. He was on his way.

Wheels on cobblestones, hooves in a rhythmic clap. He was too afraid to open the blinds, odors and sounds his only guide. Spices in the air, a fragrant bloom. The smell of coffee. Offal and manure. The scent of oats and hay, the aroma of baking bread. And then, the salty smell of the promising sea. He was near the water. The carriage stopped. He sat silently, unmoving. A door slammed. A muffle of voices, the rattle of a purse. His door opened. Holder Pratt stood there on the pavement, reaching out his hand.

* * *

"I didn't approve of what I perceived to be your advocacy of the Southern cause," Holder Pratt said. "But I was impressed with your mind and ultimately convinced that your cause was peace and your heart was with us on the slavery issue. When you came here hastily to save your friend and kinsman, a man of questionable virtue, I was inspired by your sincerity and your compassion. When you conspired with your Cousin Corbin and the Renfields to get Mary and me out of town after the riots, I felt even more respectful towards you. So you must desist, now, in these repeated blandishments of gratitude." Holder Pratt sat facing Chad in a small office alongside his workshop, a pot of coffee between them.

"I was repetitious, also, with my pronounced anti-slavery sentiments, so much so people began to think me dishonest in that regard. I'm glad that you saw the truth. My motives were first and foremost to end the war. If I were not in disgrace now I'd stand up here for real abolition, real equality, and real justice. For you and for Schuyler and for all of us. But I am, alas, a fugitive. It's to you and the others I must turn now. My fate is quite literally in your hands."

"Mary spoke of you with great affection. In our lighter moments we laughed at being privileged passengers on the Renfield yacht and the way those pompous officers tried to detain us. Corbin saved the day."

"Yes," Chad said. "I've had many disputes with my Northern family, sometimes verging on estrangement. But in all of them, there's some good. Even in my mother."

"Especially in your mother," Holder said. "Don't question everybody's motives if the results are good."

"She wants power more than anything else. She wants vengeance too. I've encountered her kind in the great Greek texts I was once privileged to study at leisure."

"Do you remember that I'm from Rhode Island, descended from an old free family, and also educated? I have sympathy for your interests. As for me, I prefer to make my way with chisel and awl, with fine woods and sculptural forms."

"I consider you to be an artist, not a craftsman."

"An artisan, perhaps. Let's leave it at that. Mr. Wales, I'm a happy man. I have my wife, my business, my son. But I fear for what will happen to all of us now, black and white, if revenge and hatred and greed take over in the wake of this terrible war. I applaud you for your prescience in recognizing the need for a negotiated settlement. Now that there has been surrender, our only hope lies in Lincoln, I think."

"Yes," Chad said. "I was reluctant at first, but I must now admit that Lincoln has become what many thought he was in the first place. He's still ruthless and determined. He's still motivated by his growing power. But he's grown wiser. What difference does it make if his motives are wrong, if his actions now may be right? Let's hope he'll bring progress for all of us. By the way, you must call me Chad."

"And for you?" Holder asked. "What is my friend Chad going to do?"

"For me, a life in England for a while if I'm lucky enough to get there. I have funds. I have various interests. I may study at Oxford. Clarissa and I are married now, Holder. I'm to be a father."

"Your mother told me about it."

"Already? I'd have thought she'd keep it quiet until I'm out of the country."

"Chad, she's prouder of you than you know. When I worked with her and Mullen over in Brooklyn, I learned a lot. I watch people. I can tell how they react to a black man who's free and educated and prosperous, for example. She was never condescending. And I can sense her inward anguish. I think she was terribly wronged somewhere, somehow. Or thinks she was."

"Did your education include a study of the Greeks?"

"I don't read Greek but I know the literature in translation and in summary."

"If you know the Greeks, then you know my mother," Chad said with a sigh.

"She'll arrive here shortly. She's to talk with you for the last time before you depart. Then Corbin will come to give you your instructions. My understanding is that you must stay hidden here, upstairs in the room where I put Schuyler and his friend, for a few days. Then you'll be taken to the docks and smuggled aboard a ship. I think that will be a few days from now."

"I've lost track of time. What is the date?"

"It's April 13th. I hope it's not unlucky. In any case, we will never forget 1865!"

* * *

After breakfast with Holder, Chad napped fitfully in the low-ceilinged chamber upstairs, where he'd once discovered the battered Schuyler, pacing the small room in shame and fear. Now he stretched out in the same bed where Marcus had sprawled, one blue eye swollen almost shut and bloodstained golden hair awry on his forehead.

He allowed himself to ponder, for the first time in weeks, his remembered verses, of love's soiled bedrolls and the blood of comrades. Of heroes with swords fighting for honor and home and family and lover. Of the cadence of their voices and the hypnotic metrics of their fabled texts. But he couldn't concentrate and his eyes grew heavy. He drifted off, feeling an unusual serenity.

He was awakened by a familiar voice. He strained to catch the words, dimly heard from the foot of the stairs. It was his mother once again, and this time he did not recoil. He moved down the stairs cautiously, afraid of a trap, but saw Holder Pratt guarding the front while his mother waited in the anteroom, primly seated on one of Holder's fine Newport chairs. He sat opposite her and waited.

"I never knew what to make of you, even as a child," Harriet said after a long silence. "You were hardly over three when you started reading. And when you were five you wrote me a poem. Four lines, perfect meter, cleverly rhymed. And when you were twelve you wrote me a sonnet! Imagine that, fourteen lines, classic structure, that pattern ... what did you call it?"

"Iambic pentameter. Like Shakespeare."

"Yes. Do you remember?"

"Vaguely."

"I was dear to you then."

"You're dear to me now, Mother. It's just that you're so much stronger than I ever realized and I'm much more susceptible to conquest that I wanted to be."

"You? No, my son, it won't do to overlook your true character. Sometimes I think I'm the only one who's on to you."

"On to me?"

"I withdrew when you sought refuge behind those poets and historians and all that. I failed to praise you for your talent. Do you know why?"

"I assumed you thought me effete. Or at least ineffectual."

"I saw something in you that was also in me. But in your case, had you been self-confident and ruthless and deeply hurt, you'd have become like me, only more so. You'd have ended up a general invading a defenseless land or a captain of industry exploiting his workers or a politician bent on ruling the world. No, I knew I should leave you alone. Let you go your scholarly way. The world is safer because of it." She crinkled her eyes and laughed, not forced this time, sounding much like the mother he remembered before he bore the brunt of her aggression and became the salt in her emotional wounds. "I never doubted for a minute your ability to blow up the armory. Only your will. Your weakened will. And it was I who weakened it. You should thank me for that."

"If I survive, and if I ever come back, I'll try to do better."

"It's too late for us as mother and son. That bond is ideally uncomplicated and overpowering. But we can, one day, I hope, be friends. Partners, in a sense."

"Partners? How?"

"Yes, partners. If you'll acquiesce to my terms."

"Terms? Is there to be a written contract?"

"There's always been a contract, and some of it's indeed written. In the wills. In the trusts. In the shareholder's agreements. In the lawsuits and secret deals and in the alleys and in the back rooms of the abortion houses."

"Mother!"

"We must first concentrate on getting you out of here. I have some papers for you. Identity forms, letters of introduction. In London, but also in Bristol and in Edinburgh, should you end up there. I have letters of credit on English, Scottish, and French banks. In case you find out your father was as dishonest with you as he was with me."

"I've seen written copies of Father's accounts. Bynum said there are duplicates on file with the banks. There's surely no doubt that he provided for me."

"Maybe. But just in case, I even have a packet of papers for your use in Paris if you visit those two lovebird friends of yours."

"Mother!"

"Hell, Chad, let's get rid of all this pretense. I've already witnessed more than you, much, much more, I suspect, than you ever will. What people do behind closed doors, with their clothes off in a bed or their clothes on around a conference table. I've seen it all and I've borne it all. Because of a childish prank with my cousin in a hayloft on Beacon Hill. An endless chain of innuendo and suppression. Why do you think I ever went to that house on West 26th Street? Out of teenaged lust? Out of wantonness? No, I went there as I've gone elsewhere, for information. To see how people behave when they think they're not being watched. To see how the people you trust the most will betray you, as my family did. As your father first betrayed and then abandoned me. And now you've almost turned against me."

"I thought our differences to be more substantive. You're running on pure emotion now, a steam engine gathering speed from an over-stoked furnace."

"You're as adept with metaphor as ever. It's not that I don't admire your brilliance—the ceaseless tempo of your fevered brain. But I think it's naive to think that you somehow see 'the whole thing' when others don't. Surely you're skilled at mastering languages, ideas, mathematics, everything abstract. But let me tell you, there's one big basic flaw in your whole position. You see, when it comes to human interaction—either in a household or in a nation—the abstract doesn't matter. In love and family and politics, nothing's really abstract. In daily life, in the things that really matter, there is no whole thing. And that, my dear son, is where you missed the boat, as Cousin Corbin might say."

Cheered by the possibility of escape, of freedom, Chad felt his mother's words like a vise around his chest. He felt a rare sensation: he was speechless.

Harriet savored the awkward moment, then plunged on, with fire in her voice. "I'm going to tell you now, before you sneak away from your reunited homeland, the rest of it. How did I know about the abortion palace? I went there because of Randall Renfield. I was with child, his child, because he gave me alcohol and when I was feeling high, forced himself on me. I suppose you could say he actually raped me, Chad. But I'm not sure. I was susceptible to new experiences. Whatever the case I have long since forgiven him, out of pity. He never really matured, and even then he was overshadowed by his older brother. Of course I had the baby killed. And I got everything in writing. Even Dr. Forrest's original report describing me as 'intact.' That's one of the many written contracts you seem to fear. I've charted this course from long ago, before you were even conceived. I kept a list of wrongs in my *escritoire*, the Goddard-Townsend chest they let me bring down to New York when they set me up in Aunt Marilyn's house and tried their best to silence me. But they lost and I'll win."

"Win what, Mother."

"Power."

"I pity you."

"And I you."

"Me? My name may be blemished. I may yet be caught and hanged. I may never see my wife again nor gaze upon the face of my child. But I'd rather be me than you."

"That's why my focus will be on my grandchild rather then you. I'll influence Clarissa in his education. I'll bind him to me. With love. With dependency. With force, if I have to. I'll make him be what I'd have been if I had been a man."

"What would you have been, Mother, as a man? A general? A conquering hero? A king?"

"Let me tell you, so you don't forget it, because if you do return—and deep down I hope you will—if you return to this country and take your place as head of the family you must remember that it's I who will rule in the name of my grandchild Renfield Laymus Wales. With Phillipse dead and Steinmann relying on me, it's I who'll call the shots. Neither has a real heir and both had previous reasons to keep me quiet, especially about their progeny, Susan and Schuyler, running off to Paris because they couldn't live openly with their nature here at home. I have control of the Renfield fortune though

Clarissa now that you've married her. Steinmann has made us richer still. I've gained control of my family trusts. I've been advised by an aide to Milliken. Have you heard of him? He's been running around New England in the wake of this war snapping up textile mills while his agents in the South are grabbing properties down there. But we're already ahead. Our textile empire will be greater than any in America. In the world, some day. And I've invested in steel and oil in Ohio and acquired land out West. I've used the connections I paid so dearly for on West 26th Street to buy into the railroads. With Corbin I control three shipping lines. We own real estate in New York and Boston and now, with the war grinding down and the South in ruins, in Richmond and Charleston and New Orleans."

"In other words Mother, you'll be rich. So what, we were already rich."

"The money is only a tool. When I was disgraced in Boston they gossiped about our family. Bringing up the molasses and rum and slave traders we started with. Whispering about the privateers in 1812, implying we were pirates as well. And then this nonsense about child labor in our mills. How else would they live, those people? But now, you see, it will be different. Renfield Laymus Wales will be a New Yorker. He'll have the best schooling possible. He'll be groomed from the start. But no one will connect him with trade, or commerce, or even banking. We're simply rich. We don't need to own things, we own money. So much of it that it can't help but multiply no matter what happens to the markets. We'll be safe behind the screen of old money. We'll be alluded to in awe. We'll be deluged with invitations. My grandson will be implored to join the very best clubs. We'll live behind the facade of our grand houses and we'll entertain only rarely, but when we do, all New York will vie for an invitation. Should anyone have the temerity to oppose us I can snuff them out with a letter or a phrase or a frown. My grandson will sit on boards, corporate as well as institutional. But he'll not chair them. He'll not run for office. He'll not make public statements. No, we shall rule from the quiet sanctity of our library and study. Our deeds will be done by accomplices, each of them more afraid of us than the last. We'll have victory, total victory. And I'll live to see the new century in, and so, I hope, will you, Chad. We'll be the most powerful family in America!"

Chad searched his mind, probably for the last time in her presence, for an appropriate Latin phrase. "*Morituri te salutamus.*"

"You can stop that nonsense now. You're safer than you know. Corbin will be here tomorrow. He'll give you your final instructions. Take these papers. Keep them with you at all times. When you arrive, you may write me in care of our Boston office. The new address is in the letters. One last thing. Do not question my concern for you, but do not oppose me."

Harriet Laymus Wales kissed her only son goodbye, and left him standing in a woodworker's shop in downtown Manhattan, while she marched off to wage her own new war on a victorious nation and a vanquished and desolate Southland.

* * *

Two days later Chad woke up to find a stack of newspapers outside his cramped upstairs room. He was unsure whether he'd be spirited off immediately or would wait for days. It was already April 15th. Mary had left some bread and jam and a tea cozy and cream and sugar. He carried the papers back to the little desk, settled down for a lonely breakfast, and spread the papers out on the bed. Each of them had huge black headlines.

"Lincoln Assassinated."

He bent over the bed and read each story compulsively, his pulse throbbing. The tall gaunt man he'd first seen in a box at the Academy of Music, enjoying Verdi's opera about political murder, was indeed dead, shot in the head by the actor John Wilkes Booth, whom he and Clarissa would have witnessed, were it not for the fires set in Manhattan by Southern agents, in *Julius Caesar*, also murdered while at the peak of power.

They'd carried the President to a room across the street where he lingered all night long. Another politician, perhaps with an eye towards immortality for himself, pronounced the epitaph. "Now he belongs to the ages."

What was there to belong? A corpse? Another murdered tyrant? Another statesman growing in power and understanding? Or an ordinary man acting out his particular role in the human tragedy?

More sinister, perhaps, were the implications. Lincoln's policies towards the South were far more conciliatory than those of Congress. Worse still, the vultures from the Northern banks and mills would add humiliation and deprivation to defeat. Booth was a Southerner, acting perhaps on the mistaken belief that he'd wreak revenge. Because of his crime, what his people might reap, instead, was the whirlwind.

Before he finished the dozen or so journals, Mary rapped at his door again, with a message from Corbin. *"Because of the reaction to late events the journey has been postponed until the 24th,"* the note said. Lincoln had been killed nine days after the war ended. More anxious than ever, he would have to wait nine more days in his crowded attic before he could find an escape, if, indeed, they were not already plotting to discover his lair and send him to the gallows, in the frenzy that ensued after the President's murder. The assassination now served as nascent symbol for five years of unparalleled suffering and bloodshed. A protracted funeral would embellish, and perhaps eventually canonize, the fallen leader.

* * *

"The truth is," Corbin said, "I have little time to spend with you here. In the wake of the conspiracy to kill the President, agents are everywhere, arresting anybody they can. Some have already been hanged, rumor has it. I predict summary courts martial and hasty executions. It may help us, though. They may have forgotten about you. In any case, the ship we wanted was delayed anyway, so it's perhaps an omen. It's the *Bristol Star*. She sails tomorrow morning for England. You'll disembark in Bristol and be taken by train to London. There'll be solicitors to meet you and guide you as you find a residence and present your credentials to the several banks we're using. And of course your father's banks. The ship's an old one but she's sound. You'll suffer some privation, but you'll be treated as well as possible on such a vessel. You may write us at the shipping offices in Boston. Be discreet in what you say and don't sign your name. The banks will notify us of your address so we can forward news to you. If it's needed."

"I'll be on my own at last."

"You may look at it that way if you must. And it won't be a wholly unpleasant life. You'll enjoy their libraries and museums and bookstores. The opera is especially fine. You can tour the countryside, and perhaps cross to Paris."

"Will I ever be able to come home?"

"I'm not sure. But we'll do our best."

"May I ask you for a personal favor?"

"If it's not seditious."

"My mother and I have had our differences. I now understand her better. But there's tension still and she's powerful. Will you keep an eye out for my wife and child? Will you write me to tell me how they are? How they spend their days. What the child looks like."

"I'll do so. But let me warn you first about the English. Don't let them know you're intelligent and educated. They consider that a defect. And don't be deceived by their manners. They'll talk softly, say little, pretend not to be interested in you while all the time they're scheming to do you in."

"Surely not."

"Perhaps. But it's advice given to me when I went to sea and it proved useful more than once. Especially now. France and Germany and Austria are stumbling towards turmoil. Disraeli and Gladstone are at each other's throats every day. The French are in Mexico and there are rumors of war. If so, it may be a war that engulfs us too, so very soon after the big one. And be careful with your money. There's talk of some kind of unified currency over there. And a metal-based standard, perhaps gold. It's all very mysterious and not to be trusted. Keep your profile low, enjoy your learning, eat well, stay strong, and hope you'll soon be back home with your wife and your child."

"How can I thank you, Cousin?"

"You'd have done the same for me, perhaps?"

"I'm not sure."

"Honest to the last!"

Epilogue: April 24, 1865

Scheduled to sail at sun-up, the Bristol Star was docked at the South Street pier. By the time Chad's carriage arrived, the Captain was already on the bridge. Stevedores loaded kerosene and bales of foodstuffs to sustain them during their arduous journey back home to the British Isles. The high masts and rigging were wrapped in wispy fog, the bow rising and falling gently in the East River swells. It was an old but sturdy vessel with a seasoned crew, ready to sweep him safely out to sea, away from his broken family and his sundered homeland.

He had done his best and he'd failed. Failed! But he stubbornly held on to his belief that at Princeton he'd learned much to help him find his way. He could read Greek and Latin, speak German and French, and Italian, knew history and mathematics and philosophy. Yet he'd impregnated his beautiful Clarissa and left her to wait for him in a city full of anger and fear. He said a confused farewell to his widowed mother, still mourning her dead husband's memory while lamenting, at the same time, the indifference of a fiery abolitionist preacher whose passion was insufficient to satisfy the scores of lonely women who swooned in his Brooklyn church.

Devastation was the theme of all his thoughts as he prepared to abandon the land of his birth. His mind's eye swelled with images of his father's long-lost Shenandoah plantation and of his father himself, buried with his comrades in the red clay of Chickamauga. Some of his classmates, unwilling to buy their way out of the gruesome nightmare, had been maimed or killed at Antietam or Chancellorsville or Gettysburg, now-hallowed symbols of a nation soaked in blood. As his carriage wound its way through the river-bound streets, banners of mourning swathed the lampposts while the President of the United States, a rigid corpse on a black-draped funeral train, rode home to the heartland on a catafalque of despair.

Bynum, relentlessly marching day by day towards the gallows, had forewarned him of disillusionment. Dr. Forrest, basking in the adulation of three generations of wealthy patients, argued that disillusionment was the first step towards wisdom. And now Holder, a wise and free Black menaced on every side throughout the war, had returned from his upstate farm with his wife and child, waiting fearfully to see if the new freedom proclaimed by senator and general alike could prevent America, ultimately, from destroying itself.

When they interrogated him he freely confessed the guilt of his own actions, labeled treason by some and valor by others. Then as now he expected approval from neither side. Instead, he merely longed to be free from the lot of them.

His mother, pained by her ruptured family and intoxicated with power, had rushed him off with both regret and hope. And it was the flickering candle of hope that beckoned to him now, across the dark bloody field of human history.

He hadn't given up. "Remember," Bynum told him, "it doesn't make much difference which side you're on if they're both wrong. Find something for yourself, keep a small light burning somewhere within, so you can find your own way."

Were both sides really wrong? There was no doubt in Chad's mind about the horror and outrage of slavery. But slavery was not the war's proclaimed rationale, not until it became politically expedient. And Lincoln himself had expressed mixed views on the subject. The British had eradicated this curse in their island nation decades ago, and ultimately throughout the Empire, using the persuasive power of the imperial treasury—an expensive policy, but no more so than this ruinous conflict, and with far less human agony—an entire generation decimated and desolate. The combat was fueled by tariffs, after all, and the battle joined by ambivalent Northern merchants and industrialists and bankers who saw either a threat to their purse or an opportunity to prosper in government contracts in the most expensive war, in both lives and dollars, the nation had ever endured.

His New England ancestors loudly and visibly preached abolition while they sold slave cloth and bought slave-produced cotton. American and international bankers provided letters of credit and massive loans guaranteed by human chattel. Ships built in New England, some of which once ferried human misery from the shores of Africa, now waited in Charleston and Savannah to take on as cargo the precious bales assembled by men and women in chains. Was it greed alone that prevented these industrialists and bankers and shipping tycoons from saying, "No, we will not buy slave-produced cotton. We will not sell you cheap fabrics to clothe them. We will not advance the money needed until harvest time. We will not transport the products of this vile and 'peculiar' institution."

He admitted such improbable sanctions would be expensive, and both rich and poor would suffer loss of income. Factories would slow down, some banks might fail, ships could float idly in the bay, in an overall action that would take several years to be effective. Even so, the nation as a whole would spend far less than either side paid in their stubbornly brutal war. A million casualties would have been avoided. And it could have been done without expanding unconstitutional Federal power, without the use of military tribunals and the revocation of habeas corpus, and the internecine corporate corruption that flourished throughout the war and would likely continue. Was the conclusion inevitable: that the real basis of war, the "first cause", was simply human greed? And did the blame stop there: could greed survive without the support of a populace either ignorant or misled or both?

He had no answer to these questions but he possessed his own fearful vision, an imagined tableau of future battles fought under the waving banners of opportunism and deceit. Of congressional powers ignored, of civil rights compromised, of corporate malfeasance and political arrogance, and always the same price to pay: the corpses of the young buried under a flag, or the legions of those who return without legs or sight or any hope whatsoever.

Bynum had laughed good-naturedly at his idealism. "Why, you're assuming man is rational!" His laughter cut through Chad's veil of hopefulness, spurring him to action, a course he admitted was wrong and which he'd regret for the rest of his life.

"E pluribus unum", his nation's motto had been. "Out of many one." Was it simply naive and wishful? "Out of nothing, something," his inner voice replied. He needn't countenance despair forever. He needn't allow himself to sink like a discarded cannon into the sea. His struggling country had founded itself on the thoughts of others, the English and Scottish and French who talked of liberty, equality and a social contract, words rendered powerless against the hangman and the guillotine. Greeks and Romans, assuming they'd immortalized their codes of justice, inscribed them for all time with a stylus fashioned by slaves.

Out of nothing, something. He'd let his private credo echo in his heart. He'd heal his own wounds. Someday, after he had combed the cities and villages of Europe, he'd return. Maybe she'd come to him instead, as she had promised, his Clarissa, slapping her black and ivory fan as she paced in her shuttered drawing room, tears in her eyes.

Now with lines cast off and sails unfurled, his wooden ship creaked down the East River towards the bay, past the waiting schooners and barks and steamships and on through the Narrows to the open sea. He stood hatless in the bow, holding onto a gnarled rope, leaning out over the rail to taste the surf and feel the salt air on his face. He watched the stars disappear as the sun first yellowed and then reddened the dawn.

He knew he had to cross this dangerous sea to find a place for himself, for now the New World had grown old while the Old World gloated in hungry anticipation. He'd swim upstream to the spawning grounds of it all in search of a new and wiser faith. As his ship picked up speed towards the brightening East, he fixed his eyes on the horizon, full of gratitude for the warmth of a fickle and indifferent sun.

The End

Previous books by C. D. Webb

The Credence of Christopher Craig

In *The Credence of Christopher Craig*, set during America's watershed years of 1968-1973, two young men, one straight and one gay, forge an intense friendship based on their mutual obsession with English racing cars. Their encounters with murderous violence, diverse sexual entanglements, social unrest and a besieged idealism herald the onset of America's ensuing decline. Writing in the *Midwest Book Review*, Ben Jonjak said, "*Christopher Craig* is a good book. It might even be a great book." He added that "*Christopher Craig* belongs in that group of works that is, at the very least, ambitious and cognizant of the make-up of a literary masterpiece." Calling the novel's characters "extremely well fleshed out and believable," he said it was "an enjoyable read" that reminded him "fleetingly" of *The Great Gatsby*.

Jake and Jasmine

In a separate review, Ben Jonjak said, "*Jake and Jasmine*, another work from the talented C. D. Webb, is a wonderfully told story." Jake is a poor white Southern boy, a musical genius on a scholarship to Juilliard, who falls in love with a fellow student, the gifted daughter of a rich and powerful Black family strongly opposed to their marriage. Mr. Jonjak wrote: "Webb is at his best when he is describing a composer's euphoria for playing and creating music. I would be hard pressed to think of a better love story for music lovers." He said it is "a wonderful piece of writing and places the most elegant of traditional literary themes, the love story, against the backdrop of classical music. It is an entertaining read and an extremely ambitious novel that succeeds on many levels." Cited in a *Writer's Digest* competition as one of the top ten genre novels of the year, one judge termed *Jake and Jasmine* "a brilliant mainstream novel." Other critics called it a "tour de force" that is "both entertaining and deep."

About C. D. Webb

Copperhead Wales is C. D. Webb's third published novel. He began his writing career, at age sixteen, as a poet. A selection of his poetry was anthologized in Rolfe Humphries' volume *New Poems by American Poets #2*, published by Ballantine Books.

His undergraduate and graduate study focused on American, British and French literature. He also has an interdisciplinary master's degree in psychology and sociology, and served on the Board of Directors of the C. G. Jung Foundation for Analytical Psychology.

As he continued to publish poems in regional journals he simultaneously launched an administrative career with cultural institutions, leaving his post as Development Consultant on the staff of the Metropolitan Museum of Art to establish The Charles Webb Company, Inc., specializing in capital funding for art and history museums, historic houses, musical organizations, and ballet, opera and theater companies. Under his management the firm acquired clients in 35 states, the United Kingdom, and Italy.

For several years he was Chairman of the Board of the Circle Repertory Company in New York, which deepened his interest in the theater. He has written five plays, which he intends to publish in a single volume in the future.

Now in the final editing stages, *The Playoff* is a murder mystery and coming of age tale set in the Southern mountains during the segregation era, in which a respected Black high school teacher is arrested for a crime he did not commit. Publication is expected next year.

C. D. Webb's new novel, now underway, concerns an evangelical fundamentalist preacher whose life becomes steadily more corrupt and licentious, resulting in his fall to, rather than from, grace.

Immortal Wounds, a volume of short stories, is nearing completion.